THE
FINAL
VOW

Also by M.W. Craven

Washington Poe series
The Puppet Show
Black Summer
The Curator
Dead Ground
The Botanist
The Mercy Chair
Cut Short (short story collection)

Ben Koenig series
Fearless
Nobody's Hero

Avison Fluke series
Born in a Burial Gown
Body Breaker

M.W. CRAVEN

THE
FINAL
VOW

C

CONSTABLE

CONSTABLE

First published in Great Britain in 2025 by Constable

Copyright © M.W. Craven, 2025

Quote on p. 363 from *Mad Max Beyond Thunderdome* (1985),
written by Terry Hayes and George Miller

3 5 7 9 10 8 6 4 2

A CIP catalogue record for this book is available from the British Library.

ISBN: 978-1-40871-753-0 (hardback)
ISBN: 978-1-40871-754-7 (trade paperback)

Typeset in Adobe Caslon Pro by Initial Typesetting Services, Edinburgh
Printed and bound in Great Britain by Clays Ltd, Elcograf S.p.A.

Papers used by Constable are from well-managed forests
and other responsible sources.

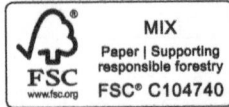

Constable
An imprint of
Little, Brown Book Group
Carmelite House
50 Victoria Embankment
London EC4Y 0DZ

The authorised representative
in the EEA is
Hachette Ireland
8 Castlecourt Centre,
Dublin 15, D15 XTP3, Ireland
(email: info@hbgi.ie)

An Hachette UK Company
www.hachette.co.uk

www.littlebrown.co.uk

For Amer Anwar, my friend.

Author's note

While the Washington Poe and Tilly Bradshaw books are written so they can be read in any order, this book *does* contain a character – and therefore a spoiler – from the previous book, *The Mercy Chair.*

I did think of omitting her entirely, but she was too much fun to write about.

Three Lights on a Match

On the first he shoulders the Bren
On the second he smiles
On the third he pulls the trigger
And then he smiles again

(Anon.)

You don't see the man in the ghillie suit.

You don't see him because he casts no shadow. There is no silhouette. He has natural cover to his front and natural cover to his rear. His ghillie suit is the same colour as the foliage he's concealed in. It breaks up his human shape. It has no straight lines. Nothing glares and nothing shines. The grasses and ferns he has stitched into the suit sway with the wind.

You don't see the man in the ghillie suit because he doesn't move. Not even his eyes. He doesn't eat and he doesn't drink. He doesn't take comfort breaks. He craves a cigarette, but he doesn't have one. He hasn't washed for days. There are no soap or deodorant smells to spook the wildlife. They crawl over and under him as if he's part of the landscape. It's like he isn't there. He might as well be invisible.

You don't see the man in the ghillie suit.

But he sees you . . .

Chapter 1

Blencathra House, Central London

There were twelve people in the police media room and that was ten too many.

Only the man and the woman needed to be there. The other ten were as welcome as professional mourners at a funeral.

The woman looked at the man, saw the grief on his face. She made a decision. 'Everyone out,' she said quietly.

She didn't need to raise her voice. She never did. The room went silent. The only sound was the crack of knuckles as the man clenched and unclenched his fists. He didn't know he was doing it.

'We have just as much right to be—' one of the ten started to say before being nudged into silence by a colleague. He pointed at the woman's expression. It said: *Don't mess with me. Not today.*

They left their seats and trooped out of the room. They glared at the man as they passed. One of them, a guy called Peter Jameson, deliberately shoulder-barged him. Stared, willing him to react.

The man didn't. Jameson was angry. They were *all* angry. The man didn't blame them.

Jameson tried again. 'This is your fault,' he said. 'She's dead because of you.'

The man continued to ignore him. Didn't even glance in his direction.

'Out!' the woman snapped.

Jameson left the room, slamming the door. The room fell silent again. The woman took a moist towelette from her bag and wiped the back of her neck. She passed a fresh one to the man, but he made no move to take it.

Despite the brutish heatwave the country was experiencing, the police media-room windows were closed. Heavy drapes covered them. It was how it was now. People suffered the discomfort. Put up with the heat. Over the last three months they had got used to it. Keeping your windows closed and your curtains drawn was the new normal. As were untended gardens. Tarpaulin screens at petrol stations. People walking in zigzags instead of a straight line. No one went outside unless they had to.

Not any more.

The man had sweated so much his suit was as wet as a sponge. He was unshaven and had red-rimmed eyes. It looked like he hadn't slept for weeks. His cheeks were shrunken, gaunt. His face was monstrously calm. Detached, almost. If he'd returned from a war zone, he'd have been described as having a thousand-yard stare. The only sign of his rage was the clenching and unclenching of his fists.

'It's on,' the woman said. She reached for a remote control and unmuted the television that was mounted on the wall. It was already on the right channel – Sky News. The anchor was called Finlay Scott and the carefully worded statement he was about to read had been drafted by the woman not forty-five minutes earlier. It had been released to the media to catch the two o'clock news. It would be repeated on the hour and be the lead story on the six o'clock and ten o'clock shows that night.

Finlay Scott cleared his throat and began reading. 'I have breaking news – police have just released the name of the twenty-first person to be killed by the sniper who is terrorising the country. The woman, who worked for the National Crime Agency's Serious Crime Analysis Section, has been named as civilian

4

analyst and the youngest-ever recipient of the Fields Medal, Matilda Bradshaw.'

At the back of the room, Stephanie Flynn, the woman holding the remote control, stared at the screen in silence. Like she couldn't believe she'd heard what she'd known she was about to hear. As if there was a disconnect between *writing* the statement and *hearing* the statement. A single tear ran down her face. She wiped it away with the towelette.

The man with the thousand-yard stare didn't look at the TV. Nor did he stay silent. That wasn't in his nature. He was an apex predator and he had never felt the urge to hunt more. He wanted, no he *needed* to be outside. The sniper wasn't in this room. He was in the hills, and he was in the woods. He was on the top of buildings, and he was underneath cars. He was everywhere the man wasn't. But they'd be in the same place soon. The man with the thousand-yard stare could feel it. He *knew* it. He could hear the beat of the sniper's heart, smell his fear. No one else was going to die. It was almost over.

So instead of staying quiet, the man threw back his head and screamed.

That man was Washington Poe.

But perhaps this isn't the best place to start.

Maybe we need to go back a few weeks . . .

The First Light

Chapter 2

A few weeks earlier

Gretna Green

The bullet that killed Naomi Etherington was a .50 BMG fired from a McMillan TAC-50 sniper rifle. It was shot from a cold barrel at a range of 1,200 yards. The sniper was using a Schmidt & Bender 5-25x56 PM II telescopic sight. The bullet was the colour of a penny and, at 42 grams, was five times the weight of the wedding ring Naomi had just slipped on her new husband's finger.

It entered her back at 800 metres per second, cut through vertebra C5, severing her spinal cord, then deflected off her ribs down into her heart. After shredding the aorta, the left atrium and the left ventricle, the bullet tore through the lower lobe of her right lung then smashed its way in and out of her liver and pancreas.

Later, the forensic pathologist would note that the entrance wound in Naomi's back was the size and colour of a fresh cigarette burn. There was no exit wound – the solid knot of the hipbone had flattened and stopped the bullet.

People still get married at Gretna Green. Three and a half thousand couples a year. It's a nod to the runaway weddings of the past when an eighteenth-century English law forbade anyone under the age of twenty-one to marry without their parents' consent. Gretna Green was an accident of geography, the first village English couples reached when they crossed the border into Scotland. Overnight, a thriving wedding economy sprang up, and businesses keep the tradition alive today. It's romantic, a lovely way to start your new life together.

But when Naomi collapsed into her husband's arms, her life's egg timer was almost out of sand. A bridesmaid, thinking the heat and the heavy white dress had caused her friend to faint, went to help. Then she saw the blood. Lots of blood. She screamed. And then it seemed like everyone was screaming. It was a full minute before anyone thought to dial 999.

It wouldn't have made any difference. By the time the paramedics arrived, Naomi had been dead for seventeen minutes.

The man in the ghillie suit didn't make mistakes.

Chapter 3

Cabinet Office Briefing Room C, Whitehall, London

The murder of Naomi Etherington was the man in the ghillie suit's third victim in eight days. In the last six months, he'd shot and killed seventeen people. He had a 100 per cent success rate. No one had survived. There was no one in hospital, hanging on, full of tubes and hooked up to twenty machines. Every one of his victims had died where they'd been shot.

Even if the sniper terrorising the country hadn't been negatively affecting the economy, the prime minister couldn't sit on his hands. He had to do something. He had to *lead*. And when the country looked to Number 10 for leadership, the quick-win, easy-to-arrange gesture was always the same – COBRA. It sounded like the PM was on top of the situation. That high-level coordination and decision-making was happening, and he was overseeing it. That when the country needed him, he was a hands-on prime minister. He was *their* guy. The public's image of COBRA resembled the White House's Situation Room. Screens on the wall, satellite links to the nuclear subs. Men in shirts, ties loosened, sleeves rolled up, toiling away day and night. That COBRA was an acronym for Cabinet Office Briefing Rooms – the media added the A to make it sexier – didn't seem to bother anyone. COBRA sounded fast. It sounded decisive. It sounded like it had bite. Like an actual cobra.

The reality of COBRA was that the prime minister was rarely present at the meetings. He might occasionally dip in and out, but that was more of a cosmetic thing. In case he was asked by the press or by the leader of the opposition at PMQs. COBRA meetings are mostly attended by the people who need to be there.

Cabinet Office Briefing Room C was typical. It was functional. Utilitarian. Nothing in it that didn't need to be there. It looked like any briefing room anywhere in the world. A table, some cheap chairs, and tough, hardwearing carpet tiles.

The seven previous meetings convened to discuss the sniper murders had been attended by representatives of the police, the Home Office, the Office of the Prime Minister and a bunch of civil contingency experts. The usual suspects.

And they were there now. Still making notes, still out of ideas. But this time someone new was in attendance. He'd been in the wings, ready for the call. Patiently waiting for the sniper to be redesignated as a threat to national security. He was called Alastor Locke, and although he looked and dressed like Snidely Whiplash without the top hat, he was one of the UK's most senior spies. Locke had listened to what was being discussed in the meeting without commenting. The sniper was a police matter. He wasn't sure there was a role for the security services yet. He'd made some notes but that was more out of habit. Locke didn't attend meetings unbriefed.

The chair was called Timothy Spiggens and he was a junior minister in the Home Office. Not the best politician Locke had ever met, not the worst. He had just reached the last agenda item – AOB. Any Other Business.

'Alastor,' he said. 'Can you bring everyone up to speed on what the security services have been up to?'

Fat chance, Locke thought but didn't say.

'The usual,' he said. 'Monitoring chatter, speaking to our friends, gross invasions of privacy, that kind of thing.'

'And?'

Locke shrugged. 'If he's a bad actor, he's working alone. No one is claiming responsibility. One of our more excitable far-right

12

groups thought it might have been one of their fringe players, someone who disappeared a year ago, but I know for a fact they're wrong.'

'How?'

'Because he's dead. Drug overdose. His body went unclaimed and he was given a pauper's funeral three months ago.'

'But if you knew . . .'

'If we knew who he was, why did his body go unclaimed?'

'Yes.'

'We're the security service,' Locke said. 'Keeping secrets is what we do. And it suits our purposes if certain groups believe we still do black sites and extraordinary renditions. It keeps them in check.'

'It's not terrorism then?' Spiggens said.

'It isn't.'

Spiggens put his head in his hands for a moment. Terrorism would give the government a target. Someone to fight. A lone wolf gave them nothing. And Mason Dowbakin, the Right Honourable Member for Preston East, was already making waves. Goading the centrist PM, forcing him to move to his right. His latest column in the *Telegraph* said he was only helping the PM – who he admired greatly blah blah blah – return to his core values, but everyone knew he was setting himself up as the next cab off the rank should there be a leadership challenge.

'This is a disaster,' Spiggens said. He opened a slim file and removed a single sheet of paper. 'These are the most recent figures. Working-from-home requests are up by six hundred per cent in the last two weeks alone, commuting is down by almost the same. When people *do* come into work, they don't leave the building until they go home as soon as they finish, so the lunch and early evening economy is tanking. The public are cancelling hospital appointments so the pandemic backlog, instead of shrinking, is getting bigger.' He put the sheet back in his file then picked up a copy of the *Daily Mail*. 'A woman collapsed in Brighton yesterday. She lay on the pavement for over an hour before someone found the courage to go to her assistance. Eighty-seven years old and she died of heatstroke in one of the most advanced countries in the world.' He slammed the newspaper on the table. 'This is absolutely unacceptable!'

'This isn't a newspaper Mrs Locke has delivered,' Locke said. 'May I see it?'

Spiggens slid it across the table. Locke picked it up and spent a few seconds scanning the front page. It was a detailed account of Naomi Etherington's murder in Gretna Green. He tilted his head. 'I know a man who lives near Gretna Green. He doesn't always play well with others, but he may be able to help.'

'What? Who is he?' Spiggens said. 'Get him on the next train, man!'

'The approach will have to come from someone else, I'm afraid. The last time we had contact there was considerable . . . unpleasantness.'

'How unpleasant?'

Locke cleared his throat. 'He said if he ever saw me again, he'd, and this is verbatim, "Take those stupid glasses off your head and stick them up your bony arse."'

'My word,' Spiggens said. 'That *is* unpleasant.'

'And truthfully, it was not undeserved,' Locke said. 'We *did* treat him rather badly.'

'Perhaps he was exaggerating.'

Locke smiled at the thought. 'This is not a man given to hyperbole, Timothy.'

'What will he want?'

'Knowing him, a crate of beer and some good-quality butcher's sausages.'

'Alastor,' Spiggens warned. 'The PM wants positive news – what will he want?'

'I really have no idea,' Locke said. 'He's whimsical.'

'Who is he?'

'Detective Sergeant Washington Poe.'

Cabinet Office Briefing Room C went from quiet murmurs to stunned silence so quickly it was like there'd been a power cut.

'Good grief,' Spiggens said eventually. 'Is he still a police officer? I thought he'd married the Marquess of Northumberland's daughter.'

'Not yet.'

'But they are engaged?'

'I really have no idea, Timothy,' Locke said. 'I certainly haven't received a wedding invitation.'

'Washington Poe,' Spiggens said, wondering if the PM would consider this good or bad news. 'I'm not sure, Alastor. We got into a *lot* of bother the last time he worked with us. All that stuff on the golf course.'

'True,' Locke replied. 'But he was right.'

'Yes, I *know* he was right. He also caused a major diplomatic incident. My counterpart in the US didn't return my calls for almost a year.'

Locke hid a smile. Unsuccessfully.

'It's not funny, Alastor!' Spiggens snapped. 'We called you in to get your take on this horrible situation and the only thing you've come up with is an unmanageable misanthrope from the far north of England.'

Locke said nothing.

'I'm not sure he's the type of person we want, Alastor.'

'Maybe not, but he is the person we *need*. He has a knack for this kind of thing.'

Spiggens sighed. '*If* I take this to the PM, can you control him?'

'Good Lord, no,' Locke said. He thought about it for a moment. 'But I know someone who can.'

'Who?'

Locke told him.

'Get her on the phone then.'

Locke removed an ornate notebook from his pocket and found a number. He pressed the speakerphone icon and dialled. His call was answered immediately.

'Modern Slavery and Human Trafficking Unit, please,' he said.

There were a couple of clicks while his call was redirected.

'MSHTU, Detective Chief Inspector Stephanie Flynn speaking.'

'Good morning, Chief Inspector, this is Alastor Locke. Have I caught you at a bad time? And before you answer, I'm in Whitehall and you're on speakerphone.'

'What do you want, dickhead?'

Locke chuckled. 'I'm thinking of putting the band back together.'

Flynn paused. Then she said, 'It's about fucking time.'

Chapter 4

HMS Lancaster, the smallest, leakiest tug in the Royal Navy, somewhere in the Atlantic Ocean

Washington Poe smelled of fish.

Not just his clothes. *Him.* It was a hard thing to admit, but he did. He smelled of fish. One of the stinkiest things you could smell of. Even fresh fish honked. If he were to compile a list – and he frequently did – of the worst things to smell of, fish would be number two. Only an *actual* number two was worse.

Cruellest of all, there didn't seem to be anything he could do about it. And he'd tried, God how he'd tried. The second he got home his clothes were off and in the washing machine. He would then scrub himself in the bath for an hour. He'd use the harshest soap he could buy, and the hottest water he could stand. And within five minutes of stepping out, he smelled like he'd used fish stock as bathwater.

His fiancée – soon-to-be wife – Estelle Doyle, didn't help. The second he was out of the bath she would say something hilarious like, 'I don't know why, but I fancy kippers for tea,' or 'We had a double-glazing salesman round earlier. He said he could do the whole house for a thousand pounds. I told him to go away . . . it seemed fishy.' And Poe would laugh because it was Doyle who'd said it and he loved her. She also had the kind of voice that would make a bowel cancer diagnosis sound sexy.

But still, he wished he didn't smell of fish.

And the reason he smelled, no *stank*, of fish was because he was being punished. His last case with the National Crime Agency's Serious Crime Analysis Section, the UK's only dedicated serial killer unit, had involved people who had been stoned to death. It had almost killed him. *Literally*. It had left him scarred and battered and with PTSD. He was still seeing his trauma therapist, and although he was getting better, the little things were still making him angry. Shops without cashiers. People who said 'holibobs'. The chip shop closing early. Flies. Adults who wished their dead relatives a 'happy heavenly birthday'. People who put LOL on text messages. People who *said* LOL. His line manager wanting regular updates on the criminal activity of drug smugglers. Raisins masquerading as chocolate chips in biscuits. Adults who said 'forever homes' and 'fur babies'. The Police and Criminal Evidence Act. The phrase 'wild swimming'. The usual shit.

He'd been temporarily reassigned to the training wing until he was assessed as being fit for fieldwork. In hindsight, or maybe it was foresight – you never knew who was pulling whose strings when these things were arranged – it was a role for which he was singularly unsuited. He'd been there for less than a month when he'd had a fistfight with another instructor, an over-educated fast-tracked idiot called Jake Burnham. Poe couldn't remember what the fight was about, but he thought an unattended Pot Noodle might have been involved. However, Burnham had also been at fault, and because he was the son of an assistant chief constable in Police Scotland they couldn't sack him. Which meant they couldn't sack Poe either. Instead, they did the next best thing: they reassigned him – again – to the stupidest inter-agency task-force ever dreamed up. His boss at the training unit had assumed he'd hand in his notice there and then, but he hadn't understood how contrary Poe could be.

So now he and three other misfits spent their working days on the smallest, leakiest tug in the Royal Naval fleet on an intelligence-led stop-and-search programme of fishing trawlers.

The half-baked idea was that the combined might of the Royal Navy, Border Force and National Crime Agency would prove a formidable weapon in the fight against drugs. Poe knew it was a half-baked idea because he was on the taskforce. Poe didn't know anything about fish. He didn't even like fish. He would tolerate cod if it was wrapped in crispy batter. Even then he'd give most of it to Edgar, his gluttonous springer spaniel. Not the batter, though. That was all his.

But lack of knowledge of the UK fishing industry aside, he wasn't the biggest buffoon on HMS *Lancaster*. The ship, which had started life as an inshore survey vessel, was skippered by the boatswain Isaac Scoplett, surely the drunkest man in the Royal Navy. He reminded Poe of a less sober Uncle Albert from *Only Fools and Horses*. Poe had no idea what Scoplett had done to get the same punishment posting as him, but he suspected gross incompetence was a big part of it. He was the only sailor Poe had met who said left and right instead of port and starboard.

If anything, the two chuckleheads from the Border Force were worse. At least Scoplett tried – not to fall overboard, mainly – whereas Amer Anwar and Clancy Bright seemed to rejoice in their stupidity. As well as that, they were mean, lazy and misogynistic. Poe had received an email from an old contact in customs. It was just their names in the subject line and ten rows of laughing emojis.

Their new line of attack was that Poe had a therapist. They thought that was funny. They didn't know *why* he had a therapist, but that didn't seem to matter. They'd been making snide comments for days, trying to get a rise, but Poe wasn't playing. He barely listened to them. It would come to a head at some point, but he wasn't ready yet.

Because, as stubborn as he was, Poe *was* getting tired of it all. He was tired of smelling of fish, and he was tired of the commute. Of the nights at sea. He missed his fiancée, and he missed his friend, Tilly Bradshaw. His *best* friend. When the last case had concluded, the dream team was split up. He had been sent to the training wing, SCAS's boss, DI Stephanie Flynn, had been promoted to DCI and gone to a Modern Slavery unit, and Bradshaw had been seconded to the security services; doing what, she wouldn't say. He knew she was as miserable as him, though.

So, in secret they'd been making a plan . . . It was a great plan and he was tempted to put it into action soon.

But not before he'd kicked the shit out of the Border Force guys.

Chapter 5

The boat they'd just boarded was called the *Aurora II*. It was a 14-metre trawler and it had been chugging its way back to Cornwall when they'd boarded it. It had taken Scoplett four attempts to bring HMS *Lancaster* alongside. Everyone had found somewhere else to look as he kept messing up what was a basic naval task. He was less Captain Cook, more Captain Pugwash.

But eventually, with the help of a lucky swell, he'd managed to get close enough to tie up and board. Scoplett nodded. Job well done. He removed his hip flask, took a swig then offered it around. No one accepted.

The *Aurora II*'s three-man crew, a father and his two sons, were sullen but cooperative. They were big men, bearded with scarred hands. Thick Cornish accents. Sounded like Worzel Gummidge. Work strong, not gym strong.

Clancy Bright asked to see their paperwork. He was smiling. Bright loved to order fishermen around. Loved to abuse the tiny bit of authority he had. Poe was surprised he hadn't used a German accent. He thought Bright would have been an enthusiastic Nazi.

Everything seemed to be in order. The father provided an up-to-date fishing vessel licence, the boat had all the required safety equipment, and Poe didn't need to weigh their catch to know it was under their quota.

But it *was* halibut and that was a problem.

'Cuff them,' he said.

'You're not in charge of me, Poe,' Anwar said. 'You fucking cuff them.'

'Actually, this is now a live crime scene, so I am in charge. If you don't cuff them, I'll assume you're part of whatever this is and, as I'm outnumbered, I'd be within the law if I belted you around the head with this fishing gaff.' He picked up a metal shaft. It had a wicked-looking hook on the end.

Anwar and Bright scrambled to get out their cuffs and it wasn't long before the three fishermen were in custody. Poe read them their rights. They didn't seem overly concerned.

'You mind telling us what the hell's just happened?' Bright said. He picked up a halibut. Held it by its gill and rubbed off some of the ice. It was about a metre long, all fleshy and fat. Looked fresh. 'Because these guys have a catch to land.'

'This boat is fitted out for purse seining,' Poe said. He looked at their blank faces and sighed. He hadn't known anything about fishing when he'd started, but he'd learned what he needed to. It was a shit job but that didn't mean he wasn't going to do it properly. 'Come on, guys, you can remember this.' He waited. Sighed again and said, 'Purse seining works by drawing a vast net around a shoal of fish. The bottom is weighted, and the top is buoyed by floats. When the shoal is in the net, the bottom is closed – or *pursed* – like a drawstring bag and the fish are trapped.'

'Yeah, we knew that,' Anwar said. 'So what?'

'So, purse seining is used for midwater fish like mackerel and sardines. The halibut is a flatfish and that means they live on the bottom of the sea. They're caught with trawler nets, not purse seines. In any case, even if they had found a way to catch a bottom-dwelling fish with a midwater net, they have no way of getting their catch onboard. That winch hasn't been used in months by the look of it.'

The father burst out laughing. 'Is that it?' he said. 'You've arrested us because you think a fish that swims on the bottom

22

of the sea *stays* on the bottom of the sea? Let me ask you something, Mr Policeman. What do halibut eat?'

'They're predators,' Poe said.

'Yes, they are. And they're ravenous. And in the waters we fish, halibuts are at the top of the food chain. That means they can venture up to feed. So yes, purse seine nets *are* used to catch them.'

'Your winch?'

'Yes, the winch is knackered and I haven't got the money to replace it. It's why I have my boys with me, dickface.'

Behind him, Poe could hear Anwar and Bright sniggering.

'Hey, Brighty,' Anwar said. 'Maybe they *didn't* catch them. Maybe there's a serial-killer conger eel down there. Maybe these guys aren't fishermen. Maybe they're crime scene cleaners.'

Bright laughed so hard, snot came out of his nose. When he'd cleaned himself up, he said, 'Just as well we have the great Washington Poe on the case then.'

'No, no, he doesn't do that any more, remember?' Anwar said, a nasty smirk on his face. 'Because he's sooooo depressed.' He clutched some imaginary pearls and Bright brayed like a donkey. He said, 'Now, can we let these poor men go? It's getting dark and I want to go home.'

'And he'll want to get back to that woman he's stringing along,' Bright said.

'Got his feet right under the table with Miss Snooty Britches, hasn't he?'

'Snooty *bitch*, more like.'

Poe didn't answer. If the last couple of minutes had been the song 'Coward of the County', it would have got to the part where Tommy was about to lock himself in the bar with the Gatlin boys.

But it wasn't a song.

Instead, Poe picked up a halibut, swung it around like an

Olympic hammer thrower, and whacked Bright over the head with it. Bright dropped to the deck of the *Aurora II* like a bag of wet towels.

'I don't see my therapist for depression,' Poe said. 'I see her for anger management.'

Bright clambered to his feet and readied his fists. Anwar rolled his shoulders, then crouched.

This fight had been a long time coming.

Poe wondered which way it would go. The Border Force guys looked like they'd fight dirty but there were witnesses. It would be fists and headbutts and kicks to the balls. When Poe was still in uniform, he'd patrolled Botchergate, Carlisle's yellow-headed pimple, and the scene of most of its alcohol-fuelled violence. He knew how to scrap in the gutter. The trick was to keep going, even when you were getting hurt. Make the other person regret it before you did.

But there were two of them. The numbers were in their favour. They had four fists to his two. They were twice as heavy and five times as stupid.

In the end it was moot.

The fight stopped before it could start when something fell out of the belly of the halibut Poe was holding.

Three hundred yards away on HMS *Biter*, a Royal Navy *Archer*-class fast inshore patrol boat, DCI Stephanie Flynn had her eyes glued to a pair of binoculars. 'Ha-ha, look at that salty bastard,' she said. 'Poe looks like Captain Haddock.'

'What's happening?'

'Nothing, they're just . . .'

'What is it?'

'I'm not entirely sure,' Flynn said, 'but it looks like Poe's just picked up a massive fish and whacked one of his colleagues with it.'

'Excuse me?'

'Er . . . I don't think I can say it any differently to be honest. Poe grabbed a fish, it might be a cod, and swung it round his head and knocked one of his colleagues off his feet. And before you ask, this is Poe; if you want logic and reason, you're in the wrong place.' She paused, tried to work out what was happening on the boat that HMS *Lancaster* had boarded. 'Uh-oh, now it looks like they're all going to start brawling.'

'Step on it,' the skipper said to the helmsman. He'd been told to take DCI Flynn to Poe and then get them both back to the mainland as fast as possible. His orders hadn't specified whether Poe had to be bloodied or unbloodied, but he was an officer in the Royal Navy; not everything had to be explicit.

HMS *Biter* surged forward as the helmsman gave it the beans. The engines growled and began churning the water in their wake. It wasn't long before they'd reached their top speed, around 25 knots. Despite *Biter* bouncing around like a roller-coaster, Flynn kept her eyes stuck on what was happening on the fishing trawler. 'Now it seems they're all looking at something on the deck,' she said.

'What?'

'I have absolutely no idea, but it's got them all excited. They certainly aren't thinking of fighting any more.'

Back on the *Aurora II*, the fisherman father said, 'That's not mine.' He glared at his sons.

'It's not ours either,' the younger one protested. 'We were told it was drugs.'

They bred smart criminals in Cornwall.

'That isn't drugs, son,' Poe said. 'That's a Glock.' He gloved up and retrieved it from the deck. The gun was shrink-wrapped with thick clear plastic. 'A Glock 17, to be precise.' He shouted over to HMS *Lancaster*'s remaining crew member, 'Mr Scoplett, can you call this in, please? The whole boat's a crime scene now and I don't want to lose evidence. But we'll take these three into our custody now.' There was no response. He risked a glance. 'Are you *asleep*?'

Whether HMS *Lancaster*'s skipper was asleep or not was immaterial: the sound of the loudhailer would have woken the dead.

'Ahoy-hoy, Captain Poe!' Flynn said. 'You mind telling me what's going on?'

Poe turned. HMS *Biter* had come alongside. No one had noticed.

Scoplett woke with a start. 'Ship ahoy,' he said.

'Well shiver me timbers,' Poe said.

Chapter 6

Cabinet Office Briefing Room C, Whitehall, London

Poe and Flynn walked into a full briefing room. A man in a suit was talking over a PowerPoint presentation. He had sandy hair, combed and wavy, the way King Charles had worn his in his forties. It was a look only posh people could get away with. He caught Poe's eyes. The man in the suit's flickered but he recovered beautifully. He gestured towards a pair of empty seats.

'I'll be two minutes,' he said. 'Then we'll do some introductions.'

Poe looked around the room. It was the first time he'd been to Whitehall. The inside, or this bit at least, was less impressive than the outside. The exterior looked like something out of *Mary Poppins*, the inside like the group activity room in a job centre. The people watching the PowerPoint presentation were a mixed bag. There were men and women in suits, men and women in jeans and T-shirts. Some were taking notes, others were on their phone tapping away at texts or emails. Two of them looked like they were taking notes for their boss. There was a guy hiding behind a copy of *The Times* who seemed to be ignoring everyone, and a woman with a scattering of acne on her forehead who was chewing on a hangnail. It looked like there was only one cop in the room. Poe had met her a few years earlier on a serial poisoner case. Mathers, he thought she was called. Good at her job. He didn't know all the Met ranks, but he thought she might be a commander by now, maybe a deputy assistant commissioner. He nodded at her. She ignored him.

The screen went blank.

'You must be Detective Sergeant Poe,' the man with the King-Charles-in-his-forties haircut said. 'Glad to have you onboard.'

'Onboard what?' Poe said carefully.

'Haven't you been briefed?'

'I haven't even had time to shower.'

'You can say that again,' Flynn muttered. Then louder, 'There were things to clear up before we could get away, sir, and Poe needed to be on the phone for the entire journey.'

'What things?' the man said. 'This has the *highest* priority.' An aide came in and whispered in his ear. She handed him a memo. 'I'm not sure this is going to work,' he said. 'It says here that not two hours ago you assaulted one of your colleagues with a deadly weapon.'

'It was a fish,' Flynn said. 'Hardly deadly.'

The man rechecked his memo. 'It says Sergeant Poe hit a Border Force agent called Clancy Bright with a halberd.'

'It was a halibut, sir.'

The man handed the memo back to the aide. 'Who wrote this?' he said.

The aide shrugged then fled. Someone was in line for a telling-off later, Poe thought.

'Regardless, this is indicative of what we were told of the man—'

'I'm out of here,' Poe said, getting to his feet.

'Sit down, Poe,' Flynn said. 'And, sir, perhaps we can start again. The reason we were late, and the reason Sergeant Poe hasn't been briefed, is because not two hours ago he broke a major gun-running operation, one we didn't even know existed. That's why he was on his phone all the way here. He was arranging for the shipment of halibut to reach its intended destination, *sans* guns, of course. That way we can pick up the buyers as well as the couriers.'

The man with the King-Charles-in-his-forties haircut said, 'Of course. Things are getting heated and I apologise. So yes, let's start again. My name is Timothy Spiggens.' Poe looked at him blankly. 'I'm a minister with the Home Office,' he added.

'And what is the Home Office?' Poe said.

'Are you serious? It's the biggest department in His Majesty's Government, man!'

'And what is a govern—'

'Pack it in, Poe,' Flynn cut in.

Mathers hid a smile behind her hand.

'Fine,' Poe said. 'I take it this is something to do with that lunatic who's shooting people?'

Spiggens nodded.

'And you're the group spearheading the strategic and political response?'

'You've heard of a COBRA meeting?'

'I have.'

'Well, this is one.'

'In that case I won't waste your time,' Poe said. 'I'm not interested.'

'You don't know what I'm going to say yet!'

'Don't I?' Poe said. 'Six months ago, I asked the man who dismantled SCAS who he was going to call the next time a monster crawled out from under the bed, and do you know what he said?'

'What *who* said?'

'A lanky prick called Alastor Locke.'

Flynn put her head in her hands and said, 'Oh, Lord.'

'I have no idea what Mr Locke said,' Spiggens said.

'Maybe you can ask the lanky prick himself, Timothy,' a voice said.

It was the guy who'd been hiding behind a copy of *The Times*.

'Hello, Poe,' Locke said, making a show of folding his

newspaper and slipping it into his briefcase. 'It's been a while. And yes, I *do* remember what I said.'

'What was it, Alastor?' Spiggens asked.

'I said, "I'm sure we'll manage."' Locke spread his arms. 'It seems I may have been a bit too nippy on the buzzer.'

Chapter 7

Flynn grabbed Poe's arm. Told him to stay calm without saying anything. He shrugged her off and got to his feet. He walked around the table and stood behind Locke. Locke turned to face him. He didn't appear concerned. The corner of his mouth lifted.

'What can you smell, Alastor?' Poe said.

Locke wafted his hand under his nose, like he was sniffing a fine wine. 'My dear boy, you appear to smell of fish.'

Poe reached up and tugged his ragged beard. 'And what's this?'

'I assume that's rhetorical?'

'Riddle me this,' Poe said. 'Who spends his life at sea but isn't a fisherman?'

Locke smiled politely. Didn't answer.

'Do you know what I was doing' – Poe checked his watch – 'not four hours ago?'

'DCI Flynn says you were heroically, and no doubt single-handedly, protecting these fair shores from those who would do us harm.'

Poe took a breath. 'Wrong. Four hours ago, I had my hand so far up a halibut's arsehole it was like I was reaching for a bingo ball.'

'Eloquently put, as ever, Poe,' Locke said.

'And the reason I was doing this was because you screwed me over. You screwed *everyone* over. I should have been on this from day one. Not seventeen bodies later.'

'Nevertheless, we're asking for your help now.' His eyes had turned steely and his voice had an edge. Locke wasn't some political lacky, he was a hard-nosed spy. He wasn't going to take Poe's shit forever.

'Well you can't have it,' Poe said. 'It's too late now. Too much evidence has been lost and whoever is doing this has got too good. No offence to the guys investigating, but he isn't going to get caught. He'll stop when he decides to stop.'

'No offence taken, Poe,' Mathers said. 'We're nowhere.'

'And I warned you this would happen, Alastor,' Poe said, his voice as flat and cold as Locke's. 'I fucking warned you.'

'You were very clear, Poe,' Locke admitted.

'I said SCAS was the last line of defence, the contingency you hoped you'd never have to use.'

'You did.'

'I'm not even talking about me,' Poe said. 'I'm a good detective but so are five hundred other cops. Two of them are in this very room. DCI Flynn is better than me and . . . I'm sorry, ma'am, I don't know what rank you are now.'

'I'm a commander, Poe.'

'And Commander Mathers is better than me.'

'I think you do yourself a disservice, Poe,' Locke said.

'I don't give a shit what you think,' Poe said. 'And the *reason* I don't is that through good judgement or blind luck the team DCI Flynn put together had the kind of alchemy never seen before in law enforcement. We were the envy of the world and that wasn't down to me, and it wasn't down to the boss, it was down to just one person. A genius, a once-in-a-generation mind who for some reason wanted to put her extraordinary mind to catching serial killers instead of solving mathematical problems. And yes, she needed time to readjust to the new world she'd chosen to work in, but with a little help from me and DCI Flynn she quickly became SCAS's golden goose. The ace up our sleeve, our silver bullet, a thousand other clichés. Within days, we were catching the kind of bad guys who never get caught. The kind of bad guys you're panicking over now. But that wasn't enough, was it? You wanted more. So what did you do? You stole the golden goose for yourself.' He paused. Took a breath. 'And then you ate it for fucking Christmas.'

'Have you heard of the trolley problem, Poe?'

Poe said nothing. Concentrated on getting his breathing under control. He could feel another episode of PTSD-related violence coming on.

'It's one in a series of ethical thought experiments,' Locke continued. 'Imagine there's a runaway trolley and five people are tied to the track. If the trolley runs over them, all five will be killed. But, and here's the sharp kick to the ankle, there's a lever that can be pulled to divert the trolley. The problem is that on the new track there is one person who will be killed. The ethical dilemma is whether it is morally wrong to do nothing and let five people die, or to intervene and sacrifice one "safe" person to save the rest.'

Poe considered that for a few beats. 'You're talking about the greater good,' he said. 'That the needs of the many outweigh the needs of the few.'

'A rather simplistic summary, but yes.'

'Do you know how much evil shit has been done for the greater good? The Holocaust, Swiss eugenics, *slavery*.'

'Yes, Poe, in your world of absolutes, I'm sure that's how it must appear,' Locke said. He tilted his head. 'But did you ever wonder *why* I took the actions I did? Because you're quite correct, your beloved Serious Crime Analysis Section was doing extraordinary work. Lives *were* being saved; justice *was* being done. And yes, a significant part of that was down to one person, your so-called golden goose. Despite this, I stole her from you. Do I appear reckless to you, Poe? Because if things *were* as black

33

and white as you say, surely only a reckless fool would have done as I did.'

'You're either part of the solution or you're part of the problem, Sergeant Poe,' Spiggens said. 'What's it to be?'

'Definitely part of the problem,' Flynn said. 'In fact, he usually makes things worse.'

'Thanks, boss,' Poe said. He turned to Locke. 'I don't think you're reckless, Alastor. I just think you see the world as your private chessboard. You spend so much time manipulating your kings and queens, your bishops, knights and rooks, that you forget about the little people. The pawns. They're an afterthought. There only to justify your actions.'

'I think that might be enough, Poe,' Flynn said.

A year ago, she'd have ordered him to stop. Today he reckoned she was silently cheering him on. He wasn't the only person Locke had screwed over.

Locke held up his hand. 'It's fine, DCI Flynn,' he said. 'Tell me, Poe; has your golden goose ever told you about the work she's been doing for me?'

Poe shook his head. Wondered why he was engaging with Locke at all. 'She won't tell me anything.'

'And I won't betray her confidence now,' he said. 'But please be assured that hundreds of lives have been saved. *Ordinary* lives. Your pawns. So, did I take your prize asset? Yes. Have people died at the hands of those you might have caught? Possibly, probably even. But the big question is – and considering where we are now, it's not as easy to answer as it once would have been – would I do the same again?' He held Poe with a look like a beartrap. 'You bet your bloody life I would.'

He took off his glasses and began polishing them. Poe thought he looked much older than the last time they'd met. He seemed tired. His hair was greyer.

'But I'm not here to convince you to help,' he continued. 'I know you well enough to know you won't be able to get past what I did. You're far too recalcitrant to forgive and forget.'

'He's an arsehole,' Flynn confirmed.

'Whose side are you bloody on?' Poe said.

'The same side you used to be on! The public's side. And in case you haven't noticed what's going on out there, it's chaos. Never mind that dickhead's the-economy-is-stagnating bigger picture bullshit – real people are suffering.'

'I've noticed,' Poe said. 'But I meant what I said: we should have been in at the start. If our shooter was going to make a mistake, it would have been when he was starting. He's too good at this now.'

'We give up, is that it?'

'*We* don't do anything, DCI Flynn. There is no *we*. We had a unit singularly equipped for events like this and now we don't.' He jabbed his finger in Locke's direction. 'Blame him, not me.'

'This is getting us nowhere,' Spiggens said. He reached forward and pressed the intercom. 'Please, send her in.'

'Right away, sir.'

'If we can't make you see reason, perhaps she can.'

'Who?' Poe said.

The door opened and a thin bespectacled woman entered. She was clutching some papers and looked like the physical manifestation of the word 'bookworm'. She was bright and she was silly and she was brave and loyal and everything that was good. Her name was Tilly Bradshaw and she was Poe's favourite person in the world.

'I'm not sure I like everyone comparing me to a goose, Poe,' she said. 'They're particularly dumb birds.'

Poe stared in astonishment. Bradshaw grinned back.

'Have you missed me?' she said.

Chapter 8

'Have you ever seen a goose, Tilly?' Poe said, smiling wildly. He hadn't seen Bradshaw for almost two months, and he hadn't realised how much he'd missed her. 'And I don't mean a cartoon one like Donald Duck.'

'Donald Duck is a duck, Poe,' Bradshaw said. 'The clue is in his surname. It's "Duck".'

'You make a good point. But here's something I bet you didn't know: Donald Duck speaks like that because he had PTSD.'

'Gosh, really?'

Poe nodded. 'It's why he keeps flying into a rage. He wears a naval uniform and was around during the Second World War. He'll have almost certainly seen active service.'

'But *you* have PTSD and keep flying into a rage, Poe. You don't speak like Donald Duck.'

Poe said, 'Quack.'

'If you're both finished?' Spiggens said irritably.

'Finished?' Flynn said. 'They're only getting started, mate. They can keep this shit up for weeks.'

Poe said, 'What are you doing here, Tilly?'

'Alastor Locke made me come,' Bradshaw replied. 'I'm supposed to help change your mind. He says you're as stubborn as a Muirkirk iron—'

'I don't know if that's good or bad,' Poe said.

'I don't either, but he seemed awfully keen for me to be here.'

'To persuade me to go and work with him?'

'Yes, Poe.'

'And do you think I should?'

'Not if you don't want to. That last case almost killed you. You're still seeing Doctor Clara Lang and you have a wonderful life ahead with Estelle Doyle. I think you should let someone else do it this time.'

'This isn't what we discussed, Miss Bradshaw,' Locke said.

Locke may as well have not spoken. Bradshaw was like a mother bear when it came to Poe. Protective didn't come close to describing how far she'd go when it came to watching his back.

'But we'd be working together again,' he said. 'That'd be fun.'

'Actually, Miss Bradshaw is needed elsewhere, Poe,' Locke said. 'It would only be you and DCI Flynn.'

Bradshaw's shoulders slumped. She tried to smile but couldn't manage it.

'Do you enjoy what you're doing for Alastor, Tilly?' Poe said.

'I hate it, Poe,' she said. 'The people I work with are nit-wits and the work is unchallenging. And I never know if what Alastor Locke orders me to do is a good thing or not. At least when I worked with you and DCI Flynn, I never doubted that what we were doing was just, even if we did upset a lot of people along the way.'

'That was mainly Poe to be fair, Tilly,' Flynn said.

'It was. But he was always honest about why he wanted me to do certain things. So were you. And then it was my decision if I wanted to do it or not. But Alastor lies all the time.'

'I'm a spy,' Locke shrugged. 'It's in my job description.' He removed his glasses and began polishing them again.

'I work with Tilly or I don't work at all, Alastor.'

'I don't think he's bluffing, mate,' Flynn said.

'Alastor,' Spiggens warned. 'I don't want to go over your head, but I will if I have to.'

'Of course,' Locke said. He smiled politely at Poe. 'If you *and* Miss Bradshaw could review the evidence, the Right Honourable Mr Spiggens and I would be eternally grateful.'

Chapter 9

Mathers took them to the incident room. The Met had assumed command because the first shooting had taken place in London, and because they were the only force with enough horsepower to manage something this big – but sixteen territorial forces were conducting their own investigations. The sniper had shot and killed multiple people but never in the same police area. Which meant that as well as leading the national response, Mathers was also coordinating murder investigations in seventeen different force areas. They needed everyone else's intelligence, and they needed to feed in their own. Each force had sent liaison officers and they all required space to work. They needed back-office staff and technical support. For every badged officer there were four or five without badges helping them do their job. A bog-standard incident room wasn't going to cut it this time. Mathers needed somewhere bigger.

She had taken the pragmatic choice and hired Blencathra House, a conference centre near the British Library. It was equidistant between King's Cross and Euston – the two main train stations northern cops would use. She'd hired the whole centre and brought in her own staff to protect it. Armed cops patrolled the grounds and checked the ID of everyone entering and exiting the building.

After they'd got through security, Flynn and Bradshaw were waylaid by someone they'd once worked with. Poe didn't know them, so he followed Mathers. He wasn't in the mood to meet new people.

'How's this working out?' Poe asked.

'It's the private sector so it's better than anything we have,' Mathers said. 'Their tech is superb. The broadband is shit hot. Everything is state-of-the-art. If it weren't, businesses wouldn't use it.'

'How many people are in here?'

'At any one time, at least three hundred. When there's a big briefing or a new murder it can double as cops from outside the area come in.'

'Anything from the hotline?'

'Nothing sensible. Lots of grievances being settled.'

Poe grunted his annoyance. Any time a hotline was set up, the public took the opportunity to ratchet up decade-long feuds. The original argument might have stemmed from their neighbour's dog shitting on their lawn, but by the time they called the hotline it was because Bob from next door was 'noncey as fuck' or he'd converted his garage into an IRA bomb factory.

'There hasn't been a single breakthrough?' Poe said. 'Maybe something you didn't want to tell the blabbermouth politician about?'

'Nothing actionable. We know the weapon and ammunition he's using, but that's it. He shoots from distance and he doesn't leave any trace evidence. Before he leaves he throws down a load of sugar. Within minutes the ground's covered in creepy-crawlies and within minutes of them turning up, a bunch of birds have arrived to eat them.'

'Clever,' Poe said. 'So even if he's left trace evidence, the wild-life makes it next to impossible to recover it.'

'Exactly.'

'What distance is he shooting from?'

'The closest was two hundred yards – from just inside the treeline of a wood – and the furthest was twelve hundred.'

'Good shooting.'

'Some of us think it's *too* good,' Mathers said. 'The current theory is that he's an ex-military sniper.'

'Is that what *you* think?'

'I'd rather hear what you think. You have completely fresh eyes.'

Mathers had stopped next to a trestle table stocked with fruit and sandwiches and pastries. Fuel for those who didn't have time to nip out for food. Poe grabbed a mug and poured himself a coffee. He took a sandwich, lifted the corner, and put it back.

'Fish paste,' he said in disgust. 'That's all I bloody need.' He took a drink of coffee. It was hot, nicer than expected. He lifted his mug in appreciation. 'Private sector providing the coffee too?'

Mathers nodded. 'Speaking of the private sector – why the hell are you still on that boat? Why aren't you doing three days a month consultancy for six figures a year?'

Poe took his time answering. 'I've thought about it,' he admitted. 'I went through some . . . stuff recently.'

'I heard.'

'I thought I was invincible. Turns out I'm not. And swimming in shit all day *is* rapidly losing its appeal.'

'Also, aren't you a duke now?' Mathers said, grinning. 'Don't you have poor people to oppress?'

Poe returned her smile. It was true that he was marrying into the aristocracy. Doyle had inherited her late father's title and estate. She was now *Lady* Doyle. 'Since we got engaged, I'd be surprised if we've spent two consecutive nights together.'

'I know what you mean,' Mathers said. 'I have two daughters I never see. I missed my eldest representing her school in the lacrosse finals this year.'

'It takes its toll,' Poe agreed. 'It's because we never have good days, only bad.'

Mathers burst out laughing. 'What a pair of moaning bastards we are.' She pushed herself off the wall she'd been leaning

41

against. 'Anyway, you're here to work. So please, tell me what you think.'

'You really want to know?' Poe said.

'Ordinarily, SCAS sticking their beak into an ongoing operation is about as welcome as genital warts. But I don't know how to catch this guy, Poe. Tell me what you think.'

'Why have you focused on military snipers?'

'Because he's familiar with weapons. Because he can shoot. Because he can hide.'

'So can gamekeepers, Civil War re-enactment weirdos, police marksmen and people who compete in biathlons,' Poe said. 'And modern sights make a thousand yards look like fifty.'

Mathers said nothing.

'But you already know this, don't you, ma'am?'

She nodded. 'I told you, we're nowhere,' she said. 'But it's a theory, and not everyone hates it, so I've assigned resources to running it down.'

'And in the meantime?'

'We do what we always do – run down every scrap of evidence, every tip that comes through the hotline, and then pray he fucks up.'

Bradshaw and Flynn rejoined them.

'That was Harold Hetherington,' Flynn said.

Poe shrugged. 'So what?'

'He smelled of wee,' Bradshaw said.

'Better than fish,' Poe said. Urine was on his list of unpleasant things to smell of, but it was well below fish.

Mathers smirked. 'Come on, I'll show you to your office,' she said.

'We have an office?' Poe said, surprised.

'The NCA does. It's got computers and coffee-making facilities and the rest of the stuff you might need. It's on the other side of the incident room.'

She opened a door.

Poe said, 'Blimey.'

The incident room was as big as an aircraft hangar and twice as noisy. It was crammed with men and women on phones and computers. The walls were covered with maps and data sets. A thousand other things. Everyone looked busy; no one looked happy. Poe had seen hundreds of incident rooms, but this was the first he'd seen without hope. Pessimism instead of optimism. The anger he felt about Alastor Locke fizzled out. These were real cops and they needed his help.

Mathers walked them through the incident room. She opened another door and took them down a long corridor. She unlocked an office and showed them inside. It was a large and airy room. A table, computer terminals, whiteboards. The blinds were closed. No surprise there. The odds of making it into the sniper's sights were astronomically high, but this was the nerve centre of the hunt. The investigation team would be an attractive target and the sniper had already demonstrated his proficiency in urban environments. He didn't always hide in the woods.

'This is you,' Mathers said.

Bradshaw took a seat at one of the computer terminals. Poe wandered over to the window and pulled a blind aside. Nice view. He could see the British Library.

Mathers said, 'I'll get you set up with accounts so you can access the data portals—'

'I'm already in,' Bradshaw said.

'Of course you are. OK, I'll get Poe and DCI Flynn set up with accounts—'

Bradshaw held up her left index finger while her right danced across the keyboard faster than the eye could see. 'They're in now as well, Commander Mathers,' she said. 'DCI Flynn's password is her son's date of birth and Poe's is PASSWORD – all upper-case – as it's the only one he can remember.'

Poe wandered over to a trestle table pushed against a wall. He opened one of the boxes. It was full of doughnuts. 'Are these anyone's?'

'They're yesterday's, but help yourself,' Mathers said.

Poe did. He bit into one then wiped raspberry jam from his chin.

Bradshaw said, 'Would it be possible to get rid of all this junk food, Commander Mathers? Poe eats like a racoon and I've just promised Estelle Doyle that I would make sure he eats five pieces of fruit a day.'

'Jam *is* fruit,' Poe said. 'And when did you speak to Estelle?'

'I texted her on the way over,' Bradshaw said. 'They're getting married, Commander Mathers. The wedding rehearsal is in two days. I'm Poe's best man! I'm writing a speech and everything. Poe's very excited about that.'

'No, I'm not. Stop saying that.'

'Unfortunately, he has hypertension.'

'I have hypertension because I have PTSD and I don't sleep, Tilly. Cutting out the occasional biscuit won't change that.'

'Oh, *puh-lease*! Your diet is the worst I've seen, Poe. Ever since we've known each other you haven't eaten a single healthy thing, not unless someone buys it for you. Even then they have to stand in front of you while you eat it. A high-fibre, low-salt, low-fat diet won't kill you, but hypertension might.' She turned back to the computer. 'At the very least you'll end up with faecal impaction. And you won't like how they treat that, mister. No, sir, you won't like that at all. It involves a rectal bulb syringe and what they do is—'

'Will you *please* stop talking to Estelle about my diet?' Poe took a breath, saw Mathers and Flynn grinning. He reddened. 'And there's nothing wrong with my bowels.'

'Well, all I know is that I wouldn't want to go in the toilet after you,' Bradshaw said.

'Oh, wouldn't you? Well, answer me this, smarty-pants: who *would* you like to go into the toilet after?'

Bradshaw paused. Turned back round. 'You make an interesting point,' she said.

Mathers snorted. She said, 'I've missed working with you guys.'

Poe said, 'I want to go back to my boat.'

Chapter 10

After Mathers had left, taking the snacks with her, they got down to business.

Flynn said, 'Tilly and I have been briefed, but you're coming into this cold, Poe. Where do you want to start?'

'I only know what's been in the press, so elevator pitch me,' he replied. 'There are two hundred good detectives out there, so the basics are covered. The *details* are covered. We're not a case review team; that spindly prick Locke wants us to think of something no one else has.'

'OK,' Flynn said. 'There have been seventeen murders so far and, as far as we can tell, he's only used seventeen bullets. He hasn't missed, he hasn't needed more than one shot.'

'What calibre is he using?'

'A .50 BMG.'

Poe whistled. 'That'll do it. That bullet's heavy enough to go through an engine block,' he said. 'Not an easy round to get hold of in the UK, though.'

'Mathers has fifty detectives working the gun angle. So far, zip.'

'Anything on how he selects his victims?'

'He's an equal opportunities killer – men, women, children, white, black, brown. No one is safe. Also, he's never been in the same force area twice. London was first, but he's killed in Birmingham, Lancashire and Cambridge. Taunton and Bristol. Warwick. Nottingham. The last one was in Gretna Green so

Police Scotland have joined the manhunt now. The only part of the UK he hasn't been is Northern Ireland.'

'He won't risk taking his rifle on a ferry,' Poe said. 'Not unless he's fashioned it into a crutch.' He waited for them to get his *The Day of the Jackal* reference. They didn't. He muttered, 'Savages.'

Flynn ignored him. 'Or he's known over there.'

'Mathers thinks there's an Irish connection?'

'She's not ruling it out.'

'We keep saying "he",' Poe said. 'Is that intentional or are we going by bullet calibre? It takes a lot of rifle to fire a round that big.'

'The crime-scene guys have measured impressions found at his firing positions, and the gap between his elbows and knees indicates the sniper's over six feet tall.'

'That doesn't rule out the sniper being a tall woman.'

'It doesn't,' Flynn said. 'And historically, some of the deadliest snipers in history have been women.'

Poe nodded. He knew that. During what the Soviets called their Great Patriotic War, and the rest of the world called the Second World War, it was all hands to the pump. Poe hadn't been surprised to learn that the ten deadliest female snipers in history were all Soviets. Lyudmila Pavlichenko, a Ukrainian who fought with the Red Army, had 309 confirmed kills. An astonishing number by today's standards.

'Tell me what Mathers is leaving out of her press briefings.'

'The empty bullet case is left at the firing position.'

'He doesn't police his brass?' Poe said, surprised.

'He doesn't,' Flynn replied. 'He ejects the casing and leaves it where it lands.'

'That's deliberate then,' Poe said. 'Sniper rifles aren't semi-automatic. They don't automatically eject the empty case and load a new one. It has to be done manually. Which means if he's ejecting his brass, it's because he wants it to be found.'

'Yes. We figure at some point he'll get in touch, and this is how he'll prove he is who he says he is.'

Poe didn't respond.

'What?' Flynn said.

'Why do you think he'll get in touch?'

'He's leaving a calling card. He's enjoying the attention. Getting in touch is the next logical step.'

'He isn't going to get in touch, boss,' Poe said. 'He's killed seventeen people without leaving a shred of actionable evidence. This lunatic is bark-at-the-moon crazy, but he isn't stupid. He won't get in touch.'

The door burst open. A fresh-faced woman stuck her head inside.

'Commander Mathers needs you in the main incident room right now, please.'

'Why?' Flynn asked, getting to her feet.

'It's the sniper,' the fresh-faced woman said. 'He's on the phone.'

Chapter 11

Mathers beckoned them over.

'He's called,' she said.

'I knew he would,' Poe said.

Bradshaw rolled her eyes. 'No, you said—'

'We can laugh at Poe later, Tilly,' Flynn cut in. 'Who took the call, ma'am?'

'No one,' Mathers replied. 'It was left on someone's voicemail not fifteen minutes ago. A North Yorkshire detective called Neil Munro.'

'How did he get his number?' Poe said.

'A question for later, I think.' She nodded at the man hovering over his computer. 'Let's hear it again.'

A mechanical voice filled the room.

'I'm the man who's culling the herd. The man who's causing the dip in GDP.' There was ten seconds of static. 'I'm the man leaving his empties at each firing position. And I'm the man sprinkling sugar so the wee beasties make recovering my DNA all but impossible.'

Poe and Flynn glanced at each other. *Wee beasties?* Very Scottish.

The voice continued. 'Now you have my credentials, here are the rules of the game. Rule one: I keep killing until you stop me. Rule two: I keep killing until you stop me. I know technically that's the same rule, but it's such an important one I thought it was worth mentioning twice. Rule three: and here's where it gets interesting. Despite what you might think, I'm not a monster. I want this to be a fair contest between bat and ball. And to *make* it fair, I leave a clue at each scene. A very small clue. If you're good enough, they'll lead you to my identity.' He paused. 'Until later.'

The room went silent.

Poe broke it. 'Either he's using voice-distorting software, or we've just heard from WALL-E.'

'I thought you didn't have a TV?' Mathers said. 'How the hell do you know who WALL-E is?'

Poe looked accusingly at Bradshaw. 'You'd be surprised at the useless shi . . . stuff I know now, ma'am. But my point is, voice-distorting software is another line of enquiry.'

'It's not,' Bradshaw said. 'There are hundreds of open-source programs out there. Unless he's as stupid as a chemistry teacher, he'll have downloaded one.'

'Untraceable then?'

'Yes, Poe.'

Mathers sighed. 'We'll run down official purchases anyway,' she said. 'But Tilly's right; this is a dead end.'

'Do we know where he was calling from?' Poe said.

'We're working on it,' the man on the computer said. 'It'll take time as it was left on a voicemail.'

'At least he's *made* contact,' Flynn said. 'Because Poe was kind of making sense; there was no upside to getting in touch. Only downsides.'

'It's how he asserts his dominance, DCI Flynn,' Bradshaw said. 'The BTK serial killer was caught after he sent a floppy disc to a television station, the Zodiac Killer left ciphers, and Son of Sam sent a letter to one of the police officers trying to catch him. It's his way of showing that he's in charge, not us.'

'He wanted us to know he's leaving clues at each scene,' Mathers said. 'Clues we've somehow managed to miss.'

'Which probably annoyed him,' Flynn said.

'Particularly if he's put time and effort into them.'

'We need to start at the beginning, ma'am,' Flynn said. 'We'll visit each scene, see what he's left for us.'

'Poe, you're being uncharacteristically quiet,' Mathers said.

Poe was rooting through a directory he'd found on the computer guy's desk, ran his finger down a list of names. He stopped, grimaced, then said, 'That's because revisiting the scenes would be a colossal waste of time, ma'am.'

Mathers blinked in surprise. 'I'm assuming that's not hyperbole?'

'No, ma'am. Looking for secret clues would be a colossal waste of time because the person who left that message isn't the killer.'

'Who *did* leave the voicemail then?'

Poe held her eye. He said, 'Wearside Jack.'

Chapter 12

'I beg your pardon?' Mathers said.

'Wearside Jack,' Poe repeated. 'That moron with a Wearside accent who sent letters and taped messages claiming to be the Yorkshire Ripper to the police. The cops bought it and moved the investigation away from West Yorkshire. Extended the investigation by eighteen months because they used the potential suspect's accent as one of the points of elimination.'

'But he knows about the sugar at the crime scene,' Mathers said. 'That's controlled information. *Highly* controlled.'

'It's a big investigation, ma'am,' Flynn said. 'And big investigations leak.'

Mathers put her head in her hands and groaned. 'This is all I fucking need. I can't ignore this and although the incident room is full of the best and brightest, I still don't have enough. The last thing I want to do is put fifty of them on a hoax phone call.'

'You don't need fifty, ma'am,' Poe said.

'I don't?'

Poe shook his head. 'Just the one.'

'Who?'

'Me.'

Flynn's eyes narrowed. 'You already know who made that call, don't you?'

'I don't,' Poe said. 'But I will in the next ten minutes.' He pulled out a chair, stood on it and steadied himself. 'With your permission, ma'am?'

Mathers nodded her approval.

Poe cupped his hands. 'OK, listen up!' he bellowed. 'My name's Washington Poe and I'm here representing the National Crime Agency. Nod if you can hear me.'

Silence. Not many nods.

'I'm not making a public service announcement!' Poe snapped. 'Ordinarily I'm as lacka-fucking-daisical as the next man when it comes to audience participation, but right now I'm not in the mood. So, if you can hear me, bloody nod. If you can't then move closer.'

Lots of nods this time.

'Thank you,' Poe said. 'Now, you've all heard the message left on Detective Munro's phone?'

More nods.

'That was left by a cop.' Poe did an Elon Musk – he let that sink in. The silence was crushing. 'A cop who's sitting in this room right now.'

Someone coughed. Someone else put down their mug. Loud in such a quiet room.

Poe cupped his ear, theatrically like he was on Broadway. 'How? I hear you ask. Well, please allow me to explain. The caller knew about the sugar left at each scene. Now, my boss quite rightly said this is a big investigation with a lot of moving parts. Things get leaked, mistakes are made. But I'm looking at a sea of the best cops this country has to offer, a group who don't make mistakes. Still, a bunch of cops this good will think I've made an *assumption*. That I'm, as Sherlock Holmes once said, twisting facts to suit theories instead of twisting theories to suit facts.'

Poe reached down for the directory he'd been looking at.

'This is a list of names and contact numbers for all the detectives working this case. And because more and more cops are joining the investigation, it's updated every morning at eight o'clock. Any officer who joins *after* eight a.m. is required to put their number on that whiteboard over there. It's where the bloke updating the directory gets the new numbers from.' Poe took a half-breath. 'Thing is, Detective Munro only joined the invest-igation today. He's not yet in the directory. It's why his number is still on the whiteboard over there.' Poe pointed towards the far wall. Some heads followed his hand, most didn't. 'Whoever made that call was in this room either yesterday or today. And, as Commander Mathers has this place sealed tighter than a frog's arsehole, it must have been someone who is *authorised* to be here.'

Poe threw the directory back on the table. He looked at the cops. No one was trying to avoid catching his eye.

'Now, when I told you my name, I could tell not everyone knew who I was,' Poe continued. 'That's fine. It's as it should be. No cop should be better known than the victims of the crimes he investigates. But those of you who don't know me *will* know my colleague, Tilly Bradshaw.'

There were audible gasps. People craned their necks to see her.

Bradshaw stood. She waved shyly and said, 'We're probably going to be here a few days, please don't give Poe any doughnuts.'

Poe rolled his eyes. 'Thanks, Tilly.' He then raised his voice and said, 'The moment I step down from this chair is the moment Tilly starts working on who sent that message. That person has between now and Tilly identifying them to step forward. Come to us and you'll only lose your job. Let us come to you and you'll lose your liberty as well.' He checked his watch. 'If you're lucky, you have ten minutes.'

He jumped down and walked back to the NCA office, ignor-ing the eyes that were on him. Flynn and Bradshaw followed him.

'You know I can't do what you said?' Bradshaw said the second Flynn shut the door.

Poe shrugged. 'I've learned to never underestimate you, Tilly.'

'But what if I can't?'

'It won't matter,' Poe said. 'Everyone in that room assumes you can.'

'Now what?' Flynn said.

Poe looked at the trestle table. He tried to will the bowl of fruit into normal food. 'As Tilly's confiscated everything edible, we may as well have a brew.'

The kettle was just starting to steam when Mathers knocked on the door and entered the room. She put a small box on the trestle table. 'I'm sorry, Tilly,' she said, 'but Poe gets a doughnut.'

'Bitchin',' Poe said, reaching for the box before Bradshaw could grab it.

'Someone fessed up?' Flynn said.

'Some prick from the Midlands,' she said. 'Came to see me within two minutes.'

'Did he say why?'

'Going through a divorce, drinking too much, a bunch of other stuff I don't give a shit about. He's been taken to Bethnal Green. I'll charge him with enough to get him remanded. I don't want him out until this is finished.' She opened her mouth and yawned, a right jaw-stretcher. 'Sorry,' she said. 'Sleep is hard to come by right now.' She took a moment then added, 'But I think I'll sleep tonight. Glad to have you onboard.' She yawned again. 'What's your plan, Poe?'

Poe shrugged. 'Wing it and see what happens.'

'The usual then?'

'He sticks to his strengths,' Bradshaw said.

Poe licked some sugar from his lips. 'We'll start where we always do,' he said. 'With the victims.'

Chapter 13

The M6 was busy around Birmingham, hectic around Manchester, and then quietened down. By the time they got to Cumbria it was like the start of an apocalypse movie. Poe found the muscles in his neck and shoulders relaxing. They always did when he saw the fells and mountains that the M6 weaved its way through. There might be more attractive sections of motorway in the UK, but Poe seriously doubted it.

Flynn was driving, Poe was in the back. Bradshaw was in the front passenger seat. She always was. She had stats to prove it was the safest place to be in the event of a crash. Poe looked wistfully at the salt store at junction 39. A few years ago, a mummified corpse was discovered there, and the chaos that followed – a serial killer burning men alive in Cumbria's myriad stone circles – had forged the three of them into the tightest team Poe had ever been part of. It felt good to be back together.

'I assume we're starting with the Gretna Green victim because it's close to where your wedding rehearsal is?' Flynn said, breaking into his thoughts.

Poe leaned forward, stuck his head between the two front seats. 'Actually, no,' he said. 'We're starting in Scotland because the people in that COBRA meeting don't understand guns.'

'And you do?'

'I'm ex-army.'

'That was years ago, Poe,' Flynn said. 'They probably don't use muskets any more.' She indicated, overtook a mud-splattered

Range Rover, then added, 'But go on, I'm listening.'

'The politicians and most of Mathers's cops might think this guy's Dead Eye Dick the crack shot, but that's because they don't understand how guns work.'

'What's to understand? You point them, you fire them. The rest is just bullshit so they can sell more copies of *Sporting Gun*.'

'Spoken like a true knob,' Poe said. 'Guns, particularly *long* guns, need to be zeroed.'

'What the hell does that mean?'

'It's where the weapon's sight and the barrel are aligned to the individual. Means that the point of aim and the point of impact are the same.'

'Aren't they all set at the factory?'

'They're not iPhones,' Poe said, shaking his head. 'People hold weapons differently. They look through the sights differently. They *fire* them differently. Put it this way, if I handed you my perfectly zeroed weapon, you likely wouldn't hit a thing. A centimetre's difference in the way we each hold the weapon could equate to two or three *metres* difference at the target end. It's that delicate.'

'Talk me through the process,' Flynn said. '*How* do you zero a weapon?'

'It's not difficult. You set up a target and you fire at it from the same distance you'll be firing from in the field. You check where your bullets are landing then you adjust your sights until you're hitting the middle of the target. Soon as they are, your weapon's zeroed.'

'His most common distance is twelve hundred metres,' Flynn said.

'Yards,' Bradshaw said without looking up from her phone. 'Yards, not metres. Twelve hundred yards is just over one thousand and ninety-seven metres.'

Flynn took her eyes off the road for a second and glared at Bradshaw. 'You can pack that in *right now*, Tilly.'

'Pack what in, DCI Flynn?'

'That pedantic arseho—'

'Boss,' Poe said, drawing it out.

'Sorry, Tilly,' Flynn said. 'I shouldn't have snapped at you.'

'That's OK, DCI Flynn,' Bradshaw said. 'You're probably perimenopausal.'

'Excuse me?'

'I said, you're—'

'I am *not* perimenopausal.'

'Anyway, that's why we're starting in Scotland, boss,' Poe said, stifling a grin. Flynn hadn't worked with Bradshaw for a while. She would need a period of adjustment. 'Zeroing a weapon can't be done in a lockup garage; it takes time, and it takes space. Can you think of anywhere else where that would go unnoticed? Eighty-five per cent of the UK's population live in England. Apart from the cities, Scotland's virtually empty.'

Flynn looked thoughtful. 'There's a lot of deer stalking in Scotland. Gunshots will be background noise up there.'

'Exactly,' Poe said. He paused, frowned. 'And it's not a one-off task. He's shooting from different ranges so it's an ongoing process. He'll *still* be zeroing his weapon in Scotland.'

'I'll have Police Scotland meet us at Gretna Green,' Flynn said.

Chapter 14

'Jesus, look at this place,' Flynn said. 'It's emptier than an English church.'

She wasn't wrong. Gretna Green, as well as the nearby town of Gretna, was usually bustling. Poe often made the quick trip over the border as one of Gretna's butchers sold full-size Stornoway black puddings. He knew there was no quiet season. Millions of visitors flocked to Gretna Green each year. They came for weddings, blacksmith blessings, marriage re-enactments and handfasting ceremonies, whatever the hell they were. They shopped in the outlet village, they drank in the pubs and they dined in the restaurants. And they wandered the streets like the gormless idiots all tourists were. Now it looked uninhabited.

But . . . that wasn't quite right. Gretna Green *was* empty, but only if you took a cursory view. When you studied it, really studied it, signs of life were everywhere. The shops were shuttered, but they *were* open. Pubs were serving drinks and meals, but tarpaulin covered the entrances and the curtains were drawn. The schools were open but outdoor activities had been cancelled. And when someone *did* have to go outside, they scrambled around like beetles whose rock had been overturned.

'I can't remember the last time I saw someone walk in a straight line,' Flynn said, watching him in the mirror. 'It's all zigzags or a crouching run now.'

'It's because he's so indiscriminate,' Poe said. 'It's like the early days of the pandemic. Unless you're at home, you don't feel safe.'

'No wonder he's been designated a threat to national security. It's chaos out here.'

'The sniper's like the Joker,' Bradshaw said. 'He was in it for the chaos, wasn't he, Poe?'

'If you say so, Tilly,' Poe said.

'Didn't you read that essay I did for New York University? It was called "Comic Book Villains and the Poincaré Map". I sent you the link.'

Flynn scowled. 'You sent *everyone* that link, Tilly,' she said.

Chapter 15

The seventeenth victim had been killed at the Mill Forge, a wedding venue two miles outside Gretna Green. Bradshaw had read out a potted history on the way up. It had started life as a grain farm in the eighteenth century, became a family home in the 1980s and was converted into a restaurant and bar in the 1990s. It became a wedding venue in 1999 and was now one of the most popular in Scotland. Which meant it was one of the most popular in the UK.

The car park was empty. Flynn parked near an old wooden wheel. It was as big as a house and had blades. Looked like the kind of thing that sat in running water, the blades turning the wheel, the wheel turning the grinder shaft, which turned the mill stone. One hundred years ago the wheel would have been used to turn grain into flour. Now it was a garden ornament.

'We're supposed to wait here for detectives from Police Scotland,' Flynn said.

'They're late,' Poe replied. 'How rude.'

'Actually, we're early.'

Poe opened the door. It had been a long trip and he wanted to stretch his legs.

'We may as well have a mooch around; this is a crime scene.'

'They won't be happy.'

'When are they ever? And look,' he said, pointing to a man waving them inside, 'that guy over there, he's inviting us in.'

'That'll be Grantham Smythe,' Flynn said through the

driver's open window. 'He's the owner. Come on then. But if Police Scotland ask, we thought we were sitting ducks in the car park.'

Grantham Smythe was middle-aged. Looked like a drinker. Good for him, Poe thought. He wore a two-tone ten-pin-bowling-style shirt. He was standing in the doorway of the bar. The tabled outdoor area in front of the bar was completely shielded by tarpaulin. Poe could see the name of a local timber merchant on the side. He reckoned tarpaulin, canvas, even plastic sheeting was in high demand right now. Seemed the timber merchant had decided it was more profitable renting out his tarpaulin than protecting his wood from the rain. Or maybe he was a good guy trying to do a good thing. Anything was possible, Poe thought.

Smythe waited for them to get out of the car then beckoned them over again. Poe noticed he didn't leave the cover of the tarpaulin shield. He didn't blame him.

'You here about my crime report?' he said. 'Still need a number for the insurance.'

'We're NCA,' Flynn replied, showing her warrant card.

Poe didn't bother. His leather wallet still smelled of fish.

'When am I going to get my crime number?'

'I have no idea, Mr Smythe,' Flynn said. 'That's not what we do. Can we come inside, please?'

Smythe begrudgingly led them into the bar. He seated them at a table. 'Can I get you anything to drink?' he said hopefully. They were clearly not going to be *free* drinks.

'We're good, thanks,' Flynn said. 'And I appreciate this is awful timing, but do you mind if we ask a couple of questions?'

Smythe poured himself a measure of whisky then joined them at the table. 'You're from the National Crime Agency?'

'We are.'

'It's terrorism then. I knew it was.'

'Why do you say that, Mr Smythe?'

'Isn't that what the NCA does?'

'We're a broad church,' Flynn said. 'The three of us are more used to investigating serial murders than terrorism.'

'Like Jack the Ripper?'

'If that's the only serial killer you know,' Poe said, 'then yes. *Exactly* like Jack the Ripper.'

'I see.' He poked his ear, examined the end of his finger, then said, 'Did they ever catch him?'

'Who?'

'Jack the Ripper.'

Poe sighed. The man was clearly an idiot. 'Yes, they caught him in Spain last year, didn't you hear? He was one hundred and seventy years old.'

Bradshaw giggled.

'How many weddings did you do that day, Mr Smythe?' Flynn said before he figured out he'd been insulted.

'We had seven scheduled.'

'And what number wedding were you on when the . . . incident occurred?'

'You mean the wedding when the best man punched the groom for sleeping with his wife or the wedding when the murder happened?'

'The murder, Mr Smythe. The NCA doesn't issue crime numbers and we aren't interested in family brawls.'

Smythe looked up, like the answer was written on the ceiling. 'It was the first wedding after lunch, so it'll have been number four.'

'The middle one then.'

'No, the last one.'

'But you said you had seven scheduled.'

'We did. But the last three were cancelled. It's why I need my crime number. I'm a victim here as well. This has left me well out of pocket. But to answer your question, it was the fourth wedding *and* the last wedding.'

Poe smiled. 'He has a point. If someone got murdered ten minutes before *my* wedding, I'd think twice about putting on my top hat.'

'You won't be wearing a top hat, Poe,' Bradshaw said. 'You'll be wearing a black suit from Marks and Spencer. And that's only because your work suits smell of fish.'

'You're getting hitched,' Smythe said. 'Congratulations.'

'Thank you,' Poe replied.

'Do you have a venue? I can do sniper's rates for you.'

'Sniper's rates?'

'That's what we're calling the discounts we're having to offer.'

'And what are you calling the welcoming drinks?' Poe asked. 'Headshots?'

'Hey, that's not bad. Let me make a wee note of that.' He tapped something into his phone. 'And I know you were joking, but ninety-six per cent of my bookings have been cancelled since the murder. Not postponed, *cancelled*. I can't even sell next year's Valentine's Day package and that's our busiest day by a mile. Gretna Green's economy is built around the wedding business, and right now, the wedding business is *tanking*. So yes, we're offering discounted packages. Do you want one or not?'

'I'd rather stand in dog shit,' Poe said.

Smythe got to his feet. Clenched his fists. Poe stayed seated.

'Sit down, Mr Smythe,' Flynn said.

Smythe didn't. 'He's a piss-taking bastard!'

'If you don't sit down right this second, I'm nicking you and making you wait for Police Scotland in the middle of the car park.'

Smythe sat.

'Thank you,' Flynn said. 'And, Poe, stop being childish.' She stared at him until he nodded. 'Now, the other question I want to ask is why didn't wedding party number four take advantage of all the protection you're offering?'

'Do you think the sneaky wee insurance bastards will claim that force mature jobby? Try to get out of paying me?'

'Force *majeure*,' Bradshaw said automatically. 'It's French for "greater force".'

'Why didn't they use the protection, Mr Smythe?' Flynn asked again.

Smythe shrugged. 'They did for most of it but when it came to the photographs, the bride insisted they go outside. Who the hell wants a grimy tarpaulin as their wedding background? Not when you can have mountains and blue sky and green grass.'

'And an ornamental water wheel,' Poe said.

'Exactly.'

'Did the preceding wedding parties take their photographs outside?' Flynn asked.

'They did.'

'Same place?'

'Aye.'

'Same photographer.'

'Aye.'

'Was there anything different about the fourth wedding?'

'They all look the same after a while,' Smythe said. 'The only weddings you remember are the ones that end in mass brawls.' He sipped his whisky. 'And even then, it would have to be a *good* mass brawl.'

While Flynn finished up with Smythe, Poe got to his feet and went to the door. He'd heard a car pull into the car park. Sounded like a diesel. He looked outside.

'Police Scotland have arrived,' he said.

Chapter 16

The detectives from Police Scotland didn't care that they'd already spoken to Smythe. They seemed focused and professional. DS Ian Ferguson was rail-thin with a shock of caricaturist ginger hair; DS Fiona Stephenson was tall and rangy. They both wore jeans and jumpers. Their practical shoes were flecked with mud. These were outdoor cops. Poe immediately liked them.

'He ask about his crime number?' Stephenson asked. Her accent was soft. Edinburgh maybe.

'Seven times,' Bradshaw replied.

'I've seen Ofsted inspectors with more compassion,' Flynn said.

Stephenson smiled, but it didn't reach her eyes. 'You here to check up on us?'

'We've just joined the investigation so we're playing catch up,' Poe explained. 'I have stuff to do in Cumbria tonight, so it made sense to start up here.'

'What do you need?'

'I want to see the shooting platform.'

Stephenson pointed at a building in the distance. 'He shot from a farm over there,' she said. 'Climbed on to the roof of the cowshed and waited.'

'For wedding four?' Poe asked.

'That's the working theory. A couple of my colleagues think he climbed up there at lunchtime, but Ian and I aren't buying that for a second.'

'Why not?'

'He isn't built that way. Snipers are meticulous. They take their time. And target selection is just as important as shooting ability. He waited for wedding number four either because he knew the victim or he was waiting for the perfect conditions. Unless there are criteria we haven't yet figured out.'

'There aren't,' Poe said. 'Tilly would have spotted them.'

'Who's Tilly?'

'I am,' Bradshaw said, giving the Scottish cops a thumbs-up. 'My geographical profile analysis came up negative, the victims have nothing in common and there is no pattern regarding dates and times.'

'Commander Mathers isn't dismissing seventeen victims as being just smoke and mirrors,' Flynn said. 'That he's hiding the intended victim in among collateral damage.'

'But?'

'But it's not the main line of enquiry. She thinks he's choosing them at random.'

Stephenson nodded. 'We think he was waiting for the perfect shooting conditions. No wind, no rain. The right light.'

'You know a lot about snipers,' Flynn said.

'We've all had to become experts,' she replied, checking out their footwear and nodding approvingly. 'Come on, I'll take you to his shooting platform.'

They jumped in Stephenson's car – Police Scotland in the front, the NCA jammed in the back like battery hens – and drove to the farm the sniper had used. It was a dairy farm. Friesians, fat off the lush lowland grass. Stephenson parked in the farmyard.

The sniper had ignored the milking shed in favour of the shed the cows bedded down in at night. It had tin sides and an asbestos roof and was the same height as a two-storey house.

'He used the farmer's own ladder to get up to the roof, then crawl boards to get into position,' Ferguson explained. 'He left everything in situ, and other than some fibres, left no usable trace evidence. We can take you up for a gander if you wish, but I can tell you that once he was in position, he had a great view of the Mill Forge. He could have picked her off any time he wanted.'

'And once he'd fired, he was only two minutes from several escape routes,' Stephenson added. 'He could have taken the A74 or any one of the minor roads. None of them are covered by CCTV or ANPR.'

'The farmer?'

'Sleeping. He rises early, naps in the afternoon. He heard the shot but didn't think anything of it. It's not an uncommon noise around here.'

'His wife? Farmhands?'

'No other witnesses.' She put her hands on her hips. 'All of which has been properly recorded and shared with the team Commander Mathers is leading.'

'Which makes us wonder why you're really here,' Ferguson said. 'You say you're not here to check our work, OK, we believe you. But you're definitely up here for something.'

Poe and Flynn exchanged a glance. The plan had been for Flynn to drive up to Tulliallan Castle in Fife, Police Scotland's headquarters, and speak to a senior officer there, while Poe and Bradshaw went to the wedding rehearsal.

'We have a theory,' Flynn said. 'And as far as we can tell, it's not a line of enquiry anyone is pursuing.'

Poe explained about zeroing. And how he thought the sniper was getting his weapon ready somewhere, and that Scotland ticked all the boxes. When he'd finished, the Police Scotland detectives looked thoughtful.

'And it's definitely an ongoing process?' Stephenson asked. 'It isn't something that's only done the once?'

Poe shook his head. 'Even if he weren't firing from vastly different distances, the sights on those rifles are incredibly sensitive. A couple of knocks, even driving over a sleeping policeman, would be enough to alter the sight/barrel alignment. And this guy's driving huge distances. Trust me, he's continually zeroing his weapon. If he wasn't, he'd miss.'

They asked questions that Poe answered as best he could. Eventually they had a plan. Police Scotland was responsible for a vast area of land. Thirty thousand square miles. Six thousand miles of coastline. Almost eight hundred islands. They had good air support. They had a modern helicopter with multi-sensor cameras. They had drones and night-vision goggles. Their searchlights could light up half a football pitch. And more importantly, they had people who knew what they were doing. They'd talk to the gamekeepers, the men and women who walked the moors looking after the grouse. Ask them to look for unusual activity. Searching Scotland for a sniper zeroing his rifle would be like looking for an Arctic fox in a snowstorm, but at least they'd now have eyes in the sky. Boots on the ground.

Stephenson drove them back to the Mill Forge where they exchanged personal phone numbers and said their goodbyes.

'You coming to the wedding rehearsal now?' Poe said to Flynn. 'I know you were using Fife as an excuse not to.'

'Why would I want to go to that?' Flynn said. 'You don't even want to go and the whole thing's for your benefit. A chance to get all your sarcastic comments out of your system.'

'I didn't ask if you wanted to come, boss. It's a wedding rehearsal. Nobody *wants* to come.'

'I do,' Bradshaw said.

'Except for Tilly, obviously.'

'I've never been to a wedding before. I imagine it will be glorious.'

Poe and Flynn took a moment. Glorious wasn't the word that sprang to mind. Ordeal did. Stuffy did. Archaic did.

'If you don't come, Estelle'll know you've snubbed her,' Poe said.

Flynn sighed. 'Fine,' she said. 'But only because I want to hear Tilly's best man speech.'

Chapter 17

The man in the ghillie suit stared at the wedding party through the Schmidt & Bender telescopic sight. It was as if he were right there. Like he could reach out and touch them. The bride-to-be wasn't wearing white, but he had no trouble identifying her. She turned everyone else into background. Natural charisma. Unlike the woman he'd killed at Gretna Green, this wedding wasn't taking place in a ten-ceremonies-a-day venue. This wedding was in a marquee. It was on private grounds. The bride's family were aristocracy. They had money and titles. Serious money, serious titles. The groom was a title-less scrote, though, allowed into the family to widen the gene pool. Make sure the family tree had more than one branch. That her children would be born with normal-looking ears.

It didn't matter to the man in the ghillie suit. Titles meant nothing to him. Money meant nothing to him. He was a change-agent. A blow to the status quo. And yes, he had an agenda, a *secret* agenda, but he thought of that as more of a byproduct. The important thing was the chaos.

He held his breath. Shooting from distance was all about a stable firing platform. That meant no breathing. No nothing. Just the sight, the barrel and the target. One-two-three. Easy. Like shooting fish in a barrel . . .

He increased the pressure on the trigger.

Then he smiled. Relaxed.

More guests were arriving. The marquee would soon be full.

It would still be an easy shot. The man in the ghillie suit decided to wait.

The more the merrier.

Poe picked up a small white dish. The caterers had put together lots of small white dishes. He was supposed to try them all then pick his favourite five. Doyle would do the same. The caterer had already selected ten wedding staples. Italian dried ham, tarts with paper-thin pastry topped with micro-herbs, smoked salmon blinis, that kind of thing. Twenty dishes for the wedding breakfast. Poe had asked why they weren't serving Cumberland sausage, cheesy mash and onion gravy. He said that Edgar didn't like smoked salmon. He certainly didn't like micro-herbs. No one did. Anything the chef had to apply with tweezers wasn't food as far as Poe was concerned. Doyle reminded him that Edgar was a gluttonous spaniel who ate sheep shit. And the last time she'd offered him smoked salmon, he'd accidentally bitten her hand he'd grabbed it so fast.

'And how did you answer when I asked how involved you wanted to be in the planning?' she said. She was wearing black jeans, torn at the knees, Golden Goose sneakers, an off-the-shoulder jumper and skull earrings. A slash of crimson lipstick. Poe thought she'd never looked more beautiful. Someone had once said that Doyle looked like a Goth Elizabeth Taylor and now Poe couldn't unsee it. She certainly had an aura about her.

'I said I was too busy,' he mumbled.

'That's right,' she said, smiling. 'You said you were too busy. This is what it's like not to be involved.' She softened and added, 'Don't worry, Poe, your only jobs are to pick five dishes tonight and make sure you say "I do" on the day. Everything else is just wedding tinsel. It's pretty, but it doesn't mean anything.'

So Poe picked up and put down white dishes like he was playing 'find the pea' at Borough Market. The one in his hand was full of vegetables but not like the ones he had with his Sunday roast down at the Crown. These vegetables were covered in red goo and smelled funky.

'What's this?' he asked Bradshaw.

Bradshaw *had* wanted to be involved in planning the wedding.

'It's called kimchi, Poe.'

'And what the hell is kimchi?'

'It's fermented cabbage. It's Korean.'

'Are you stark raving mad? I'm not eating fermented cabbage on my wedding day.' He paused a heartbeat. 'I'm not eating fermented cabbage *ever.*'

'Just try it, Poe,' Doyle sighed.

Poe picked up a spoon. Nibbled at a bit of the kimchi. His eyes widened. 'Hey, this is *really* nice.' He licked the spoon then finished the rest. 'Can I have some more?'

Bradshaw and Doyle fist bumped.

'What?' Poe said.

'We've been thinking of ways to improve your diet and Tilly suggested spicy vegetarian dishes from India and Korea and Thailand,' Doyle said. 'Seems she's on to something.'

Poe scowled. 'Don't try to change me, Estelle,' he said.

She grinned. 'Just put your little sticker by the bowl and choose another four dishes, Poe.'

'Who are all these people?' he said, gesturing at the strangers in the large marquee that had been put up in the grounds of Highwood, Doyle's ancestral home near Corbridge. He guessed it would soon be his home too. As the day got nearer, more marquees would be added to this one. A disco tent that Poe hoped to never set foot in, and a taproom run by the Carlisle Brewing Company that he hoped to never leave.

'I'm not nineteen, Poe,' she said. 'I don't have a large circle of friends any more. I have a *small* circle of friends. Admittedly, it's not as small as your circle, which at best can be described as a triangle, but the friends I do have want to be involved.'

'I get that. Why are they here *now*? Isn't tonight just to practise?'

'Practise what? Standing in a tent? Sod that. No, tonight is for you to get used to the idea of being married, to meet, and no doubt immediately dislike, some of my friends who can't make the wedding, and to choose the food we'll feed to the ones who can.'

'Why can't they come?'

'Some are on call, some are out of the country. Some are even more misanthropic than you.' She gestured at a bunch of older men and women. Looked like they were tweed fetishists. 'And that crusty lot were friends of my father's. They're not invited to the actual wedding, but they wanted to wish me well.'

'Nice of them.'

'Not really,' Doyle said. 'I've been asked three times tonight about my plans for my father's grouse moor.'

Elcid Doyle, the old Marquess of Northumberland, had owned one of the biggest grouse moors outside Scotland. He had been murdered and Doyle was accused of patricide. Eventually, Poe was able to clear her name and put the real killer behind bars. Her father's estate had passed to her.

'What *are* your plans?' Poe asked.

'I haven't discussed it with him yet.'

'Discussed it with who?'

'My future husband.'

And then she disappeared into a throng of well-wishers. She glanced back at Poe and winked. He reddened and went back to selecting his five dishes. He picked up another. It contained a perfectly cut cube of belly pork, crispy skin, layers of mouth-watering fat. He put a sticker beside the dish before he'd even tried it. Then he ate it. It was even nicer than it looked. Two down, three to go. He glanced at Doyle again, thought about how much he loved her.

Thought about how happy he was.

It was time. The marquee was full. The man in the ghillie suit didn't think it was worth waiting any longer. Another twenty minutes and light would start to be a problem. It was very rural here. It got dark quickly and stayed dark. No light pollution in this part of the UK.

He lifted his rifle and settled into the prone position. He lowered his head and put his eye to the Schmidt & Bender sight. Everyone was seated, the bride-to-be at the head of the long wooden table. Her husband-to-be by her side. They were laughing together. Happy. He adjusted the magnification until the bride-to-be's head filled the crosshair. He breathed in, held it on the way back out.

Stable.

He squeezed the trigger. Gently. One fluid motion.

Estelle Doyle exploded into laughter.

Bradshaw had just finished her rehearsal speech and it was even worse than Poe had feared. She'd discussed their first case, the Immolation Man, and she didn't spare the gory stuff. She talked about their investigations over the years: the murderous chef; the idiot who called himself the Curator; the idiot the press called the Botanist. A bunch of other idiots. She explained the science in the way only Bradshaw could: she made something complicated sound even more complicated. She spent ten minutes on Benford's law, a mathematical model about real-life sets of numerical data. But she also told everyone about how they'd met, and how their friendship had formed and blossomed. She said she'd never had a friend until she met Poe, now she had five – Poe, Flynn, Doyle, Poe's nearest neighbour Victoria Hume, and Edgar – and how she'd never thought she'd ever go to a wedding, never mind give a best man's speech. 'And I don't even have a penis!' she'd said excitedly. She explained, in detail, why pasta wouldn't be served at the wedding breakfast. 'Poe says it doesn't taste of anything and he can't go to the toilet properly afterwards.' She mentioned Edgar seventeen times. She said he didn't drink enough water twice. At one point Flynn was laughing so hard she had to go outside.

She went on to describe how he still had PTSD after their last major case but somehow made it funny – 'He wakes up screaming so loud it's as if he's accidentally drunk low-alcohol beer' – then finished with a delightful anecdote about how Poe had been drinking breast milk when he found out Doyle had been arrested for her father's murder.

Bradshaw sat down to thunderous applause. Poe doubted there'd been a best man's speech like it in recorded history. He smiled at his friend and nodded his approval. She breathed a sigh of relief and gave him a goofy wave in return. He was reaching for his fourteenth cube of belly pork when his phone began to ring. So did Flynn's and Bradshaw's.

Doyle stopped laughing. Flynn answered her mobile and listened for less than a minute. Her face darkened. She hung up and looked at Poe.

'There's been another one?' Doyle asked.

Flynn nodded.

'Go,' Doyle said. 'All of you.'

Chapter 18

The second before she was shot in the head, Jools Arreghini had been the only daughter of Archie and Clarice. The second after the .50-inch calibre bullet had blown off the top of her skull like her head was a soft-boiled egg and the bullet was a sharp-edged spoon, she became the *late* daughter of Archie and Clarice.

One shot, one kill.

Archie Arreghini was landed gentry. A junior member of the aristocracy. A baron. He had reinvigorated the family fortune when he moved into shipping – a ubiquitous term that covered everything from transporting grain to famine areas to smuggling artillery shells to Russia. According to Bradshaw he was a centimillionaire, someone with over one hundred million pounds' worth of assets. He was in his sixties, had a May–September marriage, and Jools was their only child. The article hinted at, but never explicitly said, that theirs was a marriage of convenience. He got an heir; Clarice got the lifestyle she felt she deserved. And who knows, maybe the article was speculation, tittle-tattle. But . . . Clarice was nowhere to be seen while Archie had stayed until the bitter end. He was *still* there, seated at one of the tables, surrounded by finery. He looked utterly defeated, utterly alone. Except he *wasn't* alone. Even in a marquee full of cops, a man with personal protection written all over him hovered in the background. Eyes like a bird's, flitting everywhere. A bodyguard.

Although the guests and staff had dispersed by the time they arrived, the wedding's infrastructure remained in place. It was clear Archie had spared no expense when it came to his daughter's wedding.

Poe had thought Doyle was going overboard in her preparations. Looking at the things Archie had arranged for his daughter's special day, Poe realised just how restrained Doyle was being. Doyle's marquee had been hired from a man called Mr Franks. He arrived at Highwood in a flatbed truck with 'GD Franks Marquees' stencilled on the side in peeling paint. He wrote down their order in a ratty notebook. He kept licking the end of his pencil like he was a 1920s bookie. He hand-delivered the estimate in the flatbed truck the same night.

Jools Arreghini, on the other hand, had themed her wedding around a book called *The Night Circus* by Erin Morgenstern, a phantasmagorical fairytale that told the story of two competing forms of magic. Bradshaw had made Poe read it a few years ago. He hadn't enjoyed it.

The centrepiece was a huge marquee. It was over one hundred years old and had originally belonged to the Barnum & Bailey Circus. Archie had purchased it, had it reconditioned and painted black and white. Poe thought it resembled a mint humbug. A lack of colour dominated *The Night Circus*. Everything, from the tents to the animals to the performer's outfit, was black or white, sometimes grey. According to the publisher, the monochromaticity had enriched the ambience of *The Night Circus*'s dream-state.

A succession of presumably less famous, although equally black and white, marquees formed a complex network around the Barnum & Bailey tent. Each one showcased a different form of circus entertainment for the wedding party to wander through at their leisure. Just like the Night Circus crowds had in the book. Archie had scoured the planet for the very best in performers. An American ring juggler. A Korean contortionist. Pierrot the sad clown. Firebreathers and sword dancers. In the largest of the additional marquees, the Troop of Shandong had been booked to perform skipping acrobatics at 11 p.m. And incredibly, a scaled-down Cirque du Soleil performance of *Kà* had been scheduled for midnight.

The performers were on their way home. They had come from all over the world to entertain just one person; instead, they'd witnessed her execution. Even Pierrot had looked traumatised when he'd climbed into his taxi.

Other signs of Archie's extravagance were everywhere. A live lobster tank. A purpose-built wine cellar. A humidor with hundreds of fat cigars. A teppanyaki grill. A conveyor-belt sushi station. The wedding cake had nine tiers. There were so many flowers in the marquee it looked like Elton John's downstairs toilet. A band's equipment, a *famous* band, was still on a raised dais. Poe wondered how much they charged for private gigs. They usually played arenas so he reckoned it wouldn't be cheap. Like hiring Bruce Springsteen for your twenty-first. He noticed a solitary cymbal on top of an amp. He wondered what had happened to the other one. In all his years, he'd never seen them for sale individually. He thought they were probably like socks, only ever sold in pairs. Or maybe they weren't. Maybe you *could* buy them individually. Then he thought he was thinking about cymbals too much.

A flash of white caught his eye, the way a rabbit's tail does. It was Mathers. Like everyone else, she was decked out in chic forensic white. There was something about her that made her stand out, even when wearing one-size-fits-all disposable crime scene coveralls. She had a presence. Flynn had it too, but hers was downplayed. Mathers embraced hers. Leaned into it. Made it work for her. Poe reckoned she was a future commissioner.

She was talking to the crime scene manager. She had just returned from where the sniper had taken his shot. He hadn't needed much cover; this part of Oxfordshire was empty. He'd simply found a small depression and set up his firing platform. The only thing he'd left behind was a bullet casing and the marks his rifle's bipod had made in the ground. Mathers had cast a wide net but that was mainly to say she'd done it. The sniper could be 200 miles away; he could be hiding out in the village.

The inside of the marquee was bustling. P. T. Barnum might be long dead, but the circus of a complex murder investigation was in full swing. Everyone was suited and booted, focused on their individual task. Jools Arreghini's body had been removed. *Most* of Jools Arreghini's body. One of the CSI guys had been tasked with scraping up her brain tissue and skull fragments from the dancefloor. It was a gruesome task, made no less gruesome by him having no choice but to use a dustpan and brush.

Poe approached him, more to get a sense of the sniper's line of fire than to interrupt. If the contents of Jools Arreghini's head were on the dancefloor, because he'd shot from the rolling hills to the front of the main house, the distance had to be at least 1,500 yards. Poe reckoned this was the longest shot he'd taken to date. He wondered if this was down to necessity or whether he was trying to challenge himself.

The CSI guy assumed Poe wanted to talk. He pulled down his mask and pointed at the brain material. It looked like someone had dropped some mince. 'At least he's not shooting at us any more, eh?'

Poe looked at him, nonplussed. 'Us? What do you mean "Us"?'

'The common man, the salt of the earth, the workers, the ones who make this country work. About time he started picking off the leeches.'

Poe said, 'In a few days I'm marrying the Marquess of Northumberland's daughter.'

'Ha-ha, me too, mate, me too.' He put down his dustpan, pointed at the wine cellar with his brush. 'I mean, have you ever seen anything so up its own arse?'

Poe didn't respond.

The CSI guy took that as permission to continue. He looked over his shoulder, checked no one was listening. 'Ever get the feeling you're being watched?' he said to Poe with a grin. He pointed at the wall of the famous marquee. One of Jools Arreghini's eyes was stuck to the canvas.

'Get out,' Poe said.

'Excuse me?'

'You heard me. Get out.'

'Ah, I was just having a laugh, mate.' He pulled up his mask and went back to work. Poe didn't move. The CSI guy pulled his mask back down. 'Look, I don't know who the hell you think you—'

Poe raised his hand. 'Commander Mathers!' Mathers looked up. 'Over here, please.'

Mathers came straight over. 'What's up?'

'This man has a joke to tell you.'

'He does?'

'It's about the victim's eye being stuck to the side of the tent. Something about it watching us. I didn't find it funny, but I'm known for not having a GSOH. It's why I never bothered with dating apps.'

Mathers held out her hand. 'ID, please?'

The CSI guy unfastened his protective overalls and wordlessly handed it over.

'You have twenty seconds to leave my crime scene,' Mathers said. 'If you're still here in twenty-*one* seconds, Sergeant Poe will arrest you.' The guy stood, dusted himself down. 'Oh, and in case me taking your ID was ambiguous, you no longer have a job. I just wanted to make that clear.'

'You haven't heard the end of this,' he snarled.

'No?' Poe stepped forward. Went up to him. Pushed his face into his. The CSI guy took a step back. 'Look into my eyes and

81

say that again.'

The CSI lowered his head.

'I didn't think so,' Poe said. 'Now piss off.'

The CSI guy slunk off, muttering all the way.

Flynn and Bradshaw wandered over. 'What was that about?' Flynn asked.

'Nothing important,' Poe replied. He nodded towards Archie Arreghini. 'Will he talk to us?'

'It's the only reason he's still here. He wants to talk to you, Poe.'

'Me?'

'And only you.'

'Why?'

Flynn shrugged. 'Within two hours of his daughter's murder, he had full profiles of everyone on the investigation team. He sees something in you he likes. Probably your happy disposition.'

Mathers frowned. 'Be careful, Poe,' she said. 'Archie Arreghini isn't who he seems. He might be aristocracy, but you guys have a file on him. Interpol has a file on him. *We* have a file on him, and he doesn't even live in London.'

'What's he done?'

Mathers shook her head. 'Just be careful. Don't promise him anything.'

Chapter 19

Archie Arreghini was old school; he stood to shake hands. His grip was iron-like but Poe didn't think he was making a point. It was just how he was. He invited Poe to take a seat then poured them both a drink from an almost empty bottle. His eyes were red and unfocused, but Poe didn't think he was drunk.

He picked up his glass and raised it. Waited for Poe to do the same. Poe did. They bumped glasses. Poe put his on the table. Archie put his to his lips. He drained it then clinked it against the bottle.

'Do you know what this is, Sergeant Poe?' he said.

'I don't, sir.'

'It's the Macallan M, one of the most expensive whiskies in the world. I bought the last two bottles at an auction in Hong Kong a few years ago. One for Jools and me to share on her wedding day, the second on the birth of her first child.' Poe didn't know what to say to that. He stayed silent. 'Please, take a drink.'

Archie was a grieving father and Poe could see no reason not to do as he had been asked. He wasn't a big whisky drinker, but he knew the difference between a bottle of gut rotter and the real deal. The Macallan M was the real deal. It was extraordinary. Rich and complex, delicate and warming, it had a lingering, peaty, smoky finish. If he'd been at home, he'd have finished the dram and poured another.

'Good?' Archie asked.

'Very.' Poe put down his glass. 'You asked to see me, Mr Arreghini.'

Archie raised his hand. His personal protection officer approached the table. 'This is Matthew,' Archie said. 'He's from your neck of the woods. Cumbria. Do you know him?'

'I don't think so.'

'I'm surprised,' Archie said. 'Because he knows you. Well, *of* you.'

Poe shrugged. Recent events had raised his Cumbrian profile to the point that people stopped and stared.

'Matthew works for me, has done for almost two years now.'

Matthew was a tall man. Some tall men looked like short men who'd been put on a rack. Not Matthew. He wasn't lanky. Being tall was the right height for him. He was wiry rather than thin. And there was an edge to him that Poe hadn't seen since his army days. Like Matthew hadn't quite decided whether to kill you or not. Could go either way. Poe reckoned he'd been with one of the UK's myriad special forces. Served his country well, then decided to grab some of the big bucks the uber-rich were desperate to pay people like him. And why not? Matthew, and people like Matthew, were a different kind of animal. They had a different outlook on life. An attitude, a way of seeing things that people like Archie needed. Why not be properly recompensed? Matthew put a rectangular wooden box on the table then went back to where he'd been standing. Out of earshot but within easy reach.

'Do you know what this is, Sergeant Poe?' Archie asked.

Poe thought he did, but he shook his head anyway. It seemed like a rhetorical question.

'This is the *second* bottle of the Macallan M,' Archie said. 'The one I'd planned to open on the birth of my first grandchild. Catch this man and it's yours.'

'The National Crime Agency doesn't have a transactional

relationship with victims of crimes, sir,' Poe said. 'We don't require bribes to do our job.'

Archie raised his hand again. This time Matthew brought a thin manilla file.

'You're an interesting man, Sergeant Poe,' Archie said, picking up the top sheet. 'Certainly the most interesting police officer on what I gather is the largest manhunt in the history of this country.'

Poe said nothing.

'It seems you don't always follow the letter of the law,' he continued. 'That occasionally *natural* justice trumps criminal justice.' He looked up. 'If you wish, I can give you examples?'

'I'm not a vigilante, sir,' Poe said.

Archie waved his words away. 'I don't need a vigilante, Sergeant Poe.' Poe heard the unspoken *because I have my own* as if Archie had said it out loud. 'I need a man who gets things done. A man who refuses to get tied up in red tape. Who can outsmart the people he hunts because he *thinks* like the people he hunts.'

'And look where that got me,' Poe said. 'I'm being treated for PTSD, I can't remember the last time I slept for more than three hours, and my fiancée and best friend are making me eat fermented cabbage at my own wedding.'

'I understand there will also be belly pork?'

Poe stared at Archie, astonished. 'How could you possibly . . . ?'

'How did I know what makes the man charged with catching my daughter's killer tick? I made it my business to know, Sergeant Poe. I make it my business to know everything about the people I'm going into partnership with. It's why I can afford all this . . . frippery.' He took a sip of his whisky.

'We're not partners, sir.' Poe gestured towards Flynn and Bradshaw. Flynn was talking to Mathers. Bradshaw was glancing in his direction. She looked worried. 'In any case, my part has been overplayed. I'm part of a team.'

'We may not be partners in a way that you understand, Sergeant Poe, but we *are* partners. Like it or not, our two worlds have come crashing together.'

'What do you *want*, sir?' Poe said. 'Because if that file's as thorough as it seems, you'll know I'm nobody's hero.' He nodded towards Matthew the bodyguard. 'Nobody's lickspittle.'

'I want this man caught,' Archie said.

'Caught? Or brought to you?'

'You put him behind bars, Sergeant Poe,' Archie said. 'Leave the natural justice to me.'

'You know I'll have to report this conversation?'

Archie patted the file. 'I'd expect nothing less.' He reached into his jacket, pulled out a calfskin wallet. He unfolded it, removed a gilt-edged business card, and pushed it across the table. Poe made no move to pick it up. 'This is my personal number. I can be reached at any time of the day. If I can help in any way whatsoever, I don't want you to think twice about reaching out. I can open doors that might otherwise remain shut. Get people, whose first instinct is to say nothing, to talk to the men and women who enforce our laws.'

Poe picked up the business card. Tucked it into his top pocket.

Archie refilled his glass. Topped up Poe's.

'Now, ask your questions,' he said.

Chapter 20

Poe waved Bradshaw and Flynn over. Flynn shook her head. She was deep in conversation with Mathers. Poe wasn't sure he liked that. It looked as if they were plotting. Bradshaw bounded over; her expression set to what she thought was sympathy. It looked like she was trying to lay an egg.

'Hello, Poe,' she said. 'Hello, Mr Arreghini.' She patted his shoulder, nodded sagely, and said, 'Life goes on.'

'Er . . . thank you,' Archie said, bemused.

Poe put his head in his hands, rubbed his face. Bradshaw had yet to encounter a social situation she couldn't make awkward. 'This is Tilly, sir. I think she's an AI robot from the future.'

'Is "life goes on" not the right thing to say to the recently bereaved, Poe?' Bradshaw asked. 'I checked on a funeral website.'

'Maybe not to the *very* recently bereaved, Tilly,' Poe said. 'I'm sorry for your loss is more customary.'

Bradshaw opened her omnipresent laptop. 'I shall make a note of that in my "How to be more tactful" file.' She opened a document and typed something so fast her fingers blurred. 'I doubt Mr Arreghini will be the last vilomah we talk to.'

'Vilomah?' Archie asked before Poe could stop him.

'It's the term used for parents who have lost a child, Mr Arreghini. It comes from Sanskrit, one of the oldest languages in the world. A literal translation would be "Against the natural order". Sanskrit also gave the world "widow", which means empty.'

'Vilomah,' Archie said slowly, like he was tasting the word. He nodded. 'I like it. Because you're right, Miss Bradshaw. A parent losing a child *is* against the natural order.' He topped up his whisky with the last drops of the Macallan M. He picked up his glass, swirled its contents. 'It's ironic,' he said, pointing at the blood splattered against the inside of the circus marquee. 'They call whisky the water of life. The next time I take a dram will be at my daughter's wake.'

He swigged it back. Slammed it on to the table.

Poe took his cue. He pointed towards Matthew the personal protection officer. 'You're a man with enemies,' he said. 'Tell me about them.'

Chapter 21

'Shipping and warehousing are competitive businesses, Sergeant Poe,' Archie said. 'And they are, particularly for fledgling companies, *cutthroat* businesses. You cannot be successful without making enemies. It's why I hire people like Matthew.'

Personal protection officers couldn't find gainful employment in Cumbria. The only celebrities were chefs – Cumbria was plagued with them – and Melvyn Bragg. That meant Matthew either had legitimate employment in London, or *illegitimate* employment in Cumbria. If it was the former, there was no reason why Matthew should know him. But if he had been into some shady stuff . . . well, then he'd know who Poe was. *All* the criminals in Cumbria knew who Poe was. Also, Matthew was tall. Suspiciously tall. *Sniper*-tall. Poe made a mental note to investigate him the moment he left the marquee.

'Tilly will want a list of names,' Poe said.

'Are any of the other victims in the shipping industry?'

'Not as far as I can tell.'

'Yet you're asking me about my enemies. Why is that?'

Poe tapped the manilla folder. 'You're a well-connected man, Archie. You know why I'm asking.'

'You're talking about the files the authorities keep on me.'

'I am.'

Archie stared wistfully at the empty Macallan. 'While I admit nothing, you understand, a person who built up a similar-sized shipping business might have had to cut corners along the way.'

'And what corners might those have been?' Poe asked.

'Maybe he bribed officials to look the other way. Or added something to the cargo that wasn't on the docket. Perhaps he threatened a problematic union leader. Spilled the occasional drop of blood. That such a person would attract the attention of the authorities is as inevitable as disappointment.'

'Did this . . . similar person ever order a murder?'

Archie shook his head. 'Never.'

'A beating that maybe went on a bit too long, resulted in life-changing injuries?'

'No.'

'A business deal that saw someone lose everything they'd worked long and hard for?'

This time he wasn't so quick to dismiss it. 'There is always collateral damage.'

'Funny you should say that,' Poe said. 'My boss used that exact phrase when it came to one of the prevailing theories. That someone is using randomly selected targets to hide the motivation for the *true* target.'

'You think my Jools is the C in *The ABC Murders*?'

Poe shrugged. 'I don't, but it's not something Commander Mathers will dismiss out of hand.'

Archie shook his head again. 'If Jools was the intended target, it wasn't for revenge.'

'A warning maybe?'

'No.'

'You seem very sure.'

Archie sighed. 'In the past, I have had to occasionally issue warnings. An unpleasant but necessary business strategy. And the one golden rule is that the person receiving the warning has to *know* it's a warning.'

'And you don't see one?'

'I don't. It's the same with revenge. If it really is a dish best served cold, if the sins of the father have been visited upon the daughter, why hide it? Why not let me know? Add to my pain. Would that not make sense?'

'It would,' Poe conceded. 'I'll still need that list of names.'

'How far back do you want me to go?'

'Since you were a child. Grudges and slights don't have a shelf life, they fester like fermented cabbage.'

Archie picked up his smartphone. Thumbed a text to someone. Whooshed it into the ether. 'You'll have it by the end of the day.'

'Thank you,' Poe said.

'Don't waste your time on this, Sergeant Poe. Nor you, Miss Bradshaw.'

'Almost everything Poe asks me to do is a waste of my time,' Bradshaw said.

'Thanks, Tilly.'

'You're welcome, Poe. But don't worry, Mr Arreghini; on the face of it, wasting my time is what I do. And that's as it should be. Wasting time is what makes up the bulk of science.'

'It is?' Arreghini said.

'Science is the pursuit of knowledge,' Bradshaw said. 'And ninety-nine per cent of that pursuit ends in failure. Most of the knowledge gained is how *not* to do something.'

'It sounds like a thankless task, Miss Bradshaw.'

Bradshaw's eyes shone. 'Oh, no, science is *wonderful*. Science is truth. And each time we fail, we are one step closer to finding that truth. So, when Poe asks me to correlate your list of enemies with everything we've gathered so far in the investigation, I'll do it with a song in my heart and a smile on my lips. Because I won't be wasting my time, I'll be discovering one more way he *isn't* selecting his victims. Do you understand?'

'I certainly see why you and Sergeant Poe are such a formidable team,' Archie said. 'So, tell me, Miss Bradshaw. Where would *you* start looking for this man?'

'Wherever Poe tells me to look.'

'It's not as simple as that,' Poe said. 'We have no forensics, no motive. No profile worth speaking of, and – believe me when I tell you this – Tilly is the best there is at that stuff. Other than this being the second time he's targeted a wedding, we have nothing to go on at all.'

Bradshaw coughed nervously. 'Actually, Poe, that's not quite true.'

Chapter 22

'Tell me again, Tilly,' Poe said. 'And for fu ... flip's sake, use smaller words this time. And don't say central limit theorem again. No one but you understands what that is.'

'In the sixteenth century,' Bradshaw said, 'Gerolamo Cardano, the Italian polymath, introduced binomial coefficients to the Western world. He—'

'Tilly,' Flynn warned. 'Will you please, for the love of God, say it normally?'

'Cheese and crackers, you guys are dumb,' Bradshaw mumbled. She thought for a second. 'Do you know what dice are? You might have used them if you've played snakes and ladders? Or Monopoly?'

Silence.

'Jeez-Louise,' Bradshaw said. 'They're cubes with dots that signify numbers.'

'A bit less sarcasm, please,' Flynn said. 'We know what dice are.'

'I wasn't being sarcastic.'

'Start from the beginning, Tilly,' Poe said. 'Tell us what dice have to do with these murders.'

They had moved out of the circus marquee and into a command trailer. Archie had wanted to know what Bradshaw had discovered but didn't seem too upset when he was told it would need to remain confidential for the time being. Poe was in no doubt he'd find out soon enough. He seemed to be getting his intelligence in real time. His final words to Poe had been, 'Remember, there's a bottle of the Macallan M at the end of this monochrome rainbow, Sergeant Poe.' Mathers had asked everyone to leave, and despite the murder of Jools Arreghini being a Thames Valley investigation, the cops in the trailer had quickly acquiesced.

Bradshaw started again. She chose her words carefully this time. 'If we discount that someone is hiding the murder of one victim in among a bunch of other victims, like Jools Arreghini being killed because her father's a rotten egg, then we are left with only one explanation: he's choosing his victims at random. If he weren't, I'd have found the connection by now.'

'But you've told me many times that humans can't generate things at random.'

'That's right, Poe. We can't. Our cognitive processes are simply not capable of it. It would be like trying *not* to think of something.'

'So?'

'So, the murder of Jools Arreghini has provided a large enough sample size for me to spot something in the data. Something unusual. I would have spotted it sooner but the murder in Gretna Green was an outlier.'

'Which is?'

'If you were a killer who understood that the human brain is incapable of generating things at random, and you knew that trying to would likely lead to your downfall, how would you overcome this?'

Poe thought it through. Eventually he said, 'I'd find one of those random-number generators on the internet. Or failing that, I'd roll some . . .'

'Exactly,' Bradshaw said. 'You'd roll some dice.'

Chapter 23

'You look like the kind of scamp who played dice games in the schoolyard, Poe,' Bradshaw said.

Poe rolled his eyes. 'I'm only nine years older than you, Tilly,' he said. 'I played Cops and Robbers, Cowboys and Ind . . . and Native Americans.'

'Nice save, Poe,' Flynn said.

'Thank you.'

Bradshaw waved them away. Impatient. 'If you throw one die, Poe, what are the chances it will land on a six?'

'One in six.'

'That's right. If the die is fair, each possibility is equally likely. The chance of throwing a six is the same as the chance of throwing a one. Now, if you have *two* dice, what are the chances of throwing a twelve?'

'One in twelve, obviously.'

'Don't be feebleminded, Poe.'

Mathers hid a smile. Flynn openly laughed.

'It's *not* one in twelve?' Poe said.

'It's one in thirty-six, Poe.'

'It is?'

'There are thirty-six possible outcomes when throwing two dice and only one of them is a double six.'

'No wonder my dad always beat me at Monopoly.'

Bradshaw frowned. 'That makes no sense. Monopoly isn't a game of cha—'

'Poe's stupidity aside, can we move on, Tilly?' Flynn said, recognising a tangent when she saw one.

'Of course, DCI Flynn,' Bradshaw said. 'OK, so we've established that with two fair dice, there's a one in thirty-six chance of throwing a twelve. In percentages that's a touch over 2.78. What are the chances of throwing a seven?'

Poe took his time. Did some mental arithmetic. He imagined two dice. Worked through the possible combinations of throwing a seven. One and six. Two and five. Three and four. Four and three. Five and two. Six and one.

'Six chances,' he said eventually. 'A six in thirty-six chance.'

'Well done, Poe!' Bradshaw said excitedly. She started clapping and kept it up until Mathers and Flynn reluctantly joined in. 'Three cheers for Washing—'

'Not a chance,' Flynn said.

'Can *I* do three—'

'No.'

'Aw.'

'Tell us what this means, Tilly,' Poe said.

'Do you know what an icosahedron is, Poe?'

'It's a dinosaur, isn't it?'

'Don't be ridiculous. An icosahedron is a *twenty*-sided die, rather than six-sided. Now, obviously the number range is going to be much bigger, but can you calculate the chances of throwing forty?'

'A double twenty?'

Bradshaw nodded.

'We're not all human calculators, Tilly. Why don't you tell us?'

'The chances of throwing a forty with two icosahedrons is one in four hundred, Poe. That's a quarter of one per cent. DCI Flynn, what are the chances of throwing a *one* with two icosahedrons?'

'The same as a forty,' Flynn said immediately. 'A quarter of one per cent.'

'You're an idiot. The lowest number you can throw with two dice is two. A double one.'

'Well, why fu . . . bloody ask then?' Flynn snapped, reddening.

'Because you wouldn't let me do three cheers for Poe,' Bradshaw said. 'Anyway, the reason I'm telling you this is because, just like with two six-sided dice, there is symmetrical distribution when it comes to twenty-sided dice probability. Instead of seven, with icosahedrons twenty-one is statistically the most likely number to be thrown. That means, if the dice are fair, there's a five per cent chance of them showing twenty-one. It's 4.75 for twenty and twenty-two, 4.5 for nineteen and twenty-three, and so on, all the way down to two and forty, which as I said is a quarter of one per cent. In other words, the numbers most likely to occur are bunched up in the middle. If you looked at a bar graph with two on the left of the horizontal axis, forty on the right and twenty-one in the middle, the distribution would be triangular.'

Poe nodded. 'OK, we stumbled a bit along the way, but we got there eventually, Tilly,' he said. 'But I'm not sure how throwing dice helps him randomly select his victims.'

'That's because he *isn't* randomly selecting victims, Poe,' Bradshaw said. 'He's randomly selecting *locations*.'

Chapter 24

'Please switch on the monitor, Commander Mathers,' Bradshaw said. 'Poe is nearer, but he won't know how to do it.'

Mathers suppressed a grin but did as she was asked. The screen flickered blue. The Thames Valley Police logo appeared. It bounced around the screen like it was trapped.

'This is a secure system,' Mathers said. 'I'll get you the password.'

Bradshaw snorted. She typed some commands into her laptop and the logo disappeared. In the darkened trailer the screen lit up her face like she was telling a ghost story. She typed in a few more commands and a map of the UK appeared on the wall-mounted monitor. She superimposed a series of squares over England and Wales. She leaned back and studied her work, blowing an errant wisp of hair away from her eyes.

To some people – not Poe, obviously; he was far too mature – the shape of Great Britain resembled a witch riding a pig. The witch's head and hat were Scotland. Her body extended from the north of England to the Midlands, her legs reached the south coast. The pig's arse, fittingly, was East Anglia; its head was Wales. Its front legs were Cornwall and Devon. In other words, Great Britain was an odd-shaped island. Pinched at the top, wide at the bottom.

Bradshaw leaned forward and began numbering the squares. She started in the top left with Cumbria then worked her way down to Kent in the bottom right. She missed off Scotland completely. Cumbria was square number two – the lowest number you could throw with a pair of twenty-sided dice – and Kent was forty, the highest number you could throw. When she'd finished, every inch of mainland England and Wales was covered by one of the thirty-nine squares.

Poe saw where Bradshaw was going.

So did Flynn. 'You haven't numbered Scotland, Tilly,' she said. 'Why?'

'So far, his victims have all lived in squares two to forty,' Bradshaw said. 'He's ignoring Scotland. It might be as Poe suggested – that he's zeroing his rifle up there – or it might be for reasons we don't yet understand.'

'Gretna Green's in Scotland, though.'

'That's only because England's border with Scotland isn't straight. It has a forty-five degree slope. When you put the two northern counties into squares, you also catch part of southern Scotland. If you look, you'll see that some of Dumfries and Galloway is in the same square as Cumbria.'

'Which includes Gretna Green,' Poe said.

'Yes.'

Bradshaw chewed her lip. 'The data *does* support him dividing up England and Wales this way, but this is a hypothesis. A tentative explanation for how he is choosing his locations.'

'Explain the data, Tilly,' Poe said. He knew Bradshaw well enough to know she didn't guess. Everything she said was backed up by statistics.

'The range of two icosahedrons is two to forty. That's why I've sectioned England and Wales this way. Are you following so far?'

Poe and Flynn nodded. Mathers said, 'Yes.'

'And, as we've established, there are four hundred possible combinations when two icosahedrons are thrown.'

Again, they nodded.

'But not all combinations are equal when it comes to probability. There's a one in twenty chance of twenty-one being thrown, but only a one in four hundred chance of two or forty.'

'The double one or the double twenty,' Poe said.

'That's right,' Bradshaw said. 'The highest probability numbers are the middle range, the least probable are the outer range.' She opened a small box on her laptop and typed in some commands. 'Now, watch what happens when I populate the squares with the victim's locations.'

Like a plague of chickenpox, red dots began popping up. Eighteen of them, one for each life the sniper had taken. Poe immediately saw what she meant – the highest concentration of murder victims was bunched around squares thirteen to twenty-nine. The mid-range numbers. The numbers that were statistically most likely to be thrown. On Bradshaw's map that was North Wales and London and everywhere in between. Poe counted twelve victims. More than half. Jools Arreghini was in square twenty-seven. Five of the victims *were* outside of the main bunch, but within squares nine to thirty-four.

And then there was Naomi Etherington, the Gretna Green victim. She was the outlier Bradshaw had mentioned. Gretna Green was in grid number two. A double one. Snake eyes. And the odds of snake eyes being thrown were one in four hundred. No wonder Bradshaw had waited to voice her theory.

'This is it,' Mathers said, nodding. 'Tilly's right: this is how the bastard's choosing who to shoot. He's picking a square on a map based on the throw of fucking dice.'

'And if it lands in a square he's already killed in, he'll rethrow until he hits a fresh one,' Flynn said.

'No wonder my boffins couldn't find his victim type. He doesn't have one.'

Flynn nodded. 'Then, as he won't want to leave anything to

chance, he'll just choose whatever location he thinks works best for that particular square.'

'What do you think, Poe?' Mathers asked.

'You're OK with the Gretna Green outlier, Tilly? That's a one in four hundred roll of the dice.'

'It's probability, Poe. People win the lottery every week despite the ludicrous odds against it. A two being thrown is not unexpected. If the sample size were ten thousand, it would even out.'

'Now we just need to find out who sells these . . . what did you call them, Tilly?' Mathers said.

'Icosahedrons?'

'Yes, the twenty-sided dice.'

'You can get them anywhere, Commander Mathers. Sometimes they're part of a set of mixed dice, but they can be bought individually.'

'Damn,' she said. 'I was really hoping these were incredibly rare.'

'They're not, Commander Mathers,' Bradshaw said. 'But you're missing the wider point. It's not that he's using icosahedrons, it's that he already *had* icosahedrons.'

'You can't possibly know that, Tilly.'

'How likely do you think it is that when it came to choosing locations, instead of using something like a random-number generator as Poe suggested, he thought, "I know, I'll buy a pair of twenty-sided dice," Commander Mathers?'

Mathers hesitated. Eventually she said, 'Not likely.'

'Exactly,' Bradshaw said. 'It's far more likely he used what he already had lying around. He probably saw them and thought, "I can use my icosahedrons to generate random locations."'

Poe thought about it. 'I think that makes sense. The dice gave him the idea, not the other way around.'

Flynn nodded. Eventually so did Mathers.

'I'm not sure this is actionable intelligence, though, Tilly,' Mathers said.

'You're wrong about that, Commander Mathers,' Bradshaw said.

'I'm sure I am, but please do explain.'

'Do you know which demographic uses icosahedrons on an almost daily basis?'

'Before today, I'd never even heard of twenty-sided dice, Tilly. I have absolutely no idea who might need them. Gamblers, maybe?'

'No, Commander Mathers. Not gamblers. It was in the past. The British Museum has icosahedrons dating back to the first century. But today the majority of icosahedrons are used by a specific and niche demographic.'

'Who?'

'TTRPG enthusiasts.'

'TTRPGs?' Poe said. 'What the hell is that?'

'Tabletop role-playing games, Poe,' Bradshaw said. 'I think when we catch the sniper, we'll find that he's heavily involved in the world of *Dungeons & Dragons*.'

Chapter 25

'Well, not just *Dungeons & Dragons* obviously,' Bradshaw said. 'I said that as it's the game everyone seems to have heard of. I prefer *Warlocks & Witches* – I'm a level twenty-four Avariel – but there are tens of thousands of TTRPGs out there with more being developed every day. It's a multi-million-dollar business.'

Poe remembered Bradshaw once telling him about *Warlocks & Witches*. He'd walked in on her and her geeky friends. She was wearing a pair of wings. She'd said that she was a Sky Elf and that she had hollow bones. Poe had said, 'OK,' and backed away carefully.

'He's a dork then,' Poe said. 'Which seems unlikely. If he's anything like Tilly's *Warlocks & Witches* friends, he wouldn't have the upper-body strength to *hold* a weapon, let alone carry one for miles and miles across rugged country.'

'My friends are not dorks, Poe,' Bradshaw said.

'Jonathan is,' Poe said. 'He has asthma, hay fever *and* photo-sensitivity. His doctor says he's not allowed to go outside during the day.'

'Or during spring and summer,' Bradshaw added. 'But he's the exception, not the rule. Most of my friends are very athletic. Ripley once played badminton.'

'Crikey. Badminton?'

'Yes, with his mum when he was on holiday in Devon. He had to stop when he got a nosebleed, but he still has the racquet.'

'OK, before we follow the Poe and Tilly white rabbit any

further,' Mathers said, 'can we take a step back? Tilly, you said most twenty-sided dice are used in role-playing games. That implies some are used *outside* of role-playing games.'

'It says here the US Navy use dice in wargames,' Flynn said, looking at her phone. 'Maybe he's a military strategist.' She took a breath. 'Which is obviously a worrying thought.'

'That's *sort* of correct, DCI Flynn,' Bradshaw said.

'Only sort of?'

'In that it's mainly *in*correct. The dice the US Navy use in their wargaming are pentagonal trapezohedrons, not icosahedrons.'

'*Pente?*' Poe said. 'Isn't that Greek for five?'

'It is, Poe. Pentagonal trapezohedrons have five planes on each side, ten in total. The US Navy used them in pairs as percentile dice. You throw a pair, and you get a percentage.'

'He's *not* a military strategist then?'

Bradshaw shrugged. 'I don't know. RPGs aren't all dragons and goblins and magic suits of armour. Some of them *do* deal with strategy. *Spycraft* is an obvious one. It deals with modern-age espionage.'

Mathers leaned back in her chair. She put her hands behind her head and looked at the command trailer's ceiling. 'OK, how do I develop this into an actionable line of enquiry? I can't possibly investigate every person who's played *Dungeons & Dragons* but, as it's the only lead I have, neither can I ignore it.'

Bradshaw put her hand up.

'Yes, Tilly?' Mathers said.

'I have an idea, Commander Mathers,' Bradshaw said. 'Poe and I go to the UK Games Expo.'

'And what's that?'

'It's the largest tabletop games convention in the UK and it's on this weekend. And it's not just for hobbyists, all aspects of the industry attend. From *Dungeons & Dragons* to fledgling companies wanting start-up capital, every business involved in the

TTRPG community will have a stall there. It's the only weekend of the year when they'll all be under the same roof.'

'You think the sniper might attend?'

Bradshaw shrugged. 'I really don't know. He might, I suppose. But that's not why we would go.'

'Oh?'

'No, we would go to get the mailing list of every TTRPG company that attends. I'll bet you my dinner the killer is on one of those lists. I only play *Warlocks & Witches* yet I'm on forty-seven mailing lists.'

'You are? Why?'

'Because it's not just the games manufacturers and organising bodies who attend, it's the companies that make miniatures and costumes. The replica weapons and the souvenir T-shirts. Trust me, if he's a TTRPG player, he'll be on one of those mailing lists. Probably more than one.'

Mathers said, 'How many names are we talking about, Tilly?'

'Probably hundreds of thousands,' she replied.

'That's far too many. If it were one or two thousand, I could allocate a team to it. But checking hundreds of thousands of names can't be done.'

'I'm not proposing we check the names, Commander Mathers,' Bradshaw said. 'I'm proposing we collate the list then you run them through the police national computer and the police national database.'

'And what will you do?'

'I'll run the list through some of the watchlists I now have access to. If he's come to the attention of either the police or the security services, we'll get a match.'

'There'll be more than one match,' Poe said. 'One in three men in the UK has a criminal record. It's still too many.'

Mathers stood. 'Not if we restrict the offences to ones that are indicative of a propensity for violence. In other words, we remove minor road traffic offences and drunk and disorderly arrests from when they were students. Keep in things like arson and torturing animals. Tilly, can you help narrow down the list of offences?'

Bradshaw nodded. 'I can, Commander Mathers.'

'Just how big is this convention?'

'There'll be at least twenty thousand people there. It's held at the National Exhibition Centre in Birmingham.'

'And you think you and Poe can cover it all?'

'If I can keep him away from the *Star Wars* stage, yes,' Bradshaw said. 'Poe loves *Star Wars*.'

'I don't love *Star Wars*, Tilly,' Poe said. 'I just said it was the least shit out of the films you forced me to watch.'

'Will people be in fancy dress, Tilly?' Flynn asked.

'No, DCI Flynn,' Bradshaw replied. 'But they *will* be in costume.'

'Then I think it's a brilliant idea. What will you be going as, Tilly?'

'I'll dust off my wings and go as my *Warlocks & Witches* character.'

Flynn looked at Poe, a sly smile on her face. 'And what will you go as, Poe?'

Poe looked at Mathers. He looked at Flynn. 'I'll be going as a policeman,' he said.

Chapter 26

The UK Games Expo was taking place at the weekend. Jools Arreghini was murdered on the Tuesday before. Mathers offered to put them all up in a London hotel, but Poe took the opportunity to head back to Northumberland for a couple of days. He wanted to apologise to Doyle for abandoning her during their wedding rehearsal.

There was nothing he could do in Oxfordshire anyway. His main task now was to try and get inside the head of a man who indiscriminately shot people. An intelligent, forensically aware, technically proficient man. A ruthless man. And, if Bradshaw were to be believed, a tabletop role-playing game nerd. That was quite the cassoulet of character traits. He also wanted to check out Archie Arreghini's personal protection officer, Matthew. Archie had said Matthew knew Poe, and he wanted to know how. He would get Bradshaw to run him through every database she had.

So, he took his leave and headed north until he reached the M6. He then joined a million other commuters trying to get into, or past, Birmingham. It was unusually busy at the Newcastle-under-Lyme turn-off but that was OK – a caravan had caught fire. Good, Poe thought. It was probably heading to the Lakes. It was close to one in the morning when he finally arrived at Highwood. He'd expected the grand old house to be shrouded in darkness. Instead, the lights were on. He could hear laughter. Excited barking.

A man in an old-fashioned suit appeared as the front doors opened. Doors, plural. Poe now lived in a house with a doorway so large it needed *two* doors and a portico. The first time he'd set foot inside Highwood, he'd been examining a murder scene, trying to root out the clues Northumberland Police had missed. The clues that would eventually clear Doyle of her father's murder. Now he called Highwood his home. It had fifteen bedrooms. A vestibule. The curved stairway looked like something out of *Gone with the Wind*. Suits of armour guarding internal doorways; portraits of long-dead ancestors on the wall.

Highwood also came with a butler.

His name was Richard Brunton, but he only ever answered to Brunton. Poe knew this for a fact. He'd called him Richard once and his tea had been milky for a month. Poe hadn't liked the idea of a servant in the house. In fact, he'd *hated* the idea. He'd told Doyle. She'd said if he disliked the idea that much, he could tell Brunton his services were no longer required. But she'd added that Brunton's cottage in the village was dependent on him remaining in the family's employ until he was sixty-five.

'Can't we just tell him he can stay in the cottage?' he'd said. 'Kind of like early retirement.'

'Like charity?'

Poe had nodded.

'Would *you* accept charity?'

'I suppose not,' he'd said before adding, 'But when your dad was murdered, he hadn't been using Brunton. Why do we have to?'

'My father didn't use Brunton that year because he was on compassionate leave. His wife was battling lung cancer and my father said he didn't want to see him at Highwood until she was better.'

'And she *did* get better?'

'She did. And as soon as she'd regained her strength, Brunton returned to work. Of course, that was after my father had died.'

So, Highwood still had a Brunton, who only ever called Poe 'sir' and Doyle 'Lady Doyle'. Poe quite liked the cantankerous, stuffy old man. Brunton was sixty-three, so only had two years until his retirement, and Poe saw no reason to make them awkward just because *he* felt awkward.

'Welcome home, sir,' Brunton said before he reached the door. 'They're expecting you on the south lawn.'

'Estelle's not on her own?'

'Miss Emma is with her, sir,' he replied. 'And your dog, of course.'

Brunton said 'dog' the way other people said haemorrhoids. Brunton didn't like Edgar and Edgar didn't like Brunton. Poe didn't know why, although Brunton *had* limped for a week after Edgar had moved in. Poe knew from experience there was only so much Edgar would put up with before he used his teeth to express his displeasure.

Poe made his way around the back of the house to the south lawn. It was where the marquee had been sited. Edgar rushed out to greet him. When Poe had finished getting his face washed with dog saliva, he made his way inside. Doyle and Emma were sitting at one of the tables, giggling.

'Poe!' Doyle shouted. 'Tilly texted that you were heading home. Emma and I decided to wait up.'

'Hi, Poe,' Emma said. 'Rough day?'

'I've had better,' he replied.

Emma was one of Doyle's oldest friends. She was a medical doctor who, unlike Doyle, practised on the living. Poe thought she was an oncologist. Doyle was not only a professor but a medical practitioner, too; as she was a pathologist, though, her patients were already dead. There used to be a handwritten sign on the mortuary door saying 'Pathologists have the coolest patients' but when they'd moved into a more modern suite, she'd been told she couldn't take it with her. She now had it tattooed on her shoulder. Poe didn't like most of Doyle's friends, but he did like Emma. She didn't take herself too seriously.

'What are you doing?' he asked.

The table was covered in boxes, soggy newspaper, ornate vases, ribbons and, bizarrely, what looked like plastic tubs of flies.

'I've decided carnivorous plants will make ideal wedding favours,' Doyle said. She reached into a box and pulled out two plants. 'Venus flytraps for the ladies. Huntsman's horns for the gentlemen.'

Poe stared at the phallic-shaped huntsman's horn, the red, glistening globes of the Venus flytrap. 'Subtle,' he said.

Doyle grinned. 'We think so.'

'And the flies?'

'*Drosophila melanogaster*,' she replied. 'Flightless fruit flies. The plants arrived early, so after we've potted them, we're feeding them.'

'Looks fiddly.'

'You have no idea.'

'Then why . . . ?'

'We're not doing this because it's easy, Poe,' Doyle said. 'We're doing this because we *thought* it would be easy.'

They collapsed into fits of giggles. Picked up their wine glasses and clinked them together. 'There's some Spun Gold cooling in the fridge,' Emma said. 'Why don't you grab a bottle and join us?'

Poe did. He drank half the beer in one go. It had been a long day. He pressed the bottle against his forehead.

'Do you think this is over the top, Poe?' Emma said.

'The sex plants?'

'Yes.'

'The wedding I've just come from was supposed to take place in a tent that P. T. Barnum once owned. It was themed around

110

The Night Circus. The bride's father had hired a midnight performance by Cirque du Soleil. The last venue the wedding band played was Madison Square Garden. They'd built a walk-in wine cellar.' He took another drink. Enjoyed the fresh, hoppy taste. The cool finish. He turned the bottle in his hands. Thought how he'd prefer a Spun Gold to a glass of the Macallan M any day of the week. 'They had a live lobster tank and a Michelin-starred chef to cook them.'

'And the sniper got her?'

'The marquee was open-sided,' he said. 'He shot her through a crowd of people. Almost took her head off her shoulders.'

Doyle said nothing. Emma stayed quiet too.

'Her father's almost certainly a crook,' Poe continued, 'but I don't think I've ever seen such despair. He was waiting in Barnum's tent, surrounded by his daughter's blood and bone fragments. He refused to move until he'd spoken to me.'

'Why you?'

'He had a file on me. He had a file on *everyone.*'

'Between his daughter being murdered and you arriving,' Doyle said, 'what was that? About four hours?'

'He said he's connected, but something's not adding up.' Poe shrugged. 'Or maybe I'm overthinking things. He's a rich man and rich men have powerful friends. He also had a personal protection officer who knew me.'

'He knew you? From where?'

Poe shrugged again. 'Cumbria, apparently. I have no idea who he is. There was something about him, though. Familiar but unfamiliar, you know what I mean?'

'I don't, but you have good instincts. Why not get Tilly on it?'

'I plan to.'

'Speaking of Tilly, she tells me the sniper is rolling a pair of twenty-sided dice to get random locations.'

'She proved it with maths.'

'Then it's settled,' Doyle said. 'She also tells me you're infiltrating a *Dungeons & Dragons* convention this weekend.'

Poe put his head in his hands and groaned. 'She's wearing her sky elf costume,' he said.

'You'll have fun,' Doyle said.

'Really?' Emma said.

'Hell no. He'll hate it more than he hates having a butler.'

They laughed.

'I'm glad my pain amuses you,' he muttered.

Doyle smiled. She reached across. Put her hands on his. They were cold. They always were. Sometimes Poe thought Doyle had more in common with her patients than she let on.

'There's only one thing to do, Poe,' she said.

'What's that?'

'We'll get you blind drunk then you can help us feed flies to the plants.' She picked up a tub of the fruit flies. Held it up to the vivarium-style lighting in the marquee. 'Or, seeing as they don't have wings, maybe they should be called walks?'

Edgar woofed. Poe had known his dog long enough to know he was doing something he shouldn't be doing but having a great time doing it. He looked down at the spaniel. His tail was wagging. Fast. He was licking one of the plastic tubs, like it was ice cream.

Poe sighed. 'Don't eat the walks, Edgar,' he said.

Chapter 27

Poe woke to the smell of hot lard. He reached across the bed, but Doyle was already up. He threw on a pair of shorts, a Dead Men Walking T-shirt from their 2024 'Freedom: It Still Ain't on the Rise' tour, a pair of cheap trainers. He joined Doyle in the kitchen. She was plating up bacon and eggs for her and Emma. Hangover food.

'Grab a plate, Poe,' she said when she saw him. 'I've fried almost half a kilo of bacon.'

He pointed at the block of lard on the kitchen counter. It was unashamed. Lard didn't mess about. It didn't try to pretend it wasn't the rendered fatty tissue of pigs. Poe loved lard. 'Aren't you both doctors?'

'Yeah, but we're not very good ones,' Emma said, winking. She looked remarkably chipper. Poe wasn't surprised. He'd yet to meet a hospital doctor who couldn't hold their booze. 'I'm going to eat this but take my coffee to go, if that's OK, Est?'

'I thought you were off today?'

'I am,' she said. 'I want to pop into work for an hour, though. I have patients who like to see their doctor.'

She finished her breakfast, kissed Doyle and Poe on the cheek, then left them to it. Poe ate his bacon and eggs in silence, his mind on the case. He mopped up his egg yolk with that awful bread Doyle liked. The kind with gravel pebble-dashed on the crust. When he'd finished, Doyle said, 'Walk?'

*

Poe and Doyle still split their time between Highwood and Herdwick Croft, Poe's shepherd's cottage on the bleak and desolate Shap Fell. Herdwick Croft had the advantage of isolation, something Poe had always appreciated. And now she was Lady Doyle, the late Marquess of Northumberland's daughter, it was something she was *learning* to appreciate. There was always something to do at Highwood. Elcid Doyle, her late father, had an estate manager. Estelle had kept him on but there were things he couldn't do. Decisions he couldn't make. When she was at Herdwick Croft, cut off from wi-fi and a mobile phone signal, it was as if she was having the kind of digital detox Londoners checked into two-grand-a-night spas for.

But Herdwick Croft *was* cramped. Two hundred years ago it had provided shelter to one man and his dog. Literally. A shepherd and his border collie. It wasn't built for two people. It wasn't designed as permanent accommodation. It was a waystation. Somewhere for the shepherd to hunker down when the weather got very bad very quickly. On Shap Fell, that happened a lot and without warning. Add a hyperactive springer spaniel to the mix and Herdwick Croft got full pretty darn quickly.

Highwood, on the other hand, had all those bedrooms. You could walk around the estate for days without seeing anyone. You could play hide and seek and never be found. It was the kind of house with wardrobes that led to magical wintery lands where white witches ruled and Turkish Delight was the local currency. Fifteen bedrooms meant Bradshaw could stay with them whenever she wanted. She even had her own room. She had a pair of wellies in the cloakroom.

Poe had thought it would be a wrench to leave Shap Fell for extended periods. And for a while it had been. He'd missed the wild beauty. The raw landscape. The smell of the heather, of the Herdwick sheep. The no-nonsense Cumbrians.

But he'd come to realise that Northumberland was Cumbria's

perfect cousin. It had proper cities. It had beautiful coastlines. Their sand was golden, unlike the shards of razor-thin rock found on most Cumbrian beaches. Its castles were spectacular; Carlisle Castle looked like a condemned borstal. Northumberland wasn't *better* than Cumbria, but it was different.

And, at the end of the day, it *was* the north. The people were the same. Friendly, congenial, funny. Quick to anger, even quicker to laugh.

He'd soon come to appreciate Highwood. Yes, the estate had been planned. Centuries ago, aesthetics had dictated where the giant oaks were to be planted. Woods had been cleared to give uninterrupted views of the rolling hills, even parts of Hadrian's Wall. But whoever had designed the estate had earned their fee. It was special. Poe had explored the grounds for hours and hours and still didn't think he'd seen it all.

'A groat for your thoughts?' Doyle asked.

'I was just thinking how the estate's herd of red deer don't venture too close to the house these days,' Poe replied. He hadn't been. He'd been thinking about the case. And how until the sniper was caught, he'd never *not* be thinking about it. It was the way his mind worked. It had two gears – flat out and idling. Nothing in between. Nothing healthy. It was probably why he still had PTSD. 'Do you think it's because of Edgar?'

'Oh, I *know* it's because of Edgar,' Doyle said. 'The gardener told me.'

'We can try to keep him inside.'

'No, the gardener loves him. And the deer were becoming pests. He couldn't plant anything new without them getting at it. Now Edgar the scarecrow is prowling the grounds, they're staying where we want them.'

They reached the top of a slope and looked back on the house. They were high enough to see the roof of the marquee. Edgar, sensing they'd stopped, ran back to them. Then he got bored and sprinted off again.

'We haven't discussed whether you want me to take your name, Poe,' Doyle said.

She said it casually, but Poe could tell it was a question with bite. One she'd been wanting to ask for a long time. She wanted a thoughtful, not flippant, answer.

'I don't think what I want should be a consideration, Estelle,' he said. 'It's your name and it's a good one. It's synonymous with Highwood, with Northumberland. And even if it wasn't, you're Professor Estelle Doyle, world-renowned forensic pathologist. You're also *Lady* Estelle Doyle, a member of the British aristocracy. The Poes have been scratching around in the dirt for centuries.' He paused. 'So, no, I don't think you *should* take my name.' He paused again. 'Anyway, Professor Poe sounds a little too much like Professor *Poo* to me.'

She laughed. 'I've thought about this a lot,' she said. 'There's been a Doyle at Highwood since the year dot, but—'

Poe's phone rang. It was Mathers. He tilted the screen so Doyle could see.

'Answer it,' she said.

'You sure? Seems like we're having a moment.'

'This can wait, Poe.'

'Ma'am,' he said. 'What's up?'

'How quickly can you get to the Cairngorms, Poe?'

Poe covered the mouthpiece like he was holding a rotary phone. 'The Cairngorms?' he asked Doyle. 'How far away is it?'

Doyle seemed to know where all the grouse moors were. Poe assumed it was the aristocratic equivalent of a London cabbie's 'knowledge'.

'Four hours,' she replied without hesitation. 'Take the Land Rover. The last few miles might get boggy.'

'Four hours, ma'am,' Poe said to Mathers. 'Why?'

'Your hunch paid off. Police Scotland have found where the bastard's been zeroing his weapon.'

Chapter 28

A gamekeeper had found the sniper's zeroing range in the Forest of Atholl. It was in the rural region of Perth and Kinross. Most of the forest was in the Cairngorms National Park, but the range had been found just inside Dalnamein, one of the main beats the gamekeepers kept for deer stalking. The estate was massive, almost 150,000 acres, a mixture of open hill and dense forest. Perfect deer country.

Perfect sniping country.

The kind of place where gunshots would be an everyday sound.

It took Poe four hours to drive to Pitlochry, a small town in Perth and Kinross. It was 20 miles from where the gamekeeper had found the sniper's range. Close enough to get there quickly, not so close a police presence would set off alarm bells. Poe found the police station and parked behind a mud-spattered Land Rover. He was greeted at the front desk by a prune-faced Scotsman. Big arms, an even bigger waist. He looked like Ma out of *The Goonies*.

'You the guy from London? The city slicker they've sent tae tell us carrots what tae do?'

Carrots was what cops in the cities called cops in the rural forces.

'I'm from Cumbria, mate. Pitlochry's an urban hellscape as far as I'm concerned. I'm the carrot, not you.'

Ma Goonie grunted something unintelligible. Poe doubted it was anything polite. 'I'll take ye tae to the briefing room,' he said. 'They're waiting for you.'

The briefing room was full. Poe stood at the back with a couple of bored-looking armed cops. Armed cops always looked bored in Poe's experience. He reckoned it was so they looked cool.

A uniformed chief superintendent stood up and nodded at Poe. She was a tall woman. An old scar ran from the corner of her lip to the middle of her cheek. Looked like she'd been glassed. Poe wondered if she was a local cop or if she'd been parachuted in from Glasgow or Edinburgh. Police Scotland was a national police force. It covered the whole country. The smaller regional forces had been merged for more than a decade. And with 23,000 personnel, it was the second biggest police force in the UK. Only the Met was bigger. Poe thought Police Scotland was still finding its feet, particularly when it came to balancing the expertise needed for complex operations with the need for local cops and their unrivalled local intelligence systems. It was possible, probable even, that the chief superintendent had never set foot in Pitlochry Police Station.

'Now that London have bothered to show up, we'll crack on,' she said.

She brought up some slides and took them through what the gamekeeper had found.

Chapter 29

The chief superintendent was called Ailsa McCloud and, as Poe had thought, she wasn't a local cop. She was based in Glasgow and was with the Specialist Crime Division, the unit that provided specialist investigative and intelligence functions.

'Sorry about that crack before,' she said. 'It's kind of expected. And it'll help me integrate with the natives. Local intel will be key here, we want them onside.'

'I used to work for a national unit, ma'am,' Poe said. 'I'm used to low-level resentment. Calling us in was seen as a sign of weakness by the troops on the ground.'

'What do you think?'

'I think you've found him.'

The range the gamekeeper had found was crude, but semi-permanent. A square of laminated A4 paper was stapled to an old Scots pine. Bullet holes formed a smiley face. The gamekeeper had ripped it off. Underneath were many more bullet holes. The forensic guys who'd examined the tree counted over one hundred. They dug out seven. They were .50 BMGs, the same ammunition the sniper was using. The gamekeeper recognised a target when he saw one – although he hadn't realised he'd found the needle in the haystack – and he worked backwards, looking for the firing position. He found nine. Each one had a marker and a sandbag. They started at 600 metres from the target and ended at 1,400, each one 100 metres from the next. Poe didn't have the exact figures to hand, but he knew all the victims had been within those shooting distances.

With the sniper's range confirmed, McCloud had done what Poe would have done. She put everything back as it had been, including the ripped target, and left it alone. But not before her tech people had hidden a series of live-feed, military-grade trail cameras. She now had eyes on the range and didn't have to be anywhere near it. The plan was to wait for the sniper to zero his weapon ahead of the next murder, then mob him with armed cops. Maybe even hope he resisted.

It was a good plan and Poe couldn't see any way to improve it.

Although it was a good plan, Police Scotland were now in a hurry-up-and-wait, circling-the-airport scenario. They had rushed to get everything in place, but now they were at the whim of the sniper. Poe was sure he would return to his makeshift range, but he'd be working to his own timetable, and they weren't privy to it. He might turn up that night, it might be a month.

Poe explained the situation to Mathers. She only had one question: 'Do they have it in hand?'

'They do, ma'am,' Poe replied. 'I'll hook you up with Chief Superintendent McCloud, but she's an experienced cop. She knows what she's doing. I don't think I'd add any value if I stayed.' He thought about her 'Now that London have bothered to show up' crack and added, 'In fact, all I'd do is get on their pip.'

Chapter 30

Three days later

National Exhibition Centre, Birmingham

Even as a child, Poe had never taken an interest in nerd culture. He hadn't queued to watch *Back to the Future*. *Jurassic Park* passed him by. *Men in Black* had sounded silly. He'd not seen *Star Wars* until Bradshaw had made him watch it on the Spring-heeled Jack stakeout. She'd made him watch all eleven films in the franchise. *Eleven*. Nine films and two spinoffs. It had taken two whole days. Poe didn't even do things he liked for that long.

And when the people who'd had nosebleeds as kids inherited the earth, when weird became the new black, he still didn't take an interest. That was because the people who obsessed over continuity errors in the Marvel Cinematic Universe tended not to be serial killers. He figured they vented their cruelty on elves and goblins and people Bradshaw referred to as non-player characters. Apparently, that meant any character controlled by the game, not the players. Poe had immediately tried to forget that.

Which was why he hadn't known what to expect. If he'd thought about it at all, he'd have figured it would be a slightly bigger version of the *Warlocks & Witches* games that Bradshaw and her weird little pals played.

But stepping into the National Exhibition Centre was a shock to his system. Sensory overload. Like he'd been hit in the face by a nerdstick. He'd thought the sniper situation might have kept them away. It hadn't. There were screens to protect the outside queue, and security checks were taking place inside the NEC rather than at the entrance, but the exhibition centre was rammed. Poe had never seen so many misfits, outsiders and flat-out wackadoodle crackpots in one place. And he'd once spent a week in Brighton.

Intense men and women, over-stimulated children. Pasty faces and serious expressions. People queuing to get merchandise signed by washed-up Z-list actors. Displays of movie props, of backdrops. Hundreds of stalls. Food stands. Face-in-the-hole boards, the kind usually seen at Blackpool Pleasure Beach. And everyone was dressed up. Overweight men in Spider-Man costumes, underweight men in Hulk costumes. Women dressed as Princess Leia (always the *slave* Leia, Poe noticed), women dressed as Wonder Woman. A hundred other characters Poe didn't recognise. Men drank from horns, like they'd pillaged Lindisfarne. It was louder than the bar at an airport departure lounge.

'Blimey,' he said to Bradshaw. 'This is insane.'

'Conventions like this are a complex network of interconnected and overlapping subcultures, Poe,' she replied, adjusting her elf wings. 'It's a chance for fans, game makers, creators of comic books, movies, TTRPGs and a hundred other subsets to mingle without being mocked by people like . . .'

'Like me?'

Bradshaw shrugged. 'A few years ago, yes,' she said. 'But you're far more tolerant now. You've only laughed at my wings once today.'

'But?'

'But there are still a lot of bullies in the world, Poe.'

Poe nodded. He knew that to be true. 'It's a safe space,' he said at last.

Bradshaw didn't respond. She was being unusually quiet. He thought she'd have been fizzing with excitement. He'd had a sneaking suspicion that insisting they must attend the event in person was a ruse. She asked him to go to things like this with her at least twice a year and he always found a reason not to. But he was here now, and for some reason it seemed she didn't want to be. He'd seen her pick up, then discard, a flyer for light-sabre lessons. She was being very un-Bradshaw-like. He wondered why that was.

'What's the plan then?' he asked. 'Split up, get their mailing lists then head over to one of the hog-roast stalls? Get some roast pork and a drinking horn of mead?'

'They won't give you their mailing lists, Poe. They can't, legally.'

'Then why—'

'I'll *get* their mailing lists. I've already downloaded most of them.'

'Legally?'

'Do you care, Poe?' she replied, her voice curiously flat.

'Not even a little bit. What's the matter?'

'Nothing.'

'Okaaaay,' he said, drawing it out. 'If we don't need to be here to get their mailing lists, why have we trekked all the way to Birmingham?'

'I don't know *all* the games, Poe. I know the established ones and almost all of the newer ones.'

'But there are some you don't know?'

'This convention is where brand new games are premiered,' she said. 'Games in beta development. It's where people look for start-up capital. These are the ones we need to get information on. They'll all have websites. If we pick up their details, I can get their mailing lists and backers.'

'Sounds like a plan,' he said. 'You go left, I'll go right. Meet back here in an hour? See which areas we still haven't covered.'

Bradshaw bit her bottom lip and said, 'OK, Poe.'

She walked off without another word.

Chapter 31

Bradshaw had asked him to wear the suit he wore when he was in court. Dark blue with pinstripes. She'd insisted. Doyle had picked him out a burgundy tie and a light-blue linen shirt. And *she'd* insisted. He'd wondered why.

Now he knew.

His first clue was when a guy *also* wearing a dark-blue pinstripe suit with a burgundy tie and light-blue linen shirt tried to high-five him. Poe left him hanging. Two minutes later, someone else said, 'Banging costume, man.'

Up until then, he'd somehow felt over- and *under*-dressed. Now he wondered which odd-bod character Doyle and Bradshaw had surreptitiously dressed him as. He decided to grab the next person who looked at him funny. It happened immediately. A man wearing a trench coat, a fedora and a long, multi-coloured scarf approached Poe and offered him a Jelly Baby.

Poe took a black one. Didn't care that the man scowled at his lack of Jelly Baby decorum. Hiding the black ones underneath the yellow and orange ones was a naive Jelly Baby tactic. If the man thought he'd get away with that, he had no right owning a bag.

'Who am I?' Poe said.

The man looked confused. 'Er . . . have you lost the person who looks after you?'

'I don't mean, what's my name,' Poe said. 'I mean which *character* am I?'

'Er, you're the tenth Doctor.'

Poe looked at him blankly.

'Doctor *Who*. The one David Tennant played. Although, I guess you could be the *fourteenth* Doctor.'

Before he could stop himself, Poe said, 'Why?'

'Duh,' the man said. 'Because Tennant returned to the role in 2023. I'm the iconic fourth Doctor, obviously.'

'Obviously,' Poe said. The moment the fourth Doctor had disappeared, along with his Jelly Babies, he tapped out a text to Doyle. It said: YOU 2 ARE SOOOOOO FUNNY. He got a line of laughing emojis a few seconds later. He was about to send the same text to Bradshaw, but something stayed his hand. She hadn't seemed happy when they'd split up.

Poe wandered over to a small stall. It was the first one he'd seen that didn't have a crowd of people hovering. The stall owner was painting little figurines like he was six years old.

'All right?' Poe said. He peered at the name of the game. It was in a Gothic script and had a picture of some men and women at what looked like a séance. The stall owner's name badge said BARTY. 'What's *The Liar's Club* about, Barty?'

'It's a hardboiled detective game,' Barty said. 'The player assumes the role of one of twenty cops and the object is to solve the riddle of *The Liar's Club*.'

Poe waited for him to elaborate. He didn't. It seemed that was all the information Poe was getting. 'And it's a role-playing game, is it?'

'Think *Disco Elysium*, but with a better combat system.'

'No, I don't think I will.'

'Do you want me to talk you through the rules?'

Poe ignored the question. 'Does *The Liar's Club* require twenty-sided dice, Barty?'

Barty frowned. 'What an odd question,' he said. 'As it happens, it does. A pair. The players throw them to—'

'Can you fax me your mailing list?' Poe said, holding up his NCA ID card.

'Not from here, mate.'

'Where's "here"?'

'Twenty twenty-five.'

Everyone's a comedian, Poe thought. 'Email it then.'

'I can't do that either. Data protection. I think you'd need a warrant or something.'

'Do you even *have* a mailing list?'

Barty nodded. 'Four thousand members of *The Liar's Club* get a newsletter twice a month.'

Poe picked up *The Liar's Club* flyer. It displayed the only thing Bradshaw would need to access the mailing list – the name of the company and their website. He thanked Barty and wandered across to the next stall. This one was for an RPG called *Trail of Tears*.

He listened to the guy's pitch then ran into the same problem. He soon realised that Bradshaw had been right – there was more chance of the British Museum returning the Elgin Marbles than of gaming companies willingly sharing their mailing lists. The laws on data protection were rock solid. And the stalls on the periphery were the minor players. The one-man bands. He imagined that when it came to the bigger, more established companies, he'd be given even shorter shrift.

Instead of persevering, he did what Bradshaw had asked – he grabbed as many leaflets as he could. If anyone asked what he was doing, he told them he was a games vlogger. He didn't know what a vlogger was, but he'd overheard a bespectacled girl use the term when she was asking for information. It had seemed to work.

Poe's stomach growled. He wasn't hungry but he could smell one of the hog-roast food stalls. He circled back to where he was due to meet Bradshaw and found a seat. She wasn't there. That was unusual. She was always early. He checked his watch. He was on time. He was on time and Bradshaw was late. He noticed a crowd had formed. A crowd had formed and Bradshaw was missing. The two things were rarely unrelated. He got to his feet just as a man wearing a Viking helmet started shouting at some-one much smaller.

Someone wearing elf wings.

Shit.

Chapter 32

Poe pushed his way into the crowd. It was mainly men in fake armour. They had encircled Bradshaw like hyenas. Most of them were carrying replica swords and replica axes. One of them had a longbow. Role-playing games were very violent, Poe thought. A man in his way yelled, 'Have her scrubbed and brought to my tent!' Poe dug him in the small of his back. The man turned and saw Poe's expression. He fled. Poe ploughed forward. Eventually he got to the front.

Bradshaw and an idiot in a Viking helmet had squared off against each other. Bradshaw looked terrified. But defiant. She *always* looked defiant when she was scared. She met her fears face on. Had done ever since Poe had known her.

'Hello, everyone,' he said. 'What's happening?'

The mood in the group immediately changed. Went from predatory to guilty to angry.

'Go back to your TARDIS, Doctor,' the man in the Viking helmet said. 'This is between me and the she-elf.'

The man's helmet was a touch too big for him. Underneath the brow ridge, he wore Eddie the Eagle glasses. He had piggy eyes. Poe had never seen a less scary Viking. His helmet didn't even have horns.

'Hi, Poe,' Bradshaw said, breathing out in relief.

'You OK, Tilly?'

'I am, Poe. This man was just telling me how small his penis is. I'm not sure why he's so cross.'

Eddie the Viking stepped forward. So did Poe.

'Take another step and I'll punch your face flat,' Poe said. He pulled out his ID and added, 'And if I get so much as a hangnail doing it, I'll arrest you for assault.'

Eddie the Viking stopped.

'Tilly, walk me through everything,' Poe said.

'This man told me his name was Horse and if I went with him to the accessible bathroom, he'd show me why. Except, I know his name is Horace, not Horse. He is part of a men-only group called the Norse Pantheon.'

'Horace the Viking?' Poe said. He nodded. 'Yes, that fits *very* well.'

'And then he said that the women in Droitwich call him Horse because of the size of his genitalia. And as I understand that men of low wit equate penis size with masculinity, I thought it unusual that he'd told me his is very small. I imagine he finds sexual intercourse very difficult. I really don't see what I did wrong.'

'See,' Horace said, sulkily. 'I made a cheeky comment and she took the piss. And now it's *me* who's in trouble. It's what they do.'

'Who?'

Horace spat on the floor. 'Women,' he said. 'War and war gaming is a man's business. There's no role for women. Their brains function differently. But now they're here, competing. Competing and complaining. Taking it over. *Sullying* it. And we aren't putting up with it any more, are we, lads?'

There was a ragged, half-enthusiastic cheer from the rest of the *Carry On Vikings* crew.

'Did my friend *ask* you about the size of your genitalia?' Poe said.

'She didn't have to,' Horace said defiantly. 'The only reason women attend these things is to find men. It's a known fact.'

'I'll take that as a no,' Poe said. 'But since you told her anyway, I think I'd like to hear what she has to say. Tilly?'

'The average weight of a stallion is one thousand kilos, Poe. The average length of their erect penis is fifty centimetres. That's five centimetres for every one hundred kilos. The average weight of a man in the UK is ninety kilos but the man shouting at me is morbidly obese—'

'I am *not*—'

'Don't interrupt, *Horace*,' Poe said. 'Tilly?'

'That means if he weighs one hundred kilos, his penis is five centimetres when erect,' she continued. 'That's under two inches, well below the national average of five.'

'Will you stop saying that!' Horace shouted.

He stepped forward again. Bunched his fists. Poe was surprised. The threat of hitting people combined with his NCA ID card was usually enough to stop things escalating. The *Carry On Vikings* crew took a step forward too. Safety in numbers. One of them put his hand on the hilt of his sword. Smiled, glassy-eyed. Which was when Poe saw their drinking horns were wet. Some still had dry foam on the lip. It was a touch after midday, but the mead bar had been open since ten. Poe frowned. He'd made a serious miscalculation. A drunk crowd was an affray waiting to happen. It just needed someone to set it off. To light the blue touchpaper. Something like their wannabe alpha losing face to, God help us all . . . a woman.

'Apologise,' Horace said to Bradshaw.

'Maths doesn't lie, sir,' Bradshaw said. 'I have nothing to apologise for.'

Horace's eyes narrowed. Poe didn't know what to do. He couldn't fight everyone and even if he could, he was a police officer. He wasn't supposed to get into public brawls. He was supposed to be oil on water. He was supposed to calm things down. But the *Carry On Vikings* crew didn't want to be calmed down. Even if they hadn't been drinking, the average dog turd had more brain cells than a crowd of indignant, entitled white men in fancy dress. He wondered what the male equivalent of a 'Karen' was. Kevin, maybe? Bradshaw would know, and it was Bradshaw he was thinking about. The *Carry On Vikings* crew had weapons. Yes, they were replicas, but a replica sword was still made of steel. A replica axe was still a blunt instrument. You could still get stabbed with a replica dagger. He didn't want Bradshaw to get hurt. He rolled his shoulders and cocked his fist. He'd take out Horace the Viking first. He seemed to be in charge.

Which was when a voice cut through the crowd. It wasn't loud but it silenced everyone like it was Quint's nail down an Amity Island blackboard. *Jaws* was one of the few films Poe liked, although he preferred the book. In the book Richard Dreyfuss's annoying character got eaten by the shark.

'I didn't think they let nonces congregate any more,' the voice said. 'Come on, room for a small one?' A tall man, a clear head above everyone else, was scything through the *Carry On Vikings* crowd like the great white's fin.

Poe recognised him.

It was Matthew, Archie Arreghini's bodyguard.

Chapter 33

Matthew did jazz hands.

'Surprise,' he said to Poe.

Matthew's appearance didn't put a full stop to what was about to happen, but it certainly paused it. The quiet menace Poe had sensed at Archie Arreghini's had been amped up tenfold. It was overt now. Poe felt the hairs rise on the back of his neck. Matthew was a dangerous man. And again, Poe had the feeling that he should know who he was.

Matthew threw a thumb over his shoulder. 'So, Fatty here's got a two-inch dick, has he? Surprised he was bragging about it to be honest. Then again, it'd be a dreary world if everyone thought the same.'

'This is nothing to do with you,' Horace the Viking said out of the side of his mouth. 'I'm not leaving here without an apology.'

'Fuck off, mate,' Matthew said, without turning round.

Horace put his hand on Matthew's shoulder. Poe winced. Matthew looked at the hand in amusement. Horace removed it like he'd put it on a hot griddle.

'Don't ever touch me again,' Matthew said. He rubbed his hands together. 'Now, if this two-incher is worth bragging about, I reckon it's worth seeing.'

Horace said nothing.

'Go on then, whip it out,' Matthew said. He folded his arms. Tapped his foot.

He's goading him, Poe thought. He's goading him into doing

something. Poe glanced up. Saw the myriad dome cameras on the roof. He wants to be reactive, not *pro*active. Proactive people go to prison. Reactive people don't.

Matthew was six-foot three. He was lean, didn't have an ounce of fat on him. Horace the Viking needed a bra. He looked like he'd get out of breath reaching for his family pack of cheesy Wotsits. Matthew looked like he wrestled bears in his spare time. Horace looked like he made his own Christmas cards.

But, just as Matthew had wanted, it turned out that even pretend Vikings could only be pushed so far. Particularly when they'd been drinking mead for two hours. Horace put his hand on his replica sword. It had an ornate pommel and grip. He said, 'My name is Odin, the All-Father, first of the Aesir.'

'No, it isn't,' Matthew said. 'And Vikings don't wear hearing aids.'

Horace unsheathed his replica sword and shouted, ''Til Valhalla!'

Matthew didn't hesitate. He took a step forward, grabbed Horace's jerkin and headbutted him with a ferocity Poe hadn't seen in a long time. Crushed the replica helmet against his nose. Horace dropped his sword and fell to the floor, clutching his face. Blood spurted through his fingers. He started bawling.

'Shut up or I'll stamp on your tiny mouse balls,' Matthew said.

Horace shut up.

'Gosh,' Bradshaw said.

Matthew addressed the rest of the *Carry On Vikings* crew.

'Listen up,' he said. 'I need you all to piss off. And I don't mean to another part of the NEC, I mean piss off back to your basement rooms and your call-centre jobs.' He paused. 'The next person to take even a single step in my direction gets a life-changing injury.'

A glassy-eyed man in horn-rimmed spectacles, not reading the situation as well as he ought, stepped forward anyway. He eyed his fallen comrade and said, 'I don't think you realise just how many of us are solicitors. What's your name, because you're going to prison for a long, long—'

Matthew barely moved. Just his leg. It shot out like a dart. Connected with the side of the guy's knee. There was an audible snap as the joint shattered. He collapsed. Started shrieking.

'Anyone else want to play?' Matthew said. He ran his eyes over the crowd. 'No? Then off you fuck.'

They did.

Matthew sauntered up to Poe and Bradshaw. He thrust out his hand. Nonplussed, Poe shook it.

'What the hell is going on?' Poe said.

'My name's Towler,' he said. 'Matt Towler.' He looked at the two men he'd put on the floor. 'Come on, let's get a brew.'

Chapter 34

Towler looked across at the paramedics helping the injured *Carry On Vikings* on to stretchers. He shook his head. 'All that pent-up anger,' he said wistfully.

Poe studied him carefully. Towler had committed two acts of extreme violence, but he was calm. As if he did it every week. Which didn't make sense. If he was Archie Arreghini's enforcer there'd be an inch-thick file on him. Mathers would have known about him. And if he was just a mindless thug from Cumbria, *Poe* would have known about him.

But Poe didn't think Towler was a mindless thug. Despite the blood on the ground and the men on stretchers, his actions *hadn't* been thoughtless. They'd been calculated. With a head-butt to the face and a snap-kick to the knee, he'd stopped a volatile crowd from kicking off. No one had waved around heavy replica weapons. No one had loosed an arrow. No one but two willing participants had been hurt. And as the *Carry On Vikings* crew had been crowding Bradshaw, no one else had really seen anything.

And Towler had made sure he was on CCTV when Horace the Viking had drawn his sword. No court in the land would convict him of the first assault and no camera in the NEC had caught the second. Poe had explained this to the security guards and then the attending police. He said he'd witnessed the whole thing (not a lie) and that the actions Towler had taken had been proportionate (a bit of a lie) considering the circumstances. The Brummie cops had taken his and Towler's statements. Poe had showed them his triple-warrant card. Told them if he'd thought Towler had acted unreasonably, he'd have arrested him himself. That seemed to satisfy the Brummies.

'That guy whose leg you snapped will press charges,' Poe said. 'He'll try to sue you.'

Towler shrugged. 'Probably.'

'But?'

'But nothing will come of it.' He didn't elaborate.

'You think Archie Arreghini's reach extends to the courts?' Poe asked.

Towler ignored the question. He slurped his tea, glanced at Poe then said, 'You're ex-Black Watch.'

'Yes.'

'Crap hats, but a decent bunch.'

Poe looked him up and down. Saw the maroon T-shirt and desert boots. He rolled his eyes and said, 'Oh, were you in the Parachute Regiment?'

'I was. And I did riot control in Belfast,' Towler said.

'So did I.'

'You'll know the purpose of snatch squads then?'

'To grab the individuals controlling the demonstration.'

'Exactly,' Towler yawned. He scratched his armpit. 'Anyway, I saw you and your bookworm were in a bit of trouble. I was in a position to help, so I did.'

'Which brings me nicely on to my next question. What are you doing here? And who the hell are you?'

Towler smiled politely. 'That's two questions.'

Bradshaw joined them at the tea stand. She said she wanted some fresh fruit. Poe suspected she had ulterior motives. She took a seat and pulled out her laptop.

'His name is Matthew Towler, Poe,' she said. 'I'm surprised

you don't know him. He's ex-Cumbria Police. He was forced to leave after engineering his friend's escape from custody.'

'Oh, you're *that* guy,' Poe said.

Chapter 35

Towler shook his finger. 'Careful what you say there, missy. That was never proven and my friend was later exonerated. I left the force without a blemish on my record.'

Bradshaw blew a raspberry. 'Oh, *pur-lease*,' she said. 'Everyone knows it was you. No one knows why you did it, but you definitely did.' She moved her finger over the laptop's trackpad. Brought up a new page. 'He moved from job to job for a while, Poe. Private security in the Middle East, in Africa—'

'And now the UK,' Poe cut in.

Bradshaw frowned. 'This is odd,' she said. 'He started working for Mr Arreghini twenty-two months ago.'

'Why's that odd, Tilly? That's what Archie said when I spoke to him.'

'No, it's what he did *before* that's odd, Poe.'

Poe glanced at Towler. A smile was dancing across his lips. As if he was in on the joke and you weren't. 'And what did he do before, Tilly?'

'That's just it. I don't know. He either dropped off the grid and had no employment whatsoever or . . .' She bit her lip, looked at Towler and frowned. She then closed her laptop.

'Or what, Tilly?'

'Do you want a slice of mango, Poe?' Bradshaw passed him her fruit bowl. 'It's fresh and has a lot of fibre. It'll help you move your bowels.'

Towler sniggered.

'Tilly, he either dropped off the grid or what?' Poe said, ignoring the tall idiot.

'Eat the mango, Poe.'

'What did Towler do before he worked for Mr Arreghini, Tilly?'

'Stop being such a fusspot, Poe,' she replied. 'I told you, I don't know.'

Poe let it go. Maybe it was something Bradshaw didn't want to say in front of Towler. Maybe it was something else. He'd find out later. He and Bradshaw didn't have secrets.

'You asked what I was doing here,' Towler said.

'I did.'

'Mr Arreghini asked me to keep an eye on the investigation, and as you two seem to be the only ones with fresh ideas, it seemed a logical place to start.'

'We can't share anything,' Poe said.

'Don't need you to,' Towler said. 'The bookworm—'

'She's called Miss Bradshaw.'

'But you can call me Tilly.'

'The *bookworm* figured out that the sniper's choosing his location based on throwing a pair of twenty-sided dice and you came here as it's where the dorks who *use* twenty-sided dice hang out. I take it you're after their mailing lists?'

'We are,' Bradshaw said.

'Tilly . . .' Poe warned.

Bradshaw waved him off. 'I think we should trust Mr Towler, Poe.'

'Tilly, we have a track record of not trusting anyone. Why would we trust a crook's bodyguard?'

'Because he has an honest face.'

'OK, what's going—'

'Have some mango, Poe.'

Poe scowled.

'How are you getting on with the mailing lists?' Towler said. 'Did you get everything you need?'

'We were doing OK until the Norse Pantheon surrounded me and started being rude,' Bradshaw said.

'I thought they were supposed to be Vikings?' Poe said.

'They are, Poe. The Norse Pantheon are a group of deities who appear in several canonical *D&D* works.'

Poe considered the men who had surrounded Bradshaw. They'd looked more like sex tourists than Nordic gods. The kind of men who got their wives from catalogues. 'They're *Dungeons & Dragons* fans?'

Bradshaw nodded.

Towler gestured towards the *D&D* stage. It was easily the most popular. The queue to see the actors from the recent film and the spin-off television series snaked around the inside of the main arena. The fans loved the actors and the actors pretended to love the fans. 'I guess that nerd-circle jerk is the payload?' he said. 'The *D&D* mailing list will be an amalgamation of almost every other list.'

Poe raised his eyebrows.

Towler shrugged. 'I have a daughter who likes goofy shit.'

'She's called Abigail,' Bradshaw said.

'Abi,' Towler confirmed.

'And I already have the *D&D* mailing list. We're only here in person to make sure there are no games in the start-up or beta phase I was unaware of.'

'Were there?'

'Poe found two. *The Liar's Club* and *Trail of Tears*. I've already accessed their mailing lists. We'll have a walk through the convention centre to make sure we haven't overlooked any when Poe's finished his mango.'

'Then you'll start crosschecking the lists against your databases?'

'I will.'

'Which includes the names your boss sent over?' Poe said.

Towler shook his head. 'That's the wrong tree to bark up.'

'We still haven't confirmed he wasn't targeted.'

'The random nature of dice throwing means he wasn't,' Towler said.

'That's an unproven theory,' Poe said. 'We still haven't ruled out Mr Arreghini's . . . life choices being behind his daughter's death.'

'Look somewhere else, Poe. My boss was *not* targeted.'

'I think we should trust Mr Towler,' Bradshaw said.

'All right, you're being very weird, Tilly,' Poe said. 'That's the second time you've said that – and stop pushing that plate of mango towards me. I'm not eating it. I hate tropical fruit.'

'You've found where he's zeroing his rifle,' Towler said.

There didn't seem to be any point denying it. Archie Arreghini was getting his intelligence in real time, and he was passing it straight to Towler. He was better informed than most of the cops on the investigation. 'Police Scotland did.'

'On your hunch.'

Poe shrugged. 'We came with fresh eyes.'

'They've set up trail cameras?'

'You asking me or telling me?'

Towler ignored the sarcasm. 'What kind?'

Poe told him.

Towler nodded approvingly. 'That's where you'll catch him then,' he said. He drained his tea, took a slice of mango and popped it in his mouth. 'I need to be away. Try to stay out of trouble, kids.' He took in the *Dungeons & Dragons* stage queue. He shook his head again. 'Do you know something? If they were playing that film on the inside of my eyelids, I'd tape my fucking eyes open.'

Chapter 36

Poe and Bradshaw spent the rest of the afternoon checking they hadn't missed any new role-playing game stalls. Poe said he'd rather they did it together. That he didn't have the right language to engage with the stall owners. She'd just said, 'Thank you.'

When they were halfway round, Poe said, 'So, are you going to tell me what Matt Towler was doing before he worked for Archie Arreghini, Tilly?'

Bradshaw considered his question carefully. 'I don't know, Poe.'

'You *do* know, Tilly. You said he'd done something odd before he began working for Archie Arreghini. Then you stopped talking and tried to make me eat fruit. That was weird, even for you. So, tell me what he did.'

'I have no idea what he did before working for Mr Arreghini, Poe.'

'Are you lying, Tilly?'

'I don't lie to you, Poe. I never have and I never will.'

It was true. To the best of his knowledge, Bradshaw had never lied to him. Not once. He sometimes wished she would. Her painful honesty and natural inquisitiveness could at times be . . . painful. It wasn't that long ago that they'd been in a meeting together, and the label on his new boxer shorts must have been digging into the small of his back or something. In front of everyone, she'd asked him if he was squirming in his seat because he had an itchy sphincter. They'd had . . . words afterwards.

It hadn't made any difference. She still told the truth, and she still asked the questions. But, she *had* developed workarounds for when she knew something she didn't want to tell him. She'd choose her language carefully. Make sure she could answer truthfully while at the same time telling him nothing. Poe suspected now was one of those times. And there was no point forcing the issue. She was the very definition of an immovable object when it came to certain things. Or, as Doyle put it, she could be even more stubborn than him.

'Suit yourself,' Poe said. 'Why don't you tell me about the Norse Parmesan instead?'

'*Pantheon*, Poe. Parmesan is an Italian hard cheese. A pantheon is a group of respected or important people.'

'Yes, Tilly. I was being deliberately silly. But regardless, you seemed to know who they were. Tell me about them.'

'Why, Poe?'

'Because you've been trying to get me to come to one of these things for years,' he said. 'But instead of bursting at the seams with excitement you've been subdued. And now I know why. You were expecting them, weren't you?'

'I knew of them. I had never met them before today.'

'OK, if not them exactly, someone *like* them.'

Bradshaw took her time answering. Eventually she said, 'All aspects of the gaming and comic book community have problems with misogyny. And although it *is* improving, there are still men who think women don't belong. They say war is the domain of men and unless we're camp followers, all we do is get in the way.'

'Yeah, I heard Horace spout that nonsense,' Poe said. 'Even ignoring the fact that women now serve in *all* branches of the military, that they're no longer restricted to rear-echelon roles, role-playing games are not war. They're just games. Same as *Snakes and Ladders* or *Monopoly*.'

'One famous designer went as far as to say that games were

primarily designed for men as a woman's brain functions differently. That they couldn't play to a man's standard. Some went even further and said that gamer females fake their interest to attract gamer men.'

'There's nothing as sad, nothing as vindictive, as scared white men, Tilly. We both know this. We've *seen* this. It seems they had something and they don't like that others now have it too. They'll defend what they see as their turf with sexist tripe like that.'

Bradshaw nodded her agreement. 'And as most of the older games were *designed* by these scared white men, *for* these scared white men, there were problematic representations of the female character. Her value and power lay only in her appearance. Her fighting prowess was limited so male characters had a built-in advantage. *Warlocks & Witches*, the RPG I play, still assigns a beauty score to female characters. And *Warlocks & Witches* is considered one of the safer spaces for women. So even though I'm a level-twenty-four Avariel, my abilities still include things like "charm men" and "seduce men". It's kinda gross.'

'So why . . . ?'

'So why do I play it? Because I enjoy it, Poe. Because I'm good at it. And why should a bunch of nasty pasties spoil it for me?'

'They shouldn't, Tilly,' Poe said softly. A dreadful realisation crept over him. He felt his face burn, his breath sped up. Classic signs of shame. 'When you kept asking me to attend these things with you, you weren't trying to get me into this stuff, were you? It was because you didn't want to go on your own.'

She lowered her eyes and nodded. 'There have even been incidents of drink spiking and sexual assaults.'

Poe stopped walking. 'What did I say the last time you asked me to come to one?'

'You said you'd rather eat a Linda McCartney sausage, Poe.'

'And the time before that?'

'That you'd rather watch Boris Johnson's birthing video.'

Poe nodded. He'd been proud of that one. Thought it was both funny and clever. 'It seems I've been a terrible friend, Tilly,' he said. 'You were asking for help and I kept making fun of you. I apologise.'

Bradshaw frowned. 'There's no need to apologise, Poe; you don't like comic books and role-playing games.'

'And you don't drink beer but that didn't stop you going to the Carlisle Beer Festival with me last year.'

'Yes, but—'

'And you drove me to the Boiler Shop in Newcastle to see Half Man Half Biscuit this February. You *hated* that.'

'I didn't hate it, Poe. I put in my earplugs and thought about the Birch and Swinnerton-Dyer conjecture until it was time to go home.'

'Birch and . . .?'

'Swinnerton-Dyer conjecture,' she said. 'It's one of the seven Millennium Problems. Each one has a million-dollar reward for its solution.'

'Blimey,' Poe said. 'Pity you didn't solve it, it would have paid for the petrol.'

'I did solve it, Poe.'

'You did?'

Bradshaw nodded.

'And they gave you a million dollars?'

'I didn't tell them I'd finished it,' she said. 'It didn't seem fair. It only took me an hour.'

Poe looked at his friend. 'Just how clever are you, Tilly?'

'I'm *very* clever, Poe,' she said. She looked over to where the Norse Pantheon incident had taken place. Her brow furrowed. 'But I do still have a lot to learn.'

'We'll learn it together,' Poe said. 'And from now on, I'm coming with you to every comic event you ask me to. No exceptions.'

146

'You will?'

'I will.'

'And you'll wear a costume?'

'Don't push it,' he said. He paused. He pointed at a stall. 'That wasn't there before, Tilly. Let's go and see this fool then grab something to eat.'

Chapter 37

The new stall was showcasing a game called *Empty Sky* that was still in its beta phase. The stall owner had arrived late – car trouble – which was why they'd both missed him the first time they'd walked around the NEC. Poe grabbed a flyer, although he needn't have bothered. The guy knew Bradshaw. They were at Oxford together. Bradshaw had been thirteen and he'd been twenty-one. Ordinarily a twenty-one-year-old noticing a thirteen-year-old would have been enough to get Poe's Spidey senses tingling, but, as Bradshaw had been the *only* thirteen-year-old at Oxford, she'd have stood out like a spoon in the fork drawer. The guy also knew what Bradshaw was doing now, or thought he did anyway, and he willingly handed over his mailing list.

They talked about being characters in someone else's game theory for a while, whatever the hell that meant, then the guy said, 'Here's my email address. I'd love it if we could stay in touch.'

'No, thank you,' Bradshaw replied. 'That would bore me senseless.'

Poe was still laughing when they finished their final trawl around the NEC, which happened to be, by a massive coincidence that he definitely hadn't planned, at one of the hog-roast vendors. Poe marched up to the window and, before Bradshaw could force-feed him any more mango, he said, 'A roast pig belly buster, my good man. And don't spare the crackling, the hairier the better.'

Bradshaw made some vomiting noises but didn't try to stop him.

The vendor went to work. A minute later he handed Poe a pork-filled sub the size of a javelin thrower's arm. Poe was about to take his first bite when his mobile began chirping. So did Bradshaw's. Poe ignored his, Bradshaw didn't.

Poe tore off a chunk of bread and meat as he watched Bradshaw. She had an expressive face. He'd know straight away if it was good news or bad news. Good news would mean he could carry on eating. Bad news might mean he'd have to stop. Right now, his sandwich was like that stupid cat Bradshaw kept talking about. The idiot one that had trapped itself in a box. Might be dead, might be alive. No one sensible gave a shit. Bradshaw certainly didn't. She said the cat in the box was a ridiculous thought experiment and proved once and for all that theoretical physicists were as dumb as a box of shoes.

Poe kept chewing.

And then he stopped. Because Bradshaw was clearly getting bad news. Her face was going through the wringer. She was upset and she was confused. He handed the sandwich back to the vendor. 'Wrap that for me, please.'

The vendor, sensing something was up, accepted it wordlessly.

Bradshaw finished her call.

'Who was that, Tilly?' Poe asked.

'It was Commander Mathers, Poe. There's been another shooting.'

Poe briefly closed his eyes. 'Shit,' he said. 'Where?'

'That's just the thing,' she replied. 'It doesn't make sense. The shooting was in Gretna Green again.'

Chapter 38

'Tell me again what the odds are, Tilly,' Poe said.

They were driving north. Mathers was on her way to Gretna Green too, but they had a three-hour head start. They would beat her there comfortably. They were in Poe's car, but Bradshaw was driving – he hadn't wanted to waste his sandwich. Bradshaw kept the windows open while he ate it and refused to shut them until the smell had dissipated completely.

'While accepting that each throw is an independent event, the odds of throwing two double twenties in a row is one hundred and sixty thousand to one,' she said.

'But it *wasn't* two in a row,' Poe said. 'He killed Jools Arreghini in between. It was actually two throws out of three. Gretna Green to Oxford and back to Gretna Green.'

Bradshaw nodded. 'It was, Poe. I was simplifying the maths for you. However you put it, the odds of Gretna Green coming up twice in a sample this small are so large it is statistically irrelevant.'

She took a moment.

'And that means I was wrong,' she said. 'The sniper *isn't* using dice to select locations.'

'You said the maths didn't lie, Tilly. Nothing's changed. The maths *still* isn't lying. This is just a blip.'

But it was as if Bradshaw had stopped listening to him.

'What a colossal waste of everyone's time,' she continued. 'All the wild goose chases I've sent people on.' She hit the steering wheel with the palm of her hand. 'Stupid! Stupid! Stupid!'

'Tilly, stop that.'

'I even tricked you into dressing like the tenth Doctor!'

'David Brent's one of my favourite actors.'

'It's David *Tennant*, and the last time we watched an episode of *Doctor Who* you cheered for the Cybermen.'

Poe looked out of the window, watched as they sped through Lancashire. Despite the crippling self-doubt, Bradshaw was never wrong about these things. She never voiced opinions until she was absolutely certain. If she said twenty-sided dice were being used to select locations, as far as he was concerned that was a stone-cold fact. But neither was she wrong when she said something was statistically irrelevant. It was a dialetheia. A true statement whose repudiation is also true. He thought about what that meant. Tried to square the circle.

And after a while he began to smile.

'What?' Bradshaw said.

'This isn't a bad thing, Tilly,' Poe said. 'It's a *good* thing.'

'Really?'

Poe nodded. 'Really,' he said.

Chapter 39

'He's showed us his arse,' Poe said.

'What a delightful expression, Poe,' Flynn said. 'Please don't ever use it again.'

They'd pulled over at the next motorway services and switched seats. Bradshaw was a safe driver, but Poe was a *fast* driver. As soon as they were back on the M6, Bradshaw had set up a conference call between them, Mathers and Flynn.

'All this time we've been dismissing the possibility of him hiding one murder among a bunch of other murders.'

'We have,' Mathers said. 'Were we wrong to? Did it have something to do with Archie Arreghini after all?'

Poe glanced at Bradshaw. 'No, ma'am,' he said. 'I'm confident that the murder of Jools Arreghini is unrelated to her father's business empire.'

Bradshaw nodded. *What* did *she know about Matt Towler?*

'But you think he's hidden a murder in among, how many now, nineteen?'

'I don't think that either, ma'am.'

'This isn't twenty fucking questions, Poe,' Flynn snapped. 'Tell us what you think.'

'He was hiding a *location*, ma'am,' Poe said. 'All the other murders were just to give him cover.'

'You mean Gretna Green?'

'I do, ma'am. The other locations were randomly selected with twenty-sided dice, but Gretna Green was selected using cognitive functioning. In other words, he *chose* it. For reasons unknown, the town is important to him.'

Mathers took a moment. She didn't dive in with unanswerable questions like 'Why?' Instead, she asked the only question that mattered: 'How long to collate the mailing lists you gathered today?'

Poe nodded in approval. A location and a bunch of names to cross-reference against that location was progress.

Bradshaw checked her laptop. 'It'll be finished in approximately seventeen minutes, Commander Mathers.' She clocked the WELCOME TO CUMBRIA sign. 'Make that *twenty-three* minutes, we've just entered District Twelve.'

'District . . . ?'

'It's what Tilly calls Cumbria, ma'am,' Poe explained. 'I don't know what it means.'

'I have daughters, Poe,' Mathers said. 'It's a reference to *The Hunger Games*. It's considered the least advanced of the thirteen districts of Panem.'

'They don't even have fresh jackfruit here, Commander Mathers,' Bradshaw said.

'You say that like it's a bad thing,' Poe said testily.

Cumbria was never going to have lightning-quick broadband or saturation mobile phone coverage. There were too many mountains, too many valleys. And the county *did* appear to revel in its failure to embrace certain twenty-first-century civilities. Modern farming techniques were not only shunned; in the National Park area of Cumbria, they were actively legislated against. Stepping into Cumbria could, superficially at least, feel like you were stepping back in time. It appeared old-fashioned. Backward even. Poe wasn't surprised to hear you couldn't get fresh jackfruit. Cumbria was a pastoral county. It farmed livestock, not crops. Which meant the county that until recently thought strawberry yoghurt was a 'fancy London pudding' was unlikely to embrace the idea of substituting lamb with a stringy yellow fruit.

'How many names on the list, Tilly?' Mathers asked.

'Over a million, Commander Mathers.'

'And how long to get information about the population of Gretna and Gretna Green so we can start cross-referencing it with the mailing lists?'

'I already have the online records, but the physical records will need to be collected in person. Some of them won't be online.'

'Like?'

'Hotel guestbooks for people who paid cash. Wedding venue records. Museum and visitor attraction comments books. That kind of thing.'

'Marriage records are digitised now, Tilly,' Mathers said. 'But we'll get the rest.'

'Weddings aren't the only thing they do in Gretna Green, ma'am,' Poe said. 'They also do anvil handfasting blessings. Anvil *baby* blessings. Anything they can fleece the tourists for. They do vow renewals on special anniversaries or after one of them has fu— messed up. There's no legal obligation to record any of that bollocks.'

'Are you *sure* you're about to get married, Poe?' Mathers said. 'But fair enough. I'll liaise with Police Scotland. They can do the door-to-doors. What do you want us to do with the names, Tilly?'

'If you scan them into the investigation portal, I'll access them from there,' Bradshaw replied.

'Are there any online records you haven't been able to get, Tilly?' Flynn asked. 'If you give us a list, we can start drawing up warrants.'

Flynn hadn't worked with Bradshaw for a while. She'd forgotten not to publicly ask questions like that. Bradshaw didn't answer. She looked out of the window as if she hadn't heard her.

154

The back of her neck flushed pink. A clear sign she'd been ignoring the Computer Misuse Act again. Despite the District 12 wisecrack, he decided to help her out.

'Would you like some mango, boss?' he said.

Chapter 40

The last time they'd been to Gretna Green, Flynn had said it was 'quieter than an English church'. But the pubs, restaurants and cafés *had* been open. People *were* at work; children *were* at school. The wedding industry had found ways to marry people under the threat of the sniper.

Now, Gretna Green looked like one of those abandoned towns in the Chernobyl Exclusion Zone. There was no sign of human activity whatsoever. He wouldn't have been surprised to see deer roaming the streets. Tumbleweeds wouldn't have seemed out of place.

Chief Superintendent Ailsa McCloud, the Police Scotland cop who'd briefed Poe when they'd found the sniper's range, met him at the outer cordon. Bradshaw stayed in the car, running data, doing sums. Trying to make a difference.

The outer cordon was usually where memorial flowers started to stack up. It was a focal point for the local community's grief. Anger and shock sometimes. Not this time, Poe noticed. The sniper had visited Gretna Green twice now. The pavement was clear. The local community was staying away. Poe didn't blame them.

'It's not a wedding this time?' he said to McCloud.

'Just a woman going about her business,' she said. She pulled out a notebook and read from it. 'Rachelle Callaghan. Worked in a funeral home. She was just nipping out to get a sandwich for her lunch. Bullet entered the back of her head. Blew her nose clean off her face.'

Poe winced.

McCloud stepped outside the cordon. She removed her suit and bagged it. 'Walk with me,' she said.

'Where are we going?'

'Death knock. Her dad lives in Gretna. I can brief you on the way.'

Gretna and Gretna Green were just a mile apart. A fifteen-minute walk. McCloud brought him up to speed. She said the sniper's zeroing range had so far yielded nothing. They weren't giving up, though. Still had rotating units of armed cops on standby. Highest priority.

They reached Gretna. It wasn't as picturesque as its more famous neighbour. Poe followed McCloud down the main shopping street and on to an estate. Looked like one of those put up during the First World War when the War Office had to house the thirty thousand employees who worked at His Majesty's Factory, Gretna: the largest munitions factory in the world at the time.

'Where did he shoot from?'

'We haven't found it yet, but we're fairly certain it was on the other side of the River Sark,' she said, gesturing to her right. 'It's the only place with a clean line of sight. Plenty of cover.'

Poe turned to look where McCloud was pointing. The Sark was a short river that formed part of the Anglo–Scottish border before flowing into the much larger River Esk. If McCloud was right, and he thought she was, the sniper had fired from at least 1,000 metres again. The guy never missed. It was uncanny.

'And the river's an obstacle,' Poe said.

'We don't think he crossed it, Sergeant Poe.'

'That's not what I meant, ma'am,' Poe explained. 'IRA snipers used to make sure there were obstacles between them and their target. A motorway. A row of houses. Something for the squaddies to navigate when they gave chase. Slowed them right down.'

'You think he's ex-IRA?'

Poe shrugged. 'We have no idea who he is.' He thought about what Bradshaw was doing. 'But we might soon.'

He told McCloud what they'd discovered.

'You think Gretna Green's important to him?'

'The maths supports it,' Poe said.

'His zeroing range supports it too,' McCloud agreed. 'If he's local, or semi-local, he won't have to drive a long heavy rifle through a load of built-up areas. There isn't much civilisation between here and the Cairngorms.'

She stopped outside a semi-detached house. She checked her phone. 'Here we are,' she said. 'The victim commuted from Dumfries. I think her dad lives on his own.'

'You don't say.'

In contrast to the rest of the houses on the street, Mr Callaghan's was scruffy. It had a weed-choked drive and a brown lawn. A white plastic seat, the kind that skidded across the ground in the lightest of breezes, sat underneath the front window. Even that looked neglected. McCloud walked up the path and knocked on the door. Firm but not hard. Not apologetic.

A man in shorts and a Primark *Captain America* T-shirt answered the door. He had more tattoos than Ray Bradbury's 'Illustrated Man'. He was smoking a cigarette and didn't bother to remove it when he said, 'Yes?'

'Mr Callaghan?'

'Yes.'

They identified themselves as police officers.

'May we come inside, please?'

'No. Fuck off.'

'I'm afraid we have some bad news. I would feel more comfortable delivering it inside.'

He leaned against the doorframe. 'I'm fine here.'

McCloud glanced at Poe. You couldn't force your way into someone's house to deliver the death knock.

'You know there's been another shooting?'

Callaghan nodded. 'And you're not stitching me up with it,' he said. 'Bastard cops stitched me up with theft once. You can piss off if you think I'm taking another fall for you.'

'I'm afraid we believe your daughter is the victim, Mr Callaghan,' McCloud said, ignoring his tirade.

That put a stop to his vitriol.

'Nah, Rachelle's at work. She's a morticia.'

'Mortician,' Poe said automatically.

'Aye, one of them. She works at the funeral home.'

'She's dead, Mr Callaghan. The sniper shot her when she popped out for lunch.'

Callaghan stared at McCloud. Realised she wasn't joking, wasn't trying to trick him into confessing to something. His daughter really was dead.

'But I've just bought her birthday present,' he said. He pointed to a carton of cigarettes by the door. 'She was supposed to come round and get it after work. What am I supposed to do with two hundred Marlboro Golds? I don't even *smoke* Marlboro Golds.' He pulled the cigarette out of his mouth and showed them, as if they didn't believe him. 'See?'

'Perhaps we'd better come inside, Mr Callaghan?' McCloud said.

'I suppose I could sell them,' he said, clearly not listening. 'But you never get what you paid for them. You always end up out of pocket.' He paused. 'I don't suppose either of you two want to buy them?'

Poe looked at him. Realised he wasn't joking. 'I'm good, mate,' he said.

'I think we'd better leave you to your grief,' McCloud said.

They left the still-complaining Callaghan and walked back to the crime scene. A cop with muddy boots met them before they got halfway. He was sweating.

'Have you found where he shot from, Jim?' McCloud asked.

'We have, ma'am. Other side of the river like we thought.'

'Has he left his shell casing behind?'

Jim nodded. 'Aye.'

Poe was relieved. Not for Rachelle Callaghan obviously, but at least there wasn't a copycat out there. His mobile buzzed in his pocket. A text message. It was from Bradshaw. He read it and felt his heartrate increase.

She'd found something.

Chapter 41

Not something. *Someone.*

He was called Stephen Gilbert. He was a Gretna resident and he was on Bradshaw's list. He was the *only* Gretna resident on Bradshaw's list. He was an orderly at the Dumfries and Galloway Royal Infirmary. Had been there since the hospital opened in the mid-seventies. It was his first and only job. Which didn't fit the profile Poe had built up in his mind. He had been thinking ex-military. Someone who'd maybe seen too much. Or maybe someone who'd seen too *little*. Resented not having fired his weapon in anger.

Gilbert had been caught in Bradshaw's net as he was active in the tabletop role-playing game community. He was on one of the more obscure mailing lists they'd gathered at the NEC that morning.

McCloud made some calls. Gilbert was on nights that week. His shift began at 8 p.m. and finished twelve hours later. Working on the assumption that as he hadn't yet started work, and as the pubs were no longer open in Gretna, he was probably at home, McCloud made the decision to go in. Poe wanted to wait for Mathers. He said she was in overall command. McCloud wasn't having it.

'Commander Mathers is coordinating the national response, but she's not in charge here, I am,' she said. 'Rachelle Callaghan's body is still warm, and I've been given a name for the person who might have pulled the trigger. Armed response are going in now.'

Poe couldn't argue with that logic. The jurisdiction was clear: it *was* her investigation. It *was* her call to make. Poe's job now was to get out of her way. He joined Bradshaw in their car.

'Is she waiting for Commander Mathers, Poe?' Bradshaw asked.

'She isn't.'

'Should we tell Commander Mathers?'

Poe shook his head. 'We shouldn't, Tilly. Chief Superintendent McCloud needs to be able to focus now.'

'Do you think Stephen Gilbert is the sniper? I'd be ever so surprised if he were.'

'Yeah, I'm not getting the vibe either.'

Bradshaw snorted. 'Vibe? As if I would ever base my decisions on something so frivolous.'

'OK, smarty-pants, what are *you* basing it on?'

She showed him her laptop screen. She was on an NHS website. It wasn't a public-facing page. This was an admin page. 'This is Dumfries and Galloway Infirmary's estates department, Poe. It's the department that manages the porters.'

'OK.'

'When they're on nights, the porters work a four-on, four-off shift pattern. Tonight is his third night.'

Poe did some mental arithmetic. 'So he *could* have shot Rachelle Callaghan?'

'Yes, Poe.'

'But?'

'But he couldn't have shot Jools Arreghini. He couldn't have shot seven of the nineteen victims. He was working the dayshift. And I've checked the handover notes – Stephen Gilbert didn't call in sick and he wasn't on leave. He was working when he was scheduled to.'

'Damn,' Poe said. 'This was one of those times when I was hoping to be wrong.'

Bradshaw patted his arm. 'Never mind, Poe. You can be wrong about something else. Are we going to tell Chief Superintendent McCloud?'

Poe looked over at McCloud. She was in a huddle with some of her senior officers. Looked as though she was issuing instructions.

'She's committed now, Tilly,' he said. 'I think we need to let her see this through. I don't want to confuse things. There'll be a lot of nervous energy around right now. I don't want anyone getting hurt.'

They watched as McCloud climbed into the back of an armed response Mitsubishi Shogun. It drove off. No blues and twos. There was no need. They were the only cars on the road. Poe stared after them. Bradshaw went back to her computer.

There was nothing to do but wait.

Chapter 42

Poe's mobile rang fifteen minutes later. It was McCloud. He didn't mince his words. 'Did you get him, ma'am?'

'We did.'

'Anyone hurt?'

'No. Textbook. We smashed in his front door and caught him unawares. He was heating up some soup.'

'And?'

McCloud didn't immediately answer.

'He's *something*, Poe,' she said eventually. 'But he isn't our sniper.' She sighed then added, 'I think you'd better come and see.'

Gilbert lived in a pebble-dashed terraced house. It was new, not one of the munitions factory houses. It was neat and tidy. The doorstep was black. Looked to have been freshly painted.

McCloud met them at the front door. 'I think this is more your area of expertise than mine,' she said.

She led them inside. Gilbert was perched on the edge of a blood-red sofa. He was in cuffs and leg restraints. Even sitting down, Poe could tell he wasn't tall enough to be their sniper. And even if he had been, Gilbert was squinting like he was Mr Magoo. A pair of thick spectacles were on his coffee table, out of reach. No way did someone with dodgy eyesight consistently hit targets over 1,000 metres away.

Two cops stood behind him, one stood facing him. They weren't taking any chances.

'What have you got?' Poe said to McCloud.

'Follow me,' she said.

She walked out of the house and into the back garden. Gilbert had a shed. A new one. It was green and large, about the size of a single-car garage. Poe wondered if he'd had to get permission to put it up or whether it had been there when he moved in. If he'd bought the house because it had a shed. It had sturdy doors and an even sturdier padlock. McCloud gloved up and took a key from an evidence bag. She unlocked the padlock then put the key into a fresh evidence bag.

She reached for the light switch. Turned it on.

Poe's first reaction was, 'Blimey.' Bradshaw's was, 'Gosh.'

The shed was neat and clean and organised. It was also a church to role-playing games. Poe took it all in. Noticed that it wasn't just role-playing games Gilbert collected. There were boxes and boxes of games he had played as a kid. *Monopoly, Risk, Battleships, Buckaroo!* A hundred other games he hadn't seen before.

'Weird, huh?' McCloud said.

Poe took his time answering. Thought about where he'd just come from. 'It's weird, but it's not *dangerous* weird, ma'am,' he said. 'He's a collector rather than a compulsive accumulator. Everything will have been carefully curated. If you search his house, there'll be an inventory or a catalogue somewhere. It'll probably detail where each piece was acquired.'

McCloud nodded. 'There is,' she said. 'We found a pile of them in one of the boxes underneath the workbench.'

Poe studied the bench. It was thick, wooden and clean. It looked as though Gilbert had been repairing an old *Connect 4* grid. There was a tube of superglue and some small tools beside it. Poe picked up a yellow token and dropped it into the grid.

'I used to love playing this with my dad,' he said. He added a red. 'He always beat me, though.' He added another yellow. 'What about you, Tilly? I bet you never got beaten at this.'

'I didn't like *Connect 4*, Poe,' Bradshaw said. 'It's a solved game.'

'A what?'

'A solved game. It means if both players play perfectly, the game's outcome can be accurately predicted. In *Connect 4*, the player who goes first should always win.'

McCloud cleared her throat.

'Sorry, ma'am,' Poe said. 'Tilly's quite hard to keep on task sometimes.'

Bradshaw rolled her eyes. Tutted.

McCloud reached under the desk. Lifted out a rigid plastic box. HANDLE WITH CARE – HUMAN ORGAN IN TRANSIT was printed on the side. Big red letters. It was plugged into the mains. Poe could see a green light on the top. McCloud opened the lid and took a step back.

'It was when we opened this that I called you in,' McCloud said. 'It's temperature controlled and I didn't want to unplug it until you'd taken a look.'

Poe peered inside. It was full of plastic boxes, the same shape and size as jewellery trays. Poe gloved up and lifted one out. It was a microscope slide box. Poe opened it. Each slot held a glass slide – a thin flat piece of glass with an even thinner sheet of cover glass. Each slide had a white square for labelling.

And they were all labelled.

Poe lifted out one of the slides and held it up to the light. Trapped between the two sheets of glass was a hair.

'Is that a . . . ?'

'Pubic hair?' McCloud finished for him. 'That's certainly what it looks like, Sergeant Poe. Every single slide has one. They're all neatly labelled with initials and dates. We assume the initials are the person's name and the date is when it was collected.'

Poe put it down and lifted out another. Another pubic hair. A different initial and date.

'You can see why I thought this was a job for the Serious Crime Analysis Section.'

Poe didn't say anything. He put the slide back in the box and cast his eyes around the shed. He saw what he'd expected to see in the corner. 'You can let him go, ma'am,' he said.

'These aren't a serial killer's trophies?' McCloud said. She looked disappointed. As if catching a serial killer would make up for *not* catching the sniper.

'He's not a serial killer, ma'am,' Poe said.

'What is he then?'

'He's a fly fisherman,' he said. 'Lots of them believe that the pheromones in women's pubic hair help attract fish. They tie their flies with them. If you go online there are whole forums discussing which is the most effective ethnicity, what time of the month is the best time to harvest.'

Poe gestured to the slide boxes. The top one held sixty slides and there were eight boxes. Assuming every slide held a pubic hair, that was four hundred and eighty. He shook his head in amazement. The things people did . . .

'As Gilbert works at the hospital, he'll have had ready access to . . . material. A large part of his job is taking patients to surgery, to X-ray, to a whole host of hospital departments, and a lot of them will be wearing those stupid gowns. The dignity strippers that don't cover the arse. When the patient gets out of the wheelchair or the bed, nine times out of ten, they'll leave one of these little dudes behind. He'll have slipped it into an envelope and brought it home. It's creepy but I doubt it's illegal.'

'This is a new low for me,' McCloud said, shaking her head. 'It's hard enough being a woman in this job. It doesn't matter what I achieve now – I'll be forever known as the fucking pube-thief catcher.'

Poe didn't know what to say. He thought McCloud was being hard on herself. It was a mistake anyone could have made. But

167

she was right: cops were merciless when it came to things like this. They had to be. Laughing at the silly stuff helped get them through the dark.

So he kept his own counsel. Thought about how the sniper was still out there, and how they were no closer to catching him.

Chapter 43

Poe waited for Flynn and Mathers to arrive. He briefed them, then drove back to Highwood. Bradshaw went with him. She normally stayed in a hotel in the area they were working – they both did – but they were all shut. *Everything* in Gretna was shut. He wondered how many businesses would survive. At least there had been government assistance during the pandemic. With the sniper, they were on their own.

Mathers and Flynn were heading up to Glasgow with Chief Superintendent McCloud. The Gretna connection had refocused the investigation away from London on to Scotland. They needed to discuss resource allocation. Mathers would have to send some of her detectives north. It was where the investigation was active. Nothing was happening down south.

Poe didn't bother going into Highwood. He could hear laughing and he could hear Edgar. Doyle and Emma were back in the marquee.

'They can't still be feeding flies to the dick plants,' Poe muttered.

'I beg your pardon, Poe?' Bradshaw said.

'You'll see.'

'Bloody hell, it's the Time Lord,' Emma said the second they stepped into the marquee.

More laughter. Looked like they'd been drinking again. Poe walked to the fridge and grabbed a Spun Gold. He opened a sparkling water for Bradshaw and poured it into a glass. No ice.

That was very important. Bradshaw didn't do ice. Something to do with faecal bacteria.

'Brunton's out getting an Indian takeaway for us, Poe,' Doyle said. 'I've ordered you lamb Madras. Tilly, he's getting you one of their vegan daals. Hope that's OK?'

It was.

They caught up with each other's news. Poe didn't worry about case security when it came to Doyle. She had one of the sharpest forensic brains he knew. Any input was well considered and usable. He asked for her take on it.

'I'm a pathologist, not a psychologist, Poe,' she said. 'You know the manner of and the cause of death. All the victims were killed with high-velocity bullets. I'm not sure what else I can add.'

'Emma?' Poe said. 'You're an intelligent woman, but you're also a layperson. You won't have any preconceptions. Tell me what you think.'

Emma put down her glass. 'You want my input into how you catch a serial sniper?'

Poe nodded.

'Something you and Tilly and Estelle have yet to think of?'

Poe nodded again.

She threw up her hands. 'I don't know, Poe. I'm an oncologist, not an *oracleist*.' She took a moment. 'Hey, that was good. I think I'll use it on some of my stupider registrars.' She held his gaze. 'Estelle tells me you have the best instincts she's ever seen, and Tilly is . . . well, Tilly. If this man gets caught it'll be because you two have thought of something no one else has. You don't need my input, Poe.' She reached over and tapped him on the head. 'Everything you need is in there.'

'It was just a suggestion,' Poe said.

'OK, here's a suggestion. You stop pissing around and go to see Clara Lang. If anyone has a unique insight into this man, it'll be her.'

'That's a good idea, Poe,' Doyle said. 'Plus, you haven't been for a while. You could do with another dose.'

Poe nodded. It *was* a good idea. Clara was *Doctor* Clara Lang, and she was Poe's trauma therapist. But their relationship was . . . complicated.

'Why don't you see if you can get in to see her tomorrow?' Doyle said. 'And on the way back you could pick up Uncle Bertie. It'll save me a trip to North Yorkshire.'

'Who the hell is Uncle Bertie?'

'You'll love him, Poe; he's even grumpier than you.'

'Ha!' Bradshaw said. 'There *is* no such person!'

Doyle and Bradshaw fist bumped. Poe scowled. They were always doing that.

'Don't pout, Poe,' Doyle said. 'And Bertie isn't my real uncle. He's my father's oldest friend from his shooting days. He's coming up for the wedding, but he's not allowed to drive any more. There was an . . . incident.'

'Why's he coming up tomorrow? The wedding isn't for another month.'

'Bertie's from the generation that did the Grand Tour when they came of age. They never go anywhere for "just a few days". I think he's planning to visit as many of his Scottish shooting cronies as he can between now and our big day. You'd better take the Land Rover – he won't be travelling light. He'll have at least three travel trunks. Probably some shotguns.'

'He's not staying with us, is he?'

'A couple of days maybe. He'll soon get bored.'

Poe was about to protest but he kept his mouth shut. Except for choosing five dishes for the wedding breakfast, Doyle, Bradshaw and Emma had organised the entire wedding. The least he could do was collect her crotchety uncle.

'You fancy a trip to North Yorkshire, Tilly?' he said. The thought of Bradshaw and a grumpy old Yorkshireman squeezed together in Doyle's ancient Land Rover filled him with joy. It would be hilarious.

But Bradshaw shook her head.

'Chief Superintendent McCloud has started to upload hotel guestbooks and wedding venue logbooks to the portal,' she said. 'I want to run them through my software so I can cross-reference the new names with the names on our mailing lists.'

Poe tapped out a text to Clara Lang's secure hospital. Told them he'd be visiting in the morning. He sent another text to Flynn, letting her know he'd be out of contact for most of the following day. By the time he'd finished, the conversation had returned to wedding business. It wasn't long before Poe tuned out. He got up to stretch his legs. Wandered over to the open side of the marquee. The moon was high and bright, casting a silver sheen over the spectacular Northumberland countryside. He stood with his back to everyone, sipping his beer, admiring the rolling hills, the copses, the rivers. Or, as he thought of it now – cover for a sniper. He turned back to Doyle. 'Do me a favour,' he said. 'Close this side of the marquee. I know it has the best views, but if you must have the marquee open-sided, at least have the open bit facing the house.'

'You're worried about the sniper?'

Poe nodded. 'He's out there somewhere, Estelle,' he replied. 'Who's to say he hasn't been watching the schmucks tasked with catching him?' He paused. 'I think he likes watching people.'

Chapter 44

Doctor Clara Lang was in a secure hospital on the outskirts of Harrogate. Uncle Bertie lived on a country estate near York. Poe planned to see his trauma therapist in the morning, grab a pub lunch, then pick up Doyle's uncle in the afternoon. He figured he could be back at Highwood for tea. He would then spend the evening reviewing the new data with Bradshaw.

But sometimes plans get changed. Sometimes they get cancelled altogether. This was particularly true when it came to secure hospitals. Poe had just passed Scotch Corner when his mobile phone buzzed. He checked his rear-view mirror for cops – the Land Rover wasn't equipped with modern things like a hands-free system, electric windows or power steering – and pressed accept when he saw the road behind him was dibble-free. Road cops *loved* ticketing the National Crime Agency.

'Poe speaking,' he said.

'This is Doctor Gray, Sergeant Poe. I'm afraid you'll have to postpone your visit with Clara.'

'Oh, I was hoping to talk to her about this lunatic holding the country to ransom.'

'I'm afraid there's been an incident,' he said. 'And we don't like to use the word "lunatic".'

'Neither do I, doc,' Poe said. 'But this guy is bloody nuts. I'm afraid lunatic is exactly the right word.'

'Well, like I said, there's been an incident.'

There was that word again, Poe thought. Incident. Doyle had

said Uncle Bertie was no longer able to drive due to an incident. And now Doctor Gray was using it in the same sentence as Clara Lang. And when it came to his trauma therapist, the word 'incident' usually meant someone was now missing an eye.

'Is everyone OK?'

'Doctor Lang is fine, Sergeant Poe.'

'Not what I asked.'

'But it's how I answered,' Doctor Gray said. 'I'm sorry if you've had a wasted journey, but your visit has been cancelled. *All* visits have been cancelled.'

Poe could hear yelling in the background. Alarms were still sounding. It probably wasn't the best time to be nosy. He said he'd rearrange his visit, wished him well with whatever was going on, and hung up.

'Just me and you then, Uncle Bertie,' he said to himself.

Chapter 45

Bertie was a stumpy, bow-legged man. He was puce-faced, addled with gout and shorter than a Shetland pony. Hair sprouted from his ears and nostrils like escaping hamsters. He wore a three-piece suit made from heavy tweed. His vast stomach tested the buttons on his waistcoat to breaking point. He looked like Humpty Dumpty, if Humpty Dumpty carried a stick and had a voice that would have shamed a town crier.

In a word, he was formidable.

The grounds of his estate were smaller than Doyle's, but his ancestral home was twice the size of Highwood. He had an army of staff and every one of them looked relieved to be seeing the back of him.

He pointed at Poe and said, 'You, man! Where's your uniform?'

'Excuse me?'

'You're the driver Lady Doyle sent, are you not?'

Poe turned and looked behind him. 'Excuse me?' he said again.

Uncle Bertie didn't repeat himself. Poe reckoned Uncle Bertie *never* repeated himself. It was your responsibility to hear what he said, not his.

'I'm the person doing you a favour, if that's what you mean?'

'What?!'

It seemed Uncle Bertie was also deaf.

A stern, rangy man in a black suit gestured to two young

men. They began hauling out Bertie's travel trunks and shot-gun cases. One of the men caught one of the cases on the side of Doyle's Land Rover. He got a crack across the shins with Bertie's stick.

'Idiot boy!' Bertie snapped happily. 'I'll have you horse-whipped if you've marked the wood on that Purdey.'

When the Land Rover was loaded, Poe opened the passenger door. There was no way Bertie was travelling in the back if Poe was driving. He wasn't a chauffeur. Bertie climbed in without comment.

'Now, where are you taking me?' he said when Poe got behind the wheel.

'Er, I thought I was taking you to see Estelle.'

'Nonsense. There's a pub not too far away that does a very good pie. If we're quick, we might get there before the landlord gives them away to the poor.'

Poe, who had only just eaten a pie the size of a hubcap, said, 'OK.'

Uncle Bertie was actually quite good company. Poe liked him.

He'd marched into the White Swan and demanded two pies and two pints and two whiskies. He then told two city-types that they were sitting in his seat and he said it in such a way that they picked up their drinks and moved.

'Lady Doyle tells me you were in the army,' he said when they were seated. 'What regiment?'

'Black Watch,' Poe said, sipping his pint of Black Sheep. It was a nice pint. Darker than Spun Gold, but very drinkable.

'Knew a man in the Black Watch. A captain. His Adam's apple was the wrong way round. Didn't like him.'

And that was the end of their military reminiscing. Bertie didn't offer any information on his own career, although Poe knew he'd had one. He'd been a colonel in one of the armoured regiments. Doyle hadn't known which one. Bertie looked like a tanker, though.

The landlord brought their pies over.

'It had better not be chicken, sir!' Bertie said.

'It's beef and ale, Bertie,' the landlord said, winking at Poe.

After the landlord was back behind his bar, Bertie added, 'Damn fool served me fish once. Fish! In a Yorkshire pub. I should have had him horsewhipped!'

'Do you even *have* a horsewhip?' Poe asked.

'What?!'

'Never mind.'

'Now, what's this nonsense about a wedding? Lady Doyle's finally getting hitched, eh?'

'She is, sir.'

'And which weak-chinned, in-bred, dribble-faced moron has finally tamed her?'

'That would be me, sir.'

'You!' he shouted, his eyes twinkling. 'But you're just a thief taker!'

Poe thought Bertie knew *exactly* who Lady Doyle was marrying. That he was having fun at Poe's expense. He said, 'I was a *pubic hair* thief taker yesterday.'

Bertie grabbed Poe's whisky. 'You won't be drinking this, I assume?'

Poe shook his head. 'I'm driving.'

'Good.' He rolled the whisky around his mouth before swallowing. 'Lady Doyle thinks a lot of you.'

'I hope so.'

'She does. She told me. And that's no small thing for Elcid Doyle's daughter to admit. Known her since she was a baby and she's the most wilful woman I've ever met. She also warned me not to give you any grief. She said I wouldn't like what would happen if I did.'

Poe shrugged. 'Well, I no longer carry a truncheon if that's what you're worrying about.'

An unwitting fool approached their table and asked if he could take the spare seat.

'No, you damn well can't!' Bertie snapped. 'Me and the sergeant have a lot to talk about and I want to put my feet up.' The unwitting fool skulked back to the overcrowded table he and his friends were on. Every so often one of them would glance their way. Uncle Bertie paid them no attention. 'Now, tell me about this pubic hair thief you caught yesterday. Grabbed him by the short and curlies, eh? Damned pervert should be—'

'Horsewhipped?' Poe said.

Chapter 46

If Victor Meldrew and Larry David had had a son the result would be Uncle Bertie. He said *what* he wanted to *who* he wanted, and he threatened to horsewhip every second person he met. As far as Poe could tell, his only redeeming feature was being held up as a cautionary tale about narrow gene pools.

Poe was having a great time, though. Uncle Bertie could remember every whisky he'd ever drunk, every bird he'd ever shot and, in his words, every 'filly' he'd bedded. He was appalling, but in a funny way. Poe only had the one pint but he made it last two hours. Uncle Bertie had seven whiskies, three brandies and a foul-smelling liqueur that the landlord would only pour when he was wearing rubber gloves. Poe texted Doyle a photo. She sent one back by return: YOU'RE WITH U BERTIE EARLY? He tapped out another text, explaining that his meeting with Clara Lang had been cancelled.

Three seconds after he'd pressed send, his phone rang.

'You haven't left York yet, have you?' Doyle asked.

'We're still here.'

'Good. The local tailor has been on the phone. They were supposed to deliver Uncle Bertie's suit, but they thought he was going to collect it. You couldn't . . . ?'

'I'll get it,' Poe said. 'Text me the directions.'

'More ale, landlord!' Bertie yelled after Poe had hung up.

'No more,' Poe said. 'That was my Estelle, your Lady Doyle.

She wants us to pick up your suit. There was a problem with your tailor.'

'Damn idiots should be—'

Poe grabbed Bertie by the lapels. Pulled him in. 'Listen to me, you cranky old bastard,' he said. 'We're going to collect your suit and we're going right now. You're not going to complain and you're not threatening to horsewhip anyone. Are we clear?'

Uncle Bertie grinned. 'You'll do, lad,' he said.

Bertie's tailor was in York city centre. Poe got lost in the one-way system but soon figured it out. He put Doyle's Land Rover in one of the staff parking bays. Bertie nodded in approval.

'Stay here,' Poe said.

'I'm not setting foot in the damn place.' And after Poe had got out, he bellowed, 'And tell them I expect a discount! Damn disgrace a man having to collect his own suit.'

Poe ignored him.

A fussy shop tailor met him at the door. He looked like he was about to tell Poe he couldn't park there, but when he saw who was already snoozing in the passenger seat, he perked up.

'I'll get his suit, sir. Sorry about the miscommunication.'

He stalked into the back. Poe wandered the racks, touching the expensive-looking cloth. He wondered how much a bespoke suit from these guys would cost. Poe had only ever had machine-washable suits. They were the best option for cops. And they had all been dark. Either black or navy blue. Anything that hid the blood. Poe spotted a tie rack. He thought he might surprise Doyle by buying something new for the wedding. He pulled out a jazzy-looking one. It was orange flecked with pink and turquoise and unlike anything he'd ever considered before. He grimaced at the two hundred pound price tag and draped it over his arm. He sauntered back to the till area.

A tailor's dummy caught his eye. He started laughing. It was the spitting image of Bradshaw. He snapped a picture and sent it off with the accompanying message – PUT YOUR CLOTHES ON AND GET BACK TO WORK, TILLY ☺

He was still laughing when the tailor returned with Bertie's suit. He picked up Poe's tie.

'Ah, the Great Gatsby,' he said. 'Excellent choice, sir. Did you find everything you needed?'

'Why, were you hiding things?'

'Very good, sir. Is the tie to go on Bertie's account?'

Poe was tempted to say yes, but instead he whipped out his debit card and punched in his PIN. Felt good about what he'd done.

His phone rang. It was Bradshaw. He pressed the reject icon. Slipped it back in his pocket. It immediately rang again. Poe sighed. He answered it.

'It was just a joke, Tilly.'

'Oh that, yes, ho-ho-ho, Poe,' she said. 'But that's not why I'm calling.'

'Go on.'

Poe listened. And after Bradshaw had finished, he said, 'Who the hell is Ezekiel Puck?'

Chapter 47

Bradshaw had spent the morning cross-referencing the names on the role-playing games mailing lists she'd downloaded with the names from the hotel guestbooks, wedding venue logbooks, and museum comments books that McCloud and Mathers had scanned into the investigation portal.

The first match had been the pube thief. The second match sounded like the pube thief's mischievous brother.

Ezekiel Puck.

It sounded like a made-up name to Poe. The kind you gave yourself, not the kind you were given.

Bradshaw explained how she had found it. She said that a couple celebrating their twenty-fifth wedding anniversary had wanted to recreate the original wedding. They'd chosen the Smithy's Forge in Gretna Green, one of the smaller wedding venues. The whole family was there, but on the morning of the ceremony, one of the original witnesses had taken ill. Ezekiel Puck had stepped in. There was no explanation as to why he was there. He had no connection to the venue or to the people recreating their wedding. His name didn't crop up anywhere else.

She also said that Puck's online presence was strange. That he hadn't existed on any database, until suddenly he had. He rented a house under the name. He opened a bank account. Even got a passport. It was as if he'd been born a forty-nine-year-old man. The more she described him, the more Poe became convinced that Ezekiel Puck was an assumed identity. His first thought was that Puck was a protected witness, but he immediately discounted it. The protected witness teams *did* give people new names and backgrounds, but they didn't give them *stupid* names. It would be counterproductive. And he hadn't changed his name via deed poll. If he had, Bradshaw would have had his whole life history by now.

'What does the boss think?'

'The same as everyone, Poe.'

'Which is?'

'That Ezekiel Puck is the name of his role-playing game avatar,' she said. 'And somehow he's sneaked it into the system so he's now officially known as Ezekiel Puck.'

'Is that possible?'

'I could do it, Poe. That means others can too. It would also explain why the name doesn't appear anywhere until a couple of years ago.'

Poe wasn't convinced. If Puck had been determined to adopt his avatar name, why not do it officially? It wasn't an onerous task. It cost less than a Christmas turkey. It wasn't even unusual. People did it all the time. Richard Burton had been called Richard Jenkins. Michael Caine had been Maurice Micklewhite. Elton John had been Reginald Dwight. But Bradshaw said Puck *hadn't* changed his name officially.

'Do we have an address?' Poe asked.

'We do, Poe,' Bradshaw said. 'It's in Ripon.'

'But that's where I am. Or within thirty miles anyway. I'm in York now. I've bought a tie.'

'A tie?'

'It's orange.' He looked across at the sleeping Uncle Bertie. He could be in and out of Ripon before the old soak woke. He said as much to Bradshaw.

'DCI Flynn says you're to liaise with police officers at North Yorkshire Police headquarters. She says there hasn't been a crime in North Yorkshire since Nicholas Nickleby's days and you're to make sure they don't eff-word it up. DCI Flynn and Commander Mathers will join you as soon as they can.'

'Are North Yorkshire headquartered in York?'

'Northallerton, Poe. An assistant chief constable called Christine Wilpers is expecting you.'

Poe frowned. 'I'm not driving all the way to Northallerton just to turn around and come back to Ripon.'

'But that's what DCI Flynn says you have to do, Poe.'

'Does she? Oh, well that's definitely what I'll do then.'

A pause. Then, 'Was that sarcasm, Poe?'

'Just give me Ezekiel Puck's address, Tilly.'

'I've already given it to Assistant Chief Constable Wilpers, Poe.'

'And I've been told to make sure they don't fu . . . mess it up. That means checking they have the right house to raid.'

Bradshaw told him where Ezekiel Puck lived. He repeated it twice to make sure he'd got it then hung up. He'd check out the address for himself before he got to Northallerton.

What was the worst that could happen?

Chapter 48

'Wake up, Bertie,' Poe said. 'We're going to Northallerton nick but first I'm popping into Ripon.'

'I know a nice—'

'This isn't a bloody pub crawl,' Poe said. 'I'm checking out a lead.'

Bertie belched. He was always doing that, Poe noticed. Didn't seem to care who heard him.

'What lead?' Bertie asked.

'Just a lead.'

'Not this sniper chap?'

'Why'd you say that?'

'Lady Doyle's thief taker won't just be any old thief taker,' Bertie said. 'He'll be an exceptional thief taker. And this chap's turning into quite the nuisance.'

'Indeed,' Poe agreed. 'Quite the nuisance.'

'And we're going to clap him in irons, eh?'

Poe rolled his eyes. '*We're* not doing anything, Bertie. I'm going to have a little look. See if it's worth the boss and *her* boss coming down. For all we know this "chap" could be registered blind.'

Bertie tapped the side of his nose. He winked and said, 'You don't call in the cavalry until you see the whites of the damned Indians' eyes, eh?'

'Possibly something less offensive,' Poe said, 'but broadly speaking, yes.'

Poe knew Ripon well. He had to drive through it on his way to see Clara Lang. It was a nice market town, just off the A1. The Land Rover wasn't equipped with a satnav, so Poe stopped at a newsagent and bought a Philip's *Street Atlas: North Yorkshire*. The last thing he wanted to do was telegraph his arrival by asking for directions. He bought a bag of Werther's Originals for Bertie to suck on while he waited.

'No whisky?' he moaned when Poe passed the boiled sweets over.

'Shut up,' Poe replied.

Ezekiel Puck's house was a two-minute drive from the newsagent. Poe drove 500 yards then parked the Land Rover two streets over. He would walk the rest of the way. He clambered out of the driver's seat and walked around to Bertie's side. He opened the door and said, 'I'll be ten minutes. Don't get out, don't talk to anyone, and definitely don't have anyone horsewhipped. Just eat your toffees and wait.'

'Do you want one of the Purdeys? They're loaded for deer.'

'No, I don't want a gun,' Poe sighed.

'My stick then?'

'I don't want a bloody stick either.'

Bertie offered him the bag of Werther's. 'A toffee?'

'Ten minutes,' he reminded him. 'If you're not here when I get back, I'm telling Estelle.'

Bertie gulped. 'Steady on, old chap.'

Chapter 49

Poe studied the map, then tucked it into the back of his jeans. Covered it with his shirt. If Ezekiel Puck was the man they were looking for, he would be surveillance aware. Poe wanted to look as though he was visiting friends and that meant not wandering around like he was lost.

The address Bradshaw had given him was in the middle of what Poe thought of as a mid-range estate. Wasn't cheap, but neither was it at the high end of the housing market. Three main groups of people would live there – first-time buyers, retirees and divorcees.

Poe studied the gardens. Tried to work out which group Ezekiel Puck belonged to.

Gardens could tell you a lot about an estate's demographics. The retirees' gardens would be well kept. The lawns would be green and trimmed to the bone. The borders would be packed full of flowers – perennials and annuals. Lots of colour. There would be bird baths and hanging baskets. By contrast, the gardens of the divorced group would be neglected. The divorced group would see this kind of estate as an insult to the memory of what they'd lost. And they would refuse to make the best of it. They'd grow resentful of their homes and their new neighbours. Tending their gardens would be seen as a sign they'd accepted their lot in life. The first-time buyers' gardens would fall somewhere in the middle. They were always eyeing the next rung on the housing market so their gardens would be functional and neat, ready to be shown the minute a promotion at work beckoned.

Poe was generalising, of course. There was no reason why a recently divorced dad couldn't be green-fingered, just as there was no reason a pensioner couldn't hate gardening with a passion. But it was a rule of thumb that had served him well in the past.

He reached Ezekiel Puck's house and walked straight past. Barely glanced at it. It was no help anyway. His garden was neat but not fussy. Hardwearing, evergreen shrubs and the lawn had been paved over. Low maintenance. It offered no insight into the man who lived there.

Poe decided to employ an old detective's trick. The old invent-a-frivolous-excuse-to-talk-to-one-of-the-suspect's-neighbours ruse. He chose the house next door to Puck's. Marched up the garden path and tapped on the door. No answer.

But this was Yorkshire, and that meant people stuck their beak into other people's business. Which is what happened.

"Ere, lad, you after Bungalow Joe?' a man said.

He was around seventy. Sounded like he had his granny's teeth in. He wore a flat cap. His trousers were held up with braces. Poe wouldn't have been surprised to see he had an 'I ♥ Geoffrey Boycott' tattoo.

'Bungalow Joe?' Poe said. 'Why's he called that?'

The man leaned over the fence that separated the two proper-ties. 'Because he used to live in a bungalow.'

A no-nonsense reply. *Fucking Yorkshire.*

'Is he not in?'

'No, lad. Bungalow Joe's visiting his daughter in . . .' – he paused to spit on the ground – 'bloody Burnley.'

'Not a fan of Lancashire, I take it,' Poe said, keen to get him gossiping. People like this were an absolute goldmine, but only if you didn't ask them direct questions. Ask them something direct and they'd clam up tighter than a fish's bum.

'Richard were protecting those princes when he put 'em in the Tower of London. He didn't bloody kill 'em. They were 'is own flesh an' blood.'

Poe was treated to a ten-minute diatribe on the Wars of the Roses, and why the battles between the house of York and the house of Lancaster for the English throne were all down to the house of Lancaster deliberately misunderstanding what had happened to the rightful heirs.

Poe said nothing. Lancashire and Yorkshire had been arguing about the Princes in the Tower for centuries. He let the Yorkshireman's anger wash over him. When he'd tired himself out, he said, 'I'm thinking of moving to this estate. Joe said he could show me the ropes. Which streets to avoid, that kind of thing.'

'It's a decent place to live, lad,' the old man said. 'Never any trouble and we look out for each other.'

'How well do you know your neighbours?'

'Know some better than others.'

'Joe?'

'Known Joe over forty years, I reckon.'

Poe gestured at Ezekiel Puck's house. 'What about this house? Can't say I approve of what they've done with their garden.'

'Me neither, lad. A garden should be green, not grey.'

'I think Joe mentioned him actually. Tall man?' Poe put his hand six inches above his head. 'Has a strange name?'

'That's him,' the man said. 'Ezekiel.'

'Joe said he's thinking of moving.'

'Is he? First I've heard, lad. It wouldn't surprise me, though. He must have a new job as I haven't seen him for months.'

That was enough for Poe to take Ezekiel Puck seriously. He said goodbye to the old man and waited for him to disappear back into his house. He then left Bungalow Joe's garden and entered Ezekiel Puck's.

Chapter 50

Poe cupped his hands and peered through Ezekiel Puck's kitchen window. The old man wasn't wrong. Puck clearly hadn't been home for a long time. From the kitchen, Poe could see all the way through the house. Unopened mail was piled high under the letterbox.

It could be subterfuge, of course; anyone could put a stack of mail under their letterbox. Leave the house through the back door, make it look like he hadn't been home in a while. But Poe didn't think so. Puck's neighbours all looked as though they had nothing better to do but notice things. If he'd been leaving his house by the back door every day, the old man would have said something.

No, Ezekiel Puck hadn't been home in a while.

It was time to call Commander Mathers. This was the strongest lead they'd had.

Poe took one final look then left the street. He got out his mobile and found Mathers's number. He hit call. She answered immediately.

'You at Northallerton yet, Poe?' she said without preamble. 'We'll be there in twenty minutes.' Poe bit the bullet and admitted he'd called at Ripon first. After getting his ear chewed, Mathers said, 'And?'

'I think it might be him, ma'am.'

He told her what the old man had said. That his mail was piled up. She seemed mollified.

'Get to North Yorkshire HQ as soon as you can, Poe. We'll start planning.'

Poe hung up. He rounded the corner to the street where he'd parked the Land Rover. For some reason he fancied a Werther's Original. He hoped Uncle Bertie hadn't troughed them all. He was about to call Bradshaw to tell her to go hard and heavy on Ezekiel Puck. Give him the full Bradshaw treatment.

Instead, he stopped. He blinked in surprise.

The Land Rover's passenger seat was empty.

Uncle Bertie was missing.

Poe assumed Uncle Bertie had got bored waiting. He'd been gone forty minutes, not the ten he had promised. Uncle Bertie didn't look like the kind of man who'd sit still unless there was a bottle of strong booze involved. Which reminded Poe, they'd driven past a pub on the way to Ezekiel Puck's estate. He remembered seeing the sign swinging in the late afternoon breeze. The White Hart, he thought it had been called. White something, anyway.

Mystery solved.

Poe checked his watch. He'd told Mathers he'd get to North Yorkshire's headquarters as soon as he could. He didn't have time to shoehorn a whisky-soaked, horsewhipping lunatic out of a pub. He considered leaving him where he was. Let the old fool make his own way to Highwood. But then he thought about the conversation he'd have to have with Doyle; the one where he explained that he'd screwed up the one wedding job he'd been given. He sighed and started walking to where he thought the pub was.

Which was when a van screeched to a halt beside him. The side panel opened and four men jumped out. Before Poe could work out what was happening, a hood had been pulled over his head and he was bundled into the van.

Fucking Yorkshire.

Chapter 51

Poe felt like he'd walked into a spy movie. One of the good ones like Bond or Bourne. Nothing with Steven Seagal. He didn't think he was in immediate danger. He'd been handcuffed to the rear and his legs had been tied together, but no one had hit him. No one had said anything silly, like 'You're getting too close to the truth.' His phone had been taken from him, but he didn't think it had been thrown out of the window. No one was manically laughing.

But other than *not* being in immediate danger, Poe didn't have a clue what was happening. He'd clearly been abducted, but the men who had grabbed him were well practised. They'd done it before. That meant law enforcement or military. And they weren't talking, not even to each other. Disciplined.

The van took a few turns, and when it did someone held his shoulders so he wouldn't topple over. After what felt like fifteen minutes but was probably closer to five, the road straightened and the van sped up.

As soon as it did his hood was ripped off, a camera was pointed at his face and his picture was taken. The man with the camera, a burly six-footer who looked stronger than Popeye, checked the screen then nodded at the man at Poe's side. He was hooded again.

And still no one had said anything. It wasn't until the van started to slow and turn again, a good twenty minutes after his picture had been taken, that someone spoke.

'ETA, five minutes.'

'Does anyone fancy boiling an egg?' Poe said.

No one laughed.

Poe started counting Mississippis. When he got to three hundred, the van stopped. He felt fresh air on his neck. Someone had opened a window. He heard muffled chatter – sounded as though credentials were being checked – then something being raised or lowered. Some sort of checkpoint. The van moved forward again. Then it stopped and the engine was turned off.

The door opened and he was helped to his feet. His leg restraints were loosened but not removed. He was guided out of the van and on to the ground. The echo of his boots made it sound like he was inside, but in a large building. Someone held his shoulder and pushed him forward. Shuffling and hooded, like he was the Elephant Man, Poe started walking.

The echo faded. Carpet, not tiles.

He was pushed into a room and made to sit in an uncomfortable chair. His leg restraints were removed. So were his handcuffs. Poe brought his hands round to his front and rubbed his wrists. Flexed his fists. Tried to get the blood moving again. His hood was removed.

He was in an interrogation room. He was seated on the perp's side, the side with the eyebolt on the table. He put his hands next to it, expecting to be secured. Instead, the men who'd brought him in left the room. One of them returned with a bottle of still water. Poe opened and drained it. Getting abducted by the state was thirsty work.

He checked his watch. He'd been in their custody for forty minutes and still no one had said who they were or what they were doing. Poe got up and stretched his legs. He checked the door. It was locked. He felt like banging on it and shouting about having rights. He thought whoever was watching him through the dome camera stuck to the ceiling would find that funny.

After another hour someone brought him a sandwich and a packet of cheese and onion crisps. Part of a Tesco meal deal. Poe ate the crisps but left the sandwich unopened. It was tuna. An hour later he opened it. Half an hour after that, he ate it.

He wondered where Uncle Bertie was. He hoped he wasn't still in the pub. He'd be rat-arsed by now if he was.

And an hour after that a tall gangly man walked in. He took the seat opposite and sighed.

'You really are the most bothersome man, Sergeant Poe,' Alastor Locke said.

Chapter 52

Poe's immediate thought on being abducted in broad daylight was that he'd unwittingly stumbled into a police operation. Maybe something to do with county lines, the term for organised criminal groups moving drugs from big cities to smaller towns and rural areas. But Alastor Locke's appearance meant he hadn't stumbled into a police operation; he'd stumbled into a *security services* operation.

Poe wasn't big on coincidences. He didn't think they were God's way of staying anonymous. He thought coincidences were best left to the authors of bad fiction. Poe was more in Doctor Theodore Woodward's camp – when you hear hoofbeats, think horses not zebras. Poe had chased down a suspect to a small estate in a small town in North Yorkshire, and the security services happened to be running an operation there? He didn't think so.

'Ezekiel Puck is one of yours, isn't he?' he said.

'Your timing is as impeccable as ever, Sergeant Poe,' Locke said. 'I was having lunch with the Home Secretary when I was told someone was creeping around Ezekiel's house. Have you met her?'

'No, Alastor, I haven't met the Home Secretary.'

'She's the most loathsome woman. Always serves salad for lunch.'

Poe said nothing. He hadn't voted for the Home Secretary's party and now he knew she served salad to her guests, he never would.

'Anyway, as you might have gathered,' Locke continued, 'we've been watching the house belonging to the man you know as Ezekiel Puck.'

'Is he the sniper?' Poe said. He'd found direct questions worked best with Alastor Locke. Closed, not open. Locke was the slipperiest bastard Poe had ever met.

Locke nodded. 'We think so.'

'Think so?'

'Yes, he is.'

Poe was surprised. He'd expected an outright denial. At best, pontification. But Locke hadn't denied it. He'd said yes. Right out of the blocks. Poe shook his head in disgust. 'Then you're just as culpable as him.'

'Please explain.'

'If you'd told us who it was from the start, we might have been able to stop this. Instead, you've had us chasing down every stupid clue, the most obscure leads.'

'Yes, I gather you make a very fetching Doctor Who, Poe.'

Poe started to get out of his seat. Fists clenched.

'Calm down, Poe,' Locke said evenly. 'We *didn't* know it was Ezekiel Puck. Of course, we didn't.'

Poe sat back down. Gathered his thoughts. Locke was making sense. He might even be telling the truth. If the security services had known who the sniper was, it would have been dealt with internally. MI5 would have located Puck, then when executive action was needed, one of the police Special Branches would have taken over. Still, something wasn't adding up. He didn't think Locke was lying, but he wasn't telling him the truth about everything. That wasn't unusual for him. Poe reckoned the sin of omission was part of Locke's daily routine. He'd probably been withholding information since Nanny had been stirring salt into his porridge.

'When did you find out?'

'When Miss Bradshaw put her list of role-playing game enthusiasts through one of our databases, a database she had no authorisation to access, I may add.' He shook his head in admiration. 'That woman costs this country a small fortune. Every time our IT departments beef up their security, she just waltzes right in again.'

'Alastor.'

'Ah yes, where was I?' Locke said. 'Anyway, the name Ezekiel Puck isn't on any of our databases, but it *did* raise an alert. And I've got to tell you, Poe, it's a name I hoped never to hear again.'

'Who is he?'

'Ezekiel Puck doesn't exist. It's a codename.'

'A codename for who?'

'For one of the most dangerous men this country has ever produced.'

Chapter 53

'Ezekiel Puck is one of our dirty secrets, Poe,' Locke said. 'He was someone we sent out into the world to do . . . things on Her Majesty's behalf.'

'*Her* Majesty?'

'He's long retired.'

'What things?'

'Bad things, Poe.'

He stopped. Let Poe draw his own conclusions. Poe did, and quickly.

'*How* bad, Alastor?' Poe asked. 'Because, forgive me for being blunt, your entire life is secrets and lies. It's what you buy, steal and sell. And because you have the unattainable goal of keeping us safe in our beds, you can't hold your nose at the methods you choose to achieve this. If I did a sniff test, everything would smell bad.'

'I'm—'

'And that's fine,' Poe cut in. 'It's as it should be. We need a security service and we need their methods to remain secret. And if rules have to be bent, the occasional Chinese burn administered, then I'm not going to lose too much sleep. You have a country to protect. But when *you* say Ezekiel Puck did bad things, I sit up and pay attention. Because forgive me, Alastor, if *you* think this guy was bad, the rest of us are probably going to think he's dia-fucking-bolical.'

Locke took his time responding. Eventually he said, 'And the rest of you would be right.' He reached into his briefcase and retrieved a thin file. He opened it but didn't glance at the top page.

'Ezekiel Puck, because if he's permanently going by that name now, we should probably use it as well – and I suppose the fact he took the name of Shakespeare's trickster as his code-name tells you everything you need to know about him – was born Raymond Addy. He's forty-nine years old and he grew up in Edinburgh. He joined the service directly from Cambridge, and after extensive training he was assigned to a very small, very secret department under my purview.'

'Would I be right in thinking this department didn't find its way on to any paperwork that the Intelligence and Security Committee of Parliament could check?'

'Good Lord, no. My budget came out of the discretionary fund of the discretionary fund of the discretionary fund, and so on.'

'There was no oversight then?'

'We aren't a lawless service, Poe. There was no *statutory* over-sight, but there was oversight. Every operation was authorised. All methods were approved. No one went rogue.'

'Did this department have a name, Alastor?'

'Of course. They had to be paid. They had to *exist*. Officially they were Department 17, a small unit attached to the much larger counter-proliferation division.'

'And *un*officially?'

'Unofficially, they were known as "the mischief makers".'

Chapter 54

'Mischief makers?' Poe said. 'What the hell does that mean?'

'Have you heard of the term "gaslighting", Poe?' Locke replied.

'Tilly sometimes uses it,' Poe admitted. 'Usually after Edgar has tricked her into giving him a second dinner. It means psychological manipulation. The gaslighter attempts to sow self-doubt and confusion in their victim by distorting reality. It's commonly used to obtain power and control in abusive or dysfunctional relationships.'

Locke nodded. 'It's a ghastly turn of phrase, I know,' he said. 'But, without giving you the entire megillah, Ezekiel Puck was a professional gaslighter.'

'Well, you *did* say it was something bad,' Poe said.

'We call it psyops,' Locke continued. 'Psychological operations. Or black propaganda. Psyops isn't new, of course. The Persians waged psychological warfare against the Egyptians as far back as the Battle of Pelusium in 525 BC. Churchill had whole departments dedicated to it during the war.' Locke sighed. Removed his glasses and polished them with a monogrammed handkerchief. He was always doing that. Poe wondered if he had greasy eyeballs. 'May I ask you something, Poe?'

'You can.'

'When it comes to black propaganda, whose name springs to mind?'

Poe didn't hesitate. 'Joseph Goebbels,' he said. 'His Ministry of Enlightenment and Propaganda deceived the Germans into believing that if it wasn't for the Jews they'd all be living in a utopia.'

Locke nodded. 'Goebbels *was* a gifted narrator, and when it comes to scale, there is no doubt he's the most infamous propagandist in the history of the world. But, in my small, and no doubt insular, world, it's not Goebbels that springs to mind when we think about psychological warfare; it's Ezekiel Puck. He had an extraordinary talent for winkling out his target's hopes and dreams, their fears and their deepest darkest secrets, and then exploiting them. He would push their buttons and pull their levers until there was nothing left but despair.'

'And which group of people did you designate as targets, Alastor? Trade union leaders? *Guardian* readers? The French?'

Locke flicked through the documents in the file. He picked out one but shielded it from Poe. He said, 'What do you know about Iran?'

'Just what your Ministry of Enlightenment and Propaganda . . . sorry, I meant to say what your Foreign Office tells me.'

'Very droll, Poe,' Locke said. He tapped the document he was holding. 'This British company found a loophole in the law when it came to exporting resource planning software. They were selling it as a way of coordinating humanitarian aid.'

'But?'

'But the company knew it could also be used to integrate industrial processes relating to Iran's nuclear programme.'

'Why not call them out on it? Or shut them down completely?' Poe paused then answered his own question. 'Because it would embarrass the government.'

'It would. But there was more than that to consider. The company is a major employer. Shutting them down would mean job losses. The Treasury would lose tax revenue. Far better the problem went away. Quietly.'

'Step in, Ezekiel Puck?'

Locke nodded. 'A rogue senior executive was behind the sale of the software, but he was protected by the law and if it came down to it, his board would have had no choice but to stand behind him and denounce the crackdown as government over-reach. Puck was given the task of bringing this man to order. The method was left to him.'

'He murdered him?'

'Good Lord, no,' Locke said. 'Despite what you might think, democide has never been in this country's wheelhouse.'

'Democide?'

'State-sponsored killing.'

'Well say that then,' Poe snapped. 'We didn't all go to Cheltenham Ladies' College.'

'Yes, very good, Poe,' Locke said. 'We leave democide to the Russians and the Saudis. No, Puck's methods were far more subtle. And by the time he withdrew, no one even knew that what had happened had happened by his design.'

'What did he do?'

'Nothing for three months. Nothing but study the senior exec-utive. His current life, his previous life. Eventually he decided a failed romance from his university days was his Achilles heel. It was a short-lived love affair, but Puck's research led him to believe the impact on the senior executive's life had been pro-found. That everything since – his wife, his children, even his career – had been a compromise.'

Poe thought it through. Saw where Locke was going. 'He rekindled it?'

'He did. He arranged a dinner reservation with his target. He had the paperwork to prove – paperwork that would stand up to rigorous scrutiny, I may add – that Puck was able to put a sig-nificant amount of business his way. He met him in a restaurant he already knew the woman in question would be dining at with her husband. Made sure their tables were close enough for them to see each other, but not so close they could *speak* to each other. And a week later, he gets the first email . . .'

Poe read to the end of the page. 'He thought that on seeing him, his ex-lover wanted to rekindle their relationship?'

'Puck managed her end of their digital relationship. She professed her never-ending love for him. Her dissatisfaction with her husband. That seeing him had reminded her of everything she had lost. In short, she told him everything he wanted to hear. Everything he'd been *dreaming* of. They agreed to meet.'

'And this woman had no idea?'

'She did when he gatecrashed a lunch with her mother in a Covent Garden patisserie. Later, she, or rather Puck, apologised for pretending she wasn't expecting him. Put it down to her mother unexpectedly showing up. That she had to maintain the facade until she was ready to leave her husband for him.'

'How long did this last?'

'Two weeks after the restraining order was made against him. By then Puck didn't need to do anything. The senior executive was turning up at her place of work, screaming declarations of love at her until the police removed him. He left his wife, his children, even his house in Hampstead. He moved into a hotel, convinced that one night there'd be a knock on the door.'

'And eventually he was sacked?'

'Removed by the board. They had no choice really; he was rarely at work, and when he did turn up he was drunk. He was replaced by someone with views on Iran that were much more in line with current government thinking.'

'What happened to him?' Poe said quietly. He wasn't sure he wanted to hear the answer.

'I fear that gets us neatly to the crux of the problem,' Locke replied. 'A month after being removed by the board, our disgraced senior executive threw himself under the 15:26 out of Finchley Road & Frognal.'

'He killed himself?'

'We couldn't prove it, but we think that despite the task being complete, Puck kept going. That he'd been having too much fun to stop.'

'He drove the senior executive to suicide?'

'We think so.'

'Why?'

'If you're looking for anything more nuanced than because he could, I don't have it.'

'How many?'

'How many what, dear boy?'

'You know.'

Locke did. 'In total, fourteen of his targets committed suicide. It was always a possibility, given who the mischief makers targeted and how they went about achieving their goals, but even so, by their standards, fourteen is an extraordinarily high number.' He removed another document from his file. 'The wife of an awkward ambassador of a country I won't identify took her husband's nickel-plated revolver and blew her brains out when her past as a high-end call girl was made public. He resigned his post and returned home. His replacement was much more amenable to what's happening in the South Atlantic. One of these so-called "hacktivists" was found hanged after it emerged he'd been using his credit card to download indecent images of children.'

'Jesus,' Poe said. 'And you *allowed* this?'

'I have a country to protect, Poe. I can't be sentimental as to how I go about it. And while these deaths are individually tragic, the missions that Puck and the other mischief makers conducted were authorised at the highest level.'

Poe was about to protest, but Locke raised his hand.

'But I will say this,' he said. 'The pattern of his . . . shall we say extracurricular activities didn't show itself until later. Ezekiel

Puck *did* have a flair for the work but the moment I saw he was relishing his role as the architect of someone's life falling apart, I cut him loose. Early retirement. A firm handshake and a moderate pension. In my world, ruthless is good. Sadistic is not.'

Poe took a moment. 'Then your world sucks, Alastor.'

'And fine words butter no parsnips, Poe. The facts are that Ezekiel Puck is out there, conducting an operation, the goal of which is known only to him. When I put him out to pasture, I took away his livelihood, but I couldn't take away what he'd learned. It wasn't a bell I could un-ring. I couldn't take away his proclivities for causing pain. It's a mess and I'll do my damnedest to help clear it up, but if we can leave the public inquiry until *after* you've clapped him in irons, I think we'd all be very grateful.'

Clap him in irons . . . The second time someone had said that recently.

'Alastor,' Poe said. 'Where's Uncle Bertie?'

Chapter 55

'Uncle Bertie is safely ensconced in Lady Doyle's ancestral home, Poe,' Locke said.

'You grabbed him too?'

'We did.'

'I hope he had you horsewhipped.'

'He *did* give one of my guys a crack on the noggin with that stick of his, if that's any consolation. I rather think the old chap enjoyed himself.'

'And Estelle's old Land Rover?'

'Went back with Uncle Bertie,' Locke said. 'There's a car waiting outside to take you anywhere you need to go. Where will you start?'

'Can I share what you've told me?'

'With Tilly only. She has the right clearance, the others don't.'

'Broad strokes, though? What he *is* rather than what he *did*.'

'That seems a fair compromise, Poe,' Locke said. 'And I'll send Tilly everything we have on Puck once you've explained the need for discretion. So, where will you start?'

Poe thought about it. 'Does he have a link to Gretna or Gretna Green?'

Locke leaned forward, his eyes wide. 'He does.'

'Tell me.'

'His ex-wife is from that part of Scotland. I think she might still live there. May I ask how you made that connection?'

'Puck was an official witness at a wedding vow renewal,' Poe said. 'We haven't worked out why yet. He wasn't related to the family and he wasn't part of the original wedding party. What do you know about her?'

'She's called Joanne Addy, although I imagine she'll have reverted to her maiden name by now.'

'Which was?'

'It escapes me.'

'Not to worry,' Poe said. 'Tilly will have her whole life in seconds.'

'And the range in Scotland you found. The people overseeing it are competent?'

'Chief Superintendent McCloud knows what she's doing. She's set up military-grade surveillance cameras, a covert perimeter, and her armed cops are on a two-minute notice-to-move order. If he turns up, we'll have him.'

Locke considered this. 'Now the disinfectant of sunlight has been shone upon his Ripon hideaway, I assume you'll speak to his neighbours. Get an artist's likeness? Maybe get one from his ex-wife as well. Cross-reference them?'

'We call it an E-FIT these days, Alastor,' Poe said. 'Electronic Facial Identification Technique.' He took a moment. 'Although now I've said it out loud in full, I'm sure "technique" was only added to make the anacronym catchier.'

Locke slid a business card across the table. It was white with crisp edges. Black writing. Looked like Times New Roman. A serif font. Nothing cartoony like Comic Sans for Alastor Locke. Poe didn't pick it up.

'I can always be contacted on this number, Poe,' he said. 'When you get your E-FIT, I'd like you to send me a copy.'

Which was when the thing that had been bothering Poe finally made itself known. He frowned. He was right – Locke *was* withholding something.

Something important.

Chapter 56

'You don't know what he looks like, do you, Alastor?' Poe said. 'It's why your jackboots grabbed me instead of observing me. It's why one of them took my picture.'

Locke didn't respond.

'How can you not know what he looks like?' Poe said. He grabbed Locke's file, ripped through the documents. 'Why isn't his photograph in here?'

Locke had the grace to look embarrassed. And considering the utterly shameful things Poe had witnessed him do, this was a big deal.

'*Mea culpa*, Poe,' Locke said. '*Mea culpa.*'

'I know that one, you overeducated prick. It means "my fault". So, tell me, how can MI5 not know what one of their most dangerous employees looks like? I'd love to hear this.'

'Pipe down, Poe. It's not as outrageous as you might think. The very nature of Puck's job meant that the fewer people who knew what he looked like, the better. The *safer*. He wasn't always ruining marriages *in absentia*. Sometimes he had contact with his targets. His image was highly restricted. *All* the mischief makers' images were highly restricted. If you didn't need to know what they looked like, you didn't get to know what they looked like. They were on our IT systems under their codenames. The legends they used in the field were used once and discarded.'

'I suppose it's a bit like how we manage protected witnesses,' Poe conceded.

'Then you understand.'

'Still . . .'

Locke sighed. 'Before he was managed out of the service, Ezekiel Puck breached our systems. He deleted his personnel records. And then he deleted the backups. Which in itself isn't as insidious as it might seem. The sensibilities of the public, and therefore our bandwagoner elected officials, change on an almost daily basis. What was acceptable practice last week might be deemed abhorrent the following week. You know this to be true, Poe. Just look at how hot the water got for the undercover police officer who infiltrated that environmental protest group. He was labelled *agent provocateur*, was he not?'

Poe took Locke's point. A tribunal had said that Mark Kennedy's sanctioned undercover operation had been 'an abuse of the highest order' and that by entering a sexual relationship with one of his targets, he'd 'grossly debased, degraded and humiliated' her. The National Public Order Intelligence Unit had declared Kennedy a loose cannon while simultaneously refusing to release any internal documents that supported their position.

Locke took Poe's silence as understanding. He said, 'The mischief makers were a paranoid bunch. They had to be to stay alive and that mindset never leaves you.'

'Do *you* remember what he looks like?' Poe said.

'I'd recognise him if I saw him,' Locke said. 'But I wouldn't be able to help with a visual reconstruction.'

'Great,' Poe said. 'I'll put out a locate/trace on a tall chap that no one remembers, shall I? It'll be over by teatime.'

'Don't let him ruffle your feathers, Poe,' Locke said. 'Ezekiel Puck is intelligent and he's well trained, but he's not omniscient. And in that regard, he's no different to the scores of rapscallions you've hunted down and brought to justice. Do what you do best – work the man while Miss Bradshaw works the data.'

Which was easier said than done, Poe thought. Ezekiel Puck's brain wasn't wired like anyone else's he'd come across. He was intelligent, he was sadistic, and he'd been through a unique training programme. An unholy trifecta.

Poe put his head in his hands and blew through his fingers. 'I don't know how to catch a man like this, Alastor.'

Locke took his time replying. He reached out and touched Poe's arm. 'Nor do we, Poe,' he said quietly. 'Nor do we.'

Poe's phone alerted him to a text. It was from Bradshaw. It said: WHERE ARE YOU, POE? HOW DID IT GO WITH DR CLARA LANG?

He stared at the screen for a moment then put the phone face down on the table. 'But I know someone who might,' he said.

Chapter 57

Poe had been held in a York police station. Locke had left an Audi A4 on the street outside. As soon as he was on the A1, he called Clara Lang's hospital and asked to be put through to Doctor Gray.

'I'm calling in, doc,' he said. 'I'll be there in thirty minutes.'

'Not today, Washington,' Gray said. 'Probably not this week.'

'It has to be now.'

'Are you having an episode? I know these sessions are as much for your benefit as hers.'

'I'm fine. I just need to pick her brains.'

'That's out of the question, I'm afraid,' Gray said. 'And if I could accommodate you, you know I would.'

'What's the problem?'

'I told you earlier there was an incident.'

'You did.'

'I may have downplayed it.'

'I still need to see her.'

'She's sleeping, Washington. She's had, in layman's terms, a whack on the head with a liquid cosh. She'll be out for the rest of the day at least.'

'Is she OK?' Poe cared deeply about Clara Lang. She'd saved his life. Admittedly, she was also the cause of his PTSD, but that was just semantics.

'*She's* fine.'

Poe understood what Doctor Gray was trying to tell him

without breaking patient confidentiality. There was a dark side to Clara Lang. And it didn't end well for the people who saw it. Someone had been hurt. Clara had been sedated. She would be kept that way until it was safe for staff and patients alike.

Poe said goodbye and put his foot down. He'd spend the night at Highwood then visit Ezekiel Puck's ex-wife in the morning.

'I got one of the blighters with my stick, Washington!' Uncle Bertie yelled the second Poe got out of the Audi. Locke hadn't told him where to leave it and Poe hadn't asked. If it wasn't collected in the next day or two, he'd dump it in the nearest Iceland car park. Leave the keys inside and let nature take its course.

Bertie had a crystal whisky glass in one hand and his stick in the other. It didn't look like he intended to let go of either any time soon.

Doyle linked arms with Poe. Led him into the marquee.

'Seems you've made a new friend,' she said. 'You're all Uncle Bertie can talk about.'

'Did you get his suit?'

'We did, thank you. Did he really hit someone with his stick?'

Poe nodded. 'You wouldn't believe who if I told you.'

'He said it was one of Alastor Locke's men.'

'How the . . . ?' He didn't bother finishing. Bertie and Locke were peas from the same pod. *Of course* they would know each other. They probably hunted foxes together.

Poe told her how his day had gone from pub-based lunacy with Uncle Bertie to getting abducted by the security services. He told her about Ezekiel Puck and how Locke had asked him not to tell anyone about his role in a weird, and no doubt about to be banned, unit called the mischief makers. He finished by telling her that Clara Lang had been sedated after yet another violent episode. Doyle asked several questions, all of them about Clara. She had as much invested in her treatment as he did.

'What's your plan now?' she asked.

'I'm going to ask Tilly to tear Ezekiel Puck's ex-wife's life apart. She's at the centre of this whether she's aware of it or not.' Poe's mobile rang. It was Flynn. He sighed. He'd been dreading this call. 'But first I'm going to let the boss shout at me for a bit.'

He accepted the call. Gingerly put the speaker to his ear.

'Poe, you fucking arsehole!' Flynn shouted. 'What the hell were you thinking, disobeying a direct order like that? Commander Mathers is apoplectic.'

Doyle grimaced. 'Beer?' she whispered.

Poe nodded. This could go on for a while.

Chapter 58

It *did* go on for a while.

But when Poe told Flynn that he had a file on their suspect, that Puck had been part of a shadowy MI5 unit called the mischief makers, and lastly, that there were no known pictures of him, she refocused her anger on Alastor Locke, which had been Poe's intention all along.

'That duplicitous wanker,' she snapped, then muted herself for a moment. She came back on and said, 'Can Estelle put me and Commander Mathers up for the night?'

'I'm sure she can.'

'We'll be there as soon as possible. We'll strategise tonight and hit the ground running tomorrow.'

'As soon as the E-FIT is complete, we *have* to go public, Poe,' Mathers said. 'Full press briefing. Interviews on the six and ten o'clock news. To do anything less is irresponsible.'

Poe wanted to agree. Just to piss off Alastor Locke. He'd promised him he wouldn't air his dirty laundry in public, but it wasn't a *real* promise. Not like when he'd promised Bradshaw he'd only get *one* meat and potato pie from the Chopping Block in Penrith. He certainly didn't feel bound by a promise to Locke. If the roles were reversed, Locke certainly wouldn't feel bound by a promise he had made to Poe. Promising to keep the information to himself was something Poe had said to move the conversation along. And he reckoned Locke knew that. Knew that Poe would do whatever was best for the case, not whatever was best for someone trying to avoid the scrutiny of a public inquiry.

But on this occasion, Poe didn't think going public was a good idea. He tried one last time.

'I can't stress enough how worried Locke is about Ezekiel Puck, ma'am,' he said. 'I've known him for a while now, and this is the first time he's looked worried. I got the impression that Locke was being visited by all the Christmas ghosts at once. A rogue mischief maker sounds like the live-action remake of his worst nightmare. At the minute, Puck doesn't know we know who he is. Which means he thinks he can carry on doing what he's doing. We have two decent chances of stopping him – he'll either visit his zeroing range or he'll get caught in the net we throw around Gretna. That changes the second you go public. Puck goes from predictable to unpredictable. And don't assume he'll panic. The way Locke described him, this guy can improvise. He can think his way around problems. He'll have contingencies for being identified and we have no idea what those might be. I honestly think the best play is to try and take him unawares. The only way we can do that is if we sit on his name.'

'Even if more people die?'

'Yes,' Poe said without hesitation. 'And I don't say that lightly.'

Mathers looked like she had the weight of the world on her shoulders. She glanced at Flynn. 'Steph?'

'I agree with Poe,' Flynn said. 'But we don't need to decide now. Tilly will have finished her profile on Joanne Addy, Ezekiel Puck's ex, in an hour. Why don't we wait until we've read what she has?'

It was a good compromise and Poe was reminded that Flynn was a senior manager in her own right now. He thought she would transfer back to the Met at some point. That she would soon tire of being a big fish in the NCA's small pond. And when she did, she had the personal and professional attributes, the skills and temperament, to go all the way if she wanted. There was no reason she couldn't become deputy commissioner. Maybe even the commissioner. The most senior cop in the country.

Doyle stuck her head into the parlour. Mathers and Flynn had mocked him for living in a house with a parlour until Poe had reminded Flynn that the cheapest flat in her apartment block was three million pounds. Flynn's partner, Zoe, had a job analysing oil prices. It paid well.

'Brunton's made bacon sandwiches if any of you are wanting a bit of supper?' she said.

They followed her into the main kitchen – Highwood had two – and took a seat around a table King Arthur would have said was too big. Bradshaw was already there, sipping lemon tea and nibbling a rice cracker. She closed her laptop.

'I'm ready to brief you now,' she said.

They each grabbed a bacon sandwich. Poe opened his and added the bacon from another. Brunton never got the meat-to-bread ratio right. He threw Edgar the empty bread. The spaniel gave him a dirty look. Poe didn't know why. Edgar should have been used to bacon-less bacon sandwiches by now.

Poe took a bite of his sandwich, enjoyed the crispy bacon and the even crispier rind. He poured himself a cup of strong tea.

Ready for anything.

Chapter 59

Joanne Addy opened her front door then stepped back. It was what people did these days. They opened their doors and stepped back into the shadows. Why unnecessarily frame yourself? Why make yourself an easy target?

She was a short woman who compensated for her lack of height with three-inch heels and a beehive hairdo Marge Simpson would have been proud of. Poe had expected her to say, despite living under the gun, she was on her way out. But she didn't. This must be how she dressed at home. Always ready for pop-ins.

She invited them inside. They were mob-handed so there weren't enough seats. Mathers, Flynn, and an armed cop whose name Poe hadn't caught and was too embarrassed to ask again, took the sofa. Bradshaw took the remaining armchair and Poe perched on the arm.

Joanne Addy didn't ask why a bunch of cops and NCA officers had filled her living room, which Poe thought curious.

'Is this about Conrad?'

Poe and Mathers shared a glance.

'Who's Conrad?' Mathers said.

'The wee shite who keyed my car last week,' Addy said. 'Just because I wouldn't give his jakey maw a job.'

Poe mentally translated. Maw meant mother; jakey usually meant homeless alcoholic but was used as a one-size-fits-all insult these days.

'We're not here because someone scratched your car, Mrs Addy,' Mathers said. She paused a moment, waited for the silence to get uncomfortable. 'We're here about your ex-husband.'

'Raymond? What's he done?'

'When was the last time you saw him?'

Addy looked up. 'Must be a couple of years. Maybe longer. He'd heard I'd finally persuaded Mr Douglas to sell me the Smithy's Forge and he wanted to check I was doing OK.' She looked wistful. 'He knew it was my dream. Wish he'd talked me out of it now, of course. This sniper bawbag's killing more than people.'

Bawbag – *ball*bag. Poe had to admit, Scottish slang was far more colourful than English slang. He said, 'It *does* look quiet out there.'

Addy glared at him. 'It looked quiet out there when that first wee lassie was killed. Now the bawbag's come back for second helpings, it's bloody dead. I rang round the other venues and they're all empty. I have the money for one more month of nothing coming in. After that' – she ran her finger across her throat – 'I'll be dead and buried.'

'How long ago did you buy the Smithy's Forge?' Mathers asked.

'Eight years ago. I'd been there twenty-odd years by then. Got a job as a weddings and events assistant when I left school. Didn't miss a day.'

'You must enjoy it?'

Addy smiled for the first time. 'I'm not selling weddings, I'm selling *dreams*. Even the repeat customers, the ones who see the marriage as something to endure until they feel the urge for yet another wedding . . .'

'They're addicted?' Poe said, surprised.

Addy lit a cigarette. Sucked half of it down and said, 'You'd be surprised what people can get addicted to, Sergeant Poe.'

Bradshaw nodded vigorously. 'Poe's addicted to Cumberland sausage, Joanne Addy,' she said. 'He eats it at least once a day.'

'Great contribution, Tilly.'

'Thank you, Poe.'

Addy continued as if that bizarre exchange hadn't happened. 'I have one customer who gets us to provisionally pencil in her next wedding while she's still wearing white from the current one. And that's fine. The heart wants what the heart wants. And I've loved working in the Smithy's Forge since the moment I set foot in the place. Maybe I'm an old romantic, but I knew I'd own it one day. Call it fate or something. I don't see it as a job or a career; I see it as a calling.' She tapped out a new cigarette and lit it from the old one. 'And now it's over. Of all the difficulties the Gretna Green wedding businesses face, no one had considered something like this. An eejit sniper.'

'Is there no help available?' Poe asked.

'It's not like the pandemic. There's no government assistance this time and the insurance company are claiming it's *force majeure*.'

Bradshaw had told Grantham Smythe, owner of the Mill Forge, the wedding venue where the first Gretna Green victim was killed, that *force majeure* was French for greater force. It was a catch-all phrase for when the slippery bastards in insurance were trying to deny claims. Unlike an act of God, which only included natural events that couldn't have been foreseen, *force majeure* included extraordinary situations caused by human intervention. War is *force majeure*. COVID was *force majeure*. So were striking unions. Infrastructure failures.

It seemed insurance companies had added snipers to the list.

Chapter 60

'Do you have a recent photograph of Raymond, Mrs Addy?' Mathers asked.

Addy shook her head. 'He wouldn't let anyone take his photograph. It had something to do with his job before we got married. He said it was a security issue. I thought he was talking a load of pish, bigging up his life before we met, but now I think he *might* have been in the SAS. Something like that anyway.'

'Why do you say that?'

'Because he never talked about what he'd done, not even when he'd been drinking. I asked him countless times, but he was a vault when it came to his past.' She looked at Mathers, her eyes pinched. 'And now I think I'd like you to tell me why you're here.'

Mathers glanced at Flynn and at Poe. Flynn nodded. So did Poe.

'We think Raymond is calling himself Ezekiel Puck now, Mrs Addy,' Mathers said. 'Does that name mean anything to you?'

Addy nodded. 'I don't know where it came from, but he occasionally used it. I think he may have even used it when he was roped into being a witness at a wedding renewal. Renewals aren't official ceremonies, so it didn't really make much difference. I think he used it as his character name on that stupid game he was obsessed with.'

'What game was that?' Poe said carefully.

'*Disincentivise.* No, that's not it. It was something like that, though.'

'It's called *Dezinformatsiya*,' Bradshaw said. 'It's an espionage role-playing game. It's based on the books of John le Carré. Players can play either side of the Cold War. Ezekiel Puck is the world's top-rated player and he's on a bunch of the *Dezinformatsiya* mailing lists. It's how we identified him.'

'That'll be right,' Addy said. 'Le Carré was Raymond's favourite author. Why are you asking about his joke name?'

Mathers composed herself. Aware she was about to throw rocks at Joanne Addy's life. 'We think Ezekiel Puck might be the sniper, Mrs Addy.'

There was no reaction. None at all. Mathers could have told her the Martians had landed. Or the Scottish government had banned fried food.

Eventually she said, 'I don't get it.'

'It's not a joke, Mrs Addy. There's evidence linking Raymond to the recent shootings.'

Addy lit a fresh cigarette, her third in ten minutes. She frowned. 'But why would Raymond be killing people?'

'We don't know,' Mathers said.

Poe thought he might, but he didn't want to voice his suspicion just yet. Instead, he said, 'Mrs Addy, this might seem a strange question, but please bear with me – did anyone who knew Raymond ever commit suicide?'

Mathers threw him a look. Poe ignored it and concentrated on Joanne Addy. He could tell she was about to say something along the lines of, *Of course not*, but something was staying her hand. After a few moments, she nodded.

'Davy Newport took his own life,' she said. 'He was the guy who taught Raymond how to stalk deer.'

And how to shoot from distance, Poe thought, but didn't say. *How to stay hidden.*

'What happened?'

'It turned out Davy was a thief,' Joanne said. 'Got caught

221

with his hand in the till of the charity he founded. Never got over it. Blew his own brains out.' She held a finger to her head. Pulled an imaginary trigger.

'Did he and Raymond ever have a falling out?'

'Well, yes, but it wasn't anything serious. Raymond said Davy had promised him first shot at this ten-point stag they'd been stalking for almost a month. Raymond was raging when he saw it in the back of Davy's pickup.'

Poe nodded. That fit with his theory. 'Anyone else?'

'Anyone else what?'

'Did he know anyone else who took their own life?'

Joanne frowned in concentration. 'There was . . . but no, that can't be right – Raymond didn't even know her.'

'Tell me anyway, Mrs Addy.'

'There was this lassie, a wee slip of a girl,' Addy said. 'Raymond and her mother had got into it in Asda car park. She said Raymond had pranged her car, Raymond said it was the other way around. The insurance company came out on her side and Raymond lost his no claims bonus. Two months later, her daughter took an overdose. She'd been shagging her wee boy-friend, and someone leaked the videos they'd filmed. The polis said the cloud thingamajig had been hacked.' She paused a beat. Took another long drag of her cigarette. Looked like she needed it. 'But it was odd, you know?'

'How so?'

'Because this lassie's videos were the *only* ones leaked.'

'That is odd,' Poe agreed.

'Her ma killed herself a month after her daughter's funeral. Hanged herself. Used the belt from her daughter's communion dress.'

Poe took a moment before he asked what he needed to ask next. 'We'll come back to your ex-husband if we may, but can we now talk about the Smithy's Forge? You say you've worked there

222

since you left school?'

Joanne nodded. 'Aye, since I was sixteen.'

'And it had always been your dream to own it?'

'Aye,' she said carefully, unsure where Poe was going.

Poe saw Mathers and Flynn share a glance. It was clear they didn't know either.

'Gretna Green weddings are a hugely profitable business,' he said. 'And because of that, the venues themselves are rarely put up for sale. When they are, competition is fierce, I imagine. May I ask how you funded it, Mrs Addy?'

'Legitimately,' she said.

'I don't doubt it.'

She took another drag on her cigarette. Sucked it down to the butt then stubbed it out. 'Banks in Dumfries are happy to loan to wedding venues,' she said.

'And is that what you did?'

'Aye. I had to accept a higher interest rate, as I'd never run a business before, but that isn't unusual.'

'What collateral did the bank require?'

'The venue.'

'So, if you default on your loans, the bank can seize the Smithy's Forge?'

'Aye,' she said. 'And my house.'

'Your house?'

'I had to put that up as well. The venue needed refurbishing. It was looking a bit tired.'

'The loan was secured using the wedding venue *and* your own home?'

She shrugged. 'It didn't seem such a big deal at the time,' she said. 'Wedding businesses in Gretna Green don't fail.'

'How much is there left to pay?'

'A lot. More than half.'

'Does the business have reserves?'

She shook her head. 'I used up my reserves during COVID. The government helped, but they couldn't do everything.'

'Have you missed any payments yet?'

'Three.'

'And?'

'And the bank has already called. All nicey-nice, but they mentioned options the last time they called.' She wrapped 'options' in air quotes. 'And we all know what that means.'

Poe nodded. He did. They all did. He took his time with the next question; aware he was about to suggest something probably better left unsuggested. '*If* we don't catch whoever is shooting people, Mrs Addy, and *if* the bank seizes the Smithy's Forge and your house to recover their loan, what will you do?'

She reached for her cigarettes. Lit one and said, 'Pray I get the cancer.'

Poe nodded. That's what he'd thought. 'Will you excuse us a moment, Mrs Addy?'

He looked at Mathers and Flynn and tilted his head towards the door. He got up and walked outside. As soon as they'd joined him, he said, 'We've been looking at this all wrong. This isn't an unhinged lunatic on a killing spree. Nor is it someone hiding one murder in among a bunch of other murders. And that's because the murders aren't his primary objective.'

'What are they?' Mathers said.

'They're a means to an end.'

'Spit it out, Poe,' Flynn said.

'This has been about one thing – destroying Joanne Addy's wedding business. It's about shattering her dreams. Turning her out on the street.' He glanced through the window. Addy was lighting yet another cigarette. 'Ezekiel Puck is pushing his ex-wife towards suicide.'

Chapter 61

They returned to hear the back end of Bradshaw explaining why *force majeure*, a concept that originated in French civil law, was used in the United Kingdom.

'It's an accepted standard for countries that have developed their legal systems from the Napoleonic Code,' Bradshaw said. 'And while it obviously clashes with the concept of *pacta sunt servanda*—'

'I don't know what that is, lassie,' Addy said, her mouth half open, her eyes glazed over. It was a look Poe knew well. It said: *I'm ready to swap my cigarettes for a crack pipe.*

'It's Latin for "agreements must be kept",' Bradshaw said. 'Essentially it means—'

'Why did you and Raymond split up, Mrs Addy?' Poe cut in.

She glowered at him. 'Is that no a bit personal?'

Poe said, 'Yes, but I need to know.'

'Why?'

Poe waited her out.

'Fine,' she said after a small pause. 'Raymond used to play mind games with me. I don't think he could help it. He would do things like leave the fridge open then say he'd watched me do it, that kind of thing. I used to bite for the first few years of our marriage, but eventually I got bored of it. I stopped reacting. If he said I'd left the bathroom light on, even if I knew I hadn't, I'd just apologise and go and switch it off. He stopped doing it after a bit. It was no fun if I didn't flip my lid. It was the drama

225

he craved. In the end, I think he got bored of me. One morning over breakfast he said, "You're no fun any more, Joanne." He left the same day.'

'You said you saw him a couple of years ago?'

'Yeah, he just turned up one night. Said he was in the area. He asked if that damn virus had finished off the Smithy's Forge, but I told him I'd got everyone through it. He seemed disappointed. Like he hadn't wanted me to succeed without him.'

Poe glanced at Mathers and nodded.

'We think the sniper *is* your ex-husband,' Mathers said. 'Furthermore, we think he's doing all this with one goal in mind – to crash Gretna Green's wedding economy.'

'But . . . but why?'

'To ruin your business, Mrs Addy. Ezekiel Puck wants to see you destitute and homeless. You were right – he *didn't* like that you were succeeding without him. Every person he's shot, every bullet he's fired, has brought him one step closer to this singular goal.'

'The bank seizing the Smithy's Forge?'

'That's not his goal. The bank seizing the Smithy's Forge and your home is only a stepping stone. His *ultimate* goal is you taking your own life.'

Joanne Addy stared at Mathers for a long time. Eventually she shook her head and said, 'That's sick as fuck. And my Raymond wouldn't do something like that.'

'It is sick, Mrs Addy,' Poe agreed. 'But I'm afraid Raymond *would* do something like that. He's done it before.' He waited a couple of heartbeats. 'Several times. I know this to be a fact.'

'*How* do you know?'

'I just do. I can't tell you how. But I *can* tell you your ex-husband was never in the SAS.'

'What *was* he in?'

'Something worse, Mrs Addy,' Poe said. 'Something much worse.'

'And if I *don't* kill myself?'

Poe shrugged. 'He has a sniper's rifle and he never misses.'

'I'm in danger then.'

'You are.'

'We'll have overt and covert police officers watching your house from now until he's been caught, Mrs Addy,' Mathers said. 'And with your permission I'd like to put armed officers in your home.'

'In here? With me? Where will they sleep?'

'They won't be sleeping, Mrs Addy.'

Mathers and Joanne Addy began discussing the logistics of having police officers in her home. She seemed more concerned about them blocking her toilet than she was about them saving her life. Poe didn't blame her. He'd never been on a stakeout that hadn't involved a blocked toilet at some point. He blamed the national shortfall in trained plumbers. Bradshaw blamed all the curry and pickled eggs.

Poe's phone vibrated in his pocket. He'd put it on silent while they delivered what was obviously upsetting news. He didn't know why he'd bothered. Like all mobile phones on silent, the vibration mode was loud enough to startle crows. It was a text from Ailsa McCloud, the chief superintendent leading the Police Scotland investigation. The words on his screen were: POE, WE HAVE A PROBLEM. Poe unlocked his phone and read the complete text.

Shit.

That really *was* a problem.

Chapter 62

'This twat is running rings around us!' Mathers yelled once Poe had told her what was in McCloud's text message. 'And how could she not know?!'

Which was both a fair and *un*fair question.

McCloud had told Poe that a Forest of Atholl game-keeper had found a trail camera. And it didn't belong to Police Scotland. He'd been putting up nesting boxes, hoping to attract more great spotted woodpeckers – apparently, woodpeckers were disproportionately important to woodland ecosystems – when he'd noticed the trail camera strapped to an adjacent tree. Suspecting it belonged to a poacher, he'd removed it and handed it in to the estate manager. The estate manager, the only staff member in the know, had immediately taken it to Chief Superintendent McCloud. He'd led her to the tree in question. McCloud had climbed up to the strap marks on the bark and immediately saw what the trail camera had been attempting to capture.

The mystery trail camera was aimed at Ezekiel Puck's zeroing range.

He'd been running surveillance on them. Or more likely, given how careful he was, he'd set up the camera after he'd set up his range. Made sure he wasn't walking into a trap each time he returned. Clever. But not so clever they couldn't have predicted it, Poe thought.

But now the surveillers had become the *surveillees*, one thing was certain – Ezekiel Puck wasn't coming back. The zeroing range was a bust.

'You know where we are?' Mathers said to no one in particular. 'Square fucking one, that's where.'

Poe was tempted to let her vent. It wasn't McCloud's fault. It wasn't anyone's fault. And when Mathers calmed down, she'd see that. The problem was, in this state of mind, Poe thought she was on the precipice of a mistake. That she might think she had only one option left.

So instead of letting her talk herself into a blunder, he said, 'We didn't have all our eggs in the range basket, ma'am. We've made progress. *You've* made progress. We know who he is. Where he lived and who he was married to. And I'm fairly certain we know his endgame.'

Mathers glowered, not yet ready to concede that Puck's camera was anything other than an unmitigated disaster. She held his eye as she put her phone to her ear. When it was answered, she said, 'When's that fucking E-FIT going to be ready?' The answer clearly wasn't to her liking. 'Not good enough. I want it ready to go out in twelve hours. If it *isn't* ready in twelve hours, you can go back to spray-painting dicks on railway bridges.'

'Releasing the E-FIT is a mistake, ma'am,' Poe said.

'And why the fuck would I care what Alastor Locke's lackey thinks?'

'Excuse me?'

'You heard me, Poe. I know you went through some horrific shit last year, but the Poe I knew on the Botanist case would *never* kowtow to the security services.'

'You're a very silly woman, Commander Mathers,' Bradshaw said, bristling the way she did any time someone had a go at him. 'Poe is *no one's* lackey.' She bit her lip. 'Well, maybe he's Estelle Doyle's lackey. He certainly seems to do whatever she asks of him. I think if she said he was no longer allowed to eat black pudding, he'd stop.'

'Or pretend to, at least,' Poe said.

Despite herself, Mathers stifled a grin. 'You were saying how I was a very silly woman, Tilly?'

'Poe hates Alastor Locke,' Bradshaw said. 'He says he's an eff-word underhanded idiot and that MI5 are as much use as a bread dildo.'

Flynn snorted.

'You heard that, huh?' Poe said.

'You weren't whispering, Poe. You were shouting so loud I had to put my fingers in my ears. Also, it doesn't make sense as an insult – phallus-shaped bread was used to relieve sexual tension as far back as the Greco-Roman period, and that was two thousand years ago.'

Poe knew there was a joke in there somewhere about yeast infections, but he was surrounded by three strong women, and Flynn held a second-degree black belt in Krav Maga. She could, and had, put him on his arse. Plus, whatever he said would find its way back to Doyle. She and Bradshaw were in almost constant touch. So instead of making an inappropriate – go straight to the HR naughty step – comment, he said, 'I think releasing the E-FIT is a mistake because Puck might not yet know we've found his Yorkshire hideaway. He might not yet know we've spoken to his ex-wife. The second you broadcast his image we lose that advantage.'

Mathers sucked in a breath then blew it out. 'I'm sorry, Poe,' she said. 'That Locke jibe was uncalled for. The truth is, if it wasn't for you guys, we would be nowhere.'

'I sense a "but" coming.'

'But I need to take "confidence in the police" into consideration. The public need to see progress being made. If we lose their confidence, they'll start ignoring advice. Then it moves from a public confidence issue to a public *safety* issue.'

'It's not as straightforward as that, ma'am,' Poe said. 'And while I appreciate the decisions you're making now will no doubt be scrutinised at the inevitable public inquiry, I think, tactically, the best thing to do is let the security services sit on Puck's home in Yorkshire while we sit on his ex-wife in Gretna.'

'I'll bear that in mind,' she said. 'But we're getting the E-FIT and we're getting it soon. At the very least I want to know what this fool looks like.'

'We know he's tall,' Poe said.

'So are you,' Mathers said. 'So is Lurch.'

'Lurch?'

'Sergeant Illingworth. He's one of my armed cops. My point is that lots of people are tall. Hell, even Archie Arreghini's bruiser tops out at six-three.'

Poe looked at Bradshaw. Wondered if she were about to offer Mathers some mango. 'Yes, he does, doesn't he.'

A suspicion bubble rose to the top of his mind-swamp and popped. It didn't smell nice.

231

Chapter 63

Poe had never got onboard with the working-from-home craze. He appreciated that everyone's circumstances were different, but the pandemic was over. He didn't understand why people didn't want a change of scenery. A change of pace. He didn't understand why anyone would choose to bring office equipment into their home. Why they would voluntarily blur the boundaries between their work and personal life. Be at the beck and call of their boss. He'd even heard about one hippy-dippy organisation that insisted their employees did Zoom yoga every morning. Even the staff member in a wheelchair was forced to join in. But most of all, he didn't understand why such an inherently social animal, one that relied on cooperation to survive and thrive, would willingly cut off ties with their 'pack'. When it came to the antisocial crank awards, Poe was always in contention, but even in his darkest days, he had never envisaged rejecting *all* forms of human interaction.

But he was WFH now, as Bradshaw insisted on calling it, because, with no new leads to follow, Mathers had sent them home. She didn't want them distracted by the day-to-day minutiae of a large-scale murder investigation; she wanted them doing what they'd been brought in to do. She wanted Bradshaw working on Ezekiel Puck's profile. She wanted Poe thinking about what Puck's next move might be.

Poe hadn't protested. And he had to admit that Highwood, with its expansive grounds and its game larder, wasn't a bad place to be when you were confined to barracks. And Highwood *was* conducive to thinking. To letting air into his mind. Poe felt he needed that. He needed to contribute. Other than having an untested theory about Ezekiel Puck's motive, he hadn't felt particularly useful. Bradshaw had made the big breakthrough, not him. So far, his input had been minimal, almost inconsequential. And although he knew that feelings of worthlessness were a symptom of PTSD, it didn't make them any less real. He spent the first few days walking the grounds with Edgar. He would check in with Bradshaw first thing in the morning, collect the sandwiches and flask of tea that Brunton made for him, then he and his over-excited spaniel would set off. By the time he returned, hungry, thirsty and exhausted, there was barely enough time to call Flynn for an update before he was called down for his evening meal. He, Bradshaw and Doyle would spend the rest of the night yakking away into the small hours.

That evening, while they were polishing off a chippy tea (vegan patty for Bradshaw, fish and chips for everyone else, extra battered black pudding for Poe), Doyle said, 'When are you planning to see Doctor Lang, Poe?'

Poe shrugged. 'They won't let me in. I got the impression she'd caused a disturbance. A bad one.'

'That was a week ago,' Doyle said. 'She'll be stable now. Why don't you go and see her this week? It'll do you both good. You're part of each other's therapy.'

'I'll come with you if you want, Poe,' Bradshaw said. 'I think Doctor Clara Lang will have a unique insight into Ezekiel Puck. It will be helpful for my profile.'

'I'll call the hospital first thing tomorrow.'

Bradshaw's phone rang. She tilted the screen so Poe could see. It was Flynn. Bradshaw put their boss on speakerphone.

'This is Tilly Bradshaw,' Bradshaw said. 'I am not alone. I repeat, I am *not* alone.'

'Yes, very good, Tilly,' Flynn replied. 'Is Poe with you?'

'I am, boss.'

'Good. Get yourselves in front of a TV,' she said. 'There's something you both need to see.'

Chapter 64

The something they needed to see was a Metropolitan Police press conference.

It was due to start at 9 p.m. Poe checked his watch. It was coming up to nine now. Mathers had told Flynn the press conference was happening, and Flynn had told Poe. Mathers had given Flynn enough time for them to find a TV but not enough time for them to interfere. Poe knew this was true because it wasn't a hastily assembled press conference, one put together to break urgent news. This press conference looked slick, as though it had been managed by a high-end PR agency. It had been planned, probably for a couple of days. It had a strategy.

Flynn said Mathers wasn't returning her calls. Hadn't for a while now. Flynn was giving her the benefit of the doubt. She said Mathers was running the biggest, longest-running murder investigation the country had ever seen – bigger even than the Yorkshire Ripper – and there would be times when she simply wasn't available. Poe thought Flynn was being generous. Even in the heat of the Botanist case, Mathers was always available. If she wasn't returning Flynn's calls it was because she didn't want to return them.

Poe didn't like that. He didn't like that one bit.

All the major channels had broken away from their regular schedule to show the press conference live. The BBC, ITV, Channels 4 and 5, Sky News. The desk had a forest of microphones in front of it, each with a gaudy station or newspaper logo strapped to the handle. Doyle had turned her TV to the BBC, but the press conference was broadcast like the Queen's funeral had been – it was on every channel. A rolling banner across the bottom of the screen said, MAJOR BREAKTHROUGH IN SNIPER CASE. The BBC had a split screen. The left side showed an empty desk with the Metropolitan Police backdrop behind it. Jugs of water and three empty glasses. A large LED presentation screen to the side of the desk had the same logo as the backdrop. It was bouncing around the screen like it was trapped. Very nineties. The right side was a succession of talking heads. Puffed-up wannabes, short on facts, big on conjecture. None of them knew what the major breakthrough was, though all claimed to be inside the loop. Poe wasn't inside the loop, not any more, but he knew *exactly* what the press conference was about.

Flynn called back. Bradshaw put her on speakerphone again.

'What the hell is she doing, boss?' Poe said. 'We still have things in play and she's going to out Ezekiel Puck to the whole country.'

'It won't have been her decision, Poe,' Flynn said. 'I know the commissioner and he's the biggest arse-coverer I've ever met. And you and I both know the family of the next victim are going to be screaming that their loved one would still be alive if the police hadn't sat on the E-FIT. He'll already be rehearsing his answers for the public inquiry. From his perspective, going public is the safe decision.'

'It's also the *wrong* decision.'

'It is, but Mathers also works in a command-and-control organisation. The decision will have been taken above her head.'

The clock on the top left of the screen flipped from 20:59 to 21:00. Bang on time, three people trooped in – the arse-covering Metropolitan Police commissioner, Mathers and a woman Poe didn't recognise – their expressions like tombstones. The commissioner took a seat on the end and immediately swallowed a burp. Mathers sat in the middle. *The business seat*, Poe thought. The woman Poe didn't recognise took the seat on the left of the screen. She had the carefully cultivated look of a public relations expert. The Met employed an army of them. Any organisation that gave the power of arrest to as many sex offenders, racists and ne'er-do-wells as the Metropolitan Police seemed to needed spin doctors on call 24/7.

The PR expert kicked things off by introducing the Metropolitan Police commissioner. She sat back, her inflated salary earned.

'Ladies and gentlemen,' he said. 'In a minute I'll hand the press conference over to Commander Mathers, who has a major breakthrough to announce. She'll explain what it is, how we came about it, and the support we'd like from the press in getting the message out. But first I'd like to . . .'

Poe zoned out as the commissioner spouted a bunch of adverb-heavy, communication-friendly platitudes. 'Working tirelessly around the clock' featured. So did 'incredibly demanding circumstances'.

After the commissioner had done his best to convey his command credentials, while simultaneously distancing himself from all operational decisions, he handed over the baton. Mathers picked it up.

'Thank you, sir,' she said.

Poe thought he detected a trace of sarcasm, but maybe that was wishful thinking on his part. Mathers nodded at the PR woman who pressed a clicker. The presentation screen changed from the Met logo to a series of faces.

'On your screens are E-FITs of the man we believe to be the sniper,' Mathers said.

Poe had seen the E-FITs a few days earlier. Mathers's guys had got two from Ezekiel Puck's neighbours in Yorkshire and one from his ex-wife in Gretna. They were remarkably similar, although, like all E-FITs, they looked like a cross between Herman Munster and the twins from the Proclaimers.

'The name this man is currently using is Ezekiel Puck,' Mathers continued.

She went on to say how the breakthrough had been made – which was heavy on Met investigative work, light on Bradshaw's data-driven twenty-sided dice theory – and the actions they'd taken because of it. She urged the public to remain vigilant before stressing the importance of not approaching Ezekiel Puck. Poe didn't think it was necessary to warn the public not to approach a man who'd killed nineteen people, but whatever. The public could be as dumb as a box of doorknobs sometimes. It was why bottles of bleach still had DO NOT DRINK warnings in big red letters and why hotel-room hairdryers all had DO NOT USE IN SHOWER labels.

The MAJOR BREAKTHROUGH IN SNIPER CASE rolling banner across the bottom of the screen was replaced by the hotline number.

They then went to questions. There were lots.

The commissioner didn't answer a single one.

One hundred and eighty miles away from the press conference, in a bedsit in Merthyr Tydfil, Ezekiel Puck turned off his television.

He said one word: 'Bastard.'

Chapter 65

Doyle switched off the television. For a moment the only sound was Edgar panting. Poe reached down and fondled his ears. Edgar whined in pleasure. His tail drummed the stone floor in Highwood's master kitchen.

'This is a whole new ball game,' Poe said eventually. 'I really don't know how Puck will react.'

'He won't stop, Poe,' Bradshaw said. 'My profile, as rudimentary as it is given there is no comparable data, suggests he will keep going until he's achieved his goal.'

'He will react, though,' Poe said.

'Just a minute, Tilly, I have Commander Mathers on the other line,' Flynn said over the speakerphone, her voice tinny and distant.

Poe rolled his eyes. '*Now* she's contactable,' he said.

'I'll see if I can change it to a conference call,' Flynn said.

'Let me know if you need a hand,' Poe said.

Flynn cut the call.

Bradshaw snorted. 'As if you could arrange a conference call, Poe. I asked you to mute your phone last week and you ended up sending a voicemail to my dad. It was just a load of tommyrot about why things had to be so eff-word complicated and how your eff-word pager didn't need an eff-word mute button. Even *I* don't know how you managed to do that.'

'Maybe you can Ask Jeeves.'

Bradshaw gave him a look. She shook her head and said,

'"Ask Jeeves"? Wowsers trousers, Poe. Do you still use puddles as mirrors? Ask Jeeves had the worst search engine technology in the history of the world. No wonder Google destroyed it.'

Poe grinned and winked at Doyle. 'And what is—'

Flynn called again. Bradshaw pressed accept. Mathers's voice filled the room, just as tinny and distant as Flynn's had been, but hers had an edge. Poe recognised it as the pressures of being forced into a mistake.

'First of all, I'm not apologising,' she said. 'While sitting on Ezekiel Puck's name and his E-FIT might have been the smart tactical move, it was not a *defensible* move. The public had a right to know.'

'Was this your decision or the commissioner's, ma'am?'

'It was mine.'

'You're a fibber, Commander Mathers,' Bradshaw said. 'There was a micro-pause before you answered. Poe might not have noticed, but I—'

'I noticed,' Poe said. 'It was almost long enough for you to cross your fingers.'

'Fuck you, Poe!' Mathers snapped. 'And fuck you too, Tilly! I brought in SCAS to advise. Consider me advised.'

The phone went dead.

Flynn called back immediately. 'That went well,' she said. 'And don't worry about Commander Mathers shouting, Tilly. She's under an incredible amount of stress.'

'I wasn't going to. I only worry when you and Poe shout at me.'

'We never shout at you, Tilly.'

'You shouted at me yesterday, DCI Flynn.'

'That was because you asked me if I was perimenopausal again.'

'And I still think you—'

'Is that us off the case?' Poe cut in, anxious to avoid yet another

Bradshaw/Flynn stand-off. 'Because I've only just stopped smelling of fish.'

No one replied. Doyle sniggered.

'Piss off,' Poe said. 'I do *not* still smell of fish.'

'You do a little bit, Poe,' Bradshaw said.

'I can smell you over the phone, mate,' Flynn said.

Poe scowled. 'Regardless, are we going to keep working this or not?'

'We work for the NCA, not the Met,' Flynn said. 'Until our director orders us off the case, we'll keep working it. We'll just keep it to ourselves for now.'

Poe thought it through.

'Poe?'

'Why did Mathers call?' he asked.

'Because she wanted to explain why she went public with the E-FIT.'

'Bullshit,' Poe said. 'Mathers is a commander in the biggest police force in the country. She doesn't owe us an explanation and we have no right to expect one. As she said, we're there in an advisory role only.'

'Then why *did* she call?'

'Five quid gets you six it was to wind us up. Make sure we stayed on task. She's committed to a play she doesn't like, probably been told to cut us loose. But she's not an idiot. She knows how stubborn we are—'

'Speak for yourself.'

'She wants us working Ezekiel Puck, but she doesn't want us reporting back to her. That was why she was so rude. Someone must be monitoring her emails and phone calls. Making sure she toes the party line.'

And once more Poe thought, *Tilly and I have a plan* . . . And it didn't involve toeing the party line, that was for sure.

Flynn didn't immediately respond. 'I think you're right, Poe,' she said eventually. 'She *was* unusually rude.' She paused again. 'OK, we've understood the subtext – now what do we do?'

'What we always do.'

'Fuck around and find out?'

'It's worked so far.'

'OK, so we know what *we're* going to do. Tilly hits the data. We hit the witnesses no one has thought of hitting. The usual stuff. The big question is, what will Ezekiel Puck do?'

'I think he'll do two things, boss.'

'Which are?'

'First, he'll change his appearance. Tinted lenses, cheek implants, that kind of thing. You can make yourself taller, heavier or older, but not the other way round. So, while the description and the E-FITs said to be on the lookout for a tall, thin man in his fifties, I think we need to be looking for someone two-stone heavier and twenty years older. He's already standout tall but he might walk with a stoop now.'

'OK, Tilly, can you work up some alternative E-FITs?'

'I've already started, DCI Flynn.'

'What's the second thing he'll do, Poe?'

'He'll react to Mathers releasing the E-FITs,' Poe said.

'Are you sure?'

'I'm certain. His ego won't allow him to do anything else.'

Which was strange, because for seven days Puck *didn't* react. But then he did.

And everything changed.

Chapter 66

Poe had gone to bed late. He and Bradshaw had spent the day in Gretna Green talking to Joanne Addy, Ezekiel Puck's ex-wife. When they'd arrived, the armed cops protecting her made themselves scarce. Almost as if they'd been expecting them. Poe was relieved. He liked Mathers and was disappointed by her earlier outburst. Now he understood it was the only way she could keep them involved, he liked her even more. She wasn't just a good cop, she was a *clever* cop. Poe didn't get anything new from Joanne Addy, although Bradshaw said it added depth to her emerging profile. By the time they got back to Highwood, it was past midnight. Not even Doyle and Edgar were waiting up for them. He said goodnight to Bradshaw then went straight to bed. He was asleep within three minutes.

An hour later, the grating sound of 'I'm Too Sexy' by Right Said Fred filled the bedroom. Poe reached for his phone, silently cursing Bradshaw and the new ringtone she'd given him. Every time he did something she disapproved of – which could be anything from eating sausage rolls to telling elected officials to piss off – she changed his ringtone to something he'd hate. She also did something with the phone settings so he couldn't change it. He suspected Right Said Fred was her way of letting him know that she'd found out he'd had *two* pie lunches the day he'd collected Uncle Bertie.

He stared at the screen, blurry-eyed. It was Flynn. And it was half past one in the morning. This wasn't going to be good news.

He pressed accept and said, 'Boss?'

'Good news, Poe,' she said.

'I knew it would be.'

'How quickly can you and Tilly get to London?'

Poe did some mental calculations. He'd been awake for twenty hours. Bradshaw, who admittedly didn't need more than four hours a night, had been awake even longer. Getting in his car and driving for five hours wasn't a sensible thing to do.

'Five hours,' he said.

'You sure?'

'Maybe a bit longer, I'm still in my underpants. And Tilly probably has to unplug herself from her mainframe or something.'

'I meant are you sure you don't need some sleep?'

'We'll share the driving. What have you got?'

'I've just got off the phone with Mathers.'

'Don't tell me, she's convinced the commissioner that we need to be officially involved again?'

'Better than that,' Flynn said. 'They've got the bastard.'

Chapter 67

Five hours later

The roof of 100 Bishopsgate, City of London

Poe thought 'They've got the bastard' was a *bit* of an overstatement. What Mathers had was an anonymous tip. Although, as far as anonymous tips went, it was a good one. Someone who didn't want to get involved – and really, who could blame them? – had called the hotline saying they'd seen a man matching Ezekiel Puck's description accessing the service lift in 70 St Mary Axe, a 90-metre-high office building in the City of London. Due to its ridiculous shape – oval with flat sides – 70 St Mary Axe was informally known as the Can of Ham. It was a custard pie's throw away from two other food-related architectural pisstakes – the Gherkin and the Cheese Grater.

The anonymous tip had been the forty-third that day, but something made the cop who'd answered the phone take it seriously. Before he'd hung up, the caller claimed to have been a portrait artist. He'd said he'd studied faces for years and he was as sure as he could be that the man he'd seen getting into the service lift was the same man the police were searching for. The cop had gone down to the Can of Ham himself and accessed the security footage.

He'd then called Mathers and said, 'It's Puck.'

Poe and Bradshaw joined Mathers on the roof of the surveillance building, Building 1, 100 Bishopsgate. It was a forty-storey tower, twice as high as the Can of Ham. The cops on the roof, and Poe counted fifteen, could see down on to the roof of the Can of Ham, but, as long as they didn't stick their head over the edge, they would remain invisible to anyone looking up. It was a good choice.

It wasn't yet seven in the morning, but the sun was already beating down. Gulls circled lazily overhead, screeching like mating cats. Despite being so high up, the air was morgue still. Poe loosened his collar.

Bradshaw fanned her face with her hands. 'I should have put on some factor thirty,' she said.

Mathers had her eyes glued to a pair of surveillance binoculars. Flynn was standing beside her. They were both damp with sweat. The kind of damp that turned into a rash. When Flynn saw them, she tapped Mathers on the arm. Mathers handed Flynn her binoculars and headed their way.

'Sorry about the outburst last week,' she said when she reached them. 'I needed to buy you guys some space.'

'We figured as much, ma'am,' Poe said. 'Although I gather you didn't need us in the end.'

'We got lucky,' she said. 'Any other member of the public and the call would have been logged to chase up later and we might have missed the bastard.'

'It's definitely him?'

'The E-FIT is uncanny, but we checked with his ex-wife and with his neighbours in Ripon. They confirmed it.'

'Someone's sitting on them?'

Mathers nodded. 'They won't be able to contact him.'

Poe glanced over the roof, took in the street view almost 200 metres below him. The gaps between the City of London's sky towers had wide walkways and places to sit and eat. There were food trucks and coffee carts. Trees and flowerbeds. But it wasn't quite Richard Curtis's London. The air still reeked of exhaust

246

fumes and the sound of jackhammers was pervasive. A defecating tramp was being arrested by the City of London cops. Poe wondered if it had even registered with the people down there. An army of them were ignoring everyone and everything as they hurried to work. Others were sitting down to enjoy a coffee and a breakfast muffin, oblivious, or choosing to be oblivious, to the bare-arsed tramp being frogmarched away. And for some reason they weren't bothered about the sniper. It was as if the City of London wasn't involved in the lives of the little people. They were there to make money and a serial sniper wasn't going to stop them having their morning latte. A triumph of capitalism over common sense.

Poe cast his eyes over the men and women eating and drinking below him. The people emptying bins and sweeping pavements. The high-rise window cleaners on their aerial platforms. If any of them were undercover cops, they were good. They'd have to be – Ezekiel Puck would be surveillance aware. He'd know what to look out for. 'You're sure he's coming back?' he asked Mathers.

'Oh, I *know* he's coming back.' She led them through the service hatch and into a room on the top floor of Building 1. The table was packed with laptops and tablets and high-grade communication systems. She opened one of the laptops. She pressed play and said, 'Watch this.'

The screen showed the Can of Ham from above. Poe glanced at Mathers.

'CCTV from this very building,' she said. 'And because anyone who successfully blows up a City of London skyscraper officially wins best terrorist at the terrorism awards – the IRA are the current title holders after their successful bombing of Bishopsgate in 1993 – now CCTV quality has to meet a certain standard. It's why it's so clear.' She touched the trackpad and zoomed in on the Can of Ham's roof. She pointed at two rectangular patches and pressed pause. 'The two-storey plant room is underneath the arch. It houses the cooling towers, air-handling units and two generators. But because the generators have to stay cool, the area above them is open to the elements. The two patches that cover them are made of perforated mesh, but they're coloured to look like glass. That way, when you look at the building from a distance, the entire roof will appear to reflect light.' She pressed play. 'Now watch this.'

Poe did. He watched the nearest mesh hatch open.

He watched a man climb out and lie down on the roof.

He watched that man take something from his jacket pocket and raise it to his eye.

Mathers pressed pause and zoomed in again. The picture did lose a bit of sharpness but the something the man had taken from his pocket was unmistakable.

It was the sight from a sniper's rifle.

Mathers was right. They had got the bastard.

Chapter 68

'He's scoping out his next target,' Poe said. He leaned into the screen. 'And from up there, he has a three-sixty field of fire. He'll literally have thousands of targets to choose from.'

Mathers nodded. 'Given he had a trail camera watching his range in Scotland, we haven't been up there, but I'm not concerned. We've grilled the architects and the maintenance crews, and once he's in the plant room, we can lock him up there.'

'What if someone else goes in? Routine maintenance or something?'

'We have experienced cops on the twenty-first floor and a standing instruction that the plant room isn't to be accessed by anyone. That way, no matter how he's disguised himself, once the plant room is opened, we'll know it's him. Once he's inside, my guys lock the door behind him. He'll be stuck up there.'

'Like a rat in a trap.'

'And the moment he opens the mesh hatch is the moment he gets his one and only warning. Drop his weapon or one of my snipers drops him.'

'How will you get the warning to him?' Poe asked. 'He won't hear you from the ground.'

'As soon as he's in the plant room, we'll send up a loudspeaker drone. It'll be waiting for him when he reaches the roof.'

Poe nodded. Loudspeaker drones had been trialled by Devon & Cornwall Police. They'd been found to be particularly useful in missing persons cases and in communicating with crowds at large-scale events.

'Happy?' Mathers asked.

'As Prince Andrew at a sweet sixteen.'

'Poe, are you *happy*?'

'I'm never happy, ma'am,' he replied. 'But I can't see anything I'd have done differently.' He paused a moment. 'The question is, are *you* happy?'

'I think I've thought of everything,' she said, 'which usually means I've missed something important.'

'Well, like I said, I wouldn't have done anything different.' He paused a beat. 'You know you'll have to give the order? He won't put his weapon down.'

'That's the prevailing view.'

'And are you ready?'

Her eyes turned to steel. 'You'd better believe it, Poe. He gets one warning. After that I put the fucker down.'

Poe didn't doubt it. He said, 'Good.'

But even as he said it, he knew something wasn't right. He didn't know what, but it didn't *feel* 'good'. He had said locking Ezekiel Puck in the Can of Ham's plant room was akin to a rat trap. There was only one way in and one way out. And Ezekiel Puck was a planner. He was an ex-MI5 field agent. So, why had he chosen the roof of a building with no escape route? Why put himself at risk? Everything had been risk free so far. The more he thought about it, his rat trap analogy was the only 'good' thing about this operation.

He left the operations room and rejoined Flynn on the roof.

'Everything OK?' she said.

He shrugged and said nothing. He was probably wrong.

Chapter 69

'I've known you long enough to know when something's bothering you, Poe,' Flynn said. 'Now isn't the time to develop the
subtle art of silence. If you know something, say something.'

'What? You're auditioning for the British Transport Police
now?' Poe said. 'See it. Say it. Sorted.'

Flynn didn't respond.

'Fine,' he said. 'Ezekiel Puck is a careful man, yes?'

'Agreed.'

'Mathers has photos of him entering the building.'

'She does.'

'And what's he wearing?'

'A hat and glasses.'

'No, he's wearing a disguise,' Poe said. 'Up until then we only
had an E-FIT, so it didn't need to be elaborate.'

'OK.'

'Yet when he's caught on the plant-room CCTV – a part of
the building the public can't access – he *removes* his disguise.
Why?'

'It'll be hot up there, Poe,' she said.

'Wrong. According to Mathers, the plant room is designed to
be cool. It has to be, otherwise the generators will overheat. But
even if it was hot, why remove the glasses? The hat, yes. Lots of
body heat escapes through the top of the head—'

'That's a common misconception, Poe,' Bradshaw said. 'It
originated in the 1950s when military researchers exposed

volunteers to freezing temperatures. They concluded that between forty and forty-five per cent of body heat was lost through the head, but that was simply because it was the only part of the body left uncovered. The head only represents ten per cent of the body's surface area, so it can't lose almost half the body's heat.'

Poe and Flynn stared at Bradshaw.

'How do you know all this shit, Tilly?' Flynn said eventually.

'Poe enjoys being corrected.'

'Do I fu—'

'OK,' Flynn said, nipping him off. 'He removes his glasses and his hat, which I guess is kind of weird. Why?'

'I think Puck *wants* to be seen, but only at a time of his choosing. He wears his disguise in public areas, but when he's alone he intentionally allows his true likeness to get caught on CCTV.'

Flynn's brow furrowed as she thought it through.

'And the anonymous tip is bothering me,' Poe continued. 'The caller gave us exactly what was needed to bump it to the top of the list.'

'You have a theory?'

'No.'

'A suspicion?'

'No.'

'Do you have *anything* I can take to Mathers?'

'Just a general sense of unease,' Poe said.

Flynn said nothing for almost a minute. 'Great!' she snapped. 'Now *I* have a general sense of unease.'

'You can't take it to Mathers anyway. She has snipers training their rifles on the roof of that stupid building. She has undercover cops on the ground and more inside. She doesn't need a doubting Thomas getting inside her head.'

'Agreed,' Flynn said. 'So, what *can* we do?'

'Nothing,' Poe said. 'Mathers is committed to this play now, and that means we have to see it out with her.' He took a breather then added, 'But, we keep our eyes peeled. This bastard is up to something.'

Chapter 70

If Ezekiel Puck was up to something, it didn't seem to be in the heart of London's financial district. The only thing of note that happened during the first six hours was that a bird shat on Flynn's shoulder. A big green and white splat that splashed off her shoulder and into her hair.

'Fucking seagulls!' she snapped.

Bradshaw cleared her throat. 'Seagull is a colloquialism, DCI Flynn,' she said. 'There are over fifty species in the Laridae family and they don't all live exclusively by the sea.'

'Shitehawks then! Is that acceptable terminology, Tilly?'

'I would just say "gulls", DCI Flynn.'

Poe guffawed. After a beat, Flynn did too. Mathers wandered over to see what they were laughing about. Anything to relieve the tension on a high-stakes operation, Poe thought.

'The boss has just had some good luck, ma'am,' he explained.

Mathers looked up. 'They're a nuisance, aren't they?'

Poe had spent the last ten years living on Shap Fell. Any gull stupid enough to try its luck there would be gleefully met by goshawks, peregrine falcons, marsh harriers, even golden eagles. Gulls weren't pests on Shap Fell. They were snacks.

'They're noisy,' Mathers continued. 'They're aggressive. They damage roof tiles and they block drains and gas flues, even chimneys. They carry salmonella and tuberculosis, both of which can be fatal to humans. And, as DCI Flynn can now attest, they shit everywhere.'

Poe gave her a quizzical look. 'You seem to know a lot about sea . . . about gulls, ma'am.'

'I attended a lot of idiotic community panels when I was in uniform,' she explained. 'We've been given access to one of the executive bathrooms on the thirty-ninth floor, Steph; why don't you go and get yourself cleaned up?'

'Thank you, ma'am,' Flynn said gratefully. 'If I don't get it out of my hair now, it'll harden and be there until I get home.'

'You should leave it on,' Bradshaw said. 'You bleach your hair anyway, and gull excrement contains uric acid.'

'I do *not* dye my hair, Tilly,' Flynn said.

Poe, who had noticed some darker roots on Flynn's head even before he'd been assigned to the boat, said nothing.

'She *does* dye her hair, Poe,' Bradshaw said after Flynn had stomped off the roof to the executive bathroom. 'She has an Amazon subscription for it.'

'How the hell do you know what's in the boss's Amazon basket?'

'Oh, *pur-lease*. Amazon's network firewall is weaker than your one-one-one-one mobile phone password, and I like to make sure everyone I love is healthy. It's why I think she might be perimenopausal. She put a book in her basket last month. It's called *So You Think You're Perimenopausal?*'

'Do you know what's in *my* Amazon basket?'

'You don't have an Amazon account, Poe.'

'Still sticking it to the man, Poe?' Mathers said, smiling.

Poe shrugged. 'I never saw the point. They wouldn't deliver to Herdwick Croft, and Highwood has everything I need. It even has a game larder.'

'Which makes me gag every time Poe goes in it to see what's for his tea,' Bradshaw said.

Another gull pinwheeled overhead. It shrieked like it had stood on some Lego. Poe looked up. Mathers wasn't wrong; they were noisy bastards.

Poe said, 'I guess in this part of London, which is basically a glass city, the landlords of buildings like this get particularly vociferous about the council keeping gulls under control.'

He pointed at a skyscraper a couple of hundred yards away and the window-cleaning platform inching its way down from the roof. It was long and wide, big enough for workers and their equipment. Two guys in white overalls were cleaning windows. One of them was seated, his back pushed against the safety barrier. The other guy was standing, operating the controls. Poe wondered if they'd go all the way down then work their way up, or whether they had predetermined windows to clean. Or maybe they just went to the ones the gulls had been using as faecal targets that day.

'One man's shite is another man's treasure,' he said. 'Cleaning the windows on that monstrosity must be like painting the Golden Gate Bridge – a never-ending job. Big money, I bet.'

Mathers shielded her eyes. The skyscraper had so much glass it was worse than staring at the sun. Poe wondered if it was one of those buildings that acted like a giant refractor lens, melting cars and blinding cabbies.

'That's 22 Bishopsgate,' Mathers said. 'It's the second tallest building in the UK.'

'You say that like it's a good thing,' Poe said.

They watched as the platform stopped. Which answered Poe's unasked question about whether or not they started at the bottom. The guy holding the controls had stopped the platform only a few storeys from the roof. He put the control pad in its holster and started unpacking his equipment. The guy sitting down didn't move. Poe frowned. Not only did the guy not move, he also *hadn't* moved. Not since Poe had been watching. Not even an inch. It was almost like he wasn't real.

Like he was a prop.

Oh shit.

Poe realised this at the same time he saw the glint of a telescopic sight.

'Sniper!' he screamed. He threw himself in front of Bradshaw, pulled her down just as he heard the crack of the supersonic round.

But Bradshaw wasn't the target.

Commander Mathers was.

And Ezekiel Puck never missed.

The Second Light

Chapter 71

Two weeks later

Highgate Cemetery, north London

It was atmospheric carnage. The first summer storm of the year. Thunderclaps and sheet lightning. The graphite sky congested and bruised, the air charged and dangerous. Puffs of dust rising as the rain machinegunned the parched earth. Nature reminding humans of the fragility of their existence.

It was two weeks since Ezekiel Puck had lured Commander Mathers to the roof of 100 Bishopsgate. Two weeks since he had dressed a tailor's mannequin in white overalls to avoid suspicion as he lowered himself down the outside of the second tallest building in the UK until he had the perfect shot. Two weeks since he'd punched a fist-sized hole in the back of Mathers's head, dressing the roof of 100 Bishopsgate with bits of her skull and brain.

And two weeks since he had disappeared without a trace.

There had been no reason for the coroner to hold on to the body. Everyone knew what had killed Mathers. Everyone knew *who* had killed Mathers.

Poe hadn't attended the church service. He hadn't felt able to look her family in the eye. Mathers was a senior police officer in the Met, but she was also a wife and a mother. She'd left behind a husband and two young children. Flynn had found the courage, and so had Bradshaw, but he was racked with guilt. Flynn had told him he was being stupid. That she'd had the same doubts, the same sense of unease about Ezekiel Puck being caught on CCTV at the Can of Ham. She'd said that they'd been right to keep their doubts from Mathers. Doubt wasn't actionable intelligence, and Mathers had a complex operation to manage. Poe knew she was right, just as he knew the only person to blame was Ezekiel Puck, but it still consumed him. He'd tried to book an appointment to talk it through with Clara Lang, but her doctors said she was still unavailable. He'd hung up in the middle of their mealy-mouthed excuses.

So, Poe stood alone by the empty grave – a hand-dug trench, the rain turning the earth at the bottom into a thick black paste – and waited for the committal to start, his clothes and hair unable to get any wetter. Water dripped from his nose. He made no move to wipe it away. He knew he was being watched. Highgate was the most secure cemetery in the world right now. There were cops everywhere. Poe didn't know if it had been chosen because the heavily wooded grounds made it a sniper's nightmare, or whether this had always been intended to be Mathers's final resting place. But he knew that *everyone* in Highgate Cemetery was being watched. Not that there was anyone around. Ezekiel Puck had ended public displays of grief, the same way COVID had ended low interest rates.

Poe stared at the grave spoils until his eyes blurred, a loop in his head replaying everything that had happened on that rooftop. Decisions made; decisions *not* made. There would be an investigation, of course. The Independent Office for Police Conduct would pull apart Mathers's operation like they were shredding crispy aromatic duck. Poe would be called on to give evidence. They'd all be called on to give evidence. And those blessed with twenty-twenty hindsight would conclude that Mathers had made a mistake. That she'd been too hasty in believing the evidence of her own eyes. That she should have questioned it more vigorously. And Poe knew that everyone on the panel would privately be thinking the same thing – that Ezekiel Puck had outmanoeuvred them at every turn and, if they'd been in Mathers's shoes, they'd have been on that roof too.

Over the sound of the rain, Poe heard muted voices. He stepped away from the grave – that was for family and close friends – and waited for the committal party. People in black appeared out of the rain, spectral, like something out of a Stephen King movie. They gathered around the grave, taking shelter under the trees, making sure to leave room for the family, who would follow the coffin.

Bradshaw arrived; her usual attire of cargo pants and a Marvel T-shirt replaced with a black pant suit and a crisp white shirt. He wondered where she'd bought it. Then he wondered if this was her first funeral. He thought it probably was. She joined him, her face streaked with tears. She leaned in and rested her head on his shoulder. Poe put his arm around her.

Flynn stood next to them, her face stoic, her eyes full of rage. Of helplessness.

They waited in silence. The coffin bearers would be taking their time, careful not to slip on the treacherous mud.

The vicar arrived first. He held a bible in his right hand and an umbrella in his left. Behind him, six uniformed police officers bore the polished oak coffin. It was a simple and neat design. Sarcophagus shaped with brass fittings. The family followed the bearer party. Mathers's husband, holding the hands of his two children. Brothers and sisters. Nephews and nieces. Uncles and aunts. Supporting each other the way families do during this part of the service.

The final part.

And there, right at the back, was someone Poe *hadn't* expected to see. Alastor Locke. The tall man was openly weeping. His back was bent. He seemed to have aged twenty years in the weeks since Poe had seen him in Yorkshire. He caught Poe's eye and nodded. Poe returned it but kept his face neutral.

The vicar came to a halt. As soon as the bearer party had lowered the coffin on to the putlogs, the wooden posts that spanned the grave, he began the committal service.

'I am the resurrection . . .'

Poe concentrated on the words. He wanted them to mean something.

Chapter 72

'So, now you know,' Locke said.

'Commander Mathers was your daughter?' Poe asked.

'In-law.'

'I'm sorry for your loss. Truly. I liked her. She was a good cop. A clever cop. But more than that, she was a good person.'

'Thank you, Poe. She was.'

They stood in silence, waiting for the funeral party to disperse. Locke shared a glance with Mathers's husband, his son. It looked as though he was about to walk over but Locke shook his head and stopped him.

'Your daughters need you more than you need your father, Tom,' he said. 'I'll be along presently, but first I need to talk to Sergeant Poe.'

Poe untangled himself from Bradshaw's grip.

'Give me a few minutes, Tilly,' he said.

Bradshaw nodded and joined Flynn on the path.

'Walk with me,' Locke said.

'Did you know Charles Dickens's parents are buried here?' Locke said.

'I did actually.'

'The popstar George Michael is here somewhere too.'

'I'm more into punk, Alastor,' Poe said.

'Yes, yes you are.'

The rain had stopped. The ground steamed. Water dripped

from the trees. Birds chirped. As they walked the leafy, sinuous pathways, stopping to examine the occasional vine-covered head-stone, Locke gave him a potted history of the Victorian cemetery. He told Poe it was the final resting place for over 170,000 souls. That the great and the good, the rogues and the ne'er-do-wells, all shared the same 37-acre hillside that enjoyed sweeping views of the capital.

'I want to show you something,' Locke said. 'Arguably Highgate's most famous resident.'

He led them down a winding trail, the light dappled by the trees. His long strides meant Poe had to jog to keep up. Locke noticed and slowed enough for Poe to take in his surroundings. Poe thought it was a stunning graveyard. Tranquil, a slice of overgrown Gothic beauty, a secluded funerary landscape in the middle of one of the biggest urban jungles in the world. Old graves and contemporary graves. Elaborate tombs and sweeping mausoleums. Catacombs and vaults. There was even an Egyptian Avenue, built after the nineteenth-century boom in Egyptology. The steeply wooded hill was a place where architects' imagin-ations had run amok. He thought he might come back next time he was in London. Spend a day or two exploring the city of the dead. He'd take Bradshaw. She'd love telling him about all the scientists who were buried there. Poe knew you could buy maps – and if he'd been there on his own, he'd have needed one – but Locke seemed to know where he was going.

After a twenty-minute walk through the West Cemetery, Locke led them into the flatter, more manicured East Cemetery. They soon arrived at their destination.

'Here it is,' he said. 'Highgate's star attraction – the tomb of Karl Marx.'

Poe was impressed. He'd known Marx was interred at Highgate, of course, but he hadn't realised how big his tomb was. The Grade 1 listed monument was twelve-foot-tall; a pedestal topped with a Space Hopper-sized bronze bust of Marx's head and shoulders. Poe thought Marx looked a lot like Brian Blessed. He imagined they shared the same booming voice. Inscribed in gold letters in the granite were the words, WORKERS OF ALL LANDS UNITE, one of his best-known lines.

Locke stared at the tomb for a moment then shook his head. 'Did you know Alexander Litvinenko is buried at Highgate as well?'

'The Russian spy? The one Putin had poisoned?'

Locke nodded.

Poe said, 'I didn't.'

'He has a cut-off column to symbolise a life cut short.' He sighed. 'I don't know if it's because the Father of Communism is interred here, or if it's just somewhere quiet and out of the way, but in the sixties and seventies there were so many spies meeting at Karl Marx's grave, MI5 had a permanent detail observing it.'

'That's how you know it so well?'

'The Highgate detail was a rite of passage,' Locke said. 'Somewhere to test your mettle. The cemetery, particularly the West Cemetery, is unnerving enough as it is at night, but throw in some armed KGB assets and it was a genuinely scary task.'

'What do you want, Alastor?' Poe said.

'I am a man not without considerable influence,' he replied.

'You don't have to remind me of this; I still smell of fish.' Poe held up his scarred hands. 'And some of those dorsal fins cut through my gloves.'

Locke nodded. Point taken.

'Nonetheless, I will not wield the power of the state to avenge my daughter-in-law's death,' he said. He stopped staring at Karl Marx's tomb and turned to face Poe. He took a breath and added, 'But I *will* wield you.'

'I don't know how to beat him, Alastor,' Poe said.

'If not you, who?'

'I don't know how to beat him,' Poe repeated. 'Even Tilly is struggling with his profile.'

'Alice liked you, Poe. She said you were a forward-thinking dinosaur. I think it was a compliment.' He smiled. 'You reminded her of Sylvester Stallone's character in *The Demolition Man*.'

Poe had got so used to thinking of her as Mathers he'd almost forgotten her first name was Alice. 'I haven't seen it,' he said.

'Neither have I,' Locke said. He sighed and added, 'What a pair we make, Washington. Two analogues, trying their best to navigate an increasingly digital world.'

'I have Tilly to help me.'

'And I had Alice.'

'I don't know how to think like him,' Poe said. The fuel that burned in Ezekiel Puck's engine seemed to be a mixture of cruelty and sadism. Throw in some revenge and a sprinkling of spite and you had a psyche that was beyond Poe's understanding. Beyond his reach. He simply couldn't bend his mind that far. But then he thought, perhaps he didn't have to. Not when he knew someone equally as twisted and damaged. 'I don't know how to think like him, Alastor, but I know someone who might.'

'Oh?'

'But I will need some help.'

'What do you require of me, Sergeant Poe?'

'You can get me in to see Clara Lang.'

And Locke said, 'Consider it done.'

Chapter 73

The tomb of Karl Marx wasn't the only listed building Poe had had dealings with recently. The other one was Moulsford. The high-security psychiatric hospital near Harrogate that treated Doctor Clara Lang was Grade II listed. It hadn't been called a hospital when the Victorians had built it, of course. The era that practised corpse medicine (the skull of a young woman mixed with treacle was believed to cure epilepsy) and sent eight-year-olds up chimneys didn't shirk when it came to naming things. Back then it had been called the Moulsford Asylum for Criminal Lunatics.

It was an ivy-clad, red-brick building. A central block with two wings of three storeys on either side. It had a steeply pitched roof and ornate gables. Its landscaped grounds were extensive. There was even a lake. Lots of willow trees. Low-risk patients enjoyed the sun. Staff took cheeky cigarette breaks. Gardeners gardened and deliverymen delivered. The tranquillity reminded Poe of Highgate's West Cemetery. It was an echo of a different time. A peek into the past.

Poe had been trying to see Doctor Lang for weeks, but all his requests had been rebuffed. That was unusual. Moulsford usually bent over backwards to accommodate him. Poe was part of her treatment. *Shared experiences*. But the last couple of times he'd called, he'd been told it was impossible. That there'd been an incident. There were always incidents when it came to Clara Lang, but Moulsford was a high-security psychiatric hospital – incidents were the currency they dealt in.

Poe hadn't liked going above their heads. It felt like he'd been tattling. When Locke had called to give him the go-ahead, he'd told Poe there would be conditions. That was OK. Poe was used to conditions when it came to Clara Lang. She was Moulsford's most dangerous patient. She was one of the *country's* most dangerous patients. She was so dangerous an entire wing had been allocated to her care. Before that, it had been used as an administrative wing – now it had more security than Broadmoor.

It wasn't that Clara Lang was inherently bad. But there were two sides to her. One light, one dark. The light side – the *Clara Lang* side – was a professional trauma therapist. A quiet, studious woman. The kind of woman who'd step over insects. Who'd take in injured birds and cry when they died. The dark side – the *Bethany Bowman* side – was Clara's guardian angel. If you hurt Clara, if you threatened Clara, if you even looked at Clara the wrong way, you met Bethany. And you really didn't want to meet Bethany. Because Bethany did bad things. *Very* bad things. She had an extraordinary capacity for violence and was completely uninhibited when it came to finding things to use as weapons.

Dissociative identity disorder, they called it. Two or more personalities that routinely take control of an individual's behaviour. In layperson's terms, she had a split personality. Bethany and Clara. Poe had met both the previous year. Bethany had caused Poe's PTSD. Clara was treating it. It was complex.

Poe parked in his usual spot and made his way through security. He was asked to take a seat in the foyer. As he always did when he was waiting for Clara's doctors, Poe read the 'Reasons for Admission' poster from the nineteenth century. He had read it several times. Sometimes it made him laugh. Today he wasn't in the mood. Most of the reasons seemed to be excuses for men to get rid of their wives or disobedient daughters: Novel reading; Disagreeing with husband; Nymphomania; Imaginary female trouble. Others were unisex, but equally bonkers. Deranged masturbation, whatever that was. Probably the opposite of another reason for admission – *Suppressed* masturbation. Masturbation for thirty years seemed self-explanatory. Treatments included bloodletting and purging, lobotomy, leeching, static electricity and cold-water therapy.

In the twenty-first century, Moulsford practised things like psychotherapy and counselling. Cognitive and dialectical therapy. They prescribed modern medicines and they had the most up-to-date equipment. They even had a permanent collection of art created by the patients.

A security door opened. Doctor Gray, Clara Lang's consultant psychiatrist, stepped through. He didn't look angry at Locke's intervention. Poe was relieved. He wanted to keep coming here. The help was helping. They shook hands and exchanged pleasantries.

'I need to show you something, Sergeant Poe,' Doctor Gray said. 'It will put what I'm about to ask of you into . . . context.'

Chapter 74

Doctor Gray led Poe back through the security doors and into the business side of the hospital. They stopped at a new door; one Poe hadn't seen before. It had a passport control-style face scanner built into the wall. *Fancy.* Doctor Gray stared into it then invited Poe to do the same.

'This wing is now the most secure in the UK,' Doctor Gray said. 'No one gets in unless they have an appointment and their face is preloaded into the system.'

The door clicked open. Poe stepped into yet more security. Two uniformed guards – who definitely weren't there last time – beckoned him forward. He walked through a full-body scanner that could have graced a major European airport and stood in front of them. He raised his arms while one of the guards ran a wand over his body. The other completed a full search of his clothing. When he'd finished, he gestured to a tray on a table.

'Please put all your belongings in there, sir.'

Poe did as he was asked. He put his wallet, his car keys, some loose change, even his handkerchief into the tray.

'Boots and belt too,' the guard said. 'We'll provide paper shoes, but you'll need to hold up your trousers if you've been dieting.'

'Bit over the top, isn't it?' Poe said, bending down to untie his shoelaces.

'No,' Doctor Gray replied.

There's been an incident . . .

One of the guards produced a laptop. He handed it to Doctor Gray.

'We'll have to watch this here, I'm afraid,' Doctor Gray said. 'We can't take this on to Clara's wing. We can't take *anything* on to Clara's wing.'

'I remember,' Poe said.

'No, Sergeant Poe. You don't. Things are different now.' He opened the laptop, found the file he wanted and spun it round so Poe could see the screen. 'This is an association ward. As you can see, Clara is sitting quietly. She's reading an article on recent advances in trauma therapy. She's not talking to anyone and she's not causing any problems. Watch what happens.'

Bullying. That's what happened. Poe had an aversion to bullies. He always had. When your first name was Washington you attracted the attention of bullies like Meghan Markle attracted the attention of Piers Morgan. In this case, a woman the size of a small car approached Clara, said something to her then snatched her reading glasses from her head. She snapped them, threw them in Clara's lap, then walked off laughing.

'The patient who broke Clara's reading glasses is called Veronica,' Doctor Gray said.

'New?'

'Yes. And unfortunately, she's about to find out exactly who she picked on.'

Doctor Gray closed the video and opened a new one. Same camera. Clara again. Sitting in the same seat, the same association ward. It looked like she was wearing a new pair of glasses. The timestamp suggested it was a week later. Veronica approached Clara. She reached for her reading glasses. But this time she wasn't bullying Clara Lang. She was bullying Bethany Bowman. And Veronica saw something. Something she didn't like. She reared back as though Clara/Bethany was on fire.

But she wasn't quick enough. Nowhere near quick enough.

Bethany was on her in a flash.

She grabbed Veronica's head, twisted it, then bit down on her ear. Veronica screamed – silently as the CCTV footage was either muted or it didn't have sound – and tried to pull away. Bethany let her. The incident was over in five seconds.

Veronica staggered away, her hand clutching the side of her head. And that's when Poe saw the blood. Lots of blood.

Where her ear had been.

'I don't understand,' Poe said.

'What don't you understand, Sergeant Poe?'

'Bethany bit off her tormentor's ear.'

'She did.'

'But why the big fuss? Why all the extra security? Violent encounters in Moulsford, if not a daily occurrence, can't be so rare that you need to change all your protocols. All I've seen here is a bully picking on the wrong victim. I suspect she'll be more circumspect next time.'

'That's all you saw, is it, Sergeant Poe? I think we'd better watch it again.'

Doctor Gray pressed play. 'Don't focus on *why* the assault happened, focus on *what* happened.'

Poe leaned in and studied the attack again. It was brutal and premeditated and over quickly. Maybe *too* quickly. He frowned and asked Doctor Gray to rewind to the exact moment of the bite.

Poe was a veteran police officer. He was used to seeing bite injuries. They weren't restricted to dangerous dogs and unruly toddlers. Bites were common during street fights, a primitive response to chaotic and violent situations. The nose and ears were common targets. So were the neck and cheeks. Hands and arms all got bitten. But outside of Hollywood and Mike Tyson fights, you couldn't just bite off someone's nose, ear, finger or lip. The body wasn't designed that way. Body parts could be *torn* off, but the way Bethany had chomped on her victim's ear and come away with it in her mouth wasn't natural.

'What am I missing?' he said. 'How did she bite off Veronica's ear so cleanly?'

Doctor Gray opened a file and removed a photograph. He handed it to Poe.

'That's how,' he said.

Chapter 75

'Before she attacked Veronica, Bethany spent a week filing down her incisors with disposable nail files,' Doctor Gray said. 'She did this until they were razor thin.'

Poe stared at the photograph in horror. Tried to imagine the pain Bethany must have endured to turn her teeth into cutting weapons. The pain she must still be enduring. Most people had eight incisors. Four on the upper jaw, four on the lower; the teeth at the front of the mouth that people used to cut food as they bit into it. Bethany had filed hers until the ends were thinner than paper. No wonder she'd been able to bite off Veronica's ear so easily.

'What happened to the ear?' Poe asked.

'Bethany ate it.'

'She *ate* it?'

'Bethany isn't a cannibal, Sergeant Poe,' Doctor Gray said. 'She ate the ear so it couldn't be reattached. She told me later that Veronica wouldn't be bothering Clara for her reading glasses any more. That she couldn't wear glasses when she only had one ear.'

Poe looked at the photograph again. 'Jesus,' he muttered.

'Now do you understand why the Home Office was willing to fund all this additional security?' Doctor Gray said. 'Clara and Bethany have rights. We are not able to perform surgery without her consent.'

'She won't allow you to fix her teeth?'

'Absolutely not. And that means we are legally obliged to let her keep her weapons.'

'Which must make treating her problematic.'

'It does.'

'The additional security is to ensure she isn't given access to anything else she can improvise into a weapon?' Poe said.

'If she's willing to do this to her teeth, can you imagine what else she's capable of?'

Poe couldn't. He said as much.

'Now, before I let you in to see Clara, our legal department has drafted this waiver, a release of liability,' Doctor Gray said.

'Why?'

'When the logistics of managing this new, weaponised Bethany became apparent, the Home Office authorised special measures. Guards as well as medical staff. A unique, ultra-secure interview room. It was designed by an American who specialises in the no-human-contact wings on supermax prisons. We call it the Rubicon.'

'What's the problem with it?'

'I didn't say there *was* a problem.'

'Then why the liability waiver?'

Doctor Gray sighed. 'Because it hasn't been tested yet. Not with Bethany. We've run simulations and they have been incident free, but you'll be the first person to conduct a live interview. We've built in a sizeable margin for error, but still . . .' He picked up his liability waiver. 'I can't make you sign this, and I have no doubt that the man who forced our hand regarding your visit can force our hand regarding—'

'Give me your pen,' Poe said. Poe signed the form. Didn't even read it. 'Let me see her, please.'

'Follow me.'

A guard opened another security door, an air-gapped one this time, and led them to Clara's wing. She had one to herself. It reminded Poe of 'Lonely Man of Spandau', a punk song by the Angelic Upstarts. It was about Rudolf Hess and how, for twenty years, he was the only inmate of Spandau Prison in Berlin.

Doctor Gray stopped outside yet another security door. 'Shaun will now talk you through the Rubicon rules. Please pay attention. This isn't like pre-flight safety instructions; you need to understand them. He'll then take you in and make sure you're secure. Only then will Clara be brought in.'

Shaun the guard explained what the Rubicon was and how it would keep Poe safe. It wasn't a difficult concept. When Shaun had finished, Poe said, 'Can I see her now, please?'

Shaun nodded.

'Don't let your guard down, Sergeant Poe,' Doctor Gray said. 'Not even for a second. As Veronica can attest, Bethany's got pretty good at pretending to be Clara these days.'

'That's good,' Poe said. 'It's Bethany I want to see today.'

Shaun opened the door.

Poe stepped into the Rubicon.

'Blimey,' he said.

Chapter 76

The Rubicon was a box-shaped room, about the size of a squash court. It was named after a river in north-eastern Italy. The Rubicon was the river Julius Caesar crossed without disbanding his army. Generals were required to disband their armies before entering Italy, and Caesar deliberately choosing not to made armed conflict unavoidable. The resulting civil war led to Caesar becoming *dictator perpetuo*, dictator for life. Crossing the Rubicon was now an idiom for passing the point of no return.

A 1-metre-thick red line on the floor split the room in two. It ran from the doorway to the middle of the back wall. Straight as a pencil. DO NOT CROSS was stencilled in white all the way along it. That wasn't going to be an issue; Poe couldn't have crossed it, even if he'd wanted to.

And that's because he was tethered to his side of the room.

A wire rope was secured to the back of the leather jacket into which he'd been locked. The wire rope was attached to a steel bar that ran the length of the wall on the left. The steel bar looked like a ballet barre. The wire rope wasn't fixed in place. It was on a ring that moved along the steel bar the same way curtains move along a curtain pole. Poe was free to walk anywhere in his own half of the Rubicon, but he could not cross the red line. The wire rope wasn't long enough. Poe could choose to stand, or he could sit in the plastic chair provided. The other side of the Rubicon was the mirror image of Poe's, the only difference being that Bethany's chair was bolted to the floor.

Everything was a weapon.

Poe tested his restraints. They were solid. There was no way he could step into the other side of the room. He felt as if he was in a Hannibal Lecter movie. Bradshaw had made him watch *Red Dragon* when they started working together. She'd said it was about the hunt for a serial killer named the Tooth Fairy, and that he might find it useful. Poe hadn't. Real serial killers weren't that flamboyant.

Shaun the guard tugged on the wire rope again. When he was satisfied, he went into a well-rehearsed speech. 'Don't try to touch Miss Lang. If Miss Lang slides something across the floor, don't pick it up. If Miss Lang starts to spit, go to the back of the room and wait. If you have any doubts at all, raise your hand. We will be watching. Our response time is supposed to be eight seconds. We have it down to four.'

'I'll be fine,' Poe said. 'Clara and I go way back.'

Shaun the guard grunted but didn't respond.

'One more thing,' Poe said. 'No sound.'

'Excuse me?'

'What Clara and I are about to discuss is highly sensitive. No one can listen to what we talk about.'

'You're the boss,' Shaun said. He left the room. The door shut behind him.

After five minutes it opened again. Two guards walked in and stood either side of the door. Two more walked in and stood in front of Poe. They were wearing protective clothing; the kind prison officers wear when they have to extract combative inmates from barricaded cells. They also wore neck guards. Sensible when the patient had werewolf-like throat-ripping capabilities.

A minute later Doctor Clara Lang entered the Rubicon. She was escorted by four guards. They led her to the other side of the Rubicon. She took in the room in a single glance. She nodded in approval. It seemed she liked it. She was already wearing her leather jacket. She watched as they tethered her to her own wire rope. Just as they had with Poe, they tugged on it to make sure everything was secure.

Clara was a slight woman with long dark hair and a butter-wouldn't-melt expression. Pale with haunted eyes, as if she didn't sleep, and when she did, she didn't like what she saw. Poe knew the feeling well. He didn't like going to sleep either. She stood still until the guards had left the room.

The moment the door clanged shut, Bethany, because surely only Bethany could walk like that, began prowling her side of the DO NOT CROSS line like a caged tiger. She didn't make it obvious, but Poe could tell she was testing her restraints. Just as he had. She licked her lips. Her sharpened teeth sliced into her tongue. She wiped her mouth on the back of her hand and smiled at the blood.

'Hello, Sergeant Poe,' she said. 'It's been a while.'

Chapter 77

Poe didn't scare easily, and he desperately wanted Clara Lang to find the peace she deserved, but this was giving him the heebie-jeebies. The woman on the other side of the Rubicon was looking at him like he was food.

'Who am I speaking to?' he said. 'Clara or Bethany?'

'Clara doesn't live here any more,' Bethany said in a singsong voice.

Poe nodded. Good. He said, 'I gather you've been in the wars?'

Bethany grinned. 'My therapist says I've defiled myself.' She opened her mouth. Showed Poe her sharpened teeth. 'What do you think?'

'I think you need a different therapist.'

'That's what *I* said!' She leaned against her tether and stretched out an arm. Clenched her hand. 'Fist bump?'

Poe saw that Doctor Gray was right to be apprehensive about the Rubicon being untested. At full stretch, Bethany could reach halfway across the painted red line. If they'd miscalculated the length of his wire rope by even an inch, they'd be able to touch each other. He suspected they hadn't considered how much new wire rope could stretch. Poe knew this from his work at sea. Most of the boat's equipment was secured with wire rope. When a load was applied – for example, someone pulling it – the dimension became smaller causing the rope to become longer. It was known as constructional elongation, and it remained in place until the wire rope had been subjected to a load several times.

'I'm happy where I am, Bethany,' Poe said.

'It's usually Clara you want to see, Sergeant Poe. Yet, unless I've misjudged this, it's me you're pleased to see today.'

'It is.'

'May I ask why?'

'Do you consider yourself to be a bad person, Bethany?'

'You know I don't.'

'I *do* know,' Poe said. 'Yet you *have* done bad things.'

'For her.'

Poe nodded. It was true. Bethany had murdered three people, injured several more, but, in her mind at least, it had all been to protect Clara Lang.

'For her,' he agreed.

'What do you want, Sergeant Poe?'

'Your help.' Poe had found that the only way he could get through to Clara or Bethany was by being open and honest. They both saw through subterfuge. Clara because of her training as a trauma therapist; Bethany because of what she'd been through as a child. 'There's a killer outside and he's causing havoc. I can't get in his head. I know why he's doing it, but I don't know how to stop him.'

'And you think I might?'

'I do.'

'Why?'

'Because this man is pure spite.'

Bethany raised her eyebrows. 'You think I'm driven by spite, Sergeant Poe?'

'No. I think your parents were driven by spite. It's why I think you'll have a unique insight.'

'But I don't want to think about my parents.'

'And in ordinary times I wouldn't ask you to. But this man has killed twenty people and he isn't stopping any time soon. These are *not* ordinary times.'

'And if I help you?'

'What do you get?'

'Everything's transactional in a secure hospital, Sergeant Poe.'

'What do you want?'

'Nothing.' She smiled. Waited for him to ask the right question.

'OK, what does *Clara* want?'

'The hospital can't afford the academic books she needs to stay up to date. If she gets too far behind, she'll find it difficult to requalify when she gets out.'

'I'll see she gets everything she needs,' Poe said. 'I'll pay for it myself, including registration fees, lapsed or otherwise.'

'That isn't cheap, Sergeant Poe.'

'I'm marrying a very wealthy woman.'

'OK then,' Bethany said. 'Clara trusts you, so I will too. Tell me everything you know about this man.'

Poe did. It took two hours. And when he'd finished, Bethany asked just one question: 'Who would you run into a burning building for, Sergeant Poe?'

Poe didn't have an immediate answer. He wasn't even sure he'd understood the question. But after Bethany added context, he did.

And then he knew exactly what he had to do to catch Ezekiel Puck.

He had to do what others wouldn't.

He had to file down his teeth.

'Thank you, Bethany,' Poe said. Distracted, his mind on the calls he'd have to make the second he got his phone back. He stood, readied himself to leave.

'Oh, one more thing, Sergeant Poe,' Bethany said.

'What is it, Bethany?'

'I know you mean well, and I know that you genuinely care for Clara.'

'I do.'

Poe stared at the door. There was a commotion outside. Raised voices. Urgent.

'But, when the scores are tallied,' Bethany continued, 'Clara is incarcerated because of actions you took.'

'Is everything OK?' Poe shouted. He took a couple of steps forward.

'You know everything is accounted for on this wing, Sergeant Poe?' Doctor Gray shouted from the other side of the door. 'Down to the last plastic paperclip.'

'I do,' Poe said. 'What's the problem?'

Doctor Gray said, 'We've lost something,' at the exact moment Bethany lunged for Poe. A wild stab that with empty hands would have missed him by an inch. But her hands weren't empty.

'I think I've found it,' Poe said, looking at the fountain pen sticking out of the back of his hand.

Chapter 78

Later that day

Highwood, Northumberland

The Council of Highwood. That's what Bradshaw had named the meeting that Poe had called. He'd told her it was the only *The Lord of the Rings* reference she was allowed.

He had started thinking about what to do as soon as he was out of the Rubicon, even before Doctor Gray had dressed the pen wound Bethany Bowman had inflicted on him. It was superficial anyway. Lots of blood but not much tissue damage. It would leave a nice scar, but so what? He had lots of scars, what was one more?

He'd gone to Bettys Café Tea Rooms to collect his thoughts. Hadn't wanted to be too distracted on the drive back to Highwood. And over a plate of pan-fried Swiss rösti – grated potato, Gruyère cheese, cream, bacon and a poached egg – and a pot of tea, he'd formed an idea.

He called Locke first. Told the spook he needed to drop whatever it was he was doing and hightail it up to Northumberland. Locke didn't ask why, he simply called for his assistant. Asked him to arrange transport. Poe spoke to Flynn next. Told her what he was planning. She wasn't happy. He also called the Met's new senior investigating officer, Commander Charles Unsworth. Told him some of what he planned to do. Unsworth had wanted in on the meeting, but Poe had said it was a courtesy call only. He didn't want him in the meeting. The less he knew the better.

Doyle had said she'd make herself scarce, but Poe stopped her. 'This concerns everyone,' he said.

'Even me?'

'*Especially* you.'

'Wait until he tells you this whack-a-doodle plan of his, Estelle,' Flynn said when she arrived. 'You're going to love it.'

Locke had the furthest to travel. While they waited, Doyle said, 'How was Clara?'

'Auditioning for *The Spy Who Loved Me*,' Poe replied. 'Her teeth are now deadlier than that idiot Bond villain's, the one with the metal mouth.'

Doyle frowned. 'I think you'd better explain.'

Poe did.

When he'd finished, Doyle said, 'Oh, that poor girl.'

'Will she ever get better, Poe?' Bradshaw asked.

'I think so, Tilly,' Poe said. 'But she needs to feel safe first. Only then will her doctors be able to talk to both sides of her. And weirdly, filing her teeth into razors might work in her favour. It meant Moulsford was finally able to access the Home Office funding they needed to make her part of the hospital secure.'

They settled into a tea and biscuit-filled silence. After fifteen minutes, Flynn couldn't stand it any more. 'Exactly what did Clara fucking Lang tell you, Poe?' she snapped.

'She asked who I would run into a burning building for.'

Poe didn't get a chance to elaborate. The sound of a helicopter landing drowned out any further conversation.

Alastor Locke had arrived.

Chapter 79

Poe finished his briefing. The room stayed silent. After a minute, he said, 'Well, what do you think?'

'It's a lot to process, dear boy,' Locke said.

Flynn snorted. 'It's reckless, is what it is.' She turned to Locke, clearly sensing he might be an ally. 'Alastor, do *you* think we should try this . . . lunacy?'

'Any position I form will be coming *ab irato*, my dear.'

'That's Latin for motivated by anger rather than reason, DCI Flynn,' Bradshaw said. 'Alastor Locke doesn't think he can be objective because Ezekiel Puck killed his daughter-in-law.'

Locke smiled and nodded.

'Yes, thank you, Tilly!' Flynn snapped.

'You're very welcome.'

Flynn glared at her before saying, 'And don't call me "my dear", Alastor. I'm not your fucking pet.'

'My apologies, Stephanie.'

Flynn turned to Doyle. 'Surely you're not going to go along with this shitshow, Estelle?'

'I don't know what to think yet,' Doyle admitted. 'Like Mr Locke said, it's a lot to process.'

'Damned fool is making himself the target, Lady Doyle!' Uncle Bertie yelled from the back of the room. He had fallen asleep in a plush armchair and Poe had kind of forgotten he was there. They all had. 'It's a tiger hunt and Washington is volunteering to be the tethered goat.'

'Remind me why he's here, Poe,' Locke said.

'Insight,' Poe lied.

Bertie held up his glass. 'Lady Doyle has damned good whisky,' he said. He then went back to sleep.

'Bertie's kept bigger secrets than this,' Doyle said. She looked at her uncle. 'Plus, he's bloody sozzled. He won't remember a thing.'

'Estelle?' Flynn said. 'Can you please try to talk some sense into your idiotic fiancé?'

'I agree this is reckless, Steph. I wonder why you're so surprised, though. It's entirely within Poe's wheelhouse.'

Poe glanced at her. 'You just had to get a nautical reference in there, didn't you?'

Doyle winked.

'Why does it always have to be him, though?' Flynn said, unwilling to give up without a fight.

'Tilly, what are the odds of me being shot by Ezekiel Puck?'

'I don't know, Poe,' Bradshaw said. 'You can be very annoying.'

'A normal person then. What are the chances of a normal person being shot?'

'Sixty-nine million people live in the UK, and as Ezekiel Puck doesn't discriminate when it comes to who he kills, the odds are straightforward – barring extenuating circumstances, the odds are sixty-nine million to one.'

'And what might extenuating circumstances be? Would what I'm proposing increase those odds?'

Bradshaw bit her lip and nodded. 'If Bethany Bowman is correct, it would, Poe.'

'That's why it has to be me, boss,' he said to Flynn. He turned to Doyle. 'That said, just say the word and I won't do it.'

'And what will you be like to live with when the next person is killed? No, you must do this, Poe. To deny you would be to deny who you are.'

'It'll mean postponing the wedding,' Poe said.

'Uncle Bertie!' Doyle shouted.

Bertie woke with a start. 'What is it, Lady Doyle?'

'You willing to sample our wine cellar for a couple more weeks?'

He raised his glass. *'Per ardua ad astra.'*

'Through adversity to the stars,' Bradshaw said without looking up from her laptop.

'Doesn't anyone speak English any more?' Flynn muttered.

'Uncle Bertie is fine with postponing the wedding, Poe,' Doyle said.

'He isn't our only guest.'

'They'll be fine too. We're not in our twenties. We're inviting friends, not people we go to the pub with.'

'But . . .'

'Yes, you can still invite your friends from the pub.'

Poe took that as tacit permission. 'Right, let's get down to the logistics,' he said. 'I want to do this in six days and there are a lot of things to arrange.'

Locke took an ornate notebook from his inside pocket. 'Thank you, Washington,' he said.

'I'm not doing this for you, Alastor,' Poe said.

'I know. But thank you anyway.' He licked the end of his pencil. 'Now, shall we get down to brass tacks. Sergeant Poe says we're on a schedule.'

Chapter 80

Six days later

Poe used the same press briefing room as Mathers had. It seemed fitting. It was also large enough to accommodate the world's press. And it *was* the world's press. Locke had done his bit. News stations Poe had only heard about had their cameras and reporters there. Euronews, RT, Al Jazeera and NDTV jockeyed for position with the BBC, Sky News and CNN. They were all showing it live. The written press were seated at the back, pens poised, smartphones and dictaphones at the ready. They hadn't been told what they were there for, only that they wouldn't want to miss it.

This wasn't the first time Poe had been front of camera – the people SCAS hunted were always newsworthy, and the press corps was a hungry beast – but it *was* the largest briefing he'd ever been involved in, and it was the first one he'd fronted on his own. Bradshaw had wanted him to rehearse but he didn't want his anger diluted. He needed to get emotion across to the waiting millions. Getting the public onboard was going to be key.

The low, rumbling sound of a large crowd ceased the second Poe stepped on to the dais and sat down. He filled his water glass, took a drink.

'Welcome, everyone,' he said. He'd planned to start with 'Ladies and gentlemen', but Bradshaw had explained that 'Welcome everyone' was more inclusive. 'My name is Detective Sergeant Washington Poe and I work for the National Crime

Agency. Thank you for breaking into your scheduled programming. I will not keep you long.'

He took another drink. Bradshaw had told him it was a useful way of breaking up different blocks of information. That way the message didn't get jumbled. Say hello, introduce yourself, then have a drink. Tricks of the trade.

'Today I want to talk to you about a woman named Joanne Addy,' Poe said. This was a trick of his own. Don't lead with your chin. Keep them guessing until they were desperate to know where you were going. 'Now, Joanne had a dream. Since she was a girl, she's wanted to own a wedding business in Gretna Green. She's worked at a venue called the Smithy's Forge since she was legally allowed a Saturday job, and eight years ago, the opportunity arose to buy it. She took out a large bank loan and purchased it, and because she'd worked there for years, she had her own ideas about what she wanted to do differently. She therefore took out an additional loan, this time against her own home, to refurbish it. She'd realised her dream.' Another drink. No one in the press was fidgeting. They were all stuck on his narrative. 'Now, can anyone tell me what happened on the last day of 2019?'

'COVID,' the guy from Al Jazeera shouted.

'That's right,' Poe said. 'The last day of 2019 was when the World Health Organization was informed about a cluster of pneumonia cases in Wuhan City, China. Spin forward a few months. The UK is locked down. The wedding industry is heavily affected. No one is getting married. For a long time, no one was *allowed* to get married unless they could prove exceptional circumstances. But Joanne Addy didn't lay off her staff. She didn't tell them to find work at Tesco. She used what little government support was available, she kept her business afloat, and she topped up the wages of her furloughed staff. Joanne Addy is a good employer and a good woman.' Poe took his third drink.

'Oh, one more thing, Joanne Addy is the ex-wife of a man called *Raymond* Addy.' He paused a beat. 'And Raymond Addy is Ezekiel Puck. Our sniper.'

His fourth and penultimate drink. He took longer this time. Waited for the noise to abate.

'Raymond, because I think that's what we should call him from now on, didn't like that his wife had moved on without him. So, he did what rejected men have been doing since the dawn of time – he focused one hundred per cent of his energy into destroying her happiness. And Raymond figured that if he could destroy her business, he would destroy her. Now, a garden-variety psychopath might have burned down the Smithy's Forge. Or done something horrific like throwing acid in her face. Men can be inventively cruel when it comes to women who have rejected them. We should really change the saying to a *man* scorned, don't you think? Anyway, where was I? Oh yes, unfortunately, Raymond *isn't* a garden-variety psychopath. He's an *inventive* psychopath. So instead of doing something mundane like posting a load of mean reviews on Tripadvisor, he went on a murder spree that has so far claimed the lives of twenty people. He's doing this with only one objective – to decimate Gretna Green's wedding industry. He thinks if he can stop people from getting married there, the bank will foreclose on the Smithy's Forge. That his ex-wife will be made homeless; her lifelong dream crushed. Raymond believes that if he can engineer this, Joanne will eventually take her own life.' Poe took his final and longest drink. He refilled his glass anyway. 'I don't think we should let that happen, do you?'

He nodded towards the display screen at his side. It flickered into life.

'I think it's time we showed Raymond Addy that we can be inventive too. Now, I know some of you thought this briefing was about offering a substantial reward for information leading

293

to the blah-blah fucking blah.' He hadn't told anyone that he planned to swear. Until he did, he wasn't sure he would. But it had felt right. It conveyed what he was feeling. What he hoped others were *starting* to feel. 'It's not about a reward. This meeting is about launching the "Save the Smithy's Forge Fund".

'This is the home page for the PledgePower website. The details have been emailed to everyone here. PledgePower is a company my colleague Ti . . .' Poe stopped, aware he'd almost slipped up. 'PledgePower is a company set up by my colleague yesterday. It's a crowdfunding platform with only one client – Joanne Addy, who, by the way, is unaware we're doing this. She's under armed guard in an undisclosed location without access to a phone or a television.'

Poe picked up a clicker and pressed the button Bradshaw had told him to press. The screen changed.

'PledgePower complies with all current legislation. We are asking for three million pounds, and if we don't reach that within fourteen days, all monies will be returned. Donations can be made by texting the number on the screen, by visiting the website, or via the app that . . . my colleague has just uploaded to all major platforms. On the right of the screen is a live tally. As you can see, we are already at over one hundred thousand pounds.'

Poe left the screen on. The counter started spinning, too fast to see.

'Raymond Addy, I'm now talking directly to you,' Poe said, his voice colder than granite. 'Your plan has failed. Happy couples will be getting married at the Smithy's Forge for years to come. If the British public do what I know they're going to do, your ex-wife's dream remains alive and kicking.' Poe leaned away from the microphone. 'Fucking loser,' he muttered.

But he made sure he said it loud enough to be picked up. He stood, ignored the chorus of questions, and left the dais. As soon as he was out of shot, he smiled. It had gone as well as he'd hoped.

Joanne Addy was going to be rich.

And Ezekiel Puck was going to be furious.

Chapter 81

Bradshaw had worked her magic. She'd played about with SEO – an acronym that stood for Search Engine Optimisation, a fact that Poe immediately tried to forget – until PledgePower became the most viewed website in the UK. The media – who'd been leaned on by Alastor Locke – got stuck in. Dissenting voices were shut down. It kickstarted a national debate on toxic masculinity that ended up in the House of Commons. #SaveTheSmithysForge trended on the artist formerly known as Twitter.

And the money poured in. They passed the three-million-pound point, when all donations would have had to be returned, in a day. They reached fifteen million pounds within a week.

Fifteen million daggers in the heart of Ezekiel Puck.

Now he had a big fat red target on his back, Poe was restricted in what he could do. Every move he made was planned out in advance, agreed with the cops charged with his protection. Agents from the United States Secret Service's Presidential Protection detail advised on how to secure perimeters against a determined sniper. He spent his days indoors. Edgar was with Uncle Bertie in a fishing lodge on the River Foss. The spaniel had jumped out of Doyle's old Land Rover, excited to be somewhere new. His tail had wagged like a twanged ruler until he realised Poe wasn't staying with him. No dog could sulk like Edgar.

His wedding to Doyle had been postponed, but that allowed her to take up a lecturing opportunity in Arizona. She'd been putting it off but agreed to leave the country until Puck was caught.

Flynn and Bradshaw continued to work. Bradshaw managed the website and the donations, Flynn made sure the logistical arrangements were running smoothly. They were. Flynn told Poe that in all her dealings, she could detect the hand of Alastor Locke. If someone as much as paused before saying yes to her, she bobbed him a text. Within minutes the pauser would be on the phone, effusively promising to bend over backwards.

Ten days after Poe's press briefing, Flynn finally called to say they were ready. If he was adamant that he wanted to do this, it was time to let Puck make his move.

'Thank fuck,' Poe said. He shucked his security detail, marched through Highwood's double front doors, faced the hill, ripped off his T-shirt and screamed, 'Come on then!' He panted and thumped himself on the chest. 'What are you waiting for?!'

And 2,000 yards away, Ezekiel Puck, safely hidden in his ghillie suit, smiled.

Chapter 82

Two weeks after the press conference

Southampton

Ezekiel Puck had cheered up. He'd had a setback with the PledgePower website, but that was all it was – a setback. He'd planned to drive his ex-wife to suicide, but she couldn't hide forever, and a bullet to the head was a fine compromise. It might even be better. Right now, Joanne would be daring to hope. Over forty million pounds had been donated. Her ridiculous wedding venue was safe. The retarded staff she thought of as friends could keep their jobs. She could pay off her bank loans. She would no longer have a mortgage. She might even go big – buy the holiday home in Malta she'd always dreamed of. And she'd still have an eight-figure nest egg.

He couldn't allow that. That was unacceptable.

But his ex-wife would have to wait. First, he wanted to deal with this Washington Poe character. The idiot was about to discover what happened when you got sucked into Ezekiel Puck's gravity well. Poe had fucked around. Now it was time for him to find out. Poe had thought he could turn himself into an irresistible target. That he'd miss all that over-the-top security they'd put around the policeman. The British had occasionally loaned Puck out to the Americans. Sometimes they'd had a job that could only be carried out by someone with a plummy accent and a stiff upper lip. Someone with breeding. So he'd recognised the Secret Service-style security. The onion-ring perimeters. The counter-sniping teams. Their meticulous advance work.

It wouldn't make any difference. He wasn't going to kill Washington Poe. Not just yet. That wasn't how he worked. No, sir. It wasn't his way. First, Poe had to *suffer*. And given how much he'd disrespected Puck, Poe had to suffer *a lot*.

That's how Ezekiel Puck played the game.

He had sometimes wondered if he was insane. Of course he had. How could he not? He'd shot and killed twenty people in the last six months alone, ended their dreary lives with 45 grams of lead and copper. Even as a child, Puck had preferred despair to hope. Despite never having felt it, he *understood* despair. He knew how to use it, how to bend it to his will. He understood how powerful it could be. It was the emotion that kept on taking. It gave nothing back.

It was beautiful.

Despair was why he was in Southampton instead of Northumberland. Poe had sent his woman away, far beyond Puck's reach. It wouldn't have mattered if he'd staked her to the lawn of that ostentatious house he lived in for most of the week, though. Puck wasn't interested in Lady Estelle Doyle. Poe was only into her for her money. She was replaceable. He wasn't interested in that ratty little dog of his either. The emotional attachment to pets was fleeting, in Puck's opinion. He never killed pets. The risk versus reward wasn't there. If he killed Poe's dog he could go out and buy a new one the very same day.

No, Puck was interested in the one thing that Poe *couldn't* replace. The one thing he seemed to care about more than himself. He'd filmed the shooting of Alice Mathers – he filmed *all* his shootings – and when Poe had seen him on that window cleaning galley, his instinct wasn't to dive for cover. It was to pull that weakling Matilda Bradshaw to safety first.

He'd spent a week researching Matilda Bradshaw. From her

days as a child prodigy to her early acceptance into Oxford. From her award-winning exploits in the field of pure mathematics to her curious downwards move to the National Crime Agency. To her highly unlikely friendship with the curmudgeonly Poe. She'd saved his life, literally and figuratively. Literally when she dragged the fuckwit from a burning building. Figuratively, by reversing the spiral of depression he had no doubt been in. When Matilda met Poe, he'd been circling the drain. Eating and drinking himself to death. Now he was a well-adjusted man. He had friends. He lived in a massive house. He was about to get married to some inbred entitled bitch.

He had hope.

Mr Poe, Puck thought, *it's time you were introduced to hope's adversary – despair.*

Puck checked his watch and smiled. It was time. Matilda was a creature of habit. Probably why she was so good at maths. Or maybe she was one of those idiot savants. Like Rain Man. Needed her routines. Good in front of a computer, a proper dumb-dumb in real life. He knew it was she who'd set up that crowdfunding website. Poe had almost said her name during his press conference. Puck had many reasons to hate Matilda Bradshaw; that she'd saved the Smithy's Forge was almost as bad as the *other* reason. He had been the world's top-rated player on *Dezinformatsiya*. Now he was number two. TillyB1987 was number one. Matilda must have hacked the website. Altered her scores. Inflated hers and deflated his.

Bitch.

Matilda's car rounded the corner. Exactly when it always did. It was raining but Puck could see her clearly through the driver's window. She had a distinctive shape. Thin with stupid round glasses. Hair like candyfloss. She leaned forward in the seat, her weak eyes straining to see in the poor weather. He watched as she drove into the drive of her parents' house, the remote-controlled garage door already open. As soon as she was in, the door shut behind her. She stayed in the car until it was fully closed. Careful.

Not careful enough.

Because Matilda's routine never changed. She drove home. She waited until the garage door was shut before she exited the car. She walked into the house and went straight upstairs to her bedroom. She sat in front of her computer and she worked for an hour. She then went downstairs and made something to eat before heading back upstairs to work for the rest of the evening.

Puck knew this because he'd watched her do it on three consecutive nights.

The house was in total darkness. Matilda's parents weren't home, which was a shame. He liked it when the families saw their loved ones die. He would have enjoyed their reaction as they stared in horror at what was left of their daughter.

Puck lifted the McMillan TAC-50 and brought the telescopic sight to his eyes. His hands caressed the rifle as he waited. It really was a magnificent piece of equipment. Faultless. Well worth the effort and risk involved getting it into the country from mainland Europe. When he had fewer pressing concerns, he might write an open letter to the manufacturer. Credit where credit was due.

A downstairs light came on. Matilda was out of the garage and into the house.

A shadow flashed in the half-window where the winder stairs turned. Matilda was almost at the top. She had nearly reached her bedroom, the one she'd had since she was a child. Ten more seconds and she'd be in front of her computer. Two seconds after that, she'd turn on her desk lamp.

Twelve seconds until she was lit up like a smile, her silhouette hazy through the net curtains. An easy target for a man of his skill.

Puck's finger took up the slack on the trigger as he waited for

Matilda to take the seat in front of her computer. All he had to do was apply one more ounce of pressure. One more ounce and he'd blow that nerdy bitch's glasses clean off her face.

Matilda switched on her desk lamp. She reached for the curtains. Went to draw them. After all, there was a sniper out there . . .

Target acquired.

Puck didn't hesitate. He squeezed the trigger.

The window shattered. Matilda's head snapped back, her once-in-a-generation mind splashed all over her periodic table wallpaper. She toppled and fell off her chair.

Game over.

Welcome to hell, Washington Poe.

An hour later, the landline rang at Highwood. Brunton answered it.

'I'll get him, ma'am.' He found Poe in the drawing room. He said, 'Detective Chief Inspector Stephanie Flynn on the phone for you, sir. She says it's important.'

Chapter 83

The press turned. The press *always* turned. It's what they did. Yesterday's darling is today's villain. *Build them up so we can knock them back down.* A curiously sustainable business model. They interviewed people who knew Poe. They interviewed people who didn't know him. Talking heads, all puffed up on faux anger. They camped outside Highwood. They went to his local and spoke to the landlord. Apparently, Poe was *persona non grata* now. They even door-stepped Doyle as she left her hotel in Phoenix. The idiot who refused to step aside got a stiletto down the shin for his troubles.

Reckless!

The clamour for criminal charges to be brought against Poe reached a crescendo. The opposition benches called for a public inquiry. Eventually Number 10 issued a press release.

How does this man still have a job?!

They delved into his past. Into his previous cases. Trashed his reputation. They downplayed his role while highlighting Bradshaw's extraordinary achievements. They claimed he'd built up his reputation on her giant shoulders. That he'd used her. That he had faked their friendship for the glory their combined casework was bringing him. They built her into the hero she undoubtedly was, but never wanted to be. The *Daily Mirror* led the calls for a posthumous George Medal, one of the UK's highest awards for civilian gallantry, and all the tabloids jumped on the bandwagon. The George Cross Committee explained that the medal recognised the bravery of people who put themselves at risk. And while they understood the nation's zeitgeist, being murdered didn't qualify.

Defund the George Cross Committee!

Within a week, Poe was the most reviled person in the UK. It wasn't until the *Sunday Times* exposed another BBC paedophile that the press moved on.

Poe saw none of this. He didn't read any newspapers and he ignored the social media bunfight. He issued no statement and he made no public appearances. Immediately after Bradshaw's death had been announced on television, he returned to Highwood. He refused to leave the grand old house, not even for fresh air. Leaving the house was a faff for the cops tasked with keeping him alive. Ezekiel Puck was still out there. Better for everyone if Poe stayed inside.

He withdrew into himself. He stopped eating. He lost weight, became gaunt.

And eventually he got the call.

'I'm on my way,' he said.

Chapter 84

Blencathra House, Central London

Poe sipped his tea and stared into space. He was back where it had all started – summoned to the room that Mathers had set aside for the National Crime Agency in the conference centre she'd hired as an incident room. He smiled as he remembered Bradshaw asking Mathers to get rid of all the doughnuts. He heard people, cops probably, walk past the closed door. One of them stage-whispered, 'Wanker.'

Word was out. The prodigal son had returned.

He wondered if prodigal son was even the right turn of phrase. It sounded like a positive thing, even though the word 'prodigal' was anything but. He thought the phrase might have originated in the New Testament. Maybe a parable. Ordinarily he'd have asked Bradshaw.

But now he couldn't.

He finished his tea and threw the paper cup towards the bin. It bounced off the wall and missed. Typical.

Usually a meeting like this – and given that the outcome was predetermined, Poe thought of it more as a 'panel' – would have taken place at the National Crime Agency's headquarters, but this was taking place in Blencathra House. Poe still had a target on his back and Blencathra House was the most secure building in the country. When he was called in, he'd sit in front of two men and a woman. He wouldn't even have a rep at his side. It would have been like defending Gary Glitter; no one wanted to do it. Guilt by association. The panel would read out statements and listen to his responses. His mitigation. They'd then read out the decision they'd made before he'd entered the room.

Someone knocked on the door. It opened. Flynn stuck her head through, her expression grim. It looked like she'd lost weight too.

'They're ready, Poe,' she said.

The meeting was mercifully short.

Poe was served with a misconduct notice – a smorgasbord of charges that included gross negligence, dereliction of duties, bringing the NCA into disrepute – by a senior HR manager, his line manager at the stupid joint taskforce, and some guy from communications who was tapping out his press release before the meeting had even concluded. Poe didn't contest anything. He offered no mitigation. There didn't seem any point.

The senior HR manager, a man called Ashley Barrett, delivered the punchline.

'Sergeant Poe, I am suspending you on full pay pending the outcome of the internal investigation. You have the right to . . .'

Poe stopped listening. He reached into his jacket, pulled out his warrant card and his ID cards, and put them on the table. He didn't grandstand, didn't throw them down like he'd been dishonoured. He got up and left in the middle of Ashley Barrett's waffle. He closed the door behind him.

Flynn was waiting for him.

'Suspended,' he said.

She nodded. It was what they'd expected. 'Come on,' she said. 'Commander Unsworth is waiting for you.'

Unsworth was Commander Mathers's replacement. Poe had called him to let him know he was planning to crowdfund Joanne

Addy's wedding business. Unsworth hadn't tried to talk him out of it. He'd said it was a good idea. Now he was livid. It seemed he'd quickly mastered the prevailing-wind politics of senior management. He didn't look up from his laptop when Poe and Flynn entered his office.

'We have to offer you protection,' he said. 'There's a credible threat against you and we have a legal obligation to *all* UK citizens at risk.' He stressed 'all' like it was a dirty word.

'But?' Poe said.

'But no one is rushing to babysit you, Sergeant Poe.' He looked up. '*Are* you still a sergeant, or did the NCA do the right thing for once?'

'Poe's been suspended, sir,' Flynn said. 'The NCA has processes to follow, just as the Met does.'

Unsworth grunted his annoyance. 'Nevertheless,' he said, 'we have a sniper to catch, and *Sergeant* Poe is taking up valuable armed resources. We need every cop we have.'

'Can I refuse it?' Poe said.

'Poe,' Flynn warned. 'Don't be hasty. Think—'

'Of course,' Unsworth cut in. 'This isn't a police state.'

'Then I refuse it.'

Unsworth nodded. He opened a file and pulled out a single sheet of paper. 'Sign here, please,' he said, pointing at the bottom.

'Do you have a pen, sir?'

Unsworth went back to his laptop. 'Get your own fucking pen,' he said.

'Here you are, Poe,' Flynn said, passing him a chewed-up BIC.

Poe scrawled his name above SIGN HERE.

'Oh, one more thing,' Unsworth smirked. He turned his laptop so they could see the website he'd been on. 'I take it you've seen this?'

It was the *Sun*'s homepage. The headline wasn't as crude as

GOTCHA! or FREDDIE STARR ATE MY HAMSTER! but it didn't need to be. Not when it was as personal as this.

LADY DOYLE BREAKS OFF ENGAGEMENT TO DISGRACED COP!

Unsworth smiled, delighted to be the bearer of bad news. He said, 'Now, get the fuck out of my office, Poe. I have work to do.'

It was time to go home, Poe thought.

His *real* home.

Chapter 85

Ezekiel Puck couldn't remember when he'd been happier. He'd broken Washington Poe like Bane had broken Batman's back. Poe hadn't had much but Puck had stolen it anyway. He'd destroyed his reputation. He'd taken his career. He'd broken his engagement.

The timing had taken him by surprise, though. He'd assumed it would have taken longer. That Lady Doyle would dig in. Do a Tammy Wynette and stand by her man. Maybe he'd given her too much credit. Perhaps her inbred stupidity was tempered by the animal cunning that had kept her type's heel on the throat of the working class for centuries. She'd cut bait. *Boo-hoo, Washington Poe.* He'd known she would eventually, of course. The only thing the aristocracy hated more than losing money was losing face. But even so, Lady Doyle's ruthlessness had caught him unawares. No feet under the table for Puck's free-loading nemesis. No inherited wealth teat for Poe to suckle on.

As soon as the engagement was called off, he knew Poe would grab his dog and skulk back to Herdwick Croft, the tick-infested shitpit he used to call home on Shap Fell. By all accounts, he'd been a recluse before Matilda Bradshaw had entered his life and no doubt his plan would be to become one again. To shut himself off from the world, ignore the press-fuelled bile coming his way. What choice would he have? He'd no longer be welcome at Highwood. And even when he was popular, his only real friend had been Matilda. And that freak of nature was currently in cold storage. Herdwick Croft was where Poe would reconsider his life. Maybe decide he didn't want it any more.

Puck understood this like he was inside Poe's head. It was his talent. As Alastor Locke used to say, suicidal ideation was his bailiwick. He'd sometimes thought the old spymaster had used it as a reprimand, as something not to glory in, but that couldn't have been right. He'd certainly used his services enough times. That's why his betrayal had stung so much, why his mediocre daughter-in-law had paid the price for his hypocrisy. He'd circle back to Locke after he'd taken care of more pressing concerns.

Understanding suicidal ideation was why, thirty minutes after his .50 bullet had removed most of Matilda's head, he'd headed north. And it was why six hours later he'd checked into a quiet campsite in the same grid reference as Herdwick Croft. He wasn't worried about being recognised. The E-FIT had been a decent likeness, but it was still just a drawing, a portrait of someone the artist had never met. Drawing someone from verbal cues was like trying to describe the difference between left and right – virtually impossible. A wig, coloured lenses and a memorable hat cancelled the E-FIT just as the Hindenburg disaster cancelled the Zeppelin industry. There was the CCTV still from the Can of Ham, but he wasn't worried about that. They hadn't released it, and even if they had, he no longer looked like that. Anyway, he had documentation proving beyond doubt that he was Edward Toyne, a self-employed voiceover artist from Newbiggin-by-the-Sea and self-confessed badger enthusiast.

His interest in badgers also explained why every evening he donned his thermal jacket, waterproofs and thick boots – the same gear all the other moronic fell walkers wore – and left the relative warmth of his tent to spend the night on Shap Fell. He would hoist his 70-litre navy-blue rucksack on to his back and tighten the waist straps, say goodbye to his tent neighbours and disappear until the next morning. The rucksack contained every-thing he needed – trail mix, spare socks, water and a packet of caffeine tablets. Nothing unusual. Things you'd find in every rucksack around Shap. What *was* unusual was the broken-down McMillan TAC-50 sniper rifle, the Schmidt & Bender 5-25x56 PM II telescopic sight and a MOSKITO TI laser rangefinder. Oh, and the ghillie suit that would once again turn Ezekiel Puck into the invisible man.

That evening was no different. He waved goodbye to Pippa, one half of the hippy couple in the tent next to his, and made his way on to Shap Fell. His lessons with Davy Newport, the guy who'd taught him how to shoot and stalk deer, meant he could approach Herdwick Croft unseen. Poe's shithole cottage was on a peak, no doubt so the shepherd had a three-sixty view of his flock of sheep. It only had windows at the front, noth-ing at the back, just solid stone. Probably where the prevailing wind battered through. Puck had selected a firing position 500 metres away, directly in front of Herdwick Croft's only door. If Puck was six o'clock, Poe's cottage would be twelve. Plumb straight and less than half the distance he'd been firing from recently.

An easy shot.

Dead easy.

When he was 200 metres from his firing position, he removed his telescopic sight from his rucksack and spent an hour observ-ing the surrounding area. All clear. He knew it would be. When he was satisfied that he was alone, he climbed into his ghillie suit and reassembled his rifle. He ate some trail mix and drank some water before putting his rucksack into a heavy-duty refuse sack and burying it. The only thing he needed was his ghillie suit, his rifle and some hand-loaded ammunition.

He then crawled the 200 metres to his firing position. When he arrived, he flicked open the bipod, rested the rifle against his shoulder and leaned into the sight. He wriggled to make an indent he'd be comfortable with then sighed.

Content.

Content but not happy. He didn't know why. He had Poe where he wanted. He wasn't home yet, but he would be. By his calculations he'd have been suspended today or the day before. Then, Poe being Poe, he'd creep back to Shap Fell. Puck had ample time, though. Even if it had been a morning suspension, by the time Poe had collected that yappy piece of shit he called a dog, he wouldn't get up north until close to midnight.

And Puck would be waiting.

So why wasn't he happy?

He thought it was Shap Fell itself. He hated it. Fucking hated it. Had done from the moment he'd stepped on to the pube-like grass. It was desolate, like the surface of the moon. It was hard and lumpy when it looked soft and smooth, wet when it looked dry. It was windy and it was fucking creepy. And even in the warmest summer for a decade, it was colder than a witch's tit in a brass bra. Only an arsehole like Washington Poe could find peace on something so bloody inhospitable.

Something in his sight caught his attention. He stiffened and cast his eyes until he saw it. He relaxed. It was just a fox, prowling for newborn lambs, no doubt. Puck wished it luck.

He sighed and settled down for another cold night. If Poe was going to turn up, it would be soon. If he didn't, Puck would stay out anyway. Going back to his tent would lead to questions, and Poe was such a contrary bastard he couldn't trust him not to turn up at four in the morning. Puck didn't mind the wait. He might even see a badger.

He'd just resigned himself to another wasted night when he heard it. It was faint and he might have imagined it, although he didn't think he had. He closed his eyes and opened his mouth.

312

Davy Newport had told him that was the best way to improve the sound field. Something to do with reducing internal noise like pumping blood. Puck didn't know if it was bullshit, but he did it religiously before every kill.

There it was again. The low rumble of a four-stroke single cylinder engine. Poe's quad. Only a knucklehead like Poe would live somewhere you couldn't get to by car. Puck thought the fact that Poe needed a four-wheel-drive all-terrain vehicle' to navigate Shap Fell was all the justification he needed to kill him. Stupidity like that shouldn't be allowed to live. It might breed.

The sound got louder as the engine got closer. It could only be Poe. And then confirmation. A dog barking, excited in the way only mentally ill disabled breeds like springer spaniels could get. Puck put his head to his sight and waited.

Two minutes later, the fell was awash with light. Poe had the quad's headlights on. Full beam. The glare hurt Puck's eyes. Dazzled him. He pulled back and closed them. Waited. He opened them again. Poe was almost at Herdwick Croft. He was clearly in a foul mood. He was throwing the quad around. Bouncing up and down in the seat as if he were on a bucking bronco. The spaniel ran beside him. Poe skidded to a halt in front of Herdwick Croft. Puck drew a bead. He pulled back, dazzled again. Poe was wearing a headtorch. By the time he'd cleared his eyes, the fell was dark again.

Poe and his dog were inside Herdwick Croft.

Safe.

Puck smiled, happy again.

Everything was as it ought to be.

He'd never planned to shoot Poe off his quad. Outside of Hollywood, that would have been an impossible shot.

No, Puck had something more fun planned.

In a few hours, Poe would learn the story of three on a match.

And why the *third* light was so unlucky.

Chapter 86

The sun would rise just after 6 a.m., and Puck was willing to bet Poe would rise earlier. He looked like a bad sleeper at the best of times, and these were *not* the best of times.

They were for Puck, though. He was really enjoying himself. There was no wind and there was no humidity. Perfect shooting conditions. He'd spent the early hours fantasising about how he could kill Poe's mongrel first. Blow his stupid yappy head clean off his shoulders. Or maybe put one in his hind quarters. It would be days before Poe was discovered, plenty of time for the spaniel to die horribly. But he hadn't been able to square that particular circle. He'd watched Poe grab Matilda on the roof. The guy had reflexes. *Serious* reflexes. The only way he'd be able to get them both would be to fire twice, as close to simultaneous as possible. Give Stig no chance of diving back into his dump. But it was a difficult shot. A risky shot. And he didn't take risks. It was why he would never be caught. So, as fun as it was to fantasise about Poe dying next to his fatally wounded dog, it was safer to stick to the plan. Shoot Poe in the gut then sit back and watch him die. Puck hoped it would take at least forty-eight hours. Ample time for the dog to get hungry enough to eat Poe's fingers. He didn't know if springer spaniels did that – German shepherds were known for it – but a boy could dream.

He checked his watch. It was 3 a.m. He shifted position. He did it the way snipers everywhere did. By lifting one limb at a time, an inch at a time. Slowly flexing them, letting the blood flow. A bit like a nurse massaging a coma patient. To anyone watching, it would seem as though he hadn't moved at all. He checked his watch after he'd finished: 3.20 a.m. He wouldn't move again until Washington Poe did.

Ezekiel Puck loved the superstition of 'three on a match'. Loved the fatalism. He wasn't sure if it was true, thought it probably wasn't, but so what? Soldiers believed it. That was all that mattered.

Apparently, during the Crimean War, the first war in which optical sights were fitted to rifles, soldiers believed that the third man to light his Turkish cigarette from the same match would be shot by a sniper. The theory was that the sniper would see the flare of the match, and by the time the third soldier put his head to the flame, the sniper would be ready to fire. One-two-three-bang.

Then it happened.

The first light. Poe's bedside lamp coming on.

He was awake. Puck didn't move, didn't check his watch. He thought it was about half past five. It certainly wasn't later as it was still dark. Poe's stupid dog began to bark. Excited. Across the silent Shap Fell, the sound carried all the way to Puck's expectant ears.

He steadied his breathing. Slowed it down. He moved his finger inside the trigger guard. Otherwise, he stayed perfectly still. He was good at staying still. Ever since he was a child, he'd preferred watching people to talking to people.

There would be a minute or so while Poe got up, threw on a pair of shorts and a tatty T-shirt. He'd then lumber downstairs and turn on the cottage's main light. It was actually closer to *two* minutes. He must have needed the bathroom. Even though Poe was younger than he was, Puck thought of it as an old man's bladder.

And again, right on cue, the downstairs light came on.

The second light.

Puck gently squeezed the trigger, took up most of the three and a half pounds of pressure. He took in a deep breath, let out half of it then held it. If the chest rose and fell, so would the barrel. A millimetre at his end would be inches at Poe's. Literally the difference between life and death.

The next light, the unlucky *third* light, would be Poe opening the door to let out his dog. The light would spill across the wiry grass of Shap Fell like a beacon and Poe would be framed in the doorway. A shot Puck couldn't miss.

He waited.

And he waited.

But the door didn't open.

The dog kept barking, but Poe stayed inside.

Something was wrong.

And then Ezekiel Puck realised he'd made a terrible mistake.

Chapter 87

A good sniper has the capacity to stay motionless for hours; a great one for days. They'll go into a bubble, emptying the mind of all things but the target. Nothing distracts them. Nothing.

It's the sniper's greatest strength.

It's also their biggest weakness.

Because snipers need spotters. They need them like babies need milk. The spotter's role isn't just to identify targets; it's to provide situational awareness. And protection. They're the eyes and ears of the team, vigilant because the sniper can't be. The sniper is the weapon, the spotter is the early warning system.

And right now, Ezekiel Puck's warning system was going into overdrive. It was screaming DANGER at the very top of its voice.

Even as he stared down the sight, the muzzle already starting to twitch, he realised the danger was at his end, not Poe's. Without thinking, without moving, he mentally checked his five senses. He thought that was where the answer would lie.

Nothing had changed visually. Poe was still hunkered down in his cottage. It wasn't sight that was giving him the shakes. He couldn't hear anything untoward either. Nothing had touched him and for obvious reasons he could discount taste. Smell perhaps? He didn't think so.

Maybe he'd imagined it. He'd seen Poe enter his cottage and he'd been watching the only way in and out all night. Poe was inside. His dog was inside. He could still hear it barking. There was no doubt about it. All five senses checked out. He breathed out again. Took a fresh one. Held it again, waited for Poe to open the door.

But his unease persisted. He'd forgotten something, he was sure of it. Unbidden, a memory resurfaced. It was one of his lessons with Davy Newport, the guy who'd taught him to shoot. The dour Scotsman had been a bore, but he knew his stuff when it came to stalking the most cautious prey animal in the UK. He remembered one particularly tedious lecture on a damp morning in the Scottish Highlands. Newport had told him that the nervous system's five main senses were important, but he shouldn't neglect the others.

Newport had told Puck that as far as the stalker was concerned, humans had *nine* primary senses, not five. He'd explained that proprioception was the ability to tell where your appendages were. Close your eyes and lift a finger to your nose. Proprioception allows you to find it without looking. Important if you need to reach for something but can't move your head. And what about chronoception: sensing the passage of time? The stalker had to know how long the hunt had lasted without relying on a watch. Checking your watch was unnecessary movement. Newport didn't have a name for the stalker's eighth primary sense – the ability to detect changes in wind pressure – but as changes in wind direction meant changes in *scent* direction, knowing which way the wind was blowing meant you could stay downwind. Downwind was good, upwind was bad. And finally, there was thermoception. The body's ability to sense temperature. It's how humans can tell if something is hot without having to touch it. Newport had told Puck that of all the additional four primary senses, thermoception was the most responsive to subtle changes. The most accurate.

And then Puck understood the terrible danger he was in. The back of his neck was warm. Shap Fell was cold but his neck was

318

warm. Logically, that could only mean one thing. An external heat source. Someone was standing over him.

Someone was *breathing* over him.

His brain processed this in a fraction of a second, but it still wasn't quick enough. He tried to spin round but the man standing over him was too quick. He'd seen the man's serious reflexes before, but only from a distance. When he'd grabbed Matilda Bradshaw out of harm's way on the roof of that London skyscraper. The man stamped on his arm, snapping it like a twig. He then brought his boot down on Puck's throat. Held it there, pinning him to the cold, wet moorland.

'How?' Puck managed to gurgle.

'Hello, Ezekiel,' Poe said. 'Nice to finally meet you.'

Chapter 88

Thirty-six hours later

Charing Cross Police Station, London

Poe stood in the interview room doorway and stared at Ezekiel Puck. He was breathtakingly bland. He looked like the tax accountant that tax accountants used. The kind of man who watched BBC Four documentaries. But Poe guessed that was the point. Bland had been good for Ezekiel Puck. It had worked for him.

The interview room was hot and stuffy, and Puck was sweating like an otter in a greenhouse. He was pale and his right arm was in plaster. He had a bruised throat. Poe could still see his tread marks. His hair was thinning. He had dark circles under puffy red eyes. Looked like he'd been crying. Other than that, he seemed to be in good spirits.

After Poe had delivered Puck to Kendal Police Station, trussed up like an Easter brisket, he made some phone calls while Puck's transport down to London was arranged. Understandably, an irate Cumbrian chief constable wanted Puck out of her county as soon as Westmorland General Hospital had set his broken arm. She wasn't too keen on Poe staying either, but as she had no authority over him, she was limited in what she could do. Poe avoided any awkwardness by volunteering to accompany Puck to London with the police convoy. The journey took exactly five hours, a succession of police forces providing a blue light escort all the way into Central London.

'I understand you'll only talk to me?' Poe said.

Puck smiled. 'Take a seat.'

'I'm fine here, thanks.'

'Please sit down, Sergeant Poe. There are things I need to say.'

'That may be true, Ezekiel,' Poe said. 'The thing is, I'm not in the mood to hear them. Not now, not ever. And the beauty of this is that I don't have to. We have your gun. We have your ammunition. We even have the videos you made. We have everything we need to secure a whole-life sentence.'

'Then why are you here?'

It was a good question. And the answer was that Commander Unsworth, the man who'd smirked when Poe had been suspended, had met Ezekiel Puck's police convoy at the entrance to Charing Cross Police Station. Poe was in the first car. Unsworth had flashed Poe a constipated smile then nodded for him to follow him into an office he'd annexed. He'd tried to apologise, but Poe wasn't having any of it. Anger would have been Unsworth's correct response; gloating, not so much. And the way he'd gleefully withdrawn Poe's police protection, the way he'd cruelly informed him his engagement to Doyle had been called off, smacked of someone Poe didn't want or need an apology from.

But, although Poe could refuse to accept his apology, with his suspension withdrawn, he wasn't able to refuse a direct order. Unsworth had told him to stay while Puck was being interviewed. He said he might be needed to clarify things that Puck told them. Fat chance. Puck hadn't said a word. Hadn't gone 'no comment', hadn't even asked for the duty solicitor. It didn't matter. Poe had no choice but to stay until Puck had been charged and remanded into custody. He booked into a hotel and caught up on his sleep. A day later he got the call to come into the police station. *That* was why he was standing in the doorway of the interview room. Poe wasn't going to say all that, obviously. Instead, he said, 'I like the coffee here.' He stepped into the room and slipped into the seat opposite Puck. 'I would offer to get you one, but I fear the temptation to spit in it would be too much.'

'I'm fine,' Puck said. 'Your colleagues are looking after me very well considering . . .'

'Considering you killed their commander?'

Puck shrugged. 'What choice did I have? Alastor Locke shouldn't have released my picture. As he would say, that was bad form.'

Poe shook his head. 'We didn't find you through Alastor Locke, you moron. We found you through your subscription to that idiotic table-top role-playing game you obsess over. It was your neighbours and your now very rich ex-wife who supplied the E-FIT. Alastor warned Commander Mathers *against* releasing it.' He made to stand up. 'Now, unless you have something to tell me that we don't already know, I suggest you go back to ignoring everyone, all the way to the seg wing of HMP Belmarsh.'

'I actually *do* have something to tell you, Sergeant Poe. Something you don't know.'

Poe yawned. 'And what might that be?'

'I know when you're going to die.'

Chapter 89

'Really?' Poe said. 'You know when I'm going to die? Why do I find that hard to believe?'

'I know when *all* my targets are going to die, Sergeant Poe,' Puck replied.

Poe smiled. 'Is that right?'

'Yes, that's right.'

'And *how* do you know when I'm going to die, Ezekiel? Because as far as I can tell, your little ambush failed. I'm still here.'

Puck nodded. 'It's true I wanted to kill you on that horrible little mountain of yours—'

'It's not a mountain; it's a fell,' Poe said. 'According to Tilly it comes from the Old Norse word *fjall*.'

'But that doesn't matter,' Puck said. He took a breath. Sipped from the dusty bottle of water in front of him. 'I know when you're going to die because it's what I did for a living. It's what I was good at. No, scratch that, it's what I *excelled* at. Just ask Alastor Locke.'

'I didn't have to,' Poe said. 'He told me.'

'Then you understand.'

'No, Ezekiel, I *don't* understand.'

'You fucked around and you found out, Poe.'

'I'm not the one in handcuffs, Ezekiel.'

'In a few weeks I'll be given a whole-life sentence,' Puck said. 'Yours has already started.'

'I think you'd better enlighten me,' Poe said. 'Because when I leave here, I won't give you a second thought.'

Puck laughed. Not a faux-laugh, this was a real belly-buster. The kind of laugh that gets you thrown out of the cinema.

'Your little friend is dead, Sergeant Poe,' he said when it had subsided. 'I blew the specky bitch's brains out with a bullet designed for lightly armoured vehicles. And I did it because of you, Poe. Your ego got her killed. That's why I know when you're going to die.'

Poe didn't respond.

'And that was just the first domino to fall,' Puck continued. 'Your reckless disregard for Matilda's life caused the press to turn against you. They carried the public along with them and your snooty fiancée soon followed suit. They've allowed you back to work because you somehow caught me, but that won't last long. The inquiry will push you out. No best friend, no rich woman to leech off, and no job to take your mind off it all.'

Still, Poe said nothing.

'If I had a calendar, I could mark off the day for you. It may happen sooner, it won't happen later.'

'And what exactly will happen, Ezekiel?'

'Why, you'll take your own life, of course,' Puck said. 'You're clearly a very selfish man, Poe, so you'll hold out for as long as you can, but you *will* eat a shotgun barrel by the end of the year. It is inevitable.'

'A shotgun barrel?' Poe said woodenly.

'Or something equally dramatic,' Puck nodded. 'You once were a recluse, and you'll try to become one again, but the peace you found in earlier years will elude you this time. I understand you suffer from PTSD? Well, trust me, what you went through before is nothing like what you're about to go through. Matilda's death will *haunt* you, Sergeant Poe. She'll be there when you're awake and she'll plague your dreams. If you thought your nightmares were bad before, just wait until she gets inside your head. I might even find a way of sending you the video I recorded. Would you like that? Maybe for your birthday? You won't be around for Christmas, obviously, but I'm sure I can get it to you before then.'

Poe sighed. 'I think you're labouring under a misapprehension, Ezekiel,' he said. He looked at the ceiling camera and nodded. 'Maybe the defining one of your life.'

Puck frowned at the same time as the door opened.

Tilly Bradshaw stepped into the interview room.

And there wasn't a scratch on her.

The Third Light

Chapter 90

Four weeks earlier

Moulsford Psychiatric Hospital

'Who would you run into a burning building for, Sergeant Poe?' Bethany Bowman, Doctor Clara Lang's alter ego, asked.

Poe frowned. 'I don't understand.'

'It's a simple enough question.'

'Nothing's ever simple with you, Bethany.'

She tilted her head. Smiled coyly. 'Are you flirting with me, Sergeant Poe?'

'More a reminder I'm locked in a room with a woman who has murdered three people—'

'Three bad people.'

'A woman who recently filed down her own teeth just so she could bite off someone's ear.'

'You *are* flirting with me.'

'Why do you want to know who I'd run into a burning building for?'

'Because if you can answer the question honestly, you'll have everything you need to catch Ezekiel Puck.'

'This won't be a long list,' Poe said. 'I don't have many friends.'

'*Sophie's Choice*, though,' Bethany said. 'You can only save one. Everyone else dies.'

Bethany might have been Clara's more exciting personality, but they shared the same razor-sharp brain. Bethany may have used it differently, but that was down to circumstances, not

329

choice. Who he would run into a burning building for wasn't a rhetorical question. It wasn't filler. She really wanted to know. So instead of saying something trite, like he was a police officer so he would run into a burning building for anyone, he considered the question carefully.

He would definitely run into a burning building for Edgar. No question about that. He imagined the spaniel would be in the vicinity anyway. He'd probably be the *cause* of the fire. Poe had lost count of the number of things the excitable numpty had broken. Knocking something hot on to something flammable would be entirely within his repertoire of tricks.

But, as likely as it was that Edgar would be the root cause of any fire, and therefore be the one who needed rescuing, Poe didn't think his dog would be an acceptable answer to Bethany's question.

The obvious answer was Doyle. They lived together, they were getting married, and he loved her. He liked to think that if she were in a burning building, he wouldn't think twice. He was about to say Doyle. But he held back. Realised he'd been circling the answer.

Bradshaw.

He would walk into a furnace for Bradshaw. And he knew she'd do it for him. He corrected himself. She *had* done it for him. During the Immolation Man case, she had literally run into a burning building to rescue him. He still bore the scars. And on the roof of that London skyscraper he had thrown himself in front of her when he'd realised Puck had lured them there. He hadn't thought about it. He'd just done it. Bradshaw didn't know, of course. One minute she'd been standing tall, pretending her hay fever wasn't bothering her, the next she was on the gravelled floor, a 15-stone Cumbrian on top of her.

'I choose Tilly,' Poe said.

'You're sure?'

'I am.'

'You don't want to ask the audience? Phone a friend?'

'Tilly. Final answer.'

Bethany nodded. 'Good then. That's where we start.'

Chapter 91

'What does this man do, Sergeant Poe?' Bethany asked.

'He murders people.'

'No! What does he *do*?'

'I was standing right next to Commander Mathers when he blew her head off, Bethany. He definitely murders people.'

Bethany shook her head, frustrated. The wire tether rattled. 'But *why* did he kill her?'

'Because she'd released his E-FIT to the press. Because she'd gone on television and named him. Because she was one step closer to catching him.'

'Wrong,' she said. 'Commander Mathers wasn't the target that day.'

'He's an exceptional marksman and he wasn't shooting from distance. She was the target, Bethany.'

'She might have been the person he killed, but Alastor Locke was the target that day, Sergeant Poe.'

Poe didn't respond.

Bethany sighed. 'The man you've described is vindictive and he's sadistic, but from what you've told me, killing people is just a byproduct.'

'A byproduct . . . ?'

'A *happy* byproduct then!' she snapped. She took a breath. 'But make no mistake, Alastor Locke was his endgame. Commander Mathers was just the *means* to the end.'

'But . . . but why?'

'You said Ezekiel Puck worked for Alastor Locke?'

'He did.'

'Then I imagine Puck mistakenly believed it was Locke who fed his image to the press.'

'What makes you so sure?'

'Because someone with an ego like Puck's won't ever be able to imagine they've made a mistake. Therefore, the only explanation for his E-FIT being made public is that they've been betrayed.'

'Isn't this all a bit too ... I don't know, overcomplicated? Why not just shoot Alastor Locke?'

'That's because you're thinking like a good person.'

'You're a good person too, Bethany.'

'I stoned someone to death.'

'Extenuating circumstances.'

'There you go, flirting with me again, Sergeant Poe. What will Lady Doyle say?'

Poe shrugged. Even though it was hypothetical, he wasn't feeling good about his decision to rescue Bradshaw ahead of his fiancée. And he knew he wouldn't keep it to himself. He would tell Doyle and she'd pretend to be OK with it, but secretly she'd be upset. Or maybe she wouldn't. Poe thought that might be worse. *Sophie's Choice* again.

'He didn't shoot Alastor Locke because he likes his victims to suffer. It's their despair he gets off on. And if you think I'm exaggerating, this is a man who killed twenty people just to damage his ex-wife's wedding business. It's the same man Alastor Locke employed as a ... what did you call them again?'

'The mischief makers.'

'That's right. He was employed to cause mischief. Instead, he drove his targets to suicide. Remind me why Alastor Locke had to let him go?'

'Because even after he'd achieved his goal, he kept torturing his targets. He did it for pleasure.'

'Exactly. And he doesn't always murder. He has a knack for identifying the one thing his target can't live without. Then he takes it from them. Sometimes it's a daughter, like the woman his ex-wife told you about, the one who pranged his car. He got to the mother by releasing her daughter's sex tapes. The daughter takes her own life then the mother follows suit. And in Davy Newport's case, the man who taught him to shoot and stalk deer, it was his honour. All he had to do to push him over the cliff was frame him for stealing.'

'OK,' Poe said. 'You seem to have a grip on this man's psyche that has so far eluded everyone else. And that includes Tilly, and she's the best I've ever seen at this. But you wanted to know who I would save from a burning building. You said if I answered honestly, I'd have everything I need to catch this prick.'

'I did. And you do. You're locked in a battle with this man, Sergeant Poe. It might not feel like it, but it's a game of chess. Of strategy and counterstrategy. Ezekiel Puck isn't like the people you've hunted before. Believing Alastor Locke betrayed him was a mistake; he won't make another. Not unless you force him into one.'

'How do I do that?'

'You play his game, of course.'

'That seems . . . counterintuitive.'

'You play his game, but you do it better, Sergeant Poe,' Bethany said. 'You make a move so bold he'll have no choice but to react. You pick a fight with him. Do something so egregious, you become the only thing he can think about. You make yourself his nemesis. And while he isn't thinking clearly, you set a trap.'

'A trap? What trap?'

Bethany yawned. 'Sleepy now,' she said. Her eyes fluttered then shut. And when they opened again, Bethany was gone. Clara Lang stared back. She looked at her restraints and her brow furrowed in confusion. Clara thought she was a doctor at the hospital. It was her unwavering belief.

'Hello, Doctor Lang,' Poe said.

'Washington, what are you doing tethered like that? Have you had another episode?'

'Something like that. Shall we get ourselves out of these restraints, Doctor Lang?'

'Yes, let's. Then we can have a nice cup of tea and chat about your nightmares. It feels like a long time since we spoke.'

Poe raised his hand. The signal to end the session.

'Oh, before you go, Bethany tells me she wants a quick word,' Clara said. 'She has something for you.'

The something was a pen. She stabbed Poe with it. It bloody hurt. The pen broke in the flesh between his thumb and his index finger, so he had a new tattoo. It would look like a jail dot, the blotchy prison tattoo that meant you'd served time. Poe had served time, was still serving time, but only inside his own head. On the flipside, Bethany had given Poe the means to catch Ezekiel Puck.

All things considered, it was probably a fair exchange.

Chapter 92

Bethany might have given Poe the means, but she hadn't given him the method. That was going to be down to him. So, instead of getting in his car and driving back to Northumberland, he walked to Bettys, ordered a pot of tea and a plate of fried food, and wrote down everything Bethany had told him.

Ezekiel Puck was a vindictive, vendetta-driven man. Spite personified. Bethany had said that made him predictable. That he'd be unable to let go of a grudge. That he would react to real or imagined slights. But Poe would have to be subtle. He couldn't do something obvious. He couldn't call an international press conference and tell the world Puck was a bed-wetting loser. He'd see through it. Shrug it off the same way he would.

Bethany had asked him what Puck did. Poe had said he killed people and she'd got angry. Told him the murders were a byproduct. That Puck was in the despair business, not the murder business. He pushed people to the brink then kept pushing. Stamped on their hands as they clung on to what made their lives worth living.

Poe was good at making people angry. He did it without thinking, Bradshaw said. A natural rudeness, she called it. But rudeness, deliberate or not, wouldn't force Puck into making a mistake. Poe couldn't bait a trap with an insult.

Poe thought back to the start of his session with Bethany. To her first question after they'd negotiated what Clara would get in return. She'd said that if he answered the question honestly, it would be somewhere to start. Who would he run into a burning building for? He'd eventually said Bradshaw. If he could only save one of the people he loved, it would be Bradshaw.

But how did that help? He was sure it did, he just couldn't see it yet. He poured another cup of tea then got stuck into his food. He decided to ignore what Ezekiel Puck did and how he did it. Instead, he thought about what he wanted. What was his primary goal? That was an easy one to answer. He'd wanted to destroy his wife's wedding business. To bankrupt it. Take her dreams away and make her homeless. Push her to the brink of suicide then give her a nudge.

You play his game, but you do it better . . .

That's one of the things Bethany had said. It had sounded like a throwaway comment. A platitude. Like one of those motivational posters depressed office workers put on their cubicle wall. Posters like THROW ME TO THE WOLVES AND I'LL RETURN LEADING THE PACK and BE YOU, NOT THEM. But neither Bethany nor Clara spoke like that. They weren't wired that way.

Play his game but do it better . . .

Play his game. But also, something to do with Bradshaw.

Bethany didn't know Bradshaw. Not really. Poe and Clara, in her Doctor Lang capacity, had discussed her at length obviously, but the two personalities rarely bled into each other. So when Bethany said Bradshaw was somewhere to start, it had nothing to do with her extraordinary intellect. It was something to do with her as a person. No, that was wrong. It was something to do with what she meant to him. Play his game, only better, and use Bradshaw.

Logically, that could only mean one thing. Poe needed to make Ezekiel Puck so angry with him that he became his sole focus. And when that happened, Puck wouldn't go after him, he'd go after his nearest and dearest. That's why Bethany had asked who he would run into a burning building for. Because

337

she knew Puck would go after Bradshaw. Just like he had with Alastor Locke. He hadn't killed the old spymaster; he'd killed his daughter-in-law.

Play his game but do it better . . .

Involve Bradshaw.

Speaking of the next stage in human evolution . . . Bettys was on the corner of Parliament Street. On the opposite corner was some sort of fashion shop. He couldn't quite see the name, but it began with J. Poe watched a woman dressing a window mannequin. Poe smiled. The mannequin looked like Bradshaw. Another one. He wondered if it was a Yorkshire thing. Or maybe all mannequins looked like that. He'd never really paid them any attention. This case was throwing up mannequins like a size-zero model throws up their breakfast. Every mannequin in North Yorkshire looked like Bradshaw and Ezekiel Puck had used one as a decoy after he'd lured Commander Mathers to that skyscraper roof. Everyone had had their eyes peeled for a lone gunman. Puck's mannequin had allowed him to hide in plain sight. He had set a trap.

Which made Poe think of his beautiful, eccentric fiancée. Specifically, the wedding favours she and her friend Emma were putting together. No sugared almonds for the guests of Estelle Doyle and Washington Poe. No, they were getting carnivorous plants. Venus flytraps for the ladies, huntsman's horns for the men.

Traps.

Carnivorous plants like the Venus flytrap didn't rely on disguise. They didn't hide in plain sight, didn't try to look like something else. The inner walls of their leaves were coated with nectar. So, despite looking like a miniature bear trap, the flies and the bugs and the other creepy-crawlies couldn't resist exploring the inside of the trapping structure. And as soon as they did – SNAP.

Mannequins and carnivorous plants. Ezekiel Puck and Bradshaw.

Play his game but do it better . . .

Bethany had said it was as though he was locked in a game of chess. Poe didn't play chess. But he understood the basics. She'd also said it was a game of strategy and counterstrategy. Which it was. But it was also a game of sacrifice.

And the bigger the sacrifice, the greater the reward.

Poe knew what Bethany wanted him to do. He had to do the unthinkable.

He had to sacrifice his queen.

He had to sacrifice Bradshaw.

Chapter 93

The Council of Highwood

'Obviously, we aren't putting Tilly at risk,' Poe said when he'd finished explaining what he wanted to do. 'We'll use a mannequin instead.'

His assembled audience of Locke, Flynn, Bradshaw, Doyle and even Uncle Bertie stared at him in astonishment.

Flynn was the first to break cover. 'A fucking *mannequin?*' she snorted. 'Are you out of your mind?'

Poe shrugged. 'Why not? It worked for Puck.' He didn't add that North Yorkshire mannequins looked like Bradshaw anyway. Flynn already thought he'd lost his marbles. This would tip her over the edge.

'Because Tilly moves, Poe.' She paused. Thought through what she'd just said. Corrected herself. 'Tilly *occasionally* moves. Mannequins don't.'

'I have a plan for that,' Poe said. 'It worked for Sherlock Holmes in "The Adventure of the Empty House", and there's no reason it won't work for us.'

'That's fiction, Poe!'

'The theory is sound, though,' Poe countered. 'And the execution is simple enough. Sherlock Holmes lures Moriarty's henchman, Colonel Sebastian Moran, into shooting at a wax bust.'

'Who's Mrs Hudson in this whack-a-doodle plan? Who's underneath the chair, making the mannequin move?'

Poe frowned. That was the weakest link in the chain. 'I haven't got that far,' he admitted.

'And who's the kamikaze pilot in a wig who drives Tilly's car to her parents' house?' Flynn asked. 'Because we sure as shit aren't asking Tilly to do it.'

'I haven't figured that bit out either.'

'I don't mind,' Bradshaw said. 'If Poe thinks—'

'No!' everyone yelled in unison.

'You need to be somewhere else, Tilly,' Poe said. 'But I'm not benching you. I *do* have a role for you.'

'If I've understood you correctly, dear boy,' Locke said, 'you plan to have the mannequin in place before our driver arrives at the house of Miss Bradshaw's parents?'

Poe nodded.

'Our driver enters the house via the integral garage, then goes upstairs to Miss Bradshaw's bedroom.'

'Yes.'

'They then turn on her desk light, and hide under the desk, occasionally reaching up to move the mannequin.'

'Is it crazy?'

'Fucking A, it's crazy,' Flynn said. 'It's the stupidest idea you've ever had, Poe. And given that you tried to drive across the Irish Sea in a BMW five years ago, that's quite a high threshold.'

'Yes,' Locke said. 'I fear it *is* a crazy plan.'

No one said anything.

'But?' Flynn said.

'But what, dear?'

'There's *always* a "but" with you, Alastor.'

'But this is the nation that dressed up a dead tramp as a Royal Marines captain, set him adrift in Spanish waters with some forged documents, and successfully fooled Hitler into thinking the Allied forces intended to invade Greece rather than Sicily.'

'I know what Operation Mincemeat was, Alastor,' Flynn said. 'Do you have a point?'

'My point, Stephanie, is that *all* the best plans are crazy.' He removed his ornate notebook from his inside pocket and jotted something down. 'Now, might I suggest a few revisions?'

Chapter 94

Alastor Locke's revisions were good ones. They didn't so much refine Poe's idea as simplify it. And when you were playing with live rounds, simplicity was your friend.

The first revision he'd suggested was ditching the mannequin idea completely. He said Flynn was right; a mannequin, even one being moved by the person acting as Mrs Hudson, wouldn't look natural. He said they needed to use live bait. And he knew exactly who he wanted. He made a whispered phone call and ninety minutes later another helicopter landed at Highwood.

They all stepped out to meet it. Hannah Finch, a woman Poe and Bradshaw had met when they'd been seconded to MI5 on a previous case, climbed out, her hair flapping wildly in the helicopter's downwash. She joined them at the door. Shook hands with them all.

'I'm Hannah Finch,' she said to Flynn. She grinned. 'I assume this is another of Poe's hare-brained schemes?'

Poe and Finch had endured a difficult relationship. They were both part of the team assigned to investigate a helicopter pilot's murder, a murder that might have been linked to an important trade summit. Poe had her arrested for stealing evidence. Bradshaw hadn't liked that at all. She'd thought, correctly, that arresting an MI5 field agent might have . . . repercussions. But they'd ended on good terms, both doing their bit to expose something bigger than either of them had imagined.

'I've chosen Hannah because she has the same light build as

Miss Bradshaw,' Locke said. 'She's worked with you all before so doesn't require extensive briefing and, most importantly, I trust her completely.'

One of Locke's edicts, one he said was absolute, was that the circle was kept small. The only people who knew what they were planning were now in the room. No one else would be brought inside. Poe had wanted to tell the cop who'd replaced Commander Mathers, but Locke wouldn't hear of it.

'I've spent my life keeping secrets and uncovering secrets, Poe,' Locke had said. 'And the one thing I've learned is that the more people who know a secret, the harder it is to keep. More importantly, we don't know who Ezekiel Puck is still in touch with. We don't know who he's *threatened*. But you may take it as gospel that he has an ear inside the investigation.'

'You can't know this,' Poe had said.

'Oh, but I do.'

'How?'

'Because I trained him,' Locke had replied.

Which was all Poe had needed to be told.

Locke's second revision was bullet-resistant glass with a UL 752 protection level of 10. He said 10 was rated for .50 BMG ammunition, the same kind Puck was using.

'Instead of a mannequin, we have Hannah act normally. She'll enter the house and go up to Miss Bradshaw's bedroom. She'll sit at her desk and turn on the lamp. Puck will have a clear view of her, but he won't see the bulletproof screen we'll have constructed behind the window. When he shoots, he'll break Mr and Mrs Bradshaw's window, but the bullet won't penetrate the secondary window. Hannah pretends to fall off her chair. Puck will think it's job done.'

'There'll be no pretending involved,' Finch said. 'Those bullets make quite the bang.'

Flynn scowled. 'Then what? Who's the Sherlock Holmes

shouting "Gotcha!"?'

'No one,' Poe said.

'No one? Then what the hell are we bothering for?'

'We can't take him in Southampton, boss. It's too urban. We won't know where he'll choose to shoot from, and even if we could somehow figure that out, we can't risk him going all Gomer Pyle on us. We can't risk him going out with a bang. No, we take him in an area we control. An area we know but he doesn't.'

'And where is this magical place?'

'We take him on Shap Fell.'

Chapter 95

Flynn frowned, but this time not in defiance. She knew Shap Fell. Had spent time with Poe out there. She knew how isolated it was. Poe thought she might be getting on board with the plan, regardless of how idiotic she thought it was. Or maybe she was resigned. 'I assume you know how to make Ezekiel Puck hate you? And that it's more sophisticated than just going on TV and calling him a knob?'

'What has his sole focus been these last few months?'

'Destroying his ex-wife's business,' she said immediately. 'And he's all but succeeded. The hopeless romantics aren't returning to Gretna Green. Not yet. Not ever, while he's out there.'

'Exactly,' Poe said. 'He's destroyed her dream.'

'So?'

'So how about we give it back to her? With interest. I hold a press conference, and in front of the world's press, I launch the "Save the Smithy's Forge" crowdfunding appeal. I explain why, and I let Ezekiel Puck know that when the money comes in – and it *will* come in, even if I have to fund this myself – Joanne Addy is free to do with it what she wants. She can save her business; she can sell up and buy an island in the Caribbean. She'll be a multi-millionaire; she can do whatever the hell she wants.'

Locke chuckled. He shook his head and said, 'That is as audacious as it's brilliant, Poe. Truly, you're wasted in the police.'

Poe shared a glance with Bradshaw. She hid a smile. *They had a plan . . .*

'What am I missing?' Flynn said, eagle-eyed as ever.

'Nothing,' Poe replied. 'Now, let's stress-test this. We aren't doing it unless we can answer every question.'

'I have one,' Flynn said immediately. 'This crowdfunding stunt is going to do the trick. It can't do anything else. Let's imagine you've successfully made yourself Ezekiel Puck's number-one target. And let's say that we've managed to make him think he's killed Tilly to get to you. Then what happens? He waits for you to disintegrate?'

Poe nodded. 'That's where you come in, Tilly. I want you to make sure I remain at the top of everyone's shit list. No one likes me anyway, so you're not starting from scratch.'

'I like you, Poe.'

'Great.'

'And Estelle Doyle likes you too, don't you, Estelle?'

'I do, Tilly.'

'Anyone else?' Poe said.

Bradshaw thought about it. 'Edgar,' she said eventually.

'Great. Two people and a dog.'

Locke laughed. 'And I'll speak to a friendly journalist. Make it clear that you do not enjoy our protection.'

'You'll be a pariah, Poe,' Doyle said. 'The press will crucify you.'

'I know. I need them to. Puck has to believe I've reached rock bottom.' He took a deep breath. 'And after a few days, I need you to publicly call off our engagement.'

'Absolutely not!'

'You have to, Estelle. As long as I have you, I have something.'

'I will not quietly sit here while the gutter press goes to town on you. It's out of the question, Poe.'

'I know.'

Doyle blinked in surprise. 'You do?'

'I do. You won't be sitting here at all. You'll have taken that lecturing gig in Arizona that you keep putting off.'

'I—'

'I can't have him wondering who to target, Estelle. He saw me dive on Tilly in London, so I think that's who he'll choose anyway, but we have to narrow down his options to one.'

'Well played, Washington!' Bertie said from his armchair. He raised his glass.

'Keep out of this, Bertie!' Doyle snapped.

'No, Lady Doyle, I don't think I will,' Uncle Bertie said, his voice firm and clear. 'This is a high-risk operation, and it must be distraction free. And, like it or not, you are a distraction. A very pretty one, I may add.'

While Doyle simmered, outmanoeuvred, Flynn said, 'What about me? We've known each other a long time. Are you sure he won't look in my direction?'

'You live in a secure penthouse. You have an underground car park. You're a hard target, boss. Tilly lives in the burbs.'

'But just in case he isn't sure who to use to get to you, Poe, I have a small suggestion,' Bradshaw said.

'What is it, Tilly?'

'I learn how to play *Dezinformatsiya*. He's the world's top-rated player. I think if you give me a little time, I can knock him down to number two. And I'll leave enough breadcrumbs that he'll be able to find out my identity.'

'Can't you just hack into their database and change all the scores?'

'Where's the fun in that, Poe?'

'Beats me. How long?'

'I'll be world number one by the time you go on TV.'

She said it with such confidence, Poe didn't bother following it up. If Bradshaw said she could master a game in a matter of days that Puck had spent a lifetime perfecting, then Puck was about to lose his crown. Poe grinned. Puck would hate that. Almost as much as his ex-wife becoming richer than Posh and Becks.

'OK, you've lost your best friend and you've lost your fiancée, Poe,' Locke said. 'What else do you have in your life? What else do we need to take from you?'

'My job,' he said emphatically. 'If I lost that, I probably would reach rock bottom and keep going down.'

'You might get suspended anyway,' Flynn said. 'A plan this reckless, with seemingly catastrophic results, will provoke a response with our senior managers. It'll have to.'

'I'll have a discreet word with the Home Secretary,' Locke said. 'Tell her it would be advantageous if you became the nation's scapegoat.'

'Won't she suspect something?'

'Of course. But she'll be wise enough not to ask.'

Doyle sighed. 'I can't believe we're doing this,' she said. 'But if we are, we're doing it right. I'll prescribe you some diuretics, Poe. They'll help you lose a load of water. It'll give the temporary appearance of weight loss.'

Poe nodded. It was a good idea.

'A word of caution: they might bung you up a bit.'

'If Poe eats fibre, it's entirely by accident, Estelle,' Bradshaw said. 'I imagine his bowel movements are something of an ordeal.'

Poe scowled. No one else did. Everyone else laughed, even the grieving Locke. Doyle and Bradshaw bumped fists. He wished they would stop doing that.

'And I'll arrange for Joanne Addy to be taken into protective custody,' Flynn said after she'd wiped away tears of mirth. 'Is there anyone else he might lash out at?'

'I don't think he'll come after me, but just in case I'll keep a low profile,' Locke said.

'What about Edgar?!' Bradshaw said.

'Uncle Bertie,' Doyle called out. 'Do you have somewhere safe we can stow Edgar for a week or so?'

'That damned hooligan spaniel of Washington's?' Bertie said.

'The very same.'

'I'll take him back to Yorkshire with me. I have a fishing lodge that no one knows about by the River Foss. Used to take the odd filly there when I wore a younger man's clothes. He'll be safe. And if that scoundrel thinks he can come for him on my land, he'll quickly learn three things: I have several guns and they're all loaded for deer; I won a silver medal shooting clay pigeons at the Olympics, so he's not the only one who doesn't miss; and last of all, I'm a confused and scared old man. I shoot first, I don't bother asking questions later, and there isn't a court in the land that would convict me. Washington's dog is safe with me, Lady Doyle. You can count on it.'

Doyle nodded at Bradshaw. 'Uncle Bertie won't drink another drop of alcohol until this is over, Tilly. He's as safe with him as anywhere.'

'But, Washington,' Bertie said, 'you mentioned there might be a bottle of the Macallan M in this for you?'

'There is,' Poe said. 'Archie Arreghini promised me his last one if I found his daughter's killer.'

'I'd love a dram, if you have one spare?'

'You can have the whole damned bottle, Uncle Bertie.'

'I think we're drawing to a close,' Locke said. 'I have a house to secure with bullet-resistant glass, and Hannah will need to discuss Miss Bradshaw's routines with her so she can mirror her actions.'

'We'll beef up Tilly's car too,' Finch said. 'Just in case he tries for me on the street. He won't, but it's my head on the block.'

Locke made a note. 'I'll get our people on it. Make sure the driver's window is reinforced. We'll use the same stuff the PM gets. You'll drive the route before Poe goes on television?'

'I'll know it like the back of my hand. If there are any pinch points, I'll fix them.'

'Is there anything else, Poe?' Locke asked.

'Actually, there is,' Poe said. 'I was in the army, but I wasn't a sniper. I need someone to walk me through what Puck will look for in a firing position.'

Locke grinned. 'I know just the man,' he said.

Chapter 96

Herdwick Croft, Shap Fell, Cumbria

Most people experience nature as scenery. Something pretty. A postcard, or a fleeting moment captured by a smartphone camera. They go back to their cities and talk about how quiet it was. How dark the skies were. That the air smelled different. Cleaner. They talk about how they loved their wild camping weekend and that they *couldn't wait to go back again*, their stories carefully edited to avoid mentioning the glamping pods, the shower huts, the free wi-fi, the amenities they'd never admit to being addicted to.

Glampers didn't glamp at Shap Fell, though. The harsh moor wasn't Beatrix Potter's Cumbria. It wasn't photo friendly, not in the way that Catbells or the Old Man of Coniston were. It was unforgiving. It was a fell with teeth and attitude. The kind of landscape where Grendel, *Beowulf*'s monster, might have summered. Most of the year, as Poe would be the first to admit, it was a bloody wretched place. A wet desert, steeped in mist and misery. The only people he saw hiking up and down Shap Fell were serious about what they were doing. They had the right equipment, the right footwear. They knew what to do when things went wrong. They were Poe's kind of people, people he would share a pint and a tall tale with in the Greyhound Inn.

Everyone else's experience of Shap Fell was the ominous moorland they drove over at 85 miles per hour and a thousand feet above sea level; the M6 motorway neatly bisecting the fell the same way the Thames bisects London.

But Poe loved it. Had done since he was a boy. The untameable beauty. He loved that the whole area was littered with prehistoric history. The stone circles, the strange monoliths, the barrows and the henges. Loved that thousands of years ago Cumbria was a cultural hub, a place of great importance. Now, you could walk 20 miles without seeing a soul. A land forgotten. Poe hadn't been able to believe his luck when he finally got to own a small part of it. When he went from being a wide-eyed visitor to a custodian. And after a year or two, he started to *understand* the fell. Became attuned to its secret frequency.

Which was why, when he crested the hill that brought Herdwick Croft, his once dilapidated shepherd's cottage, into view, he knew something was wrong. He couldn't see anything, but he knew it, the same way he knew when a suspect was hiding a terrible secret. Edgar knew it too. They hadn't been to Herdwick Croft for a few weeks, and the spaniel was ridiculously excited to be going home. Had probably been looking forward to bullying the sheep and scaring the foxes. But the moment he saw the cottage, his tail stopped wagging. Went straighter than a ruler. He let out a low growl. Poe tapped the brakes on his quad, his transport from the Shap Wells Hotel, and turned off the engine. He put his hand on Edgar's back. 'I feel it too, mate.' He got off the quad. Pocketed the key. Said to Edgar, 'Think you can be quiet?'

The spaniel replied with another long, low growl.

Poe wasn't due to ruin Ezekiel Puck's life for another three days. There was no reason for Puck to have turned his sight Poe's way yet. Plus, Puck was a sniper, not an ambush predator. He didn't get up close and personal with his victims.

Someone else was in Herdwick Croft.

Poe didn't know who it could be. His neighbour, Victoria, sometimes popped in, made sure everything was as it should be. But she didn't visit this late at night, and if she did, she wouldn't sit in the dark. And everyone else he knew was back at Highwood.

The first-floor light flashed on and off. Whoever was in his cottage had moved upstairs. Poe set off towards it, at a half jog. He wanted to get there before the mystery person was downstairs again. 'Let's surprise this prick, Edgar.'

Poe knew the land around Herdwick Croft better than any living person. Even in the dark, he knew the location of every crevice, every ankle-turning rock granite, every bit of standing water. He knew where to walk and where not to walk. And he knew how to approach his cottage in silence. He reached it in under a minute. He listened at the door but heard nothing. He turned the handle and nudged it open with his foot. Still nothing. He stepped inside and quickly made his way to the sink. He reached underneath and grabbed his skillet. Twelve pounds of cast iron. A skull-crushing weapon, more useful than a baseball bat. He gripped it in his right hand. Tested the heft, the weight.

Which was when someone turned on the downstairs light. Poe shielded his eyes for a moment. When he opened them, he saw Matt Towler, Archie Arreghini's bodyguard, sitting on his sofa. He had a bottle of Spun Gold in his hand. He wiped some froth off his top lip.

'Let's not get melodramatic, Poe,' he sighed. 'Put the fucking frying pan down.'

Chapter 97

'You?' Poe said. 'You're the person Alastor Locke sent?'

'Didn't that lanky streak of piss tell you I was coming?'

'No, he did not.'

But Locke *had* said, 'I gather you make a very fetching Doctor Who.' He'd said it to Poe in that interview room, right after he'd been detained by the security service. He thought it had been a flippant remark. He should have known better. Locke didn't do flippancy. Everything was a chess move. He'd been letting him know he had a man on the inside and Poe was so caught up in his own shit, he'd completely missed it. Bradshaw hadn't. She'd said right from the start that Towler was on the side of the angels.

'He will play his little games,' Towler said.

'You're Locke's blunt instrument?'

'And you're his sniffer dog.'

'You work for him?'

'Sometimes.'

'What about now?'

'Mr Arreghini is selling stuff he shouldn't have to people who shouldn't have it.'

'And you're working undercover. Making sure it doesn't happen?'

'Oh no. I'm making sure it does,' Towler said. 'The British government can't always be seen to be interfering in the affairs of others. But we do, all the fucking time. We do this by ignoring the activities of certain people. And right now, the eyepatch is turned in Mr Arreghini's direction.'

Poe got himself a Spun Gold from the fridge. Offered Towler another. He nodded. Poe opened both bottles and carried them over. He drew up a chair and sat down. Edgar sniffed Towler suspiciously.

'Nice dog,' he said. 'I have a springer of my own.'

'You do know I thought it might be you for a while? You were the right height, you're ex-army so know how to shoot, and you work for a man with . . . dubious connections. If Tilly hadn't kept offering me fresh mango, I'd have brought you in.'

'I know.'

'And that didn't bother you?'

'Everything bothers me, mate. That didn't. All that did was demonstrate what Locke was trying to tell me.'

'Which was?'

'That you don't care who you upset, you don't care who you suspect, and you'll follow the evidence wherever it takes you. He said if I gave you time, I'd see you for what you were.'

Poe raised his eyebrows.

'A ramped-up version of my old DI, Avison Fluke,' Towler said. 'And he was the best cop I've ever met. The best *person* I've ever met.'

'He's the guy you broke out of prison?'

'He was framed for murder.'

'So I heard. You helped him get exonerated?'

Towler shrugged. 'I did. We had a . . . job to do and getting him off the murder charge was a necessary byproduct.'

'Sounds like an interesting story.'

'It is,' Towler said. 'But not one for tonight.'

'How's Fluke doing?' Poe asked.

'Happy.'

'Then he's found the Holy Grail.'

Towler nodded. 'He got there in the end.'

They clinked bottles. Poe took a long drink. Towler did the same.

Towler yawned. 'Anyway, I was predisposed to like you.'

'You were?' Poe said, surprised. It didn't seem like Towler would be predisposed to like anyone. Poe knew the type. He *was* the type. 'Why?'

'Because you pulled my old mate Jefferson Black out of a hole. Definitively proved he hadn't killed his girlfriend. Up until then, suspicion had followed Jefferson around like an eggy fart.'

'He *was* a bit of a mess,' Poe admitted. 'He was drinking so much he could only have been a few months away from permanent liver damage.'

'He doesn't drink at all now. Tea only.'

'It seems his newfound sobriety gave him the lucidity he'd been sorely missing,' Poe said. 'It's propelled him to the top of Carlisle's criminal food chain.'

Towler rolled his eyes. 'And you were doing so well . . .'

'You're saying he *isn't* a crime boss?'

Towler didn't immediately answer. He took another drink, then shrugged. 'Why not?' he said. 'Locke says I can trust you.'

'Trust me with what?'

'We had a problem—'

'Who's "we"?'

'*We*. I won't tell you who. The problem we had was a man who called himself Smith. He was the head enforcer for an extremely intelligent crime boss called Nathaniel Diamond. Smith was as bad as they come. War crimes, genocide. Extrajudicial killings. He was lying low in Carlisle, but he crossed paths with me and Fluke on a contract killer case we worked. I recognised him. I was tasked with removing him, a proper black-bag operation. Dead of night, me and some men in balaclavas, with zip ties and a propensity for violence, picked him up. Whisked him away to a place that doesn't exist. Somewhere he can see out his days without committing any more atrocities.'

Poe nodded. Sometimes the state had no choice but to take executive action. That occasionally the rights of the individual were secondary to the rights of the whole. He didn't like it, but he wasn't supposed to. That was the point. 'Which left a power vacuum?' he said.

'Not really. Nathaniel Diamond was a thug in his own right. A nasty man. But with Smith gone he was vulnerable to a hostile takeover. So, I arranged one.'

'You put Jefferson Black in the hotseat?'

'I did.'

'Why?'

'Because my daughter's talking about studying film and television at the University of Cumbria when she's older,' Towler said. 'Now, I don't know if this is just a phase she's going through, but, if it isn't, by the time she's eighteen, Carlisle will be the safest city in the UK. I guarantee it.'

'Black works for you?' Poe said incredulously.

'He does. He'll keep a lid on things until I give him the nod. Then it'll be like the Night of the fucking Long Knives. Every dickhead in the city will be taken off the streets.'

Poe didn't say anything. It barely seemed believable. Yet, he knew Jefferson Black. Knew him to be a principled man. A moral man. Poe had always struggled with his move from top chef to top boss. Now it kind of made sense. 'What's your daughter's name again?' he said eventually.

'Abi.'

'Nice,' Poe said. 'You should have brought her with you. Edgar loves children.'

'So does the fucking sniper,' Towler replied. He finished his beer and looked at his watch. 'You'll be doing this in the dark, so we need to do that too. Come on, time to go to work.'

Chapter 98

Poe and Towler made their way out of Herdwick Croft and on to the cold and damp moor. Towler stamped his feet and smiled. It was clear he preferred being outside. Edgar saw a fox or a badger and tore off like Linford Christie, barking wildly.

'He likes a scrap then?'

'I don't know why,' Poe said. 'He never wins.'

Herdwick Croft sat on the lip of a circular, crater-like basin. Towler waited for his night vision to catch up, then did a slow three-sixty as he surveyed the surrounding land.

'You're blessed with geography here, Poe,' he said. 'As long as you choose to do this on a clear night, you have a significant advantage.'

Poe, who'd been having second thoughts, breathed a sigh of relief. 'I do?'

'Unless he shoots you as you arrive, obviously.'

'I'll be coming in fast,' Poe said. 'I'll have my spotlights on and I'll be wearing a headtorch. And even if I don't dazzle the bastard, the ground is so bumpy he won't risk a shot. No, he'll wait until I'm standing still. He'll wait until the morning. Shoot me when I let Edgar out.'

Towler thought about it. He nodded. 'You're right. It's too difficult a shot. He *will* wait until morning.'

'What advantage of geography do I have?'

'Your cottage is on the edge of a natural depression.'

'I call it the Shap crater,' Poe said. 'It looks like a meteorite thumped into the ground a billion years ago. Wiped out the dinosaurs.'

Towler nodded. 'The cottage will have been situated at the edge so the shepherd could watch the surrounding fell for predators, but also so he could keep an eye on his sheep as they sheltered in the natural protection the crater provides.'

That was true, Poe thought. When the wind got up, which it did most days, the sheep congregated in the depression. There was even an ancient, horseshoe-shaped sheep fold down there.

'It means that this Ezekiel Puck wanker is going to have to get down into the crater when he takes his shot,' Towler continued.

'Why won't he sit on the lip?' Poe asked. 'Surely, he'll have a better shot there? He'll be at the same height, and he can stay as far back as he likes.'

Towler shook his head. 'He doesn't have a shot. The lip of the crater is only five or six yards then it dips back down again. That means he'd have to be on the lip itself to have a direct line of sight. And he won't do that.'

'Why not?'

'Because he'll stand out like a racing dog's balls,' Towler said. 'That's why you have to do this on a clear night. Moonlight will help. He'll have no choice but to get into the crater. That limits his range to, say, four hundred, five hundred metres. An easy shot, but at least we'll know where he is.'

'And where will he be?'

'Let's go and look, shall we?'

As they walked to the opposite side of the crater, Poe asked Towler how he knew so much about anti-sniper tactics.

'You know how,' he said. 'I was in the Parachute Regiment.'

'And given who you work for now, were you perhaps in something more specialised than the Paras?'

'There *is* nothing more specialised than the Parachute Regiment,' Towler said.

Poe rolled his eyes. He'd never met a Para who didn't think that way. He was in the Black Watch, a tasty, highly skilled infantry regiment, but he'd never felt the need to make a song and dance about it. 'You know what I mean,' he said.

'Can you keep a secret?'

'Of course,' Poe said.

'So can I.'

Chapter 99

'Here,' Towler said, getting into a rocky, V-shaped wedge 10 metres below the ridgeline. 'This is where I'd shoot from. It's perfect. It's not obvious cover, but there's protection. The firing platform is lightly covered granite so it's stable, and it has a great view of your front door.'

Poe thought he was right. This was the fourth potential site Towler had identified but was easily the most promising. And the best thing was, Poe would have to pass the first three en route anyway.

Towler got to his feet. Studied the rest of the area. 'No, this is it,' he said. 'You'll be in dead ground until the last twenty metres or so, so you can make decent time. No need to crawl.'

'And the last twenty metres? I'll be exposed. And he'll be hyperalert.'

'He will, but not on what's behind him. He'll be in the sniper's bubble by then. Your light will have come on. He'll be waiting for your front door to open. One hundred per cent of his brain power will be focused on taking that shot. You could march up to him whacking a great big drum and he wouldn't hear you.' Towler shook his head. 'No, just make sure you're in position when your lights go on. Do that, and you have him.'

He rubbed his wet hands on his smock.

'I only know what I've been told about you,' he continued. 'So, I'll just say this – when it comes down to it, you don't muck about reading him his rights; you finish it faster than a knife fight in a phone booth. His instinct will be to hold on to his weapon. It's a gun. He has one and you don't. But that's going to be a mistake. Sniper rifles are Gucci as fuck at distance, but they're shit up close. They're too long, too unwieldy. So, while he's trying to turn it round and aim it, you kick him in the fucking head. And you keep kicking until his skull is mushy and his brain is coming out of his ears.'

'I'll bring my frying pan,' Poe said.

'I don't know you well enough to know if you're joking,' Towler said.

'I was joking.'

'Pity. Now, I have a gap in my schedule. I assume you want me here with you?'

Poe shook his head. 'Just me.'

'You sure?'

'I know this fell. Puck doesn't. And with the greatest of respect, neither do you. Also, Puck knows what you look like. He'll have seen you when he murdered Archie Arreghini's daughter. You can't even be in the same postcode.'

'What support *will* you have?'

'Nothing. We can't tell anyone what we're doing. Locke says he'll have eyes and ears inside the investigation tent. He might be right, he might be wrong, but we can't take the risk. It has to be just me.'

Towler frowned, unhappy. Eventually he said, 'I can't see any other way. Just you and him it is then. "Two men enter, one man leaves."'

'What's that?'

'It's a line from *Mad Max Beyond Thunderdome*. Have you seen it?'

'I don't have a TV.'

Towler's eyeroll could have powered Herdwick Croft for a year. 'Of course you fucking don't.'

Poe mentally rehearsed what he would need to do. Decided he'd have as many dry runs as he could fit in. The grass was tough enough and wiry enough to spring back. He wouldn't leave a trail.

'How are you planning to turn yourself into a target?' Towler asked.

Poe told him.

'That'll do it,' Towler grinned. 'I might even donate a tenner myself.'

'Come on,' Poe said. 'Let's have another beer. Make sure we've thought of everything. And while we do that, you can help me loosen the roof slates at the back of the house. I need to be able to get them off silently on the night.'

They removed four slates from his bathroom roof, a gap big enough for Poe to crawl through and drop to the soft ground without making an 'Oof' sound. They put them back on, examined their work from the outside. Even up close you couldn't tell they were no longer fixed to the roof.

When they'd finished, they had another Spun Gold.

'Nice beer that,' Towler said. He held out his hand. They shook. 'Let's hope we get to share another.'

Towler kept hold of his hand. He looked Poe in the eye and said, 'You have PTSD.'

It wasn't a question.

'Who told you?'

'No one *told* me, Poe. It's as clear as the spots on my arse.'

'What a lovely phrase.'

'You can't give that bastard an inch,' Towler said. 'When this is over, me and you are going to talk about it.'

'Why?'

'Because talking about it is how you fix that shit.' He let go of Poe's hand. 'Now, go and catch this prick, you fucking mental bastard.'

Chapter 100

So Poe went on television and he appealed to the British public and he made Joanne Addy a multimillionaire and Hannah Finch played her dangerous role flawlessly and Ezekiel Puck shot her through Bradshaw's window and the bullet-resistant glass that Alastor Locke's specialists had fitted stopped the .50 BMG bullet in mid-air and as Finch had predicted the noise was loud enough for her to fall off Bradshaw's desk chair without thinking about it and then the BBC broke the news that Bradshaw was Ezekiel Puck's twenty-first victim and Flynn made Poe sit in the media room even though it was hostile because his colleagues thought he was a reckless arsehole and he looked grim and he looked angry and there wasn't any acting involved because even the *thought* that someone might hurt Bradshaw just to get to him made him sick to his stomach and then the press turned as they were supposed to and from the bowels of an MI5 building Bradshaw manipulated social media while he prepared for the tsunami of hate that came his way, which it did, even more virulent than anyone had predicted, and when he became public enemy number one he hunkered down in Northumberland with his protection detail, every one of whom hated him, and he took his diuretics and they made him look gaunt and they *did* make him constipated, not that he told anyone that, and he waited for Estelle Doyle to play her part and call off their engagement even though she hated the idea and he was summoned to London to get suspended from the National Crime Agency for gross negligence and at his own request his protection detail was withdrawn, and as soon as all that happened he collected Edgar from Uncle Bertie's riverside retreat and slunk back to Cumbria, making sure that he arrived at night and that it was dark and his quad's spotlights were on and his headtorch battery was fully charged and he didn't stop for a second and he made himself into an impossible shot and then he stepped into Herdwick Croft and he shut the door and at the end of the day he didn't give a fucking shit about any of what had happened during the week because he'd got Ezekiel Puck on to Shap Fell and that was all that mattered.

Chapter 101

Poe had sweated through his hat, the one the headtorch was fitted to. He wasn't surprised. Ezekiel Puck was almost certainly out there, and he had a gun the size of a broomstick, a sight like the Hubble Telescope and bullets like walnuts. Poe had told Towler that he had planned to come in hard and fast and bumpy to negate the risk. Towler had agreed that Puck was unlikely to engage a moving target, but there was a point when Poe had to step off and walk to his cottage. He couldn't rush that. It had to look natural. He and Towler had discussed how to do this as safely as possible. In the end, the simplest solutions were always the best. Towler said as far as Puck was concerned, Poe hadn't been home for weeks. It would not be unreasonable for him to have brought supplies. Food and beer, fuel for the generator. Logs for his wood-burning stove.

And dog food.

A big old bag of dog food. One that had to be carried in on his shoulder. Edgar's kibble wouldn't stop a .50 BMG round, not from the distance they thought Puck would be shooting from, but it might deflect it. Turn a headshot into a miss. Plus, Towler figured, Puck had no way to tell what was in the bag. It could be rocks for all he knew.

Poe threw the kibble – a 10-kilo sack of James Wellbeloved High Protein Adult Chicken & Turkey – on to his stone floor and shut the door behind him. He leaned against it, breathed in and out ten times to calm himself. He hadn't felt that exposed since his final tour of Belfast. When he was back in control, he removed two items from his deep jacket pockets. Timer plugs, one for his bedside lamp, one for the downstairs light. Bradshaw had pre-programmed the times for him, even though it had looked simple enough. She said it would make her feel better. She had even labelled them upstairs and downstairs in big red letters. She didn't want the lights going on in the wrong order. Poe let her fuss without comment. This was tough on everyone.

Towler had insisted he bring Herdwick Croft's generator inside so Poe didn't have to go back outside to turn on his power. It was a massive fire hazard, but it was only for one night, and there were more dangerous things to worry about. And the chug-chug-chug would help cover the sound of him climbing out of the roof.

When the generator's orange light had turned green, Poe unplugged his downstairs light, a cheap thing from IKEA. He put the timer into the electricity socket and the plug into the timer. He turned on the light. Checked the timer was working correctly. It was. Bradshaw had programmed it to go off in twenty minutes, then come back on a couple of minutes after his bedside lamp in the morning. To Puck, it would seem like he had woken up then gone downstairs.

He had a quick snack – some cold Cumberland sausage in a bun, lots of brown sauce, lots of mustard – and drank a litre of water. He moved upstairs and fitted the timer to his bedside lamp, checked it was doing the business like its buddy downstairs. It was, of course. With his neck on the chopping block, Bradshaw had triple-checked the timers then triple-checked them again. He left the lamp on while he got Edgar settled. When Edgar finally dropped off, Poe stroking his head and enjoying the sound of his gentle snores, he carefully moved into his bathroom. He shut the door behind him. The last thing he needed was Edgar following him through the hole in the roof, thinking they were about to embark on another silly adventure.

Before he and Towler had left Herdwick Croft, they'd piled

up some wet and spongy bog moss underneath the loosened roof tiles. Poe had planned to lift them and bring them inside and place them in the bath, but as he'd be doing this in near total darkness, they had factored in human error. Which was just as well because Poe dropped the first one. Prehistoric man had used slate as a bladed weapon, as its edge could be as keen as a razor-blade, and the first roof tile Poe grabbed sliced the web between his thumb and index finger. The roof tile fell to the ground, landed in the bog moss, and made no sound whatsoever. The next three were easier as the quarter moon had lit up the bath-room like mood lighting lights up a jazz bar. Poe carefully placed the tiles on a towel in the bath.

He was ready. Towler had told him that on no account was he to leave the safety of Herdwick Croft unless he was abso-lutely sure. He'd said that the bravest leaders were the ones who called off operations when they didn't feel right. So Poe did exactly that. He mentally rehearsed the route he would take, the obstacles he'd navigate. He thought through that final 20 metres. Debated whether to rush Puck or sneak up. Towler reckoned he'd only know what to do when he got there. There was no point second guessing. But Towler had reiterated just how focused on Herdwick Croft's front door Puck would be. He said Poe had this: that he was ex-Black Watch, ex-uniformed cop. Brawling was in his nature. He'd then finished by saying, 'I'm soooo fucking jealous of you, right now.'

Poe checked the luminescent hands on his Timex. He'd been inside Herdwick Croft for an hour. The first timer would switch on his bedside lamp in another five.

Plenty of time.

Poe put his hands on the edge of the hole he'd made in the roof and hoisted himself up and out. He waited, made sure there were no surprises, then quietly dropped down to the soft Shap Fell.

So far, so good.

Chapter 102

The moment Poe stepped away from the back wall of Herdwick Croft was the moment he knew Puck was out there. Watching his cottage, his sight trained on the front door. He couldn't explain how he knew, just that he did. It was like the air was charged. Or maybe it was because the hair on his arms and on the back of his neck was standing up.

Poe got down on his belly and crawled to the edge of the ridgeline, the lip on which Herdwick Croft perched. Made sure he kept to a ninety-degree angle. That way, the cottage watched his back. Puck wouldn't be able to see him, wouldn't be able to *shoot* him. It was only a 10-metre crawl, but it took Poe five minutes. When he reached the lip, and slithered into the safety of the dead ground behind it, he had sweated so much his T-shirt was soaked through. Towler had said that would happen. He'd said that there was no rush. That as soon as he was over the ridge, he should stay still for thirty minutes. Get reacclimatised to the sounds of Shap Fell. Learn that night's rhythm. He said Poe would hear things he hadn't heard before and that was normal. That his senses would be heightened to unprecedented levels. Poe hadn't believed him. Now he did.

He'd left his Timex in his soap dish as he hadn't wanted the luminescent hands giving him away, so he counted out thirty lots of sixty in his head. It was weirdly therapeutic. Calmed him down. Steadied his breathing. After his final sixty seconds, he got to his feet and made his way down the slope. He then bore left and followed the lip of the basin-like crater. Poe had learned

370

to move quietly in the army, and he'd perfected it on Shap Fell. He liked to walk at night, and he liked to see the wildlife. The badgers and foxes, the rabbits and hares, the voles and shrews. Plus, ewes in lamb were easily spooked.

When he rehearsed it for the first time, the three-quarters of a mile walk to the opposite side of the crater had taken him twenty minutes. He'd told Towler. Who had said Poe was walking too fast. That it should take two hours. Poe tried again. Made sure he thought about every single step. And the time went up. He tried again. It went up again. After seven rehearsal journeys, it was taking him ninety minutes. Good enough, Poe thought. Towler hadn't truly understood how well he knew Shap Fell. That there were parts of the walk he didn't need to tippytoe. A 300-metre sheep trail, a well-worn, animal-made track, forged by generations of Herdwicks as they trekked from one grazing ground to the next, meant he could move quickly and silently for almost a third of the way.

Poe walked carefully, though. Nothing to be gained by rushing. He tested each step before he put his weight on it. He avoided the boggy areas. Lifting his boot out of a bog would make a sucking sound that would carry all the way to Ezekiel Puck. For the same reason, he avoided the granite outcrops that littered Shap Fell like acne. He might pick up a pebble in his boots' thick rubber treads. A pebble on granite would be loud and unnatural, like the metal segs he used to hammer into the heels of his school shoes. Tried to impress the girls by kicking them off the ground, making sparks. Which probably explained why Poe had been a girlfriend-free zone at school.

Ninety minutes. That was what Poe had allowed. He wasn't wearing his watch, but he reckoned he was close to where he'd been on his last two rehearsals. When he and Edgar were roaming the fell for hours and hours at a time, he'd got pretty good at measuring time by tracking the moon's passage. Everything in the sky with an orbit was like the hand of a clock. They all measured time.

'When you get into position, you sit for an hour,' Towler had said. 'Don't be tempted to look for him straight away. Trust that he'll be there. You might have spooked an animal. As quiet as you think you've been, he might have heard something. You sit still and you don't move. If he *did* hear something, he'll dismiss it if he hears nothing to back it up.'

It was good advice. Poe ignored it. Towler had identified four potential firing positions. He'd said the fourth was by far the most likely. It was the perfect sniper's nest. But Poe didn't want to get to the fourth position to find Puck wasn't there, not without having checked the first three positions. Anyway, he figured crawling over the edge of the crater's lip would be good practice. Rehearsing this was fine, but he was playing with live bullets now. It would be different.

Poe rolled on to his stomach and belly-crawled to the edge of the Shap crater. He peered over the edge. Waited for the moon to clear the wisp of cloud it was hiding behind. When it did, he saw position number one was empty. No Ezekiel Puck.

He crawled back and skirted along to the next one. Repeated the action. Found he was more confident this time. Same result, though. The nest was unoccupied. Third time lucky, maybe? Not for Poe. The third position was emptier than a pandemic bog-roll shelf.

Poe made his way to the final position. The one Towler said he'd have chosen. If Puck wasn't there, he was going to have to do all this again the next night. And the next night. *Ad infinitum.*

Now he could take Towler's advice. He could rest. Make sure his breathing was steady. The sweat had cooled. His head was clear. Focused on the task in hand. He closed his eyes and counted to five hundred. He opened them and checked the position of the moon. He reckoned it was coming up to 5 a.m.

Time to move.

Chapter 103

Poe had approached the first three positions knowing in his heart that Puck wouldn't be using them. That Puck was good enough to select the same sniper's nest as Towler. The first three positions had been dry runs.

Now it was the real thing. On the other side of the Shap crater was a man with a gun. Poe was sure of it. He found he was breathing hard again. He wished Towler was with him. Strength in numbers. A problem shared. Useless clichés, but at least he wouldn't have been up there alone. He found he was scared. That he was rerunning that night with Clara Lang, the closest he'd ever come to dying. Maybe he wasn't up to this. Maybe he should carry on walking, get to Shap Fell and call in Towler. Use the ex-Para as the weapon he clearly was.

But then he thought of Bradshaw. She was officially dead. And unofficially she would be pacing her room in the MI5 building she was using. She would be terrified. As would Doyle, all the way across the pond in the desert state of Arizona. Even Flynn would be mildly concerned.

No, it had to finish tonight.

Poe gritted his teeth, ignored the blood pounding in his ears and got to his knees. He dropped to his belly. He crawled on his elbows and his knees to the lip of the Shap crater, an inch at a time.

He saw Herdwick Croft's silhouette. The cottage looked closer than the 500 metres he knew it to be. He moved another inch. As silent as the moon lighting his way.

Then he moved another inch.
And another.
His head was completely over the crater.
He waited for his eyes to adjust to the shadows.
He stared into the last firing position. And saw nothing.

Chapter 104

'You'll see nothing, Poe,' Towler had said. 'If he's wearing a ghillie suit, you won't see him. Not if he stays still. If he knows what he's doing, and we have to assume he does, he'll have collected vegetation and attached it to the suit. He'll look like the ground. He'll blend in as if he's part of the fell. But that's OK.'

'It is?'

'*He'll* blend in. *He'll* look natural. But the thing is, a sniper's rifle is long and it's thin and it doesn't look like part of the landscape. It looks like a fucking gun. He'll try to break up its shape by tying bits of hessian and shit to it, but he can't do too much as he needs to be able to see through the sight. You look for the gun, not him.'

So, Poe *didn't* look for Puck. He looked for the straight edges, the unnatural shapes. The loathsome thing that shouldn't be there.

And there it was. A barrel. Unmistakable when you knew what you were looking for.

And hunched behind it, a clump of moss and heather that Poe knew hadn't been there when he and Towler had looked over the lip of the crater. For a moment, he marvelled at how well Ezekiel Puck had melded into Shap Fell. He stared at the man for five minutes and Puck didn't move an inch. It didn't even look like he was breathing. He was good. *Very* good.

Poe carefully backed up until he could only see Herdwick Croft. His cottage would be his starter pistol. He formed a basket with his hands and rested his head. Fixed his eyes on his bedroom window.

Time grew still.

Then it stopped.

Poe didn't take his eyes off his cottage.

And after an age, Bradshaw's timer worked its magic. His bedroom light came on. Edgar started to bark. He could hear him like he was right next to him.

Poe started to move. He had two minutes.

He crawled to the edge of the crater and got to his feet. The path down was wiry grass. He couldn't walk on it silently, but that didn't matter. Puck was in the zone now, oblivious to anything but Herdwick Croft's front door.

He had two minutes to cover 10 yards. He kept one eye on Puck, one eye on the ground.

The downstairs light came on.

Puck moved. Poe saw him inflate his chest. Filled his lungs so he could hold his breath. Made sure he had a stable firing position.

And then Poe was standing over him.

Towler had said he had to finish it faster than a knife fight in a phone booth. That he should stamp on his head and keep stamping. Then throw him down an old mineshaft.

That was a good plan. A safe plan.

But Poe didn't want to do that. Puck was going to answer for his crimes in a prison, not a hospital for people with acquired brain injuries.

He waited. Wasn't sure when to do it.

Not to worry, Ezekiel Puck decided for him. Some sixth sense made him spin round. And just like Towler had said, he kept hold of his weapon.

Stupid.

Poe stamped on Puck's right arm. He heard it crack. He

brought the same boot down on Puck's throat. Enough pressure for him to know he wasn't fucking around. Puck was wild-eyed with panic.

'How?' he gurgled.

'Hello, Ezekiel,' Poe said. 'Nice to finally meet you.'

He then bent down and punched him in the face. A jab. Stunned him. By the time Puck's eyes had stopped watering, Poe had handcuffed him to the rear and called it in.

It was over.

Chapter 105

Puck looked at Bradshaw in astonishment.

'But . . . but I shot you,' he said.

'You're a very silly man, Ezekiel Puck,' Bradshaw said.

'It was on the news! In the papers!'

'Haven't you been paying attention to the autocrats, Ezekiel?' Poe said. 'The mainstream media can't be trusted.'

'But *how?*'

Poe held his eye. Saw nothing but self-pity. Poe yawned. Bored of the man. Tired of thinking about him. 'You'll have plenty of time to wonder how, Ezekiel. But I will say this; you're a psychopath and you're a narcissist. As soon as we got our heads around that, you weren't particularly difficult to catch. You've never formed an emotional attachment to anyone so it's unsurprising you don't understand how you were caught. But let me be clear – there are no circumstances in which I would knowingly put anyone in danger. Tilly was never in your sights.'

'It was a trick.'

'No trick. We knew how you would react to your wife becoming an overnight millionaire. We knew it would *consume* you.'

Puck slumped in his seat. Beaten. Then he smiled.

'If you do know me, Poe, you'll know I'm part of your life now. I'll *always* be part of it. We might not meet again but know this – I will never stop thinking about you. *Never.* And manipulating people is what I do best. I've done it to sophisticated, wary people – what chance do you think His Majesty's incarcerated population have against me? At some point, one of them will seek you out. Seek out this bitch here, that bitch of a fiancée. Maybe I'll let you live with the pain for a bit. Maybe I won't. Deciding what to do and when will keep me warm at night, Poe. This isn't fucking over!' He screamed the last bit. Got a bit foam-flecked and ranty.

Poe sighed. 'You've got bigger things to worry about than silly revenge fantasies, Ezekiel. You killed Jools Arreghini. And her father is a man with . . . let's say, some very dubious business partners.'

'You're lying,' Puck smirked. 'Nice try, though.'

'I really don't care if you believe me or not,' Poe said. 'But just so you know, when I get home a bottle of Macallan M will be waiting for me, a gift from Archie Arreghini. It's a very expensive whisky. What did Archie say to me, Tilly?'

'He said if you caught the man who killed his daughter, he would send you the bottle, Poe.'

'Anything else?'

Bradshaw nodded. 'He told you he would take care of everything else.'

'What do you think Archie meant by that, Ezekiel?' Poe said.

Puck gulped. 'I demand protection.'

Poe shrugged. 'And you'll get it. I don't think there's a segregation cell safe enough, though. Maybe I'm wrong, maybe the father of the daughter you killed will be in a forgiving mood. You're the expert in despair, Ezekiel. What do you think?'

Puck put his head in his hands. He started to weep.

'I'll get you for this, Poe. I don't know how, but I will. I'll get you.'

'Jolly good,' Poe said. 'But can it wait a couple of days?'

'Why?'

'Because I'm getting married tomorrow.'

Chapter 106

Billy Idol's 'White Wedding' blasted out of Poe's powerful car speakers. He hadn't planned it. He hadn't selected artist, then album, then song, the way Bradshaw had showed him. He'd just got in his car and pressed shuffle. He and Edgar had left Shap listening to The Raven Age, hit the M6 with Spear of Destiny and turned on to the A69 with the title track of Glen Matlock's *Consequences Coming*. It wasn't until he was a mile from Highwood that Idol began sneering about how it was a nice day for said white wedding. And although Poe disagreed with the song's sentiment – it was starkly *anti*-marriage – he had to admit that Idol was bang on about it being a nice day for it.

The sky was denim-blue, and last night's wind had blown itself out. It was warm, not hot. Summer was hanging on, but its colours were changing. Green leaves now tinged with yellow. A solitary kestrel hovered over a field of golden wheat. Death from above. A trio of buzzards worked the thermals, riding the invisible columns of rising air. Poe had once said to Bradshaw that an empty sky was a rare and beautiful thing. She'd replied that an ounce of air contained one thousand billion trillion atoms. Poe had asked if she'd personally counted them, and she'd delivered a tedious lecture on how scientists counted things that couldn't be counted. He smiled at the memory. It was one of his favourites.

He wondered if she'd still speak to him.

Bradshaw was at Highwood now. She had decided to spend the night with Doyle rather than take a room at Shap Wells.

She'd said that he should enjoy his last night of freedom, ha ha ha. So, Poe had spent the night with Edgar. Alone and brooding. He'd tried to take his mind off everything by forcing the spaniel to have a bath. Edgar hated baths. Absolutely hated them. But, as he'd decided the night before Poe's wedding was the night he would roll in a dead fox for the first time, he'd left Poe no choice. Poe had lathered on the dog-friendly shampoo, avoided Edgar's snapping jaws and ignored his howls of indignance, washed it off and rubbed him dry with a towel. Edgar had sulked for five whole minutes.

Poe turned on to Highwood Road. It was actually called Oak Tree Avenue, but he'd always thought of it as Highwood Road as Highwood was the only house on it. He stopped in front of the cast-iron gates. Remembered the first time he'd seen them. They'd been locked then. Doyle incarcerated for her father's murder. The house a crime scene. Poe had tried to pick the padlock until he'd realised he had no idea how to do it.

It was during that case that he and Doyle had gone from being adversarial friends to something more. She would be up there as well. Probably getting dressed. She and Emma sharing a bottle of fizz as they giggled and laughed and gossiped about the things friends do when their minds are elsewhere. He wondered if Doyle would be wearing white. She had been curiously secretive about her dress. He didn't think she'd be so Goth as to wear black, although he wouldn't put it past her, but white . . . maybe not. Poe would be surprised if Doyle owned a single item of white clothing.

The guests had arrived. He could hear them. Excited chatter, the occasional burst of laughter. All but one had been able to rearrange their diaries after the wedding had been postponed. Uncle Bertie was up there. His big booming laugh was distinctive and loud. He was probably threatening to horsewhip one of the caterers. He wondered if he'd found the Macallan M.

Poe was supposed to text Bradshaw. Tell her he was outside Highwood. She'd said that as his best man it was her job to escort him to the marquee. He'd said he was perfectly capable of finding it on his own, but she had insisted. She'd said it would be her *honour*. Poe had hugged her.

He opened the car window. Eager to take in Highwood one last time. The smell of freshly cut grass detonated softly in his memory. Took him back to more innocent times. To short trousers and scraped knees and endless summer holidays. It took him back to the days before Clara Lang.

To the days before Ezekiel Puck.

I will never stop thinking about you . . .

That's what Puck had said. And although Poe had dismissed it out of hand, he'd only done that because Bradshaw was standing next to him. He didn't want her to worry. But Poe was worried. Because Puck was right. His Majesty's prisons were full of the gullible, the dim of wit, the easily influenced. They were full of men who hated cops. Hated them with a passion bordering on mass hysteria. And Puck was the right person to exploit that. He had the skills and the rest of his life to ply them. Poe didn't doubt that he would bend someone to his will. To exact his retribution. And Puck being Puck, he wouldn't come after him. Not immediately. He'd go after those he loved.

Poe wouldn't, *couldn't*, allow that to happen. He couldn't involve Doyle in the revenge fantasies of others. He couldn't involve anyone. Not Bradshaw, not Flynn.

'How can I marry Estelle?' he said to Edgar. 'How can I be so selfish?'

The spaniel wagged his tail. Thump thump thump. Helpful.

'Do you think she'll ever forgive me?'

Edgar whined.

'Me neither,' Poe said. He started the BMW's engine. Put it in reverse. 'Come on, Edgar. It's time to go home.'

Epilogue

Two minutes later

Poe screeched to a halt. There was a Honda Jazz blocking the road. Bradshaw's car. She had a new one. Replacing the driver's side window with bullet-resistant glass hadn't been reversible.

He got out of his BMW. Bradshaw got out of her Honda. She was wearing a dress. A sensible one. No superheroes print. They walked towards each other like it was *High Noon*.

Bradshaw pulled out her phone. Pressed a button and said, 'Operation Scaredy Cat is a go.' She ended the call, said, 'Where are you going, Poe?'

'Home.'

'Why?'

'You know why, Tilly. You heard what Ezekiel Puck said. No one is safe around me. Not you, not the boss, and definitely not Estelle. How can I get married? How can I put the people I love at risk like that?'

'Who are you, Batman?' Bradshaw snorted. 'Anyway, Ezekiel Puck isn't going to be a problem. Not any more.'

Poe blinked in surprise. 'He isn't? How?'

'He was assaulted in his cell last night. Two inmates on a life sentence stabbed him in the eyes and ears with a sharpened toothbrush. They then cut off his tongue for good measure.'

See no evil, hear no evil, speak no evil. The signature punishment of the men with whom Archie Arreghini did business.

He thought about it. Decided it changed nothing.

383

'There'll always be an Ezekiel Puck, Tilly,' he said. 'Someone willing to do the unthinkable. To exploit our weaknesses.'

'They're not weaknesses, Poe. They're strengths.'

'You know what I mean.'

'No, I don't,' Bradshaw said. 'But as soon as Estelle found out what Ezekiel Puck had said to you, she knew it would get in your head. That you'd stew on it, decide an irrational decision was in everyone's best interests. We decided to take precautions.'

'Which is why you're blocking the road?'

'It is, Poe.'

'But what if I hadn't reversed? What if I'd kept on going into Corbridge?'

'DCI Flynn would have stopped you.'

'There's a sideroad, I could have—'

'Poe, I'm just going to stop you there,' she said. '*All* the roads are covered. Alastor Locke has surveillance drones in the air. We've been watching you since last night.' She paused. 'By the way, what was it Edgar found to roll in?'

'You don't want to know.'

'I do.'

'A dead fox.'

'Oh,' she said. 'You were right. I *didn't* want to know.'

'I'm that predictable?' Poe said.

'You are, Poe. Estelle says it's because you're a good man.' She reached into her pocket and handed him an envelope. 'But, just in case you're still having doubts, I have a letter for you.'

It was a cream envelope, thick paper, sealed with red wax, Doyle's family crest stamped in the middle. Poe read it. He smiled. Couldn't help it. It was short and sweet and *very* direct. 'Have you read this?' he asked Bradshaw.

'I have, Poe.'

'It says, "If you think you're leaving me at the altar, Poe, I'll track you down and kick you so hard in the balls they'll shoot out of your fucking nose."' He folded up the letter. Put it back in the envelope. It was a keeper. '"Fucking" is in capital letters,' he said.

Bradshaw nodded.

'So is "nose".'

She nodded again.

'She's underlined them too.'

'I know.'

'You're my best friend, Tilly,' he said. 'What do you think I should do?'

'Do you love Estelle Doyle, Poe?'

'You know I do.'

'And do you want to be married to her?'

'I do.'

'Then shouldn't you be saying those words to someone else?'

Poe frowned. 'When did you get so bloody wise?'

'I watch a lot of *Star Trek*, Poe.'

Poe thought that might have been the Bradshawiest answer to any question he'd ever asked her. He chuckled. Then he stopped.

She saw his expression change. 'Shall we go up?' she said.

But still Poe hesitated. He still had doubts.

Bradshaw sighed. 'Look, I was waiting until my speech to tell you this, Poe, but I suppose now is as good a time as any.'

'Time for what?'

'What have we been talking about for the last six months, Poe?'

'My PTSD?'

'No, our plan.'

Their plan. Of course. Their plan to leave their jobs and go into business together. It had been something to think about, to dream about, when he'd been at sea and Bradshaw had been in the bowels of MI5 or GCHQ or wherever the hell Alastor Locke had hidden her. It was a total fantasy, though. A non-starter.

'I can't ask you to give up your career for me, Tilly,' he said. 'I just can't.'

'You're not asking me to give up my career, Poe. I've already left. I'm asking you to give up yours for me.'

'You've already left?'

Bradshaw nodded. 'I handed in my notice to Alastor Locke last night. I hate working for him, Poe. *Hate it.* I told him I would finish my current assignment but, after that, I'm unemployed. Unless . . .' She reached into her dress pocket and removed a slim piece of cardboard. It was the size of a credit card. She handed it across.

It was a business card. Navy blue, gold letters. Poe stared at it until his eyes became wet.

Washington Poe & Tilly Bradshaw
Gumshoes For Hire

'You actually used "Gumshoes",' he said, his voice breaking. 'I was only half serious when I suggested that.'

'You're only ever half serious, Poe,' she said. 'I think it's because you have a sunny disposition, although DCI Flynn says it's because you suffer from mild retardation.' She chewed her bottom lip, worried. 'Don't you like it?'

He looked at the business card again.

'It's perfect, Tilly,' he said. 'Absolutely perfect.' He took a deep breath. 'I guess I'm leaving the National Crime Agency then,' he said. He tucked the card into his top pocket. Patted it like he was in an Ealing comedy. 'Funny, I thought I'd be sadder.'

'It's the right time, Poe,' Bradshaw said.

'It is, Tilly.' He checked his Timex. 'Speaking of time,' he said. 'Don't you have a groom to escort to the altar?'

'I do, Poe.'

'Come on then. Let's not keep the lady waiting.' He paused. 'Oh, and Tilly?'

'Yes, Poe?'

'There's no reason Estelle needs to find out about any of this, is there?'

'No reason at all, Poe.'

'You've already told her, haven't you?'

'I have, Poe.'

Epilogue 2

Oh, and Poe was wrong. She *did* wear white.

Acknowledgements

Thank you for reading *The Final Vow* – I hope I didn't scare you. As always, there are several people to thank for helping to turn my inane ramblings into something semi-cohesive. My former editor, Krystyna Green, who has gone wherever it is editors go when they retire (I think Krystyna might be in Surrey – she certainly keeps inviting me to a house there anyway – which, to be honest, isn't the natural stomping ground of a northerner . . .) will always get a thumbs up for kicking off this dog and pony show by taking a chance on a book called *The Puppet Show*. Thanks, Krystyna. I'll be forever in your debt. But please do stop inviting me to stay at your house – I don't care how many bogs you have ☺.

Thank you to my new editor, Gina Luck (I would say you have big shoes to fill, but Krystyna has tiny feet, arguably the smallest I've ever seen, so maybe not. Figurative shoes, maybe?), for not flinching when you stepped into the breach. Here's to the next few years, Gina. Let's see how much mischief we can get up to . . .

My brilliant editorial team – Rebecca Sheppard and Amanda Keats, Martin Fletcher and Howard Watson, Lizzy Melbourne and Joan Deitch – and the heroes in marketing and publicity – Beth Wright, Kirsteen Astor and Brionee Fenlon (and yes, that *is* how you spell their names) – all have my undying gratitude for the continued effort and enthusiasm they've shown from the very beginning. Thank you, one and all.

Thank you to everyone else at Little, Brown who has worked on the book, specifically those of you in sales. We never get to meet, but I am very aware of the work you do. And for those of you who haven't yet worked on the Poe or Koenig books, what's wrong with you?

David Headley, my long-suffering agent, gets a special nod because he'll only moan if he doesn't. We're coming up to a decade together now, David. What are you getting me? (Modern ten-year anniversary gifts are diamonds, in case you don't have the internet. A first edition of *Diamonds Are Forever*, maybe?) It's been fun, let's keep doing it.

My beta readers, attention-seeking nerds that they are, always ask for a shout. So here it is: **THANK YOU, SIMON COWDROY, ROGER LYTOLLIS AND ANGIE MORRISON!!!!!!!** Was that loud enough?

The biggest thank you, as always, goes to my wife, Joanne. You're the first person to read the book, the first person to say there's too much swearing, and the first person to not get the jokes. You're also the *last* person to check the book before it gets signed off – thank you for your diligence. For those of you thinking this is just me tooling for brownie points, Joanne has spotted – at the very last pass – howlers like Poe telling a Tommy *Copper* joke, and pewb instead of pube.

And finally, the big one – a massive standing ovation to the readers, librarians, bloggers, vloggers and floggers. A book's not a book until it gets to you guys.

Same time next year? Tell your friends.

Mike